THE WOLF HUNT

Jack Pembroke Thrillers
Book Two

Justin Fox

Also in the Jack Pembroke series
The Cape Raider

THE WOLF HUNT

Published by Sapere Books.

24 Trafalgar Road, Ilkley, LS29 8HH,
United Kingdom

saperebooks.com

Copyright © Justin Fox, 2022

Justin Fox has asserted his right to be identified as the author of this work.
All rights reserved.

No part of this publication may be reproduced, stored in any retrieval system, or transmitted, in any form, or by any means, electronic, mechanical, photocopying, recording, or otherwise, without the prior written permission of the publishers.
This book is a work of fiction. Names, characters, businesses, organisations, places and events, other than those clearly in the public domain, are either the product of the author's imagination, or are used fictitiously.
Any resemblances to actual persons, living or dead, events or locales are purely coincidental.

ISBN: 978-1-80055-765-9

To Tracey

ACKNOWLEDGEMENTS

Although I did serve as a citizen-force naval officer for a short period, I spent no meaningful time on anti-submarine vessels or submarines, but I have been an enthusiastic delver into archives, libraries, museums and the arcane nautical bilges of the internet, especially sites such as convoyweb.org.uk and uboat.net. Most of what I've learnt about submarine warfare has been liberally and gratefully borrowed from others.

For an understanding of the role of South Africa's 'little ships' during World War II, I'm indebted to K.G. Dimbleby's *Hostilities Only*, John Duffell-Canham's *Seaman Gunner Do Not Weep*, Ronnie Erskine's *The Sea Was Kind to Me*, Joe Tennant's *The Red Diamond Navy* and George Young's *Salt in my Blood*. In addition, *Proud Waters* by Ewart Brookes and *Trawlers Go to War* by Paul Lund and Harry Ludlam gave me a better grasp of the activities of the 'little ships' further afield. Richard Compton-Hall's *The Underwater War 1939–1945*, John Costello and Terry Hughes's *The Battle of the Atlantic* and S.W. Roskill's definitive *The War at Sea* provided the context.

To gain an understanding of the U-boat war from the Allied perspective, I read D.A. Rayner's *Escort*, Terence Robertson's *Walker R.N.*, Anthony Watts's *The U-boat Hunters*, D.E.G. Wemyss's *Relentless Pursuit* and Edward Young's *One of Our Submarines*. For the German perspective, I'm indebted to Ermino Bagnasco's *Submarines of World War Two*, Luc Braeuer's *German U-Boat Ace: Carl Emmermann*, Lothar-Günther Buchheim's *U-boat*, Wolfgang Ott's *Sharks and Little Fish*, Robert C. Stern's *Battle Beneath the Waves* and Gordon Williamson's *Wolf Pack*.

For the story of South Africa's naval war, I read J.C. Goosen's *South Africa's Navy*, H.R. Gordon-Cumming's *Official History of the South African Naval Forces during the Second World War (1939–1945)*, C.J. Harris's *War at Sea*, Evert Kleynhans's Stellenbosch doctoral thesis, *The Axis and Allied Maritime Operations Around Southern Africa, 1939–1945*, and L.C.F. Turner, H.R. Gordon-Cumming and J.E. Betzler's *War in the Southern Oceans 1939–45*.

To learn more about wartime South Africa, I read Lucy Bean's *Strangers in Our Midst*, the many evocative accounts by Lawrence Green, and *Just Nuisance AB* by Terence Sisson. For the story of local spies and Afrikaner resistance, I consulted *Hitler's Spies* by Evert Kleynhans, *U-Boats and Spies in Southern Africa* by Jochen O.E.O. Mahncke, *For Volk and Führer* by Hans Strydom, and *Lives and Deaths of Memorials* (an unpublished University of the Western Cape master's thesis) by R.B. Uys.

Adrian Rowe kindly sent me his unpublished manuscript, *The Final Hours of Convoy D.N. 21*, and Evert Kleyhans granted me access to his archival treasure trove, including the U-boat documents, personal diaries and letters of the Union War Histories, housed by the Department of Defence in Pretoria. The South African Naval Heritage Trust's regular *Digest* publications, as well as those of the Simon's Town Historical Society and Cape Odyssey also proved invaluable.

The naval fiction of authors such as C.S. Forester, Alexander Fullerton, Alastair MacLean, Nicholas Monsarrat and Douglas Reeman has been an abiding inspiration.

I spent many happy hours in the British National Archives at Kew, the British Library, South African National Library, University of Cape Town Library, as well as the archives of the Imperial War Museum, Simon's Town Museum, Simon's

Town Naval History Museum and those of Snoekie Shellhole, the M.O.T.H. attached to the Simon's Town Museum (especially its meticulously recorded personal accounts of South Africans who served at sea during the war).

In particular, I would like to thank my dedicated, talented editors, Amy Durant and Rear Admiral Arnè Söderlund (Rtd), as well as those who generously gave of their time to read the manuscript, offer advice and help with research: David Attwell, Brian Austin, the late Rear Admiral Chris Bennett, Lynton Burger, Cameron Ewart-Smith, Grethe Fox, Suzanne Fox, Brian Ingpen, Captain Glen Knox (Rtd), Steve McLean, Paul Morris, Wim Myburgh, Elizabeth Parker, Robert Plummer, Rear Admiral André Rudman (Rtd), Luke Stevens, Commander Leon Steyn, Stephen Symons, James van Helsdingen, Alison Westwood, Captain Kristian Wise (Rtd) and Tracey Younghusband. A special thank you to the Sapere Books team, and to my wonderful agent and friend, Aoife Lennon-Ritchie.

The principal ships and characters of this tale are entirely fictitious.

PROLOGUE

Berlin, 15 December 1938

Gerhardus Kruger, accompanied by a group of fellow students from Stellenbosch University, stepped off the train at Friedrichstraße Station and into the heart of the bustling capital. The young man from the West Coast was immediately awed and captivated. The neatness of Berlin's streets, the beauty of its architecture, the militarism, the Swastikas draped from every vantage — here was a proud and confident nation on the rise. Although the air was icy, the sky was blue and brightly decorated Christmas trees adorned shop windows along the grand boulevards.

The *Afrikaanse Nasionale Studentebond* group of undergraduates from Afrikaner institutions had come to the Reich on a cultural tour during the university holidays and was to be housed in the Olympic Village in Wustermark on the outskirts of the city — a comfortable environment for the Germanophile visitors from South Africa.

Opened two years earlier to accommodate athletes from around the world, the village was now used mostly by army personnel. All twenty-two students were lodged in one of the former athletes' villas and Kruger found the whole set up to be efficiently run with two stewards playing attentive hosts, chosen for their ability to project the Nazi philosophy to the impressionable young foreigners. The grounds were attractive with rolling lawns, pine forests and lakes patrolled by swans and ducks.

Each day was filled with sightseeing trips and cultural events; tours took them along the Via Triumphalis and Unter den Linden, through the Brandenburg Gate, and to all the important museums and monuments, including a visit to the vast Olympic Stadium which they all knew from the newsreels.

One of the stewards, Albert Schulze, working undercover for the *Abwehr*, was tasked with determining whether any of the South Africans might be useful to the Nazi cause. He singled out the tall, serious, athletically-built Kruger as a promising candidate and one evening invited him for a drink in a nearby beer hall to sound out his politics.

'Your German is exceptionally good, Herr Kruger.'

'*Danke*, I learnt it at school and then did one year at university. There is German blood in my family too.'

'And what do you think of the new Reich we are creating?' asked Schulze, lighting a cigarette.

'I am truly in awe, Herr Schulze. There is such discipline and industry, especially among the youth, and such patriotism. There appears to be a unity of purpose in the Reich, something we lack in South Africa.'

'Why do you think that is?'

'We are a divided nation. The British are effectively occupiers. They even have one of their biggest naval bases at the Cape. The Jews control the mines and the blacks are a constant threat.'

'How would you like to see things changed?'

Kruger took a long draft of his Berliner Weiße, then wiped his moustache before answering. 'If the Afrikaner were in power and we had a National Socialist system like yours, we could be one of the greatest nations on earth. South Africa is the world's largest producer of gold, diamonds and platinum.

Just think what we could achieve if we followed the Führer's example.'

Schulze was impressed by the young man's ardour. 'You seem to be strongly opposed to the British.'

'A hundred years ago, my people trekked into the interior to get away from the British, for lebensraum, for freedom. They conquered the native tribes who stood in their way and built farms from nothing, just like the pioneers in America, but the British always came sniffing at their heels. If there was anything worth taking, like gold or diamonds, they annexed the land for Queen Victoria. The bastards fought the Boer War to steal the Transvaal's gold, burnt our farms and herded our women and children into concentration camps where 26,000 died.' His jaw was set and his eyes spoke fury: Schulze was delighted.

'There are many similarities between our two nations, don't you think?' said Schulze.

'I do. The British humiliated the Germans with the Treaty of Versailles in 1919, just as they humiliated the Afrikaners with the Treaty of Vereeniging in 1902.'

'I read in the *Völkischer Beobachter* that a great monument is being erected to the Afrikaner volk in your capital.'

'*Ja*, the cornerstone of the Voortrekker Monument was laid last week on Dingaan's Day. The sixteenth of December is a holy day for us, marking our victory over the Zulus.'

'I read that 100,000 people gathered for the ceremony.'

'One tenth of the Afrikaner nation made the trek to Pretoria. I wish I could have been there; it must have been like one of the Führer's Nuremberg rallies. Our grandchildren will look to this moment and this monument as the birth of our greatness as a volk.'

Before the student group was due to return to South Africa, Schulze took Kruger for another drink, this time with a proposition in mind. There had been a light snowfall the night before and they walked to the beer hall through streets enchantingly decked in white.

'Perhaps, with German help, the Afrikaner could finally be free of the Union Jack and the Jew,' said Schulze, hunched over his beer in the loud, smoky interior. 'I have spoken to some influential people and I want you to think about whether you might be interested in coming to study further in Germany. It would be a chance for you to travel, meet Germans and get to properly understand the new Reich.'

'That would be a wonderful opportunity!'

'There are bursaries available for appropriate candidates like yourself and we would no doubt be able to place you in one of our universities or colleges.'

'Thank you, that is enormously generous.'

'We will be in touch, Herr Kruger…'

It was a quite different city that greeted Kruger as he stepped off the train once more in cavernous Friedrichstraße Station eight months later. High summer and muggy, with a feverish air of anticipation hanging about the city and war clouds boiling in the humid air and, seemingly, in everyone's hearts.

Kruger had dropped out of university halfway through his final year of Agriculture and set sail for Germany on a whim that had the feeling of destiny about it. His parents, knowing their son's passions and being supporters of Hitler themselves, had not stood in his way.

This time, he was arriving in Berlin alone, but there was Schulze, waiting on the platform to welcome him.

'You have come, Herr Kruger. We are so pleased.'

'*Danke schön*, Herr Schulze. I feel this journey was meant to be.'

'And, perhaps, just in time.'

It was indeed just in time. Within weeks, the world was utterly transformed. England and France had declared war on Germany and three days later South Africa joined the fight. Kruger took it as a personal blow: Smuts, once a Boer hero, was now a betrayer of the Afrikaner volk. The young South African wandered Berlin in a daze, through streets thronged with soldiers and slogans appearing everywhere on walls and hoardings: '*Sieg oder Chaos* — Victory or Chaos'. His mind was all chaos and dreams of victory, but victory over the British Empire in Africa still seemed a very remote possibility.

Kruger had hardly had time to enrol at the *Reichsakademie* and find digs before war broke out and his plans were now in turmoil. Should he make his way to Italy and find a ship back to South Africa or should he remain in Berlin and try to serve the Reich? A few days later the answer presented itself, once again in the shape of Herr Schulze, who invited him to the *Abwehr* headquarters on Tirpitzufer.

'Do not abuse yourself about the situation in your country,' said Schulze, seated behind a wide mahogany desk. 'After all, Smuts only won the war debate by thirteen votes, so the anti-war sentiment is obviously strong in South Africa.'

'Exactly, Herr Schulze, it was a pro-British faction in parliament that declared war on Germany, not the Afrikaner people. Most of the police and civil service are anti-war, even some of the military, and the *OB* is gaining more support by the day.'

'*OB* — please remind me?'

'The *Ossewabrandwag* is a cultural organisation founded on National Socialist principles and has a deep admiration for the Reich.'

'Yes, of course. We can capitalise on this. All we need is a couple of thousand men in the right positions at the right time, and who knows what we might achieve?'

'Even more promising than the *Ossewabrandwag* are its militant splinter groups that operate a bit like Germany's *Sturmabteilung*. It is to one of them that we should turn for action.'

'Good, good, Herr Kruger. I have spoken to my superiors and we have a proposal for you. We need a trusted man on the ground in South Africa, someone trained by us in the arts of espionage, propaganda and sabotage. Smuts and his cabinet must be removed, assassinated if necessary, along with Jewish leaders like Oppenheimer.'

'I wholeheartedly agree.'

'The idea would be to start a sabotage campaign that cripples the Union: telephone exchanges, factories conducting war work, railway networks and harbours to disrupt British shipping. We need a sharp, powerful blow to destabilise the Union. It must happen throughout the country and sow panic. We will need strong, committed leaders and, most critically, someone to guide the first phase of attacks. Would you be willing?'

'I am at a loss. I don't know exactly what to say … but, yes, yes, it would be a great honour.'

'Good. Excellent.'

'But how?'

'First, you will need training.' Schulze paused to light a cigarette and offered one to Kruger, but he declined.

'I am fit and strong. I play rugby and I'm a good marksman — we shoot a lot on our farm.'

'All Afrikaners can shoot; this we know from the Boer War when your commandoes ran rings around the British. If only Germany had helped you more back then, who knows what the outcome might have been? But to the present: you will undergo intensive training aimed at the tasks ahead and then we will wait for the right time and opportunity to insert you back into South Africa.'

'What kind of training exactly?'

'You will need to learn how to handle all kinds of firearms as well as close combat, explosives, telegraphy and Morse code, even how to produce propaganda pamphlets.'

'Why telegraphy?'

'We need intelligence on shipping movements fed back to Germany to assist our commerce raiders and U-boats. You will have to learn everything about wireless transmitters. The German consulate in Lourenço Marques is able to supply fairly good information on shipping that passes through Mozambican waters, but we are finding it hard to source reliable intelligence on Union ports. We do have spies; however, their efforts need better coordination. Also, to get you properly trained, you will need to join the Wehrmacht.'

'But how can someone from an enemy nation join the German army?'

'If you are in agreement, we will make arrangements for you to become a German citizen. You will doubtless be aware that joining the Wehrmacht makes you guilty of treason and liable for execution if you are caught…'

'I am willing, Herr Schulze. It is my patriotic calling and an opportunity to serve Adolf Hitler, my fatherland and the cause of National Socialism.'

The German's eyes bored into Kruger's for a few moments, then he smiled broadly. 'First you will undergo basic training, followed by a spell at the Führer Leadership School in Neustrelitz to be taught propaganda, speechmaking and the theory of National Socialism; then you will join the sabotage school at Quenzsee in Brandenburg.'

'When do I start?'

'Your enthusiasm is admirable. I am pleased to inform you that you have already been given security clearance from the *Sicherheitsdienst* and the *Abwehr*. Your training can begin next week.'

They stood up and shook hands.

'I think this is an important moment in the history of your country,' said Schulze.

'I think so too.' Kruger's voice was filled with emotion.

CHAPTER 1

Simon's Town, 2 July 1941

Out of breath from the climb, and feeling a twinge from his old leg wound, Jack Pembroke found a comfortable rock to rest and watch the Royal Navy's largest base in the southern hemisphere slowly come to life. The sun had just risen from the Hottentots Holland Mountains on the opposite rim of the bay and coated the encircling crags in soft white light. There was not a breath of wind on this winter morning and tendrils of sea mist hung about the shoreline adding an ethereal quality to the scene. Sunbirds voiced their high-pitched trill and a pair of Cape sugarbirds, long tails streaming, fell upon the blossoms of a nearby protea bush. Further along the ridge, a troop of baboons made its way towards Red Hill Road, the leading male letting out an occasional bark to urge the stragglers. From somewhere on the lower slope, he could hear faint musical notes of a navy band beginning its practice.

From left to right Jack's gaze took in the big guns of Scala Battery pointing their 9-inch barrels at the mouth of False Bay and far below them a train, looking like a child's toy, clattering along the shoreline towards Simon's Town, the last stop on the African continent. Beside the station lay the white stripe of Long Beach ending at the Admiralty's garden and 200-year-old house that his illustrious father refused to stay in, preferring a rented villa south of the town.

His gaze came to rest on West Dockyard with its cluster of fine buildings, some dating back to the time of the Dutch, the old clock tower and slipway where he could see his own ship, the converted whaler HMSAS *Southern Gannet*, and her sister HMSAS *Southern Belle*, on the hard undergoing their refit. Further to his right lay East Dockyard, its basin crammed with ships including, just discernible behind a large building, the masts and funnels of the County-class cruiser HMS *Dorsetshire* in the graving dock, flush from her recent success against the *Bismarck*. To the southeast, he could make out the tank farm at Seaforth and beyond it the behemoth rocks of Boulders Beach. Round the headland, out of sight and isolated from the bustle of the town, lay his father's house, Milkwood, above its own private beach.

Jack glanced across False Bay and noticed the Royal Navy minesweepers *Immortal* and *Kirstenbosch* heading south on their daily round, keeping the channel clear of mines. He smiled as he recalled his initial, ham-fisted attempts at sweeping that very channel at the beginning of the year, when he'd first taken command of *Gannet*. But his little flotilla had proved its worth and, although two minesweepers had been lost, they had sunk a German raider. For once, his father had been pleased, perhaps even unequivocally pleased.

He remained on his sandstone perch for a long time, enjoying the sights and sounds of Simon's Bay, feeling a sense of contentment. Yes, many parts of the world were being torn apart and he had suffered terribly the previous year, both at Dunkirk and after his mother's death in London, but here in the Union of South Africa, in this strangely English town at the foot of the continent, he'd found something to hold onto, something that had taken the shape of belief, conviction even.

It had been the right decision to join his father and sister at the Cape, to take command of his beloved *Gannet*, and it was at the Cape that he had met Clara Marais, the beautiful and intelligent Afrikaans student who filled his dreams and fed his desire in a way he had not experienced before. The war in the southern oceans was at ebb: the pocket battleship *Graf Spee* had been dealt with, the heavy cruiser *Admiral Scheer* had hightailed it back to Norway and the occasional commerce raider could be handled. There was little doubt that the U-boats would eventually head south, but for now it felt like the Phoney War all over again, a period of pseudo peace, a time to breathe and love again.

He closed his eyes, stretched his arms wide and drew a long draught of air into his lungs, smelling the sweetness of the fynbos.

The sonorous booming of a dockyard tug echoed off the sandstone cliffs. It was time to descend the mountain and start the working day. Jack took the path back down the slope towards Belleview House and the next-door cottage that was his lodging. Perhaps his landlady, Miss Retief, had once again left a basket of produce from the garden on his doorstep, along with a jug of milk and the *Cape Times* if she was done reading it.

An hour later, Jack strode through West Dockyard's iron gates, adorned with the curlicue 'VR' of Victoria Regina. A Hawker Osprey floatplane sat ungainly on the wharf in front of a hangar and on the adjacent Patent Slipway, *Southern Gannet* and *Southern Belle* lay one behind the other undergoing the final stages of their transformation from minesweepers to anti-submarine vessels. Not exactly chrysalis to butterfly, thought Jack, but a sleeker look without the sweeping paraphernalia on their quarterdecks.

He ran his eye appraisingly over his own ship: flared bows, tall masts, jaunty upright funnel, boxy boat deck and a now more graceful poop deck. She looked uncomfortable and out of place on the hard, her under-parts bared for all to see. On land she was a beached whale, a hulk of iron robbed of light and power, of the life-giving beat of her engine. How he longed to free her from this indignity and return *Gannet* to her element.

Welding teams, technicians and workmen were everywhere upon and about her, their filthy boots, slovenly ways, and in some cases light fingers, infuriating PO Cummins. Jack would have to find a way, yet again, to leaven his bosun's anger. In truth, it also pained Jack to see *Gannet* thus served. Her hull was blotched with red lead, the ship's boat had been damaged and the decks were littered with packing cases, spare parts, hoses, cans of paint and coils of rope; there was even a man who looked suspiciously like a tree feller dangling halfway up the mainmast. But Jack also registered a growing excitement: his ship was being given new teeth to take the fight to the enemy once more and each day of industry brought her final transformation closer. Since his last inspection, the big whaling winch had been removed. It had been more than useful for minesweeping, but now its absence created additional storage space for depth charges.

'Lieutenant Pembroke, just the person I was looking for,' said a short, trim officer emerging from behind the rudder. The man was gaunt and beetle-browed with jet-black hair.

Jack saluted smartly. He knew by reputation that anti-submarine expert Lieutenant-Commander Dalgleish — or The Black Death — was the hardest of taskmasters. Dalgleish and his staff of eight RN ratings, some of them specialists in depth-charging, others in Asdic, had arrived at the Cape the previous year, along with mountains of instructional equipment. They had set up a small anti-submarine school, along with a training simulator and plotting table, in a spare building in Cape Town Docks. Dalgleish also supervised the fitting of AS gear to ships during their conversion, with *Gannet* and *Belle* being his current responsibility.

'You're the admiral's son, RNVR, aren't you?' said Dalgleish, appearing to masticate his words. 'Got yourself a gong after that scrape with Jerry off Agulhas?'

'Yes, sir, DSO, she was the *Sturmvogel*.'

'Jolly good show, but U-boats pose a very different set of problems. You were at *King Alfred*, not so?'

'Yes, sir. And I believe you served at the anti-submarine training base up in the Hebrides.'

'Just so, first at the AS school in Portland, then the Isle of Mull.'

Jack had heard daunting tales of the battle school at Tobermory and the standards of efficiency demanded there. It was rumoured that captains had been removed from command and junior officers reduced to gibbering wrecks by the eccentric but ruthless Commodore Gilbert Stephenson who, like Jack's father, had been brought back from retirement to whip the convoy escorts into shape.

'I believe you were under the Terror of Tobermory,' said Jack.

'Yes, Puggy Stephenson, also known as the new Lord of the Western Isles or, less charitably, Electric Whiskers. The commodore is a master of the small-ship trade — an exemplary officer, a true gentleman and, I like to think, a friend. He taught me almost everything I know about AS warfare. Always scrupulously fair, within the parameters of the levels of excellence he sets. A rod of iron, mind, and I think that's the right and proper way, don't you?'

In the spirit of his mentor, Jack had heard that The Black Death had once thrown a bridge chair clear across the wheelhouse at an inept midshipman, whose terrified leap prevented serious injury.

'Quite so, sir.' Jack felt his cheeks flush. Another prig to join the ranks of Commodore O'Reilly, SNO of Simon's Town and sparring partner of his father. Oh well, the more antagonists the merrier.

'Listen very carefully, Pembroke, the newly fitted Asdic dome houses a quartz oscillator and is henceforth your most valuable possession. The contraption is a vulnerable, fragile and temperamental creature. Come and have a gander.'

Bent double, the two men walked under the hull and crouched beside the streamlined, pear-shaped metal pod protruding from *Gannet*'s keel. 'The sonar transducer is under the dome to ensure it's kept in still water to eliminate, or at least reduce, turbulence and flow noise as *Gannet* moves through the water.'

'How fast can we go before the Asdic starts becoming ineffective?'

'About twelve knots, give or take.'

'Ah, that's all right then, sir, the old girl doesn't enjoy cruising much faster than that.'

'Believe me, Lieutenant, when she's chasing a U-boat, she'll want to go a lot faster.'

Jack grinned at the wily commander. 'And what is its range, sir?'

'In ideal conditions, about 2,500 yards, but you seldom get ideal conditions off the Cape. It's often less than a thousand yards, particularly when there are fluctuations in water temperature, salinity or plankton. Rough seas also affect the readings.'

'And propeller wash from other ships?'

'That too. Now, I'm going to ask you very nicely to treat this dome and its contents with the utmost care and to tell your skippers to do likewise,' said Dalgleish. 'There'll be no ramming or running aground or resting on the bottom at low tide or any such nonsense, do you hear me?'

'Of course, sir, we'll treat them like babies.'

'Good. I'll load you up with forty depth charges apiece to start with, but we've made room for more in the refit. When you're on convoy duty, and the Hun comes snooping, you'll certainly be needing more.'

After a day in the dockyard, Jack visited his father at Milkwood House, snug among granite boulders overlooking a cove of luminous green water. It was cool and blustery with westerly squalls patching the bay as they sat in the shelter of the stoep enjoying a whisky before supper.

'How are things on the Seaward Defence Force front, Father?' asked Jack.

'It's relentless, and the time pressure keeps mounting,' said the admiral, running a hand across his forehead. 'We're expecting the Hun to send his infernal U-boats our way any time now and we simply aren't prepared. As you know, with raiders our primary concern, our initial focus was on minesweeping, which is why I nudged you in that direction —'

'Shoved,' said Jack with a smile.

'Encouraged. We got lucky — thanks to you and your flotilla — with that mine-laying raider, but U-boats —'

'Which is why we're converting *Gannet* and *Belle*.'

'And rushing to prepare as many other AS vessels as possible, fitting them with Asdic as soon as the bloody sets arrive from Britain — all too slow. But we also need to put the other measures in place, such as improving boom defences at all five Union harbours, creating more lookout posts around the coast and beefing up underwater defences. Our aim is to have round-the-clock AS patrols, especially when large convoys are in port and the overflow has to anchor in Table Bay or the Durban roadstead.'

'They are so damn vulnerable in the anchorages,' said Jack.

'There are times when we have as many as forty merchantmen anchored in Table Bay awaiting berths with only a handful of AS vessels to protect them.'

'What about anti-submarine loops?' said Jack, referring to electrical cables that could be stretched across the entrance to a port or roadstead to provide early warning of U-boats.

'Yes, they're on the drawing board. Commander Goodlet is constructing loops for Cape Town and Durban, and hopefully Saldanha Bay. So it's in the pipeline, son, but everything takes too damn long.'

'And what about radar?'

'That too. Very hush-hush, of course, so we shouldn't even be talking about it, but the Bernard Price Laboratory at Witwatersrand University has been turned into a rudimentary radar factory. Installations are being erected around the coast as we speak. We even have one planned for False Bay —'

'Where?'

'Seal Island — a steel tower 200 feet high. Radar scanners will also be fitted on towers above Glencairn and inside East Dockyard. But this is secret stuff and still a way off.'

'Mum's the word. I just wish we could fit radar to at least one of our escorts. It would make a tremendous difference.'

'We've got HMS *Birmingham* in dock at the moment being fitted with radar, but it will be a while before the South African ships get any. *Gannet* and *Belle* will soon be joined by *Waterberg* and *Langeberg*, also converted whalers, to form a local convoy-escort group under your command. You'll all train together, just as you did with sweepers.'

'But, Father, I have no AS experience.'

'You've cut your teeth commanding a flotilla in combat. It's *that* experience we need. You'll learn on the job and Commander Dalgleish will be there to hold your hand.' The admiral smiled impishly.

Jack sighed and took a swig of whisky. There was no point arguing with his father.

'Both *Waterberg* and *Langeberg* are similar to the Southerns — about 150 feet in length, slower at fifteen knots and similarly armed,' said the admiral. 'I want yours to be a group without portfolio, able to be drafted into any task at hand, or to be a strike force if the need arises. Escorting duties will be mostly under the control of SNO Simon's Town, as he's in charge of convoys.'

'Oh dear, so I'll be reporting to Commodore O'Reilly again.'

'I'm afraid so.'

CHAPTER 2

Next morning, Jack returned to *Gannet* to start working his way through the pile of paperwork associated with the refit and impending return to sea. He climbed the ladder and, as he stepped over the rail, had to duck to avoid a dock worker swinging a spar like an axe. The decks were still a site of low-grade bedlam, but the steward ushered him into his cabin which was a sanctum of peace and cleanliness. Fido, the ship's incongruously named female cat, lay on Jack's cot and although she did not deign to get up, her baritone purring suggested she was pleased to see *Gannet*'s other captain.

'Fido has had a hard time of it with the dockworkers, Captain,' said AB Hendricks. 'So she's spent most of the time in her cabin … beg pardon, your cabin, sir.'

A clean towel, vase of flowers, the photograph of his mother in a silver frame, fresh blotting paper beside his *Birds of South Africa* by Austin Roberts and the comforting smell of wood polish. Home. 'God bless you, Hendricks,' Jack murmured. Neatly piled on his desk were letters, recent signals, a thick anti-submarine warfare manual and a morass of refit documentation. Jack sighed: once more into the paper breach, nibs fixed.

Fido hopped onto the desk and began assisting Jack by prostrating herself across the files and correspondence. He worked around the inconvenience until he came to a curious memo: 'Here, Fido, you'll be interested in this one. It's about your old nemesis, Just Nuisance.' The famous Great Dane and Fido did not see eye to eye and had once come to blows.

'It reads, "The commanding officer of HMS *Afrikander I*, Simon's Town, respectfully asks the heads of all service canteens, institutes and hotel managers to cooperate in controlling the canine rating known as Able Seaman Just Nuisance from partaking of excessive amounts of alcoholic drinks in their establishments. My regulating staff in the guardroom report that on several occasions he has required the assistance of other ratings to maintain his balance due to being drunk. This overindulgence is the result of ratings buying Nuisance too many drinks (his lager allowance is six quarts per night)." Aren't we lucky you're a teetotal sea cat, not a drunkard land dog, Fido?' Stretched full length across Jack's papers, she had dozed off. He did not have the heart to wake her and continued the paperwork from the comfort of his lap.

There was a knock at the door and PO Cummins stepped in. 'Cap'n, I think I'm going to blow a fuse.' The bosun's tomato-like face had turned a shade of purple. 'The dockyard lackeys are criminals of the lowest calibre. If you would permit me to wring just one of their necks, sir, I think it might set an example.'

'What now, PO?'

'Well, apart from mucking up my decks and everything, I checked the Carley float on the boat deck. As you know, sir, each raft has a keg of water and sealed tin of provisions for survivors. Well, the tin has been stolen — food that could save lives. That's murder, sir!'

'I completely agree, PO, but let's not make too much of a scene now that we're so close to being done with this lot. Perhaps we should get back in the water, and then give her a good going over ourselves, bring everything up to *Gannet* standard, with a quartermaster preventing any more dockies returning on board.'

'S'pose that's best, sir, but my blood pressure. I don't know how much more I can take.'

'I hear you, PO, I hear you.'

A little later, another tap at the door. It was the coxswain, PO February.

'Sorry to bother, sir, but there's a young subby on the slip, claims he's our new second watchkeeping officer.'

'Thank you, February, that will be Sub-Lieutenant Geoffrey Robinson, invite him aboard and send him to me directly.'

'Aye, Captain,' said the coxswain, touching his forelock.

A few minutes later, Jack heard voices followed by a knock.

'Enter.'

A tall figure neatly turned out in his black number ones stepped into the cabin and saluted. Jack's initial impression of his new officer was of spindly gawkiness, perhaps a certain foppishness. The smile was ready enough but seemed to betray haughtiness — that would soon get knocked out of him on *Gannet*. Perhaps this is precisely the first impression he'd made on the crew when he stepped aboard six months earlier: an aloof Englishman just arrived at the Cape with an admiral for a father and a silver tablespoon in his mouth.

'Sub-Lieutenant Robinson reporting for duty, sir.' His accent was almost as toffee as Jack's.

'Welcome aboard the *Gannet*, Lieutenant. You're fresh out of officer's course, I believe.'

'Yes, sir, just passed out.'

'Did you enjoy the course?'

'Yes, sir, six weeks ashore at the old RNVR base at the Castle under Commander Copenhagen and six weeks practical, much of it aboard HMSAS *Africana*.'

'And what did you do before joining up?'

'I was at the University of Cape Town studying architecture, got one year under the belt and decided to pack it in and join the navy, do my bit. I can always pick up where I left off after the war.'

'Good, well, our Number One isn't here so let me give you a quick tour of the ship. PO February can fill in the details.'

'He's already shown me the officers' cabin and had my luggage stowed.'

'February is a good man, the lynchpin of this ship. You can ask him anything.' Jack grabbed his cap and the two officers stepped out onto the foredeck. 'Through that hatch and underneath our feet is the seamen's mess and, below that, the bosun's store and ammunition store. Up on the forecastle is our main armament, a twelve-pounder, reliable but not very hard hitting. It's mounted where the harpoon used to sit when *Gannet* still hunted whales.'

Jack led Robinson up a ladder, through the wheelhouse and onto the open bridge. 'You'll be spending much of your life up here. We'll start with a watch-on-watch system with myself and the Number One taking the bulk of the load. When I think you're ready to handle the ship on your own, we'll switch to a three-watch system. In the coming weeks I want you to be a sponge, soak up every detail about *Gannet* as quickly as you can so you can pull your weight as soon as possible.'

'Certainly, sir, like a sponge.' Did Jack register a note of sarcasm in the young officer's voice? — a bit early for that and he'd better not have.

The pair continued aft past the captain's cabin and adjacent wireless room, wardroom, petty officers' mess and galley. 'Below our feet is the engine room, the denizen world of Chief ERA McEwan and home to his triple expansion three-cylinder steam engine powering a single prop. Above us on the boat deck we've got a Carley raft, the ship's boat and a single-barrel, two-pounder pom-pom which makes a lot of noise and deigns to fire the occasional shell.' They continued aft. 'Here on the quarterdeck is where all the fuss is at present. The dockyard chaps have been hard at work extricating our minesweeping gear and replacing it with two depth-charge racks on the stern, holding six drums each, and two depth-charge throwers on our quarters. Any questions?'

'Not yet, sir, but I'm sure there'll be lots in due course.'

'Very well, now I need to get back to my paperwork. Get settled in and report to the Number One as soon as he comes aboard.' Jack turned to go, then turned back. 'And, Robinson, on my ship never forget your OLQs.'

'Beg pardon, sir?'

'Officer-Like Qualities: being at all times punctilious, honourable, fair, dependable, brave and gentlemanly.'

'Ah, yes sir, of course.' Robinson blushed.

Jack walked back to his cabin not knowing quite what to make of the curious doppelgänger that had just made a home aboard his home.

The sailors of *Gannet* and *Belle* began to return to their ships, fresh from a generous helping of leave, and were put to work by both bosuns: scrubbing, chipping, painting and making ready for going back into the water.

Sub-Lieutenant Jan van Zyl climbed the slipway ladder and stepped aboard *Gannet*, having been recently promoted to first lieutenant, and reported directly to the captain's cabin.

'It's jolly good to have you back, Jannie, pull up a chair,' said Jack.

'Thank you, sir,' he said, taking off his cap.

'A pleasant leave?'

'No, not really, sir.'

'Still the family troubles?'

'Yes, still my wayward brother, Hans. He's getting more and more involved in the *Ossewabrandwag* — they're really just jumped-up Nazis trying to foment trouble.'

'That's no good, but we've got plenty to keep you distracted here. The refit is almost done and you'll have to take full responsibility for the ship from now on. As Number One, you'll be in charge of the day-to-day running of *Gannet*. You will be the intermediary between the crew and I, having my ear and mediating my authority. In many ways it's harder to be a good first lieutenant than a good captain and, you will find, almost requires a sixth sense. All the ship's problems get funnelled through you. Your first loyalty is to me and your second loyalty is to the men, a precarious balancing act. It's my job to look one way, but you need to be looking both fore and aft at all times. One does not want to speak ill of the dead — and your predecessor had many fine qualities — but Smit was not a good first lieutenant.'

'I think I'm ready for the challenge, sir.'

'I know you won't let me down… All right, Number One, the first thing you can do is take this crew list — you'll notice lots of new names — and prepare a watch-and-quarter bill before the new men arrive. I want them to see that even though we're still on the hard and undergoing surgery, this is a working ship that's efficiently run and means business.'

'Aye, captain!' Van Zyl said, rather too loudly and both men smiled, aware of the excitement in each other's eyes at the start of *Gannet*'s next chapter.

The new intake, replacing those killed in the action with *Sturmvogel*, arrived in Simon's Town on the back of a Bedford lorry with a first stop at the administration block to take their red-tab oath in the presence of a grey-whiskered lieutenant.

'Listen up, my hearties, I'm going to read out the South African oath of allegiance to serve anywhere on the African continent for four years or the duration of the war, whichever is shorter. When I'm finished, you raise your right hand and say, "I will." Then you'll be ready for drafting to your ship, which is to be HMSAS *Southern Gannet*, currently on the slip in West Dockyard.'

After a mumbled 'I will', the little party, draft chits in hand, was marched along St Georges Street, through the Victorian gates and down to the Patent Slipway.

'*Goeie fok*, she's a bit of an ugly duckling, hey boys?' said Seaman Malan, eyeing the ex-whaler. 'Lekker for fishing, but for fighting a war?'

'Better give her the benefit of the doubt, Fanie,' said Seaman Conradie. 'After all, she is our new home.'

Climbing aboard, the ratings were shown their bunks — three tiers lining the port and starboard bulkheads of the forward mess deck. They were hardly granted a moment to acclimatise before Cummins chased them out of their uniforms and into overalls and mustered them on the upper deck for chipping and scraping duties. Seaman Malan was set to work scrubbing the foredeck with a broom and pushing the excess water out through the large scuppers.

'What's with these *moerse* big holes near the waterline, PO?' he asked.

'Oh, lad, you'll find out soon enough,' said Cummins. '*Gannet* is seaworthy all right, but with no bilge keel to stop her rolling, and a bloody low freeboard, she's a wet ship — a bit like a submarine. Takes half the Atlantic on her decks and those scuppers release the tons of water she ships.'

'But the hatch to the seaman's mess is right here, PO!'

'Aye, Malan, as I said, a wet ship.'

Refit completed but still on the hard, the upper deck was at last free of all but a few dockyard workers applying the final touches. A flustered Chief McEwan arrived at Jack's cabin with a sheaf of papers to be signed, certifying that *Gannet* was ready to be returned to the briny, that no inlets had been left open and that their dockyard bedfellows had not, to their knowledge, shifted any ballast such as might alter the trim.

An hour later, *Gannet* slid slowly on her dolly back into the waters of Simon's Bay.

'At long last,' sighed Jack on the bridge.

The whaler was passed into the hands of the tug HMS *St Dogmael* and a smaller companion, which ushered her past the hulk of the old cruiser training ship *General Botha*, through the harbour's bullnose, across the basin and back to her regular berth beside the jetty in the south-eastern corner. Jack was pleased to see his Number One in a fit of high tension as he harried fender parties this way and that to prevent even the slightest scratch to their new paintwork. Soon after, *Gannet* was joined by *Southern Belle*, her giant Norwegian captain, Lieutenant Alstad, waving a greeting to Jack from the opposite bridge. Two out of four escorts were ready to start their working up and Jack was done with waiting.

CHAPTER 3

Jack woke to the shrill twittering of a sunbird outside his window, its call taken up by a pair of rock pigeons behind the cottage. He lay for a long time listening to the sounds of Simon's Town bringing itself to wakefulness: the dipping and wailing call of a muezzin from the mosque, the whispering of the sea on the sands of Long Beach, the deep throbbing of a launch heading out on patrol. Now a posse of guinea fowl clucked their way across the lawn, followed by the castanets of a train rounding the last bend and the squeal of its wheels as it drew to a halt in Snoek Town station. He had grown to love these early-morning sounds of his African home.

There was a tap on the glass of his French doors. 'Jack, my dear, are you awake?' came the voice of his elderly landlady. 'I've brought you a mug of *moerkoffie*.'

He got up and opened the doors in his striped pyjamas. 'Good morning, Miss R, and thank you.'

'A beautiful sunrise this morning,' she said, handing him the steaming mug. 'These windless, winter days are the best of the year on False Bay. Clear and golden, simply idyllic.'

Jack put on his leather slippers and crossed the lawn, ducking under the low boughs of the fig tree, to look at the town far below and the majestic sweep of the bay. The low sun cast a shimmering path across the sea to illuminate the old house, its tall, whitewashed façade greeting the new day. One of the shutters swung open to reveal Miss Retief moving about inside, adjusting the canvas on her easel, preparing her palette, choosing her brushes.

The stone terraces below the stoep were planted with olive and lemon trees or left feral with fynbos, reminding him of Greece. He watched a malachite sunbird in iridescent green livery land on the yellow orb of a pincushion protea like an avian Little Prince. Scanning the anchorage, Jack noticed that the harbour was again full to overflowing and a number of ships, including a cruiser and two destroyers swung at their anchors in the bay. 'Perfect targets,' he muttered, downing his coffee and heading inside to don his badly-ironed uniform.

The past weeks had been filled with an intensive spell of anti-submarine lectures and theoretical training. Today, the flotilla would be going to sea together for the first time. With *Gannet* and *Belle* back in the water, and *Waterberg* and *Langeberg* having joined them from Cape Town, Jack and his flotilla would now have the chance to put theory into practice and learn the dark art of AS warfare.

He cast his mind back over the preceding weeks of classroom training, followed by simulated war games. The officers and AS teams had sat at desks in a small, West Dockyard classroom with views of the anchorage. Lieutenant-Commander Dalgleish had been their principal lecturer and his classes were grim, rigorous, uncompromising affairs burdened with a considerable tonnage of theory that Jack struggled to stuff into his overloaded brain.

'As you will have noticed, control panels have been mounted in the wheelhouses of all four ships — that's where the operator will sit,' said Dalgleish as the class took notes. 'Each whaler has been fitted with an Admiralty Type 123 Asdic which can detect submarines to a maximum distance of 2,500 yards. The transmitter-receiver can be trained through 360 degrees using a turning wheel and the operator can read off on the compass the bearing of a returning echo from the transmitted ping. A good operator quickly makes the call of "Sub" or "Non-Sub"; a bad one sends his captain chasing shadows all over the shop. Given that the speed of sound in water is about 4,900 feet per second, the length of time between the outgoing transmission and the return echo provides your distance from the target, although this can vary depending on temperature and salinity. If the target is moving towards you, the pitch of the echo increases, and vice versa — a phenomenon known as the Doppler effect.

'Asdic also acts as a hydrophone, allowing you to listen to underwater noises such as dolphins, propellers and whatnot. The thing you really don't want to hear is the HE sound of a torpedo coming in your direction.' There were a few uncomfortable chuckles.

'How does one determine the depth of a U-boat, sir?' asked Sub-Lieutenant Robinson.

'One doesn't. Unfortunately, the navy's boffins have not yet found a way to determine exact depth. Your captain or AS officer will rely on his own judgement — more instinct really — in choosing how deep to set the depth charges.'

In his lectures, Dalgleish always stressed the need for prompt action and swift pursuit. 'If you get a U-boat report — say from a patrolling aircraft — you need to get there at your best possible speed as every minute counts. Assuming the enemy remains submerged and you arrive at the scene after one hour, you'll need to sweep an area of fifty square miles. An hour later, the area will have increased to two hundred square miles. A flotilla like yours can probably cover a patch of ocean of no more than ten square miles in one hour, but all the while the area you need to search is increasing exponentially. Of course, a landmass or other obstacle might help your cause, but you can appreciate the need for haste and good intuition, or a decent dollop of luck.'

The theory lectures completed, they progressed to war games conducted at the AS school adjacent to the Fish Market in Cape Town docks. The 'attack teacher' consisted of a glass plotting table covered with thin paper. A lantern projected a moveable spot of light on the underside of the paper to represent the escort. A mirror and beam of light under the glass represented the Asdic beam, while a submarine was indicated by a moveable cross on the plotting table. An adjacent room housed the kind of Asdic equipment found on an escort and it was from here that the trainee Asdic operator controlled the instruments and received an echo in his headphones if his beam passed over the submarine. There was also a voicepipe through which the AS officer could give orders to the convoy and escorts. Changes in course and speed were applied to the plotting table by an AS Wren of cold demeanour and striking beauty. Her aura alone contributed to the loss of many imaginary ships.

A third room housed a vast plot laid out on the floor with model ships representing the convoy and escorts. On a shelf sat dozens of models representing all the warring nations that might be encountered off the Cape, allowing The Black Death to mix and match his attackers and defenders (demonically, it seemed to Jack) as he saw fit. Officers sat in cubicles around the edge of the room and looked through slits that only offered as much as they were likely to see from the bridge of an escort in various light conditions.

Every morning, a new game was begun and soon sighting reports, foul weather and sunk ships added to the drama as each captain was given the chance to mount a defence or use his escorts to counterattack. The statuesque Wren was on hand to move the ships or bring the 'latest signals', continually upping the ante, and all the while Dalgleish loomed large, adding sarcastic comments and breathing too loudly through his nose. The officers' decisions, tactics and the speed of their reactions were noted down for brutal subsequent analysis.

When it came to Jack's turn, he found that he was surprisingly nervous. There were so many elements to take into account, so much to be wary of, and he was conscious of the need to make a good impression on his two new captains, Cowley and Fourie. But there were times when even helm orders seemed perplexing and the Wren looked at him with a mixture of boredom and mild pity as the handsome Englishman stumbled over his commands. To be fair, given the barrage of U-boat attacks unleashed by The Black Death, all the officers and Asdic ratings suffered regular losses. As senior officer, Jack was usually chosen as leader of the escort group protecting the convoy and whenever he lost a model ship he was painfully aware, as was everyone else in the room, that in a few weeks' time the ships would not be models.

Nevertheless, the attack teacher was a great help to Jack and his team, allowing them to understand convoy defence and gain some insight into the mind of a U-boat commander. Perhaps most useful were the smoking-room discussions between sessions during which Dalgleish encouraged robust debate and chipped in with his own elucidation.

While the officers and Asdic teams tried to sink U-boats on the plotting table, depth-charge parties from each whaler were taught the ins and outs of the dustbin-sized canisters filled with Amatol that had found a home on their quarterdecks. They learnt that the charges exploded under the hydrostatic pressure of water and that the depth dial on each drum could be set to six different-sized holes that allowed water into the pistol chamber. The size of the hole determined the speed of the seawater entering the chamber. When full, a spring was released, thrusting the detonator against the primer which exploded, detonating the Amatol. Teams from each ship competed against each other and were drilled until they could fire full patterns at twenty-second intervals.

Now it was time for the four whalers to begin training together in the relatively calm waters of False Bay. But The Black Death had far more in store for them than mere anti-submarine exercises and the next fourteen days would test the nerves and resilience of every sailor in the flotilla.

It was 0600 and still dark in Simon's Town, but for the crew of *Gannet* it was time to prepare for sea once more. High above the harbour, Jack made his way along the garden path, beneath the pomegranate and custard apple trees, through the farm gate and down the gravel track. At the bottom of the hill, he stepped onto St Georges Street and turned right, making his way into town past the RN Officers' Club with its tall white gable and arches, the pedimented Runciman's grocer and equally grand British Hotel, then Eaton's haberdashery, Rowland's fish shop and Cader's barber shop — the world of a British naval town so familiar to him from his time in places such as Hove and Portsmouth.

Just beyond the Dutch Reformed Church with its striking white pinnacles, he showed his pass and entered East Dockyard gates, making his way through the bustling base to his flotilla in the far corner of the basin past warships great and small, the white dashes of their ensigns set against the dark ramparts of Simonsberg. He passed Just Nuisance, coming down the gangplank of a cruiser where he'd no doubt been requisitioning food or terrorising a ship's pet. February had mentioned that Nuisance recently killed a dog mascot on a corvette, but was banned from *Gannet*, where Fido ruled the roost.

Jack reached the brow of his ship and paused. *Gannet* had become the centre of his life, both a moral force and a weapon with which to hit back at the enemy, to put right the wrongs that had vested on him and the world. She was an extension of him. 'My ship,' he said under his breath, feeling a sense of possession, but also of being possessed, as he stepped across the brow.

Robinson, the bosun and a small party of seamen stood on the foredeck awaiting his arrival. They came to attention and saluted as he crossed the narrow strip of water and stepped aboard to the fluttering trill of a bosun's pipe. Its sound had come to mean so much to Jack, signifying his place in the system and his command of this feisty little ship. It was a call that connected him to his brother serving on a destroyer in the North Sea, to his admiral father, his grandfather and all the other Pembrokes that stretched back into the Royal Navy's foggy past.

At such moments, he felt that he was a link, perhaps even a worthy link, in a long chain of history and custom. These moments never lasted, and his frustration with his father's overbearing nature, the Andrew's inefficiencies and with the weighty burden of tradition would reassert themselves soon enough. But these precious, uncomplicated seconds of being piped aboard his own ship, of taking command and making ready for sea once more, of preparing to fight the enemy again, filled him with a strange joy and behind it, always, the shadow of fear that he would fall short of the mark.

When had he heard the bosun's piercing call for the first time? It must have been as a little boy, watching his father being piped aboard his cruiser back in Pompey. The high-pitched trilling, the ceremony and pomp attendant upon it and his father, a chest full of medals and a vision in his best uniform, like a lord, stepping across the brow to take command. Perhaps that's where the seed had been planted. Perhaps Oxford and London and his brief venture into journalism had all been digressions. Or perhaps *this* was the great digression.

An hour later, *Gannet* was ready for sea. The stokers had flashed up their boilers to raise steam earlier that morning, the fuelling and storing had been completed and the last of the ammunition taken in, a job for most of the hands with shells and depth charges being hauled aboard and securely stowed under the watchful eye, and spicy tongue, of PO 'Guns' Combrink.

The flotilla's three other captains reported aboard *Gannet* for a final briefing and were now seated around the wardroom table upon which Jack had spread a chart of False Bay and Hendricks served tea.

The tall blond Norwegian, Sven Alstad, captain of *Southern Belle,* Jack knew well. He was a former whaler who had hunted southern rights and fins from Donkergat on the West Coast before the war — a man he could completely depend on. Angus Cowley, captain of *Waterberg,* was RNVR (SA) and a weekend sailor at Royal Cape Yacht Club — good-humoured, pipe-smoking and quick with a quip but not up to scratch in the discipline department on his vessel, or so Jack surmised. Bearded Jacques Fourie of *Langeberg* was the son of a farm foreman in the Groot Drakenstein Valley and had been a

General Botha boy, receiving a decent naval education on the training ship — he appeared to be solid and reliable, if unimaginative.

After a short discussion about the training ahead, each captain giving his input, Jack addressed the group: 'To effectively protect our anchorages and convoys, we need to learn how to defend and to hunt as a team in the coming weeks. We will need to find out how and when to parry and when to thrust. That's part of what these working-up exercises are about. We will need to find out where our strengths lie, and if we have weaknesses, eliminate them. Rest assured, Commander Dalgleish will be probing every chink in our armour and I'm going to be leaning hard on the three of you, but I am certain you're up to it. Any questions?'

There were shakes of the head and a few cautious, or perhaps nervous, smiles.

'Right then, let's get to it, shall we?'

CHAPTER 4

The black Citroën drew up beside a vast concrete structure that looked more like a bunker than a harbour installation.

'This is it, Herr Kruger, through the big steel doors and left under the first arch,' said the uniformed driver. 'I will bring your luggage aboard shortly.'

'*Danke sehr*, and be very careful with the steel cases,' he said, unfolding his lanky body and stepping out.

It had been a long and wearisome journey by train from Berlin to the sleepy French port of Lorient. A breeze from the Atlantic took the edge off the heat and the seaweed tang reminded him of his family farm on the West Coast of South Africa. At long last, he was about to take the first step that would bring him back home.

Dressed in a dark brown suit and homburg he made an impressive figure as he strode across the tarmac and through the tall doors. The interior was dimly lit, cathedral-like, filled with the thunder of industry — the throb of a generator and hollow clang of riveting hammers — and occasionally brightened by the dancing sparks of welding torches.

Turning a corner, he came upon the U-boat, floating in its pen like a sinister, elongated whale. Gerhardus Kruger stopped short and stared, dismayed at the thought that this steel tube was to be his new home. He hated confined spaces and even as a boy on the farm when searching for those mysterious cave paintings left by the Bushman his grandfather had hunted, he'd felt claustrophobic. A constriction in the chest, a burning need to escape, like a leopard in a trap, thrashing at the cage as it waited for the farmer's bullet. For how many agonising weeks, or months, would he be stuck in the belly of this creature before he could breathe African air once more?

'May I help you, sir?' asked a passing sailor burdened by a sack draped over his shoulder.

'Is this *U-68*?'

'*Jawol.*'

'I'm looking for Fregattenkapitän Brand.'

'He is not yet aboard, but the first lieutenant is. Ask for Oberleutnant zur See Lingen. There, that is him, the tall one on the bridge.'

Kruger walked slowly along the wharf scrutinising the leviathan whose body swarmed with men loading stores and making final adjustments to equipment; torpedoes lay in cradles on the dock ready to be lowered through the forward hatch. A sentry with a submachine gun slung across his chest directed Kruger down the gangway and up a ladder on the side of the conning tower. As his head came level with the bridge he was met by a big, smiling face with full, sensuous lips. 'So, you are Herr Kruger, our precious cargo?'

'*Heil Hitler!*' Kruger gave the straight-arm salute as soon as he'd drawn himself upright. The lieutenant touched his cap with two fingers in response.

'Oberleutnant Lingen?' Kruger stuck out a hand.

'*Ja*, welcome aboard *U-68*.' Lingen sized up the mysterious guest they would have to make room for on the long voyage ahead: a tall man, with a dark complexion, imitation Hitler moustache and coal-black eyes. He had a defined jaw, dimples that looked like duelling scars and thin lips that appeared familiar with cruelty. Lingen surmised that those lips would have difficulty smiling. 'Have you ever been on a U-boat before, Herr Kruger?'

'No, and I would have preferred never, but one does what one has to do for the fatherland.'

'Your fatherland or our fatherland?' asked the lieutenant with a quizzical smile.

'What do you mean?'

'Your accent, Herr Kruger, you are not German.'

'Both fatherlands,' he said curtly.

'Good.' Lingen chuckled. 'Very good. All will be revealed in due course, no doubt. Come, let us go below and get you settled. The *Kapitän* will come aboard later. It is my job to prepare the boat for sea. Your luggage?'

'My driver is bringing it, but he might need help with the steel cases. They contain a radio transmitter and explosives.'

'I will ask the *Steuermann* to stow them carefully.'

They climbed through the hatch and down a ladder via the conning tower into the control room. To Kruger, its dim interior presented a confusion of dials, wheels, gauges and pipes of which he could make no sense. His nostrils were assaulted by a mixture of oil, bilge fumes, boiled cabbage, new paint and unwashed clothing; he breathed shallowly through his mouth to avoid the worst of it. The cramped spaces were already exerting a familiar pressure on his chest and he glanced up the conning tower to the circle of light from the oval hatch: his only escape. Although the submarine was tethered and all but immobile, Kruger felt unsteady on his feet.

'This is the heart of our boat, the *Zentrale* — just like the wheelhouse of a ship,' said Lingen. 'Here is the helm, the controls for the diving planes, the main ballast-control valves and periscope. And this is Leutnant zur See Klaus Seebohm, our handsome second officer and romantic Aryan hero, elegantly draped over his navigation table. Klaus, meet our passenger, Herr Kruger.'

The blushing officer's eyes were furtive as he shook hands, his white-blond hair and matching eyebrows giving him a bleached look.

'Come, Herr Kruger, let us continue our tour,' said Lingen. '*U-68* is a Type IX U-boat, built in Bremen in 1940. These craft are bigger than the usual Type VIIs you will have seen on all the newsreels and they have a much longer range. A top speed of eighteen knots on the surface, seven knots submerged. Type IXs have good fangs too: four torpedo tubes in the bows and two in the stern, as well as a 10.5-centimetre gun on the foredeck and two anti-aircraft guns.'

'How many crew?' asked Kruger.

'Including you, we will be fifty-one. You look a little pale, are you feeling all right?'

'*Ja, ja*, quite all right, I'm just getting used to the new environment. It's very, er, confined.'

'Not at all, you should try a Type VII.'

'No thank you.'

They moved forward through a hatch, passing the radio and hydrophone alcoves opposite the captain's quarters. Kruger brushed the green curtain aside and saw a narrow bunk, a small washstand with a lid that could convert into a table and, above the pillow, a photograph of a pretty young woman with a cautious smile.

They stepped through into the officers' sleeping quarters which also served as the wardroom with handsome wood panelling, black-leather fitted settee and bookshelf. Kruger ran his eye over the spines: Goethe's *Italian Journey*, Baudelaire and Karl May, *All Quiet on the Western Front*, Nansen's *In Night and Ice*, a few out-of-date *Deutsche Allgemeine Zeitung* and *Le Figaro* newspapers, *The Brothers Karamazov* (perhaps problematic since the launch of Operation Barbarossa the previous month) and a well-thumbed copy of *Murder on the Orient Express* (also unpatriotic, although the old English duck was certainly harmless).

'This will be your bunk — port side, bottom, and you can put your things in this cupboard.'

'But they'll never fit!'

'What does not fit we throw overboard.'

Kruger looked shocked: 'But —'

'I am only joking with you, Herr Kruger.' He beamed an enormous smile. 'We will make a plan, ha, ha!'

The two men brushed past cured sausages and polonies hung from the deckhead like grotesque penises and hammocks packed with loaves of bread. They skirted the tiny galley — source of the pervading cabbage smell — past a small head that was already reeking even before they'd put to sea, and into the non-commissioned officers' accommodation. The pair stepped through a final hatch into the junior ranks' quarters, a space crammed with men busy unloading crates and stowing sacks and cordage wherever space could be found between the bunks and hammocks. Sleek, gleaming torpedoes filled much of the interior; photos of scantily clad UFA film stars adorned the open lockers.

'We have a hot-bunking system, so these twelve bunks are home to twenty-four sailors: torpedo-men, stokers, telegraphists, seamen. We carry twenty-two eels, so until we have fired off a few, the surplus ones have to be stored here,' said Lingen. 'As you can imagine, their lordships are always keen to take some shots at the enemy to make their boudoir a little more capacious. Come, let us go aft and I will show you the engine room.'

They retraced their steps through the sleeping quarters and control room to the engine compartment where Kruger was introduced to Leading Engineer Hoppe, custodian of the U-boat's electric motors and powerful MAN diesel engines. Lingen explained that the electric motors, which didn't require external air, drove the boat when submerged and were powered by batteries, which were charged by the diesels when surfaced. On the starboard side stood a large compressor for recharging the boats high-pressure air supply. *Our lifeblood*, thought Kruger, feeling sweat breaking out on his brow as he eyed the confusion of rheostats, ammeters and voltmeters.

'When we are on the surface and the diesels are running at full speed, you cannot hear yourself think in here, and hot!' said Lingen. 'Dante's inferno without the poetry.'

They stepped through another hatchway into the junior ranks compartment and stern torpedo room, even more cramped and hellish than the accommodation in the bows. Here was the boat's second head, but the cubicle was filled to bursting with perishables and would only be functional once they'd eaten their way through its contents. So there would be only a single toilet for fifty-one men for how many weeks? Kruger gave a shudder and tasted bile at the back of his throat. He'd seen enough to know that the coming voyage was going to comprise a series of trials, colourful in their variety, texture and horror.

'Now I will let you unpack, Herr Kruger. Kapitän Brand will be aboard shortly and hopefully the final stragglers. Last night was a bit, ah, shall we say, *chaotisch*. Some of the men are still being dragged from the arms of the local whores and their Schnapps bottles. A painful separation, as you can imagine.'

'When do we set sail?'

'At 1800, so there is lots to be done.'

As Kruger unpacked and tried to stuff his belongings into the tiny locker, the last of the crew came aboard, all reeking of alcohol. One seaman, slurring a bawdy shanty and swearing profanities, had to be carried to his bunk. Kruger took out his Afrikaans Bible, his most precious possession, and slipped it under his pillow.

'So, you are to be my guest for this little cruise of ours,' said a voice behind him.

Kruger swung round to meet the eyes of a stocky man with a white cap perched askew on his head. A chubby face, strawberry blond hair, big white teeth fit for a toothpaste advertisement, pale blue eyes and a voice that was surprisingly high pitched.

'*Heil Hitler!*' Kruger saluted. 'Fregattenkapitän Brand?'

'It is I. Welcome aboard. I am sorry I was not here when you arrived, but I had my final briefing with Konteradmiral Dönitz.'

'Of course, Kapitän, your first lieutenant has been very helpful.' He hesitated. 'I take it you have been briefed on my mission?'

'Yes, in general terms. My sealed orders are only to be opened once we have left Lorient. I will tell my men once we are at sea, but not all the details. We will be slipping shortly, come up to the bridge when you are finished. There is normally a bit of fanfare and fuss on the quayside when we depart.'

By now, the boat's interior was humming with activity as the final stores were hurried aboard and the last of the anti-aircraft ammunition was stowed in its compartment beneath the galley. Items were being dumped in the alleyways and men squeezed past each other looking for places to squirrel items away. The coxswain and quartermaster bellowed orders and chivvied their charges, many of them the worse for wear from the previous night. To escape the confusion, Kruger climbed the ladder to the bridge.

'Ah, there you are,' said Brand, rubbing his hands together. 'Fully provisioned, ammunition loaded, tanks full. *U-68* is ready, Herr Kruger, as ready as any boat can be.'

'God willing, we will make a safe passage, Kapitän.'

'We have no place for God on this boat. Here, I am God,' he chortled and slapped Kruger on the shoulder. 'Don't look so worried, *Kamerad*!'

The wire-handling party had assembled on the dock and the metal gate to the pen stood open. 'Let go all lines, hold on the forward spring!' called the captain as dock workers slipped the hoops from their iron bollards, lines splashed into the oily water and were hauled aboard to the sound of scraping on the casing as *U-68* edged away from the slimy green wall.

'All clear aft, sir!'

The U-boat reversed out of the pen using her electric motors and emerged from the concrete womb into the honeyed light of late afternoon. On the wharf, a brass band in steel helmets struck up a jaunty martial tune punctuated by loud cymbal clashes. The crew mustered on the casing smiled at the small crowd that had gathered, including a few officers from the base, dock workers in dirty overalls, a handful of young women in uniform and a group of nurses who waved and cheered as *U-68* slowly turned within her length. A bouquet of white flowers landed on the foredeck, another bunch fell in the water and swirled along their grey flank before being sucked under. A nurse called Lieutenant Seebohm's name; he blushed and looked away as Lingen elbowed him in the ribs.

'Stop starboard, half ahead port,' said Brand.

With a shudder the port screw thrashed at the dirty water contained by the basin as *U-68* turned to face the mouth of the Scorff Estuary.

'Stop port motor.'

The low, bass pulse of brass instruments reached them like the wheezing agonies of a dying animal.

'Slow ahead together, starboard ten.'

U-68 gave a mournful hoot as she drew away from the pens, answered by a distant tug.

'Steer course two-one-zero.'

Kruger glanced back at the submarine bunkers, an enormous complex still under construction and swathed in scaffolding. There were scars from recent bombing, but although the town had taken a pasting, the pens appeared unscathed.

'The roof is ferro-concrete seven metres thick,' said Captain Brand, noticing Kruger's gaze. 'Our boats are safe in there, but it is out in the Bay of Biscay — the RAF's hunting ground — that we are so damn vulnerable.'

As *U-68* gathered way, heading for the buoyed channel out of the estuary, Kruger scanned the array of vessels tied up along the quays: harbour-defence craft, battered trawlers serving as patrol boats, lighters and oil barges. They slid past a row of seaside villas on the Kernével Peninsula, their façades burnished by the low sun.

'Do you see that pink, three-storey house?' asked Brand.

'The one with the gable and top-hat roof?'

'*Ja.*'

'Looks like a little château.'

'That is Villa Kerlilon, from where Konteradmiral Dönitz controls his marionettes. We all dance to the strings that extend from that building to every corner of the Atlantic.'

'Do you know the admiral well?'

'Not very, no one can know him well, but he is like a father to me. He knows everything about his U-boat captains and there is a great deal of trust between us. I truly believe he is one of the Reich's greatest leaders. We call him Der Löwe, the Lion, and he calls us his Grey Wolves. It is a very special bond.'

Kruger heard the squeak of halyards and turned to watch as the scarlet flag emblazoned with black cross and swastika was lowered by a signals rating, who bent the cloth over his arm and neatly folded it. He felt a surge of emotion: his second home was Germany and perhaps one day, God willing, that great nation would be umbilically linked to his first home, South Africa. His reverie was interrupted by a whining sound, then a cough, followed by the loud bubbling of diesel engines. He rested his hands on the bridge casing, feeling the submarine's pulse and sensing his own anticipation, mixed with the reciprocal pulse of his apprehension. Beneath his feet, the deck vibrations increased as *U-68* picked up speed past the grey ramparts of the citadel of Port Louis, fired by the sun's last rays.

'Here comes the *U-Bootbegeleitschiff* to lead us through the minefield and give us cover from aerial attack,' said the captain. 'The British are getting increasingly brazen and we are not even safe inside our own approach buoys.'

The stubby vessel bristling with anti-aircraft weapons reminded Kruger of an alarmed porcupine. As they took up station behind the minesweeper, the bollards on their upper deck were retracted and the wires, basketwork fenders and boathooks stowed away; sailors took down the ensign staff and went about tightening the clips on every hatch with spanners.

'If you want to spend time on the bridge, you will have to sing for your supper and assist with watchkeeping, Herr

Kruger. An extra pair of eyes is always useful, especially when we are within range of enemy aircraft.'

'I would like that, Kapitän.'

'Good. If the weather is bad, you can use the black oilskins hanging on hooks in the control room and the coxswain will see that you get leathers and boots.'

The sun was melting on the horizon; seagulls dipped and wheeled around them emitting an unearthly crying; the U-boat's bow wave gleamed like liquid metal as they sailed into the west. The wind had turned chilly and Kruger decided to go below. Climbing down the ladder, he found the control room a haven of order: the quartermaster at the wheel, the two planesmen bent to their dials, Lingen standing behind the periscope with his arms folded and Seebohm leaning over the chart, a pencil in one hand and a slide-rule in the other.

With the help of Coxswain Fischer, Kruger acquired stiff grey leathers and sea-boots with thick cork soles. He sat on his bunk to drag on the heavy footwear, but was overcome by a sudden dizziness, the sensation of hands clawing at his throat, of air being sucked from his lungs. He needed to get out, get back to the bridge, to daylight, but his legs had turned to concrete. The cave's dark interior contracted, its grotesque paintings of stick figures dancing towards him across the rock, taunting him … the escape hatch jammed, the boat sinking into the icy depths, his chest tightening, water pouring in and filling this death chamber, bodies pressed to the ceiling gasping their last.

Out, out! He must get out!

Closing his eyes, he sucked in deep breaths, the sweat beading on his face. He must grab hold of himself, concentrate on the simple act of putting on the boots, pulling on the leathers and climbing slowly, deliberately, back up the ladder.

Through a force of will, he managed to reach the bridge, where he found the land shrunk to a grey smudge and the sun set. The U-boat rose and dipped into a larger swell, the engine noise rhyming with the seesaw motion, falling when the exhausts were awash, increasing when they emerged and the diesel fumes could escape.

Kruger felt the queasiness rising and clung to the bridge rail while the captain, a bemused smile on his face, flexed his knees and swayed to the Atlantic's rhythm, not needing a handhold.

'Keep your eyes on the horizon and breathe deeply,' said Brand. 'You'll get used to it.'

But he felt helpless as the nausea grew, coming in waves that rose in his throat, threatening with each lurch to fell him. Eventually, he could hold out no longer and leant over the side to retch, but found that he could not be sick. He spat repeatedly onto the casing and rested his cheek on the cold steel of the rail, then hunched at the back of the bridge, feeling utterly miserable as the sky painted itself into fiery shades of crimson and orange.

Upon reaching the hundred-fathom line, the minesweeper made a signal, wheeled around to pass within hailing distance and flashed a farewell.

'Good hunting!' came a cry from her bridge.

Captain Brand grimaced and waved. 'Fools,' he said under his breath.

The U-boat increased speed, following a zigzag course southwest across the bay and into the darkness, lunging into the troughs as curtains of spray wafted over the bridge and the swell rumbled along the saddle tanks. Kruger tasted salt on his lips and thought once more of home: the cove where, as a boy, he'd fished for galjoen, hottentot and crayfish, and used a metal bar to prize plate-sized perlemoen from the rocks.

'Here, make yourself useful, it will take your mind off being sick,' said the captain, handing him a pair of binoculars. 'Stand next to Seemann Borchers and copy exactly what he does. Each lookout takes a quadrant and sweeps the sea and sky. You will soon get the hang of it.'

'I … I will try,' said Kruger, his voice thin and dry.

'The British have the knack of knowing exactly when we leave port. It can hardly be kept secret: increased traffic at the brothels whenever a U-boat arrives or departs is all the spies need. A randy German sailor is like a red flag to the RAF.'

Just twenty minutes later, Brand's predictions were confirmed.

'*Alarm!*' yelled Seaman Borchers. 'Aircraft, green one-six-zero!'

A startled Kruger could see nothing in the direction the lookout was pointing.

'Clear the bridge! Dive, dive, dive!' yelled the captain.

Kruger stood transfixed. The Hudson was suddenly upon them, swooping out of a cloud like a vengeful albatross, white in its apocalyptic vestments. The lookout had spotted it too late. Machine-gun rounds pinged off metal and pecked at the conning tower. One sailor let out a scream as his shoulder and chest exploded into roses of scarlet.

'Get below, *verdammt!*' cursed Brand.

Kruger was grabbed by the arm, yanked through the hatchway and fell down the ladder, twisting his ankle as he landed in the control room. Borchers crashed on top of him and the two rolled away as the next two lookouts tumbled down carrying their screaming, blood-soaked mate. Only then did Kruger became aware of the klaxon filling the boat with fearful howling.

The diesel engines stopped, casting a moment of eerie silence before the electric motors were hastily engaged. Through the conning tower hatch, Kruger could hear the growl of the aircraft mixed with the roar of air being forced from the ballast tanks.

'Forward, everyone forward!' shouted Coxswain Fischer as crewmen rushed to the bows to assist the crash dive and Kruger bent himself into a corner of the control room.

On the bridge, the captain snapped shut the cocks on the voicepipes, took a last glance at the sharply banking aircraft, dropped through the hatch and spun the brass locking wheel just as the sea breasted the coaming and inundated the bridge. He slid down the ladder, fingers slipping on blood, and a rating pulled closed the lower hatch with a loud clang. Perhaps taken by as much surprise as themselves, the pilot had not dropped his depth charges on the first run and was describing a tight turn to administer the fatal blow.

Crushed by an overwhelming sense of doom, Kruger's mind was in turmoil: how long did they have to live? '*Onse Vader wat in die hemele is...*' he began reciting the Lord's Prayer, then broke off to curse under his breath, '*Fok* this, give me a Mauser, a full bandolier and a Tommy at two hundred yards, not this *kak*: bobbing in a barrel, waiting to be shot.'

'One hundred metres, full ahead together, hard a-starboard!' called Brand, his eyes flashing. 'Shut off for depth-charging!'

The Hudson completed its circle and came in low, aiming at a spot just ahead of where the conning tower had just submerged, its frothy wake providing a perfect target. Kruger imagined bomb doors opening as the aircraft dived towards them. Bile climbed in his throat and he scrambled to his feet making for the head, but he was not fast enough and left a trail of vomit along the alleyway. Wiping his mouth with the back of his hand, he crawled instead onto his bunk and curled into a ball.

'Four *Wabos*, very close!' shouted the hydrophone operator, ripping off his headset to protect his ears from the anticipated blasts. There was no way the depth charges could miss: fish in a barrel indeed.

Kruger had only just begun his mission to liberate the fatherland ... and now it was to end abruptly, prematurely, perversely, like this.

CHAPTER 5

Jack climbed to the open bridge and saluted Lieutenant-Commander Dalgleish, who had got there before him and would be overseeing the exercises. As Jack looked down at the mooring lines and checked the wind speed, he recalled the first time he'd taken *Gannet* to sea and, trembling with nerves, nearly collided with *Belle*. It had been a display of shoddy seamanship and he felt renewed embarrassment at the memory. A repeat was *not* on the cards today.

Jack turned to the quartermaster and said, 'Pipe "Hands to stations for leaving harbour".'

The call echoed around the ship followed by a clatter of boots that filled Jack with excitement, and mild butterflies. His first lieutenant, signalman and two lookouts were beside him on the bridge, as was The Black Death, peering down his nose at proceedings from the starboard rail. The forecastle party was mustered and PO February stood at his post one deck below, his calloused hands bent around the wheel's spokes.

'Hello harbour master, hello harbour master, this is *Gannet*, request permission to leave port, over,' said Leading Seaman 'Sparks' Thomas in the wireless cabin below the wheelhouse.

'Hello *Gannet*, this is harbour master, you are clear to leave, over.' Thomas cut the power to the transmitter, opened the voicepipe cover next to his desk and said, 'Bridge, we have permission to leave harbour, sir.'

'Very good, thank you, Sparks,' said Jack, before picking up the speaking trumpet and calling, 'Let go stern rope, Bosun!'

Dalgleish was at his shoulder, hands behind his back, looking nonchalant but obviously taking a keen interest. Jack turned to the foredeck and shouted down to Sub-Lieutenant Robinson, 'Let go head rope, but keep her on the spring. Slow ahead.' Into the voicepipe he said, 'Ten degrees, starboard wheel, Coxswain.'

'Aye, Cap'n,' February's voice rumbled up the pipe.

The stern swung slowly away from the jetty. 'Stop engine. Let go spring! Slow astern.'

Gannet eased past *Belle* as fenders were hauled aboard. She slid stern-first into the basin to a low throbbing, described a neat turn, stopped, aimed her bows at the bullnose and then, piping the senior ships as she passed, chugged slowly towards the entrance.

On this first outing, Dalgleish would supervise tests to the new Asdic equipment in the wheelhouse, to the depth-charge racks and throwers, and make sure that all the AS fittings were watertight. Either Van Zyl, Robinson or PO Combrink accompanied him at all times to learn the ropes and each one reported back to Jack looking the worse for the encounter.

'Demanding, is he?' Jack asked.

'Aye, Captain, you might call it that,' said Van Zyl.

Dalgleish was transferred to each ship in turn to supervise their tests and the flotilla only returned to port after sunset.

Next morning, *Gannet* once again led the anti-submarine flotilla out of Simon's Town harbour and, sailing line astern, headed east-southeast, leaving Roman Rock Light to port. Jack leant over the rail and looked aft to see *Belle* keeping perfect station, but *Waterberg* and *Langeberg* were still finding their feet. He resisted flashing them a badgering signal just yet: he would give Cowley and Fourie another day to adjust.

Appearing on the bridge, Dalgleish was scathing about their station keeping and, as if to punish them, initiated a series of drills that sowed chaos throughout the flotilla: stop engines and send away boats to pick up survivors; signalmen to dismantle the aerial and rig a temporary one; prepare to take a merchant ship in tow; *Belle* to send a boarding party to *Waterberg* and *Gannet* to send one to *Langeberg*; drop anchor … and now let go a second anchor. They fought imaginary fires, closed up for action stations against a stopwatch, and put armed landing parties ashore on Glencairn Beach.

Over the ensuing days, they were worked to a standstill carrying out repeated anti-submarine exercises. On some nights, they formed up to protect an imaginary convoy, sailing south out of False Bay until the early hours, then slowly back to arrive at dawn. Halfway through their trials, they spent a night at anchor between the harbour and Lower North Battery. The crews were utterly spent and fell into their bunks, but a good night's rest was not to be.

At 0100, Dalgleish came alongside *Gannet* in a motorboat. 'Officer of the watch!' he bellowed.

'Yes, sir!' A befuddled Robinson popped his head over the bridge rail and peered down in trepidation.

'You have been rammed amidships, your stern is on fire and a U-boat is preparing to attack the anchorage. *Do something!*'

As the alarm bells clanged through *Gannet*, the motorboat was on its way to the other whalers, bent on a similar capsizing of the peace.

To Jack's dismay, the next day Commodore O'Reilly joined them in a borrowed motor yacht to oversee the business end of their AS training as senior referee officer. At times, the yacht represented a convoy and the four whalers had to form a protective screen around her. Acerbic remarks fluttered from her stays and flashed from her Aldis lamp, chivvying Jack's charges into different formations, only to change the orders and tactics in an instant, from defence to attack to simulated sinking.

Robinson was in command of *Gannet*'s depth-charge crew and had yet to come to grips with either the task or his men. At least his key rating — Seaman Rademan, who saw to the settings and dropping — appeared up to scratch. Much of the heavy lifting aft involved reloading the throwers, which needed skilful teamwork, but Robinson didn't seem able to galvanise his motley crew of off-watch stokers, a signalman and the cook. To Jack, it appeared his young sub-lieutenant viewed the task as somehow beneath him and in the drills *Gannet* was consistently slower than the other three ships.

'What the hell is going on, Sub?' he demanded of Robinson at the end of a depth-charging practice. 'Are you hosting a teddy bear's picnic party back there?'

'No, sir, it's just —'

'I don't care a tuppenny damn for your excuses! If we get the chance to chase a U-boat, the quarterdeck drill will need to be seamless and for Christ's sake don't forget to set the depths *before* removing the lashings from the charges ... like you did this morning. Take control of your crew, take a tougher line with the slackers. I want those throwers reloaded in under twenty seconds, do you hear me!'

'Yes, sir.' Robinson's face was flushed as he looked down at the deck.

During the next drill, conducted alongside, the situation hardly improved. Robinson presided over a catalogue of mistakes and delays; his crew appeared increasingly disgruntled and intractable, perhaps even deliberately sabotaging his efforts. At the end of one exercise, Van Zyl overheard Robinson's half-hearted chastisement: 'I'm afraid that wasn't entirely successful, chaps. I think we need to hurry things up a tad.' Dalgleish unloaded on Jack, who seethed at the inefficiency of his quarterdeck. Time was what Robinson needed, he told himself … his new officer would come right in the end.

Returning to harbour after exercises the following day, *Gannet* was passing Roman Rock Light when one of the depth-charge throwers accidentally fired. It was on a shallow setting and, as *Gannet* had been moving slowly, the thunderous explosion lifted her stern and caused *Belle* to swing wildly to port to avoid the water cascade.

'Good God!' Jack gasped in a moment of terror that spirited him back to the Stukas of Dunkirk, their 550-pound bombs striking the water around HMS *Havoc*. *Howl, howl, a terrible upending of the world!* Just as quickly it passed, and he registered a strange sense of relief that he was in Simon's Bay and not the Channel.

Commodore O'Reilly was just sitting down to tea on the stern of his yacht, moored near the town jetty, and his colourful tirade at the accidental firing, Jack later discovered, was both unprintable and audible from Jubilee Square.

Robinson had to report to the captain's cabin as soon as they came alongside. 'We're just bloody lucky there was no serious damage, Robinson, but I'm going to relieve you of your depth-charge duties and let PO Combrink take over.' Jack's voice was impassive but his eyes flashed with anger.

'I'm terribly sorry, sir. I don't think the men really respect me. Whether I encourage or chastise, they remain indifferent.'

'Listen to me, Robinson, leadership comes with experience, perception and intuition. Respect on a ship like *Gannet* needs to be earned and you're not doing a very good job of earning it. I learnt the hard way when I first joined her; you're learning the hard way now. And that's not necessarily a bad thing.'

The next round of training involved the firing of live depth charges in mock attacks. When Dalgleish reported a fake echo and the imaginary course and speed of an enemy submarine, *Gannet* raced to intercept, delivering a pattern of six depth charges — two off the stern, one fired from each flank and another two off the stern.

Jack strode to the side of the bridge and looked aft as the canisters splashed into the sea, their detonators set to various depths. He imagined them sinking into the deep trailing bubbles and eagerly anticipated the magnesium-white explosions that would tear holes in the ocean. He watched the surface heave up a few feet as though discomforted, then an almighty bang that split the air followed by a mountainous eruption of water. Now *that* was the correct and proper way to hit back at the enemy.

'Impressive, isn't it?' said Dalgleish, a gleam in his eye.

'Aye, Commander,' said Jack, his voice quavering.

'Itching to have a crack at the Hun?'

'Yes, sir, you read my thoughts.'

Dalgleish smiled but made no reply.

CHAPTER 6

Next day, Dalgleish organised a gunnery competition, preceded by hours of drill, Jack with stopwatch in hand bellowing as he mixed various combinations of his crew. After the carnage of Dunkirk and his two scraps with the German raider, he knew the vulnerability of the gun crews on the forecastle and how important it was to have competent hands to replace the dead or wounded.

The competition commenced with a star shell fired from the lead ship — a rotated position — which burst 6,000 yards off the starboard beam. The second whaler in line got to fire six fused rounds against the clock. Jack had set up a ring sight on *Gannet*'s bridge and marked the shell bursts as one would on a rifle range. He forced himself to focus on the puffs of smoke, not the shortened breath and flashback images the bangs elicited. Would there ever come a time when he could hear gunfire without the need to batten down emotional hatches, without a tremendous act of will?

Later in the day, *St Dogmael* plodded out of Simon's Bay towing the battle-practice target and each ship had a crack. Next, the lighter weapons were given a chance, first down the port side, then starboard. *Langeberg*'s and *Waterberg*'s Oerlikons fared better than *Gannet*'s and *Belle*'s older pom-poms, and everyone's Lewis machine guns were somewhat haywire, but Jack wasn't entirely displeased with the performance.

'Pickles' Brooke — a timid, underage rookie when Jack joined *Gannet* — had been put in charge of the pom-pom and was getting to know the vagaries of his weapon. One hand controlled elevation while the other hand traversed the gun, actions that had to happen instinctively, especially in the heat of battle. Even with the help of tracer, Pickles initially struggled to land the two-pound shells anywhere near the target, but he persevered and in time he was handling the gun as though it were an extension of his body.

Gannet's new boy-seaman, Achmat Booysen from District Six, was appointed loader and Pickles had taken him under his wing, just as Lofty Fitzpatrick had done to him before being killed in the action with the raider. It was Booysen's task to keep feeding the short, heavy belts of shells — a job he did with growing speed and efficiency as training progressed.

At the end of shooting practise, Jack was surprised to find *Langeberg* the winner. 'Bunts, make to flotilla: "Bravo Zulu — well done to *Langeberg* on your fine shooting."'

As luck would have it, a non-operational, Odin-class submarine had docked in Simon's Town and was made available to Jack's flotilla for training purposes. Dalgleish wanted to perfect the teamwork between Asdic operators, depth-charge crews and captains, and Jack relished the chance to have a real live quarry, referred to as a 'clockwork mouse', to outwit and 'destroy'.

Leaving port an hour before the flotilla each morning, the submarine would dive in the middle of the bay and trail buff floats on the surface so the flotilla knew exactly where she was; later came the cat-and-mouse games without buffs.

On one occasion, the submarine sneaked inshore, drawing the flotilla close to the bouldery stretch between Windmill Beach and Buffels Bay, and successfully outwitted all four captains. Not only was it imperative that manoeuvres be conducted safely, but there were continual echoes to be investigated, 'contacts' that mostly turned out to be 'non-sub':

rocks, wrecks, floating kelp, shoals of fish and, on two occasions, a southern right whale.

The Asdic pingers were learning that it required acute hearing to distinguish the subtly different pitch of the echoes and it was found that AB Potgieter, who had briefly played the violin in his high-school orchestra, possessed the most nuanced ear.

At first, the submarine easily evaded the pursuers. Her captain was a crafty RNVR commander of considerable skill who zigzagged, dived deep, ran silent and constantly varied his speed to the frustration of the hunters. At one point, he managed to penetrate the whalers' escort screen, surfacing behind the flotilla and signalling, 'Peekaboo', to Jack's mortification. The submarine also carried out a number of attacks, successfully 'sinking' two whalers and Commodore O'Reilly's yacht, leaving Jack red-faced and inwardly fuming.

Attack and defend, hunt and protect, the exercises continued. Having picked up an echo, *Gannet*'s Asdic operator — with Dalgleish at his shoulder — would estimate the course and speed of the submarine. Jack then steered full ahead on an attack course to deliver a dummy charge whose detonator produced a harmless explosion. Each ship was given a chance, but the game proved harder than expected and the submarine a slippery customer. The contact had to be held throughout the run in: Asdic operators keeping focus, course and engine revolutions constantly altered, the correct signals hoisted and depth-charge crews on their toes. With the commodore's yacht in attendance, all eyes were on Jack, all responsibility rested on his shoulders. By the end of the second afternoon, only *Langeberg* had scored a hit and a lucky one at that.

Dining at Milkwood, Jack lamented the situation. 'I've got Dalgleish and O'Reilly breathing down my neck at the same time. It's like charting a course between Scylla and Charybdis.'

'And your Ithaca is submerged and moving,' said the admiral, chuckling.

'Not funny, Father. I can't seem to keep focus, what with all the moving parts and the ghoulish pair second-guessing everything I do, either vocally or with their silences. My captains are just as demoralised and you can hardly blame them. I think we've all got stage fright and although they try to cover it with feigned indifference or good humour, I can see it's taking its toll. Even our Norwegian Viking, Alstad, is showing the strain and that bally submarine keeps slipping from our grasp.'

'It's all part of the game. Just be thankful you're not in Tobermory.'

'Actually, I don't know how the Terror could be worse than the combination of The Black Death and Adolf O'Reilly.'

But on the third day, the flotilla began to have more success. Jack was learning the idiosyncrasies of his Asdic set and how to anticipate the 'enemy' commander's moves. Each ship took it in turns, then worked in pairs — hunting as a team with the second whaler standing off, maintaining contact and providing cross-bearings. It was good practice for convoy duty when more than one escort might be dispatched to hunt a U-boat.

On the fourth day, they moved the training ground to the wilder waters south of Cape Point where conditions were more taxing and the submarine was able to use differing temperature layers to elude her pursuers. Even so, out of seven runs, the flotilla managed to locate the submarine and hold her until the kill on four occasions.

'All right, Lieutenant Pembroke, I think your flotilla is just about ready to take on the Kriegsmarine,' said Dalgleish. 'It's the absence of shouting and confusion, even when under considerable duress, that tells me your men are up to the mark. Your training is done.'

'Gosh, thank you, sir!' said Jack, genuinely relieved.

'I know, I know, you thought you'd never be rid of me. Let's turn this gang around and head back to Snoek Town.'

'Aye aye, sir,' said Jack.

Back in port, Commodore O'Reilly came aboard *Gannet* with some of his staff and congratulated Dalgleish, Jack and his escort group. 'I suppose you'll do, Pembroke,' he said with that maddening twinkle in his eye.

'I wish we'd had more time, sir,' said Jack.

'Me too, but the local patrols are stretched and we might need to form coastal convoys any day now. You'll find your feet on the job. You've done it before with sweepers.'

'Thank you, sir.'

'I would have liked to keep your flotilla here for the moment, but your father's lot are hard pressed on every front. You'll remain nominally under my command, but I will be releasing you to help with patrols until more AS ships are commissioned.'

'Where do you want us to begin, sir?'

'Cape Town. That is where there's the most pressing need with so many convoys passing through. Right then…' O'Reilly turned to Dalgleish, 'billiards again this evening, Commander, same time?'

'I'll be there, sir, gloves off.'

Once both senior officers had been piped ashore, Jack turned to Van Zyl, removed his cap and dramatically wiped his forehead.

'The Nazis have got nothing on those two,' muttered Van Zyl, overheard by Signalman 'Bunts' Behardien who stifled a snigger.

'I'll not have you say anything disrespectful about a senior officer,' said Jack, then softly, 'but how bloody right you are.'

It was a few days before the flotilla was needed in Table Bay, which gave each ship time to prepare. Working up had put *Gannet* back into a proper routine — just the way Jack liked it.

Each morning at 0715, he poured his second cup of coffee and, weather permitting, finished the sports section of the newspaper on Belleview's terrace. At 0725 he brushed his teeth and hair, leaving the house five minutes later. At zero hour, 0800, he stepped aboard and the working day began.

First, Leading Seaman Thomas would arrive at his cabin with recent signals, then Van Zyl with his arrangements for the day and a list of request men, followed by Chief McEwan wanting to know the orders for steam. There would be Gunner Combrink needing extra ammunition, or Robinson with the latest navigation signals, or the steward wanting to go shopping in Simon's Town for something critical to the outcome of the war. It was like a West End performance and after the interval (a cup of tea), they all made another appearance with their lines differing ever so slightly.

Sparks stepped into his cabin a few days later with a signal from SNO Simon's Town stating that a large troop convoy was due in to Cape Town. In advance of its arrival, *Gannet* and *Belle* were requested to conduct anti-submarine patrols covering the area between Cape Point and the approaches to Table Bay.

'And so it begins,' said Jack. 'Number One!'

CHAPTER 7

Kruger slowly awoke through layers of suffocation. He had gone too far into the cave, fallen into a fissure and the rock had begun swallowing his body as he slipped deeper into its black sandstone crush. The stench of diesel, cloying heat, the rattle of his toothbrush in a mug, fingertips hard against the Bible beneath his pillow. Gasping for air, his eyes snapped open and he looked around, barely able to credit this tiny wardroom lit by naked bulbs somewhere beneath the waves in the Bay of Biscay. Absurd.

It came back to him in a rush: the ear-splitting detonations as depth charges shook the U-boat, tormented moments of impending death, the captain's maddeningly calm face and their angled plunge to escape the onslaught.

Somehow, they had survived.

After the ordeal, *U-68* had surfaced to recharge her batteries using the diesel engines and gain some distance during the hours of darkness — precious few in midsummer — then remained submerged during the day to avoid the RAF's attentions.

Kruger closed his eyes again, trying to find escape from the misery, but continued to loiter in the shallows of half slumber. What he knew about submarines he did not like: too slow to outrun enemy ships, no armour plating and under-gunned. Just one hit could puncture the pressure hull and send them to the bottom. He pictured their boat sailing through a twilight world surrounded by whales and giant squid, deep-sea fish manufacturing their own light and penumbral sea monsters too grotesque to imagine.

Everything disturbed him: men brushing noisily past his bunk at the change of watch, the clanging of bulkhead doors, the smells from the galley and reek of the head. If only he could return to sleep, but no position was comfortable as the submarine pitched, yawed and corkscrewed its way across the bay. Each time the bows crashed into an oncoming swell there was a terrific jolt. He knew the gentle rhythm of waves in the cove at Steenbokbaai and the rush of water on the beach, but these ocean sounds were an entirely different kind of scraping and thumping. All of it was compounded by the infernal noise of the intercom — radio programmes from Germany, endless Beethoven and Wagner, irksome dance music — how would he ever get used to it? And always the tidal nausea, coming in waves that soared and dipped, tormented him day and night.

'You are awake at last,' said the captain, taking a seat opposite his bunk at the wardroom table. 'Don't worry, Herr Kruger, the Hudson attack was nothing — just the usual nuisance in Biscay. Sound is five times louder underwater. We were in no real danger.'

The wounded watch keeper had been placed in one of the PO's bunks adjacent to the wardroom and just then let out a pitiful groan. 'Unfortunately, Seemann Baasch is very badly injured. I do not think he will see Germany again.'

Kruger sat up and rubbed his head with both hands. It felt as though he'd been run over by a tram.

'You look terrible,' said the captain.

'Thank you.'

'The WC is free. I would grab it while you can.'

Kruger stood up groggily, snatched his toilet bag and toothbrush and made his way down the alleyway. Pulling open the door, he was met by a stench so foul it seemed visible. Holding his breath, he opened the tap that allowed a dribble of freshwater into the basin to wet his toothbrush, but soon began to gag and quickly returned to his bunk without having accomplished any ablutions.

'Not successful then,' said the captain, trying to contain his mirth.

The burial of Seaman Baasch took place at dusk and Kruger, still feeling queasy, watched proceedings from the bridge. It was cold and blustery on deck and the sunset had left in its wake a restless sky, slashed with crimson clouds. The body had been sewn in canvas and hauled up through the conning tower, a difficult and intimate act for the messmates of the deceased, then lowered onto the casing where his feet were weighted with a loop of cable.

The off watch was assembled, waiting for the captain to begin, and the body lay draped with the red naval ensign. The coxswain piped the still and the engines stopped. Not daring to use a torch, Captain Brand said the short committal prayer by heart and appeared to struggle over the verses as Kruger strained to hear words that were shredded by the wind.

The canvas body bag was lowered by rope down the side of the saddle tank and splashed into an oncoming wave. All at once it vanished, the carry-on was sounded and the thudding of the diesel engines resumed. Kruger pictured the corpse — Baasch, the fresh-faced youngster — wrapped in a death cocoon sliding to the ocean floor many hundreds of metres below their keel. The image sent a shudder through him and he felt the chill wind keenly.

Although by the fifth day at sea, Kruger was still hitting his head whenever he tried to walk upright and kept stubbing his toes on the boxes of canned fruit, bags of sugar and tinned milk that lined the alleyways, he had largely overcome his nausea. He spent much of his time lying on his bunk, alternately reading the Bible and *Mein Kampf* — the only two books he carried with him. 'Now the Lord had prepared a great fish to swallow up Jonah, and Jonah was in the belly of the fish three days and three nights,' he read once again with fervour but little solace.

Day and night, the U-boat's ceaseless bustle continued to disturb him: the constant movement of sailors to and from the forward accommodation, the cook clattering about in the galley, the flow of signals bleating from the WT alcove — weather reports, distress calls from ships under attack, homing instructions for wolf packs from the *BdU*.

How he longed for fresh air and earth underfoot, for the wide-open *vlaktes* of the farm and for the West Coast. The first hints of spring weather would be waking the veld right now: carpets of daisies and vygies transforming the semi-desert into swathes of colour. He pictured the dancing heads of a billion flowers stretching as far as the eye could see. His whole being ached for the splendour of his father's land.

Kruger opened a file and read through the details for the umpteenth time. First, he must try to sway *Ossewabrandwag* leaders into taking decisive action against the Smuts government and adopt a sabotage campaign, but he already knew this part of the plan was unlikely to succeed. Hans van Rensburg, the *OB*'s head, was a prevaricator and appeaser … a lowlife politician. It would be far better to approach the *OB*'s militant wing, the *Stormjaers*, and then only its most fanatical members. Kruger wanted no hangers-on, no doubters or *hensoppers*.

He intended to form a splinter group of hardliners — he already had the name, *Weerlig* — men he could trust, guide and control. First, he would try to enlist some of the ardent

Stormjaers he had known at Stellenbosch University. His old friend Hans van Zyl would also be able to pick out young men of the right calibre to forge a small band of dedicated National Socialists ready to give their lives for the cause. He would insist that all recruits sign a blood oath of loyalty to both himself and the Führer.

Kruger ran an eye over his inventory: fake identity papers, explosives, radio transmitter and receiver, 600 pounds in South African currency and 25,000 dollars, clocks for time bombs, invisible ink, Luger pistol. He read the code words to be used in radio transmissions as well as the frequencies and times to make contact, trying once again to commit them to memory.

The documents included a letter from the *Abwehr* to be shown to the leader of any right-wing group prepared to join the cause. He read it through once again.

The German Government will, upon the declaration of peace with the Union of South Africa, recognise and guarantee its territorial sovereignty, along with the three protectorates of Swaziland, Basutoland and Bechuanaland. The German Government will also have no reservations should the Union decide to increase its territory by incorporating Southern Rhodesia. Germany is not considering the establishment of a separate state in Africa, and recognises the Union as the leading white state in the South African sphere of influence. In the event of armed resistance breaking out against the war effort in South Africa, and if weapons be required for the resistance, these will be provided. The German Government wishes to maintain contact with any resistance movement that will facilitate the transition of power.

Kruger glanced up when a blond sailor entered the wardroom and gently opened the green curtain shrouding

Lieutenant Seebohm's bunk. 'Ten minutes to your watch, sir,' he said softly.

'What? *Oh Gott ... danke*,' came the muffled reply, followed by a leg that emerged slowly from the curtain, then the puffy, sleep-deprived face of the young officer.

'Not enough shut eye?' asked Kruger.

'Never enough,' he groaned.

'Man on the bridge?' Kruger shouted up the conning tower.

'*Ja*, come!' called Brand.

Kruger climbed past the helmsman hunched over his compass card in the conning tower and poked his head above the coaming. Sky and clean air again — a reminder that there was life beyond the fetid purgatory below. Kruger blinked, felt the low sun on his face and closed his eyes.

'He emergeth from Nibelung's Cave,' said the captain.

'I don't understand?'

'*Mein Herr*, do you not know your Wagner: *Der Ring des Nibelungen*? In Norse tradition, Grimhildr is lured to the cave of treasures and gets sealed inside.'

'I'm afraid not.' The U-boat gave a lurch and he felt a moment's queasiness. 'Anyone getting sealed in a cave is not my cup of tea.'

The captain looked at him quizzically, then burst out laughing. 'You are a very amusing fellow, you know that? It is such a pity we have to abandon you in Africa. The voyage home will not be the same.'

Kruger realised he was being made fun of but refused to take the bait. He knew, too, that spending time on the bridge was good for his mind and his health, which is why he had begun to volunteer for lookout duty, despite the onerous nature of the task. Not for an instant was he allowed to take his eyes off his designated quadrant. During four long hours, he would sweep his Zeiss binoculars across sea, horizon and sky, back and forth, up and down. Seagulls were the bane of his spells on watch. Swooping out of the sun with rigid wings, they looked exactly like aircraft. He'd already received a dressing down from the captain for false alarms and been told that if he didn't 'educate his eyes' he might as well stay in his bunk.

Night fell, Brand had long since gone below, but Kruger remained on the bridge at the end of his watch, gazing astern at their wake as swirls of foam formed, twisted and dissipated, and the metal deck vibrated comfortingly beneath his feet. Cape Finisterre was lit by a faint sweeping glow on their port beam and attended by the dancing glitter of Spanish fishing boats. Kruger watched the rise and fall of their bows, carving the sea like a plough turning over sods of earth, reminding him of the farm and their vast potato fields. He realised that his father would be preparing those very fields right now for spring planting.

After supper, the captain called a meeting of his officers in the wardroom and Kruger was invited to attend. 'I have brought you together to provide you with more details about our secret operation, one that Konteradmiral Dönitz has taken a personal interest in. Some of you may have noticed that we have a passenger on board who is not entirely German.' There were a few chortles. 'For those benighted among you who have not yet realised, Herr Kruger is a South African on a very special mission of sabotage and destabilisation. There is a strong sentiment in favour of the National Socialist cause among the Afrikaner people, a race that has been under the British yoke for generations. Our first task will be to land him and his equipment safely in South Africa.'

'Where exactly, Kapitän?' asked Lingen.

'On the West Coast, north of Cape Town, but we will be guided by Herr Kruger…' He turned to the passenger.

'*Ja, danke schön, Kapitän*. The farm of my family is on the coast in a very isolated spot near Lambert's Bay. Our people have been briefed and we will not be bothered by the British.' There was an uneasy silence as Kruger appeared reluctant to divulge more.

The captain took up the narrative: 'Our second mission, once we have deposited our guest on the beach, is to strike a blow at the shipping around the Cape of Good Hope that supplies the armies ranged against Generalleutnant Rommel in North Africa. We are the lead boat of Gruppe Savanne, a flotilla of five travelling independently but in concert down the Atlantic.'

'Are we free to attack ships en route, Kapitän?' asked Seebohm.

'Yes and no. A compromise of sorts has been struck between Dönitz and the pen-pushers at *SKL*. In order to achieve the maximum surprise in South Africa, we are forbidden from sinking anything but the most valuable targets between five degrees south of the equator and Cape Town. Complete radio silence is also to be maintained on that leg of our approach.'

'Can we decide what is "most valuable", sir?' asked Lingen.

'If it were up to you, we would sink fishing boats, IWO. But no, "most valuable" means an aircraft carrier or battleship, perhaps a troopship if it is one of the giants like <u>Queen Elizabeth</u>. Nothing else, do you hear, Lingen?'

'Party poopers,' muttered the first lieutenant.

'We should be able to catch the enemy napping at the Cape. Our hope is to cause such confusion that sea traffic around South Africa is brought to a standstill and her ports become clogged with merchant ships seeking shelter. It will also serve as a diversionary tactic, drawing enemy defences away from other areas. By spreading himself thin, he makes himself vulnerable everywhere.

'Dönitz wanted to allow us to sink anything we liked en route. Tonnage sent to the bottom is all he is interested in and I cannot say I disagree. He has no time for *SKL*'s tactics and its need for a *Paukenschlag* and "strategic surprise" in a "virgin area" like the Cape. The *Konteradmiral* told me to my face when we met at Kernével: "The grand strategists are out to tickle the enemy, but unfortunately I do not know of a single case in which an enemy has been tickled to death."

'But at least until we reach five degrees south we are free to hunt. I will be discussing our course with Leutnant Seebohm and communicating with the other boats via the *BdU*. Suffice it to say that we will pass to the west of Madeira and Cape Verde, then southeast towards the Cape. We will remain at our economical, 'diesel-electric' cruising speed of seven or eight knots. It should take us about six weeks to get there: plenty of time to brush up on your French for the girls back in Lorient.'

'Or your Afrikaans,' said Kruger, attempting a joke, to the polite chuckles of the others.

Brand continued: 'Gruppe Savanne will form an extended-harrow patrol line south of Cape Verde, with the U-boats travelling abreast at wide intervals, and angle towards Freetown where, as you know, many British convoys congregate. Let us see what we can rake up in our net. Questions anyone?'

'We do not have enough provisions and fuel for anything but the shortest patrol in South African waters, sir,' said Leading Engineer Hoppe.

'You will be happy to know that we are to be resupplied by a *Milchkuh* in the South Atlantic.'

'A milk cow, Kapitän, what's that?' asked Kruger.

'It is a new kind of U-boat, known as a U-tanker, designed to replenish others at sea. With the sinking of the raiders *Kobra* and *Sturmvogel*, both of them meant to be our resupply ships, the *BdU* has resorted to the safer option of replenishment from submarines that have a huge capacity to carry extra fuel, food and ammunition. All five boats of Gruppe Savanne will rendezvous to replenish from *U-459*, sailing from Bordeaux.'

A daily average of 170 nautical miles eventually brought them into tropical latitudes, the regular northeast trade winds off the Sahara giving the horizon a reddish tint. The crew was allowed on deck for long spells during daylight hours and lounged on the aft casing in the evenings, filling the air with rousing songs like the '*U-boot-Lied*' and '*Torpedo Los*', or the more sentimental 'Rolling Home' with Seaman Detmers accompanying them on his accordion.

The off watch entertained itself as best it could with card games such as rummy and skat or chess and sharing novels of a romantic or adventurous ilk. Photographs of family, wives and sweethearts were passed from hand to hand. Conversation often turned to home or the last run ashore and there were many tales, growing taller by the day, of sexual exploits and legendary drinking bouts. The beer and prostitutes of Lorient had allowed them to forget, for a while, the stresses of the previous patrol and would doubtless do so again after this one. Anecdotes were repeated ad infinitum and the stale jokes, mostly scatological, kept doing the rounds, growing staler and fouler with each circuit.

As to naval discipline, any semblance of orderly dress had long since been dispensed with and the men wore an odd assortment of clothing: old flannel trousers, checked shirts, gym shorts and sandals or plimsolls.

Kruger ate his meals with the officers and had begun to learn their ways. He considered Captain Brand a gifted but highly eccentric man, given to temper fits, sarcasm and moments of generosity. He found IWO Lingen haughty and aloof, and always perfectly groomed; Lieutenant Seebohm appeared to be a thinker, nervous where it came to decision making, but a competent navigator; the boat's 'old man', unkempt Leading Engineer Hoppe with his scruffy, balding dome and level-headed ways was just the person to stick close to in a crisis. The Chief had lost his first boat off Jutland, surviving for three days in a dinghy with a handful of his mates, and was lucky to be picked up by an E-boat. If the enemy began tossing the kitchen sink at them, he would be the man to watch.

Kruger had also slowly got to know the crew and was by now able to put names to most of the faces. There was Muller the cheese maker from Emden, Jung the ticket collector from Cologne, Isenberg the schoolboy fresh out of Bavarian nappies, Sablonski the joker from Mainz. They were simple, brave young men, a species of bravery alien to him, and very few of them were fervent Nazis, which he found strange in such an elite arm of the service. These were men able to spend months in each other's pockets, trapped in a steel tube under the sea, men who had to form close bonds, tolerate and understand each other, but also be prepared to slam a watertight door on a friend and drown him to save the others.

The routine on board remained constant and, as they were travelling through a relatively safe part of the Atlantic, *U-68* remained mostly on the surface. Each day, there would be a trim dive, during which Brand would occasionally order the checking and servicing of the torpedoes. 'Unlike shells or machine-gun rounds, our torpedoes are our children — they can be a bit temperamental and need regular attention,' he explained to Kruger. 'If you think about it, each one is a tiny submarine crammed with technology — a miniature version of *U-68* — launched from our womb and sent swimming off towards the enemy. God speed, little one, make mommy proud!'

During one trim dive, Kruger went forward to witness the servicing procedure as sailors stowed away hammocks and prepared the block and tackle and loading rails. Next, the rear door of the first torpedo tube was opened and the greasy, phallic, two-ton object with shiny brass propellers was withdrawn. Hoisting rings supported its weight as the sweating, straining men did their work, topping up compressed air, checking the propulsion unit, hydroplane and rudder, making sure all shafts and bearings were moving easily. Then, with a storm of foul language, the eel was prepared for reinsertion.

'Make sure your shaft is properly lubricated, lads.'

'Stick it in, Heinz, as deep as you can go!'

'Ooh, I love it Max, harder, you horny old dog!'

'Don't the British prefer it up the stern, just like you Isenberg?'

Out came the second torpedo and the performance was repeated, the comments more colourful with each extraction, each reinsertion.

'Prien was our greatest ace,' said Brand as they sat around the wardroom table drinking coffee after supper one evening. 'To creep into Scapa Flow, sink a battleship like *Royal Oak*, and escape again unscathed was an astonishing feat. The British could not believe his audacity. But Prien, Schepke and Kretschmer — our best commanders — were all taken from us earlier this year. Maybe the time of the aces is over and it is now the time of hiding, of running, of dying.'

'How so?' asked Kruger.

'We have entered a dark period for the U-boats, certainly in the North Atlantic. Nowadays, corvettes provide close-in escort around the convoys, destroyer groups rush about keeping us at bay and the British have even converted freighters into small aircraft carriers to give aerial support. They are making it harder and harder for us.'

'What about the South Atlantic?' asked Kruger.

'Yes, I am hoping that South Africa will offer us another happy time, like the early days of the war when pickings were rich, patrols were poor and our commanders returned to a hero's welcome in Lorient. U-boats are the only hope for Germany. We have too few capital ships to take on the British and now with the *Bismarck* gone —'

'But she sank HMS *Hood* —'

'A pyrrhic victory, Herr Kruger. What a hopeless sortie, sending her out with only one cruiser for escort, and then leaving her on her own to face the might of the Royal Navy. Madness. Anyway, it is down to us, to Konteradmiral Dönitz, to win this bloody mess by waging a war of tonnage — a slow, merciless campaign of attrition. If we can sink more merchant ships than the enemy can build, we win. If not, we lose, and there goes our thousand-year Reich.'

'It's not that simple.'

'Oh but it is.' There was an uncomfortable pause as they both took a sip of coffee. Brand continued: 'So far, this has been a pleasure cruise, far from the North Atlantic routes where all is red in tooth and claw. Here we can sunbathe! The crew needed this after our last patrol — things got a bit ragged.'

'And how about you, Kapitän?'

'Me?' He looked at Kruger as though he'd asked the strangest question. 'Oh, I can take it, nothing bothers me.' He said it with such nonchalant conviction that Kruger almost believed him.

'What about you?' asked the captain, taking a sip of his ersatz coffee.

'On land, I suppose I am like you, nothing bothers me. But out here in this thing…'

'Thing! Our beloved home!' He guffawed and slapped Kruger on the shoulder. 'You are comical, my South African friend.' Brand poured more coffee into both mugs. 'Tell me, why are you taking on this fight? There is no conscription in your country: you could have nothing to do with the war and enjoy an easy life on your farm.'

'My father fought with General Smuts in the Boer War, back when Smuts was still a hero. They conducted a very successful commando campaign on the West Coast near our farm and up into the northern Cape. Then the leaders sold out and surrendered to the English, but the burning passion for liberty that was bred in my father has passed on to me and I will carry the light forward until South Africa is free.'

'Unlike you, Herr Kruger, I am a pragmatist, I fight when I have to. I saw what the trenches of Verdun did to my father. Yes, I love my country too, but you are quite a different animal to me. Patriotism comes in many colours.'

'True patriotism comes in only one colour.'

'Let me guess, Herr Kruger, red.'

Kruger offered a wry smile.

On the eleventh night out of Lorient, the lookouts spotted a liner, lit up like a carnival and approaching on a converging course from the northeast. Although she was almost certainly neutral, the captain ordered a dive and mock attack to give the crew practice.

'Clear the bridge! Dive, dive, dive!' shouted the captain. 'Twenty metres.'

From his bunk, Kruger heard the main engines stop and the electric motors take over as lookouts dropped like firemen into the control room.

'Check main vents,' called Chief Hoppe.

'All main vents clear!'

Control-room hands opened the vent levers and the air that gave *U-68* her buoyancy escaped from the ballast tanks with the sound of stampeding horses. Kruger stepped into the control room and watched as the planesmen tilted their foreplanes to hard-a-dive and the after-planes to ten degrees. He felt the bows lean towards the ocean floor, watched as the needle on the depth gauge crept slowly round and listened as the sound of the sea slapping against the hull was replaced by silence — no diesel thumping, no wireless noise, no droning of ventilation fans. It was like being part of a magic trick.

The control-room lights had switched to red and the waiting lookouts donned dark glasses to accustom their eyes when they resurfaced. Brand allowed Kruger to take a quick look through the periscope. The liner's portholes were strung like pearls, her upper decks glittering with the lights of peace, and the big Portuguese flag painted on the ship's side was brightly illuminated, announcing her neutrality. To Kruger, the brief vision seemed bizarre, unnatural, as though people had no right to be moving boldly and fearlessly about the Atlantic. For a moment, he had the reckless desire to put a torpedo into her belly.

'Down periscope,' said the captain as the gleaming column sank back into its well. The two vessels traced converging courses and after twenty minutes, Brand said, 'Stand by to surface; open lower hatch,' while in the engine room, the stokers primed their diesels for starting.

'Do you want all the gunners, Kapitän?' asked Lingen.

'*Ja*, always best to be safe,' he said, gripping the ladder's aluminium rungs. 'You never know with these Portuguese, if they really are Portuguese. Herr Kruger, you may follow me up after the watch keepers. Surface!'

'Fore-planes up ten, after-planes up five!' called Chief Hoppe. 'Blow all main ballast!'

Compressed air hissed from steel bottles into the tanks and Kruger pictured the U-boat breaking the ocean's meniscus, seawater cascading off her flanks. The captain raced up the ladder, swung open the top hatch with a reverberating clang, followed by the lookouts and gunners with Kruger tacked on the end of the queue, climbing towards the stars.

By the time he reached the bridge, the four lookouts were in position, the guns were manned, the motors were silenced and the diesel engines had begun their thudding. The night was warm and tropical, like fine wine, and the approaching liner had the fantastical air of a dream creature. Phosphorescence danced along their saddle tanks, lending an increasingly festive air to the mid-Atlantic encounter. Kruger could faintly hear a band playing and saw dancers dressed in tuxedos and ball gowns gliding back and forth on the upper deck. He pictured wood-panelled saloons, beautiful women smelling of heaven, sparkling chandeliers, waiters with trays of champagne and buffet tables overflowing with food.

U-68 flashed a signal and the liner slowed to a stop; a second signal ordered the Portuguese not to use their wireless and for her master to report on board the U-boat with the liner's papers. The band had ceased playing and passengers lined the rail.

'We have sent a signal to Kernével to ascertain her particulars and whether she is really neutral, but no reply yet,' said the captain.

'And if she isn't entirely neutral?' asked Kruger.

'Then we sink her.' A strange thrill ran through Kruger: the power exuded by this man at this moment was intoxicating.

'And if you get no reply from the *BdU*?'

'Then her captain is going to have to prove that he is what he says he is and not carrying any contraband. But these Portuguese are slow to take up my invitation.' An uneasy fifteen minutes ensued during which Brand's patience visibly diminished.

'I have had enough of this nonsense, they are playing for time,' said Brand. 'A shot across her bows, if you please, IWO.'

Lingen barked an order, followed by the loud crack of their main gun as cordite wafted across the bridge. The round passed well ahead of the ship and anointed the darkness with a pillar of white water.

'For the next one, aim at the wireless cabin,' said Brand. 'We do not want them sending a distress signal.'

There was consternation on the liner's deck now, distance making the shouting sound to Kruger like the bleating of sheep returning to the kraal at sunset.

'Flood number one tube,' said the captain, his anger barely contained.

'But, sir, they —' interjected Lingen.

'Do not question my orders, IWO!'

Kruger looked from one officer to the other, the liner neatly framed between them like a laden platter, an offering.

'They are lowering a launch!' cried one of the lookouts as relief tinged with disappointment coursed through Kruger. He watched the marionette boat jerking unevenly from the davits until it splashed down, followed by the coughing of an engine trying to start, then rhythmical puttering as a sleek white launch carrying a party of six bobbed across the wave tops towards them. The U-boat's spotlight tracked its progress, as did the 20mm gun in the *Wintergarten* aft of the conning tower. The launch caught a wave, surfed for a moment, then slewed around, knocking a gentleman in a white suit off his feet as it wallowed up to the submarine's flank.

Fenders had been lowered and two of the foredeck gun crew held the launch off with boathooks, like harpooners dealing with a whale. There were confused shouts in Portuguese before the diminutive gent in the suit was handed across the gap. He slipped, wetting his ballroom shoes, and would have been squeezed between saddle tank and launch had Coxswain Fischer not lent a meaty arm.

'*Obrigado!*' he gasped.

'Jesus Christ, have mercy on us,' muttered Brand then, looking at Kruger, 'Sorry, blasphemy comes easily.'

'*Boa noite*, my name is Vasconcellos, *capitão* of the *Santa Teresa*,' said the rotund visitor as he heaved himself onto the darkened bridge.

'Good evening, I am captain of this U-boat,' said Brand in his best English. 'You have brought the papers of your ship?'

'Of course, *senhor*!' his voice was tremulous as he opened an oilskin bag and handed over a folder.

One of the watch keepers held a torch as Brand ran his eye over the documents. Kruger looked at the face of their guest, eyes darting from one giant German to another, and thought what a savage band they must seem to him, fresh from a black-tie dinner and floating ballroom ... and how badly Kruger and his shipmates must smell to those refined Lusitanian nostrils.

'So, the *Santa Teresa*, 12,000 tons, home port Lisbon,' said the captain, opening his register and flipping to the S's.

'Yes, Capitão, we carry 980 passengers and we are bound for Rio de Janeiro.'

Brand ran his finger down a column, then glanced up and said in a matter-of-fact tone: 'These papers are fake. You are now a prisoner of the Third Reich and we will sink your ship. Lingen, prepare to fire number one torpedo.'

A look of horror crossed the Portuguese captain's face and he let out the wailing sound of a balloon leaking air. Clasping his hands as though in prayer, he gasped, 'Capitão, I beg you, please, please, on my word of honour —'

Wearing one of his broad, mischievous grins, Brand failed to contain his mirth. 'I am only teasing you, my dear Captain Vasconcellos.'

Kruger watched in fascination as their guest's facial expressions ran through a catalogue of emotions that would have done a Hollywood star proud, from shock and fear to incredulity, followed in short order by relief, joy and, finally, high-pitched laughter. Like a conjuring trick, a bottle of Schnapps and two glasses appeared in their midst. After four toasts — to Hitler, Salazar and the two fatherlands — and professions of eternal gratitude, the captain was helped down the ladder and into his launch.

Brand gave engine orders for full ahead to gain distance lest the encounter were reported, before going below.

Kruger stayed on the bridge and watched the liner's lights slip astern, unable to staunch the upwelling of emotion it evoked. 'Ships that pass in the night,' he whispered to himself, then took one last look around at the vast blackness that enveloped two pinpricks of diverging humanity, before climbing down the ladder to partake of the prosaic supper of beef rissoles and red cabbage that awaited him.

CHAPTER 8

Gannet and *Belle* sailed down the western flank of False Bay on a grey winter's morning, their passage shielded from a cold front sweeping off the Atlantic by the sandstone crags. As they passed Windmill Beach, Coxswain February handed over the wheel to the duty-watch helmsman. Picking up his binoculars, Jack scanned the shore until he found his father's villa above its enchanted crescent of beach, but could not make out the grey head of the admiral on the stoep. Rounding the Point, they were into the Cape's notorious rollers and both whalers began to pitch and yaw as they followed the swept channel north towards Table Bay.

Jack was easing his way back into the feeling of open ocean, of having *Gannet* beneath his feet. In the wheelhouse below, only the monotonous pinging of the Asdic apparatus and the occasional creak of the helm disturbed the peace. The convoy was due to pass that evening and although there had been no reports of submarines south of the equator, an AS patrol was deemed necessary given the importance of the approaching ships.

Through the rest of the day, they conducted a general search up and down the western flank of the Peninsula. Both whalers had reduced speed to seven knots to improve the efficiency of their Asdic equipment.

As the afternoon drew to a close, a blanket of cloud stole in from the west to obscure the sunset, save for a few scarlet stains amid the dying embers. After dark, the lonely beams of Cape Point and Slangkop lighthouses provided orientation and solace to those on deck.

'Bridge, aft lookout!' Seaman Booysen's voice was high-pitched, breathless. 'Ship, a *moerse* big one, sir, passing astern at 180 degrees!'

'Thank you, Booysen,' replied Van Zyl. 'Keep your eyes peeled — the rest of the convoy should be astern of her.'

Immediately, there came a succession of flashes from *Gannet*'s bridge sending the night challenge, followed by answering flashes from the dark shape identifying herself as friendly.

One by one, the convoy's black silhouettes ploughed past *Gannet* and *Belle*, both whalers continuing their beat as the convoy followed the swept channel, rounded Green Point and entered Table Bay.

'Message from SNO Simon's Town via Port War Signal Station, Captain,' said Leading Seaman Thomas, scuttling up the ladder to the bridge.

'What's it say, Sparks? I don't want to turn on a torch.'

'We've been ordered to maintain this patrol until the convoy has refuelled, taken on stores and sailed for Britain, sir.'

'Goodness, that's at least another two days at sea for us. Number One, please make the necessary arrangements.'

'Aye aye, sir,' said Van Zyl. 'Lucky that we provisioned properly before leaving Snoekie, although two days' steaming beam-on to this sea will be bumpy.'

'Yes, it's going to be uncomfortable but a good shakedown for the new lads.'

'S'pose so, although it's a pity us old hands have to hold their hands. Couldn't we just watch them hammer up and down from shore, sir? The Sea Point Pavilion offers a nice vantage.'

'Where's your team spirit, Number One?'

'Awol, sir.'

For the rest of *Gannet*'s crew, the next two and a half days of plodding up and down the Peninsula's windward doorstep passed in a dreary haze, punctuated by four-hour watches and meals served by the indefatigable Porky Louw, forever clad in blue-serge trousers and filthy white T-shirt. They got to know every contour of the shore from Signal Hill to Lion's Head, the Twelve Apostles, Chapman's Peak, Grootkop, Bonteberg and finally the grey crags of Cape Point. They saw it in rain and shine, in fog and gilded by the rays of sunset; they felt more than saw its brooding hulk during the long hours of winter darkness. Jack was growing to love its graceful, cursive outline, its sandstone battlements and powder-white beaches, its ocean life and bountiful seabirds that surfed the swells' updraft or soared above the cliffs.

Finally, a recall signal from SNO Simon's Town crackled through on the radio. *Gannet*'s and *Belle*'s last task was to lead the replenished convoy down the northern swept channel to the hundred-fathom line and send them on their way to Sierra Leone; only then could they dock in Cape Town.

Passing Green Point Lighthouse, February took over as quartermaster for the last stretch to the elbow. The two whalers chugged past East Pier, across Victoria Basin, through the narrow Gap flanked by the clock tower and into the sanctum of Alfred Basin.

Once alongside, Jack reported to the operational depot of the Seaward Defence Force, housed in an old red-brick cargo warehouse on North Quay. The off-duty watch was given liberty and hastily changed into shore-going blues. Most chose to have a meal at the nearby Harbour Café before returning to the depot where the canteen's small bar saw to their needs without having to trek into the city. No one had been granted an overnight pass so they had to forgo a bender, much as they thought they deserved one after their recent discomforts.

With some of Cape Town's regular AS vessels out of service for boiler cleaning and repairs, Jack's flotilla — now joined by *Waterberg* and *Langeberg* — took turns patrolling the approaches to Table Bay. The two main routes were known as Mary (between Green Point and Robben Island) and Sheila (between Blaauwberg and Robben Island). Each pair of whalers spent forty-eight hours at sea, travelling back and forth at slow speed, their Asdics perpetually pinging. It was dreary work and all the crews felt the weight of the monotony and strain, particularly given the harsh winter conditions. Returning to harbour, both port and starboard watches were given a night's liberty, and often a day off, before the next forty-eight-hour patrol.

Shore leave would usually see a flock of Gannets heading into town to invade a pub or hotel, the Texas Bar on Adderley Street being a favourite. PO Cummins was often first to the counter, slapping down a note and buying a round of Castles for the sailors gathered about him: oppos and shipmates, seamen and NCOs, laughing and slurping their beers, faces glowing with the joys of liberty and their cares, for the moment, at ebb.

For his overnight leave, Jannie van Zyl returned to his fractured family home in Stellenbosch, but the train was delayed and he arrived just before supper. He'd been dreading this visit, as his brother Hans had recently returned from one of his *Stormjaer* camps, but the young lieutenant hadn't seen his parents in a while and this was the only opportunity. It would be good to spend time with his mother, who he adored, and be back in the old Victorian house on Neethling Street, despite the presence of his troublemaking brother.

Inevitably, dinner conversation turned to politics and the two siblings were soon at each other's throats, nearly coming to blows once again. Mrs van Zyl restored some semblance of peace with lashings of admonition and milk tart, but she could see that neither of her sons was in a compromising mood.

After dessert, the family retired to the lounge to listen to the wireless and read *Die Burger*, *Huisgenoot* and *The Outspan*. Hans, supported by his father, insisted on tuning in to an Afrikaans programme, laced with Nazi propaganda, broadcast from Berlin on Radio Zeesen. Later, when the turncoat announcer, Lord Haw-Haw, began spouting fascist filth, Jannie said a hasty goodnight and left the room, ignoring his brother's snide remarks.

On Jack's day ashore, he arranged to meet Clara, who he'd grown increasingly captivated by since their first meeting at an Admiralty House dance. Although he knew that the war and his duty stood between them, he nevertheless longed to spend time with the beautiful Afrikaans student.

Jack waited for her under the great iron girders in Cape Town station and, as she stepped off the train, his heart did its inevitable skip. She wore a blue T-shirt, canary-yellow skirt to match her hair and white tennis tackies for the coming walk.

They took the bus up Kloof Nek, disembarked at the top and followed a footpath that led through stone pines that offered views of Camps Bay and Clifton Beach, then spiralled back around Lion's Head. Jack paused to admire a jackal buzzard — chestnut breast, rounded wings, short tail — gliding past at eye level.

After a scramble to reach the summit, they sat shoulder to shoulder admiring the panorama of Table Mountain and Devil's Peak cradling the city below with its central Garden, grand City Hall, Castle and the arms of the harbour reaching out towards Robben Island, set like an upturned saucer in the bay.

'If I were a German spy, I'd monitor the comings and goings of every convoy from up here,' said Clara.

'Yes, my father is worried about exactly that: spies passing on shipping intelligence, sabotage in the harbour, Nazi sympathisers in the Afrikaner community —'

'Not *my* section of the Afrikaner community.'

'Of course not, but you see the problem. No ship movement can be kept secret; even making Simon's Town a no-go area to the public doesn't help much. There are just too many vantage points around the Peninsula to —'

'Are those yours?' she interrupted, pointing to two vessels heading out past Mouille Point.

'No, those are port minesweepers. That one zigzagging far out towards Robben Island is one of ours, doing its anti-submarine patrol. And there's another one in the distance moving between Blaauwberg and the island.'

'Like toys in a bathtub.'

'Not when the northwester is howling and there's a meaty swell running. It gets jolly uncomfortable.'

'Look up there, out to sea,' she said, pointing. 'That's an Anson, isn't it?'

'Yes, it could be your brother.'

'Or my brother's pal, Henry.'

They watched as the aircraft with dark-green and brown camouflage and SAAF roundels, completed a lazy turn and came in over Sea Point to the unsynchronised throb of its twin 350hp Armstrong Siddeley Cheetah engines, a sound lately as familiar to Capetonians as the noonday gun.

'What do you think when you see an Anson on patrol, knowing it might be Pierre?' asked Jack.

'Proud, afraid, worried that he might be sent north. Things are so terrible up there with Rommel rampaging through the desert.'

They watched the cable car making its way up the face of Table Mountain to the station on top.

'Last week, my ma foolishly invited a colonel off one of the troopships to join us on our usual Sunday morning walk on the mountain, not thinking that their convoy would still be in port on the weekend. He readily agreed — too readily, as it turns out — and asked if a few of his men could join us. Well! Ma and I ended up leading 136 gunners up Platteklip Gorge.'

'You'd need sheep dogs to keep that lot together.'

'Too right. After six weeks at sea and little exercise, they lagged terribly and most were panting like steam engines when we got to the top. One sergeant suggested it might be a novel experience for a few of them to take the cable car back down the mountain. My ma and the colonel led the walking party and I corralled the cableway party. Needless to say, Ma and the colonel had only a handful of takers.'

'I'll bet.'

'Turns out the hike was offered as an alternative to church parade, hence the big uptake. After the convoy sailed, Ma received a bouquet of flowers with a card cheekily signed the "Alpine Anglicans".'

The cable car reached the upper station and Jack and Clara sat in silence admiring the view. Jack was slightly behind her on the rock and struggled to take his eyes off her delicate, aquiline profile: a tendril of white-blonde hair tucked behind an ear, the down of her cheek catching the sun, the slight flush to her complexion and a few tiny beads of sweat.

Clara turned her pale blue eyes on him. 'Penny for your musings?' she said.

'You'd need to rob a bank.'

'Two pennies then?'

'I'd always thought the war would be my only mistress; that I must not get side-tracked or waylaid by emotional stuff.'

'Two mistresses: the war and *Gannet*.'

'Yes, *Gannet* too. I saw the task at hand as requiring single-mindedness. I thought that one needed to be free of tenderness or anything that might weaken one in the face of the brutality. I suppose it was a symptom of the dark hole I was in last year after Dunkirk and, to an extent, my feelings of revenge. But then I came to the Cape and found myself in command of a ship I love … and I met you.'

'And now you're not so sure of your convictions because you find me irresistible.' She scrunched her nose and winked.

'Something like that. At least you are part of it. I think you understand me and might possibly tolerate my eccentricities.'

'Possibly. I have a good mind, says my ma.'

'I trust your mother.'

'I don't suffer fools gladly.' She smiled.

'And you're still here, sitting beside me.'

'I am.'

After three weeks in Cape Town, the flotilla returned to Simon's Town and began contributing to the False Bay AS patrols. Every few days, Jack spent a night ashore in his lodgings at Belleview, where Miss Retief cooked hearty farm-style meals of *boerekos* and offered a sage ear and interesting perspectives on every topic of conversation.

Alternatively, he would join his father and sister for supper at Milkwood. One evening, the men sat on the stoep with preprandial whiskies while Imogen sprawled on the big leather sofa sipping a port-and-lemonade cocktail, reading a magazine and half listening to the endless navy talk. There was a bite to the air, but the bay was like a mirror reflecting scraps of pink cloud. Jack noticed a pair of black oystercatchers with distinctive red legs and bills stalking the rockpools below.

'How was your trip to Walvis Bay?' asked Jack.

'Rather eventful, as it turns out. We flew up in one of these new Lockheed Lodestars to assess the port's defences. The original War Plan didn't include Walvis as a defended harbour, but the situation has changed so much that the C-in-C South Atlantic has asked that Walvis be used to bunker ships and relieve the congestion he's experiencing in Freetown.'

'Isn't the large German presence in South West Africa a problem?'

'It is, and many are pro-Hitler, so safety is a bother, but we've agreed to handle a maximum of three ships a day up there. I've sent a pair of minesweepers, *Aristea* and *Goulding*, to keep the channel clear, and four sixty-pounder field guns to protect the port. I wanted to check on progress and inspect the new SDF detachment — a lonely posting in the desert with very primitive accommodation.'

'A successful trip?'

'Yes, it all went splendidly until the return journey when the runway at Rooikop was fogged in and the pilot didn't want to take off. Then it cleared up a tad and we all climbed aboard rather reluctantly. Flying back down the coast, a stupendously thick fog bank rolled in off the Atlantic once again. Our pilot couldn't see any features whatsoever, so we descended into the murk. I asked what the hell he was doing and he said "looking for landmarks".'

'Not very encouraging.'

'I'll say. Suddenly, out of the gloom, a cliff rears up in front of us —'

'Oh God, where?'

'North of Saldanha Bay — Baboon Point they call it. If the pilot hadn't been jolly quick, we'd have crashed smack bang in the midst of said baboons. We missed the crest by a whisker.' He made a swooping gesture with his hand. 'Even the pilot needed a stiff one when we landed at Wingfield.'

'Papa, you have to take more care!' protested Imogen.

'Hardly my department, the air, my dear,' he said.

'I don't care which bally department!' she snapped, followed by an awkward silence.

'And how are things with the fleet?' asked Jack.

'As you know, we've got two cruisers in Snoek Town for partial refit, *Dido* and *Orion* — both of them smashed up off Crete in May.'

'I watched *Orion* coming in a few days ago.'

'Yes, a brave ship. She was bombed while evacuating troops and received direct hits on her bridge and "A" turret. Many grim reminders of the 300 killed have come to light as dockworkers start patching her up.'

'An awful business,' said Jack. 'Any news yet of U-boats heading our way?'

'It's maddening how we're kept in the dark. I've been pestering Freetown, but it's blood from a stone. There has been some U-boat activity in West Africa, but the C-in-C can't tell us if the enemy is venturing south or concentrating his efforts around their convoy assembly point.'

'Even if a wolf pack is coming this way, we simply don't have enough anti-submarine vessels for patrols, let alone convoy escort,' said Jack.

'Precisely. Creating convoys for all the shipping around our coast is unfeasible and the majority of merchantmen will have to continue travelling independently.'

'Isn't that a disaster waiting to happen?' said Imogen, looking up from her magazine.

'Quite so,' said the admiral. 'To make matters worse, we don't have nearly enough aircraft to cover the South African coast and the SAAF crews are unschooled in anti-submarine warfare. The situation is so precarious that Smuts has asked Churchill to step in. I currently have 380 ships on my tracking chart either approaching or leaving the Cape, including two troop convoys. As we speak, there are twenty-two ships anchored in Table Bay unable to find berths.'

'A U-boat boldly handled could slip in at night, sink half a dozen of them and be long gone before dawn,' said Jack.

'Even Simon's Town is getting chock-a-block. We just need a couple of big boys like *Carnarvon Castle* or *Devonshire* gumming up the works and the overflow has to anchor in the bay. The state of affairs in Durban is even worse.'

'So, you need more AS vessels, more aircraft and expanded port facilities to get your ships out of harm's way,' said Imogen, cutting to the chase.

'Exactly, my dear. All of it is in the pipeline, but everything happens too damn slowly. It's a race against time.'

'A race you seem to be losing, Papa,' she said standing up. 'Now, let's go through to dinner, I'm starving.'

CHAPTER 9

Along with the rest of the crew, Kruger had finally settled into the rhythm of a U-boat on long patrol. All the extra food and crates that had clogged the alleyways and second head had at last found a home or a stomach and Kruger had also found a way to treat *U-68* as a form of home.

Their underwater world nevertheless continued to feel like an alternative reality, an unpleasant dream that occasionally turned to nightmare. On land, he was a fearless *boer* prepared to endure almost anything for the cause of freedom, but here his conviction, and legs, found less purchase. The fact that he was so ignorant — not understanding how any of the pipes, valves, levers and gauges worked — and thus utterly dependent on his shipmates, added to the sense of helplessness.

He could not help but think of the submarine as a whale-like creature filled with veins and arteries, nerves, lungs, a complex circuitry connected to the brain of its commander with a single eye on the end of a long tentacle that reached above the waves. And he was extraneous to all of it.

One morning sailing south of Cape Verde, Lingen was handed an urgent, secret signal from the *BdU*. The first lieutenant hauled the boat's Enigma machine from its locked cabinet and placed it on the wardroom table. After checking the settings, he carefully typed the keys, then handed the decoded signal to the captain. A look of pleasure spread across Brand's face: 'Gentlemen, we might be in luck.'

'What is it, Kapitän?' asked Kruger.

'*BdU* reports that a big convoy has just left Freetown and is thought to be coming our way.'

Kruger pictured the grand villa in Lorient and the admiral staring at a wall map in his bunker as someone shifted the five little red flags of Gruppe Savanne onto an interception course.

That night, all lookouts were on high alert for the convoy as they headed southeast. Kruger was assigned the port aft sector and, coming from the dimmed control room, his eyes were already adjusted to the darkness.

'Do not for a moment lose focus, do not get distracted, stick to your quadrant,' warned the first lieutenant for the umpteenth time. 'Enemy destroyers are almost smokeless and their masthead lookouts are much higher than us, which gives them the advantage. Every second counts.'

The night sky was black and sleek as satin; *U-68* rose and fell to an easy rhythm. A sickle moon hung low on the water casting the faintest trail of light; each star was a defined pinprick. What were those shapes on the horizon, Kruger wondered? Ships or … no … low tropical clouds. The big Zeiss binoculars grew heavy and his biceps started to ache. He lowered them for a few seconds, stretched and flexed his arms, then back up to his eyes to scan the same sector of sea and sky yet again.

In the east came an easing of the night from slate to pewter, then the first pale washes. The dawning of a new day was God's gift and he revelled in the banishment of the dark, the slow revelation of the light. Out there, somewhere far off their port beam, lay Africa: how he willed the weeks to pass quickly and bring him once more to its shores.

A voice came from below, as from the ocean itself: 'Man on the bridge?' The relieving watch at last, but Kruger lingered, waiting for the sun to lift from the ocean, turning the sky orange, then yellow, and coating the hull in gold. It was only through God's grace that a deadly weapon of war could be transformed into something so handsome. He looked at the watch keepers, all of them bathed in the same holiness, their faces carmine — like timeless *brandwagters*, keepers of the sacred flame.

The first lieutenant stood in the doorway of the wireless cabin watching Wichmann as he listened to the incoming Morse — thin bleating from the other side of the world. Headphones covering his ears, the petty officer bent over a notepad and wrote down the unintelligible stream of letters. Lingen pulled the paper from the PO's hands the moment he was done, stepped through to the wardroom and set up the cipher machine again. The captain came and stood over him: 'Faster, IWO.'

'But, sir, imagine if I got the decoding wrong and sent us to Brazil?'

The captain sniggered, then snatched the sheet from him. 'From C-in-C to *U-68*, *U-156*, *U-159*, *U-172*, *U-504*,' he read aloud. '*U-156* reports convoy sighted, several columns, flank protection, grid square EJ7612, course three-two-zero, speed eight knots.'

'Well done to Kapitän Nagel!' exclaimed Lingen.

'We have them!' said Brand. 'Steer one-two-zero, full ahead both.' The orders were repeated, the engine-room telegraph rang and the throbbing of the diesels rose to a thunderous roar.

Kruger climbed to the bridge and immediately felt the change — the rush of speed and expectant mood among the lookouts. After weeks of plodding, *U-68* was powering forward at eighteen knots, tearing southeast into an undulant swell. The Atlantic was a heavenly shade of cobalt and flying fish leapt from the wave crests like sea sprites. The air played warm and the day was golden: what a way to race into battle. Their prow sliced into the swell, carving great peels of white water and sending sheets of spray over the bridge. Kruger looked astern at their seething wake — a boiling white trail shrouded by blue diesel fumes stretching into the distance — and prayed the convoy did not have air cover.

'Gets your heart pumping, does it not?' said Brand, arriving on the bridge.

'Yes, it does, even for a land animal like me.'

After a dull lunch of tinned sardines and canned bread flavoured with the vague taste of diesel, Kruger consulted the chart, noting the pencilled crosses that marked the convoy's last reported position and estimated location of each converging U-boat. By the look of it, *U-68* should be in touch with the enemy in a matter of hours.

As if reading his mind, the captain's voice crackled over the intercom: 'Do you hear there? This is your captain speaking. We are approaching a convoy out of Freetown heading for England which we expect to intercept at about 1800. We will wait for the rest of our wolf pack to assemble and then attack. That is all.'

Excited chatter came from every compartment and for the rest of the afternoon the men went about their duties with raised heads and broad smiles. To Kruger, it appeared as though even their complexions had added colour. He found the transformation from lethargy to purpose quite remarkable, or perhaps it was more a case of bravado to fend off their fears. Either way, these were men to fight beside … just a pity it had to be inside a steel cylinder beneath the waves.

'Kapitän, I must caution you, this full-speed business of yours is gobbling my fuel reserves,' complained the chief.

'Do not worry, Hoppe, it is for a good cause and the *Milchküh* will be waiting for us in her pasture just south of the Equator.'

'Let us hope so, sir, otherwise we might be paddling back to France.'

Kruger was on the bridge again at sunset, the lookouts keyed up for the first sighting of the convoy. A scarlet sun slid into the deep astern of them and the sea ahead was grazed by dark thunderclouds, some of them leaking curtains of rain.

'The last report says about twenty-five ships with a relatively light escort,' said Brand. 'I hope the other U-boats are close so we can attack this evening, but no news of them yet from the *BdU*.'

Tension rose on the bridge as dusk pressed in.

'Masthead on the starboard bow!' bellowed a lookout, a foot from Kruger's ear. He peered ahead as the captain raised himself onto the step at the front of the bridge and trained his binoculars at the gloom.

'*Ja*, I see it!' exclaimed Brand, 'Very well done, Dietrich!' Then into the voicepipe: 'Hard a-port, steer three-two-zero!'

Kruger braced his legs and scanned the squall-shrouded horizon as the U-boat rose on a crest, describing the tightest of turns to take up station ahead of and to starboard of the convoy. There! The white feather of a bow wave topped by the vaguest whisker of a mast. Above the throb of the U-boat's diesels he thought he could hear the beating of his own heart.

'Herr Kruger, you are going to see fireworks tonight,' said Brand. 'I would not want to be sailing in one of those merchantmen right now. They cannot travel faster than the slowest ship and given the size of the convoy, their zigzagging is clumsy — not enough to pose a problem for us. What is more, these African convoys usually have a much weaker escort than the North Atlantic ones.'

'How will the rest of the pack find us?'

'*U-156* is on the other side of the convoy transmitting bearing signals and squash signals while we wait for permission from Kernéval to attack.'

Kruger felt a prickling at the back of his neck and kept looking over his shoulder, expecting to see an enemy escort looming out of the murk.

'Look there!' said Brand. 'Must be one of the corvettes or destroyers on the starboard screen. *Verdammt*, I think it is turning in our direction. Perhaps part of the zigzag or perhaps they have spotted us. Diving stations! Open all main vents!'

In one bound, Kruger was through the hatch, sliding down the ladder to the control room and stepping smartly aside as the lookouts tumbled after him.

The captain landed neatly and called out, 'Periscope depth, Number One!'

They were submerged in a matter of moments, the noise of the dive replaced by silence, save for the gentle hum of the electric motors. Chief Hoppe closely watched the water level in his Papenberg, indicating the rise and fall of the swell, and soon restored the trim.

'Propeller noises on the port quarter, sir,' said the hydrophone operator, leaning out of his cubbyhole. Then a few minutes later, 'Now moving slowly astern.'

'Up periscope.' As the captain pressed his face against the rubber eyepieces, Kruger pictured a submerged ostrich poking a big-eyed head above the waves and had to stifle a nervous laugh. After scanning the horizon to make sure the escort had moved away, Brand called for the submarine to surface. They had to remain in contact with the enemy and needed their superior surface speed to keep slightly ahead of the convoy, awaiting the signal to attack.

'Man on the bridge?' called Kruger.

'*Ja*, come, and bring my night sight with you.'

He emerged on the bridge and handed over the apparatus which Brand fitted onto the master sight.

'I can't see them, Kapitän,' said Kruger.

'Over on our port quarter. They are formed up in a rectangle of six columns with the most valuable vessels, like tankers or troopships, in the middle for protection.'

'How strong is the escort?'

'We don't know yet, but we will find out very soon!' The big whites of Brand's teeth were clearly visible in the dark.

The telegraphist's head appeared in the mouth of the hatch. 'Message from C-in-C, sir.'

'*Ja*, Funkobermaat, what is it?'

'The other U-boats have all made contact with the convoy, sir. Permission granted to attack.'

'Excellent! Right then … action stations! Flood tubes one to four and prepare for a surface attack.'

'Bridge firing with calculators to follow master sight,' called out Lieutenant Seebohm from his position in the conning tower.

'Attacking now!' snapped Brand. 'Hard a-port, full ahead both!'

U-68 reared like a racehorse and carved towards the convoy, aiming just ahead of the lead ships.

Kruger watched, mesmerised, as the enemy, inked dreamily in the blotting paper of the night, began to take shape. It appeared as though the captain was stalking the second ship in the starboard column — a fat, juicy freighter. While Brand kept tabs on all the convoy's moving parts, Lingen's eyes were glued to the UZO mounted binoculars, linked to the attack computer below.

'Open bow caps of tubes one and two,' said the captain.

'Enemy speed eight knots,' said Lingen into the voicepipe. 'Angle on the bow, three zero left. Range 900.'

Lieutenant Seebohm punched the values into the electromagnetic calculator which immediately provided the requisite information for launching the torpedoes. Kruger's breath came in jerks, his heart firing like a piston.

'Tubes one and two ready, Kapitän,' said the first lieutenant in a matter-of-fact tone.

'All right, IWO, a double hit on that freighter.'

'*Ja*, Kapitän,' he said, peering into the sight. 'I will aim for the leading edge of the bridge and the main mast.'

'Very good.'

Kruger's mind was in turmoil as he scanned the ocean, looking for hunting escorts, the rest of the convoy, the other U-boats, the moon that threatened at any moment to elbow its way through the clouds and wreck their party.

'Lock on tubes one and two, bearing two-four-zero,' said Lingen.

'Tubes one and two, fire when ready,' said the captain, almost casually.

'Tube one: *los!*' Lingen shouted down the hatch, followed by a short pause. 'Tube two: *los!*'

'Both torpedoes running!' called out the hydrophone operator.

Kruger could feel, hear and see nothing of the two projectiles as they left the mother ship and raced towards a point ahead the freighter. Hopefully the darts and target would converge at a spot divined by the mathematics of their electromagnetic calculator.

'Shift target, port twenty,' said the captain. 'IWO, prepare to attack the next ship in the column.' Just then, Kruger saw bright flashes on the far side of the convoy, followed by hollow thunder.

'Excellent, our boys are getting to work over there too,' said Brand.

Their prow swung away from the doomed ship and Kruger held his breath, listening to the seconds counting themselves off in his head as the captain stared intently at his stopwatch. Any moment now...

A blinding sheet of orange light tore open the darkness, followed moments later by a second blast. The shock wave hit Kruger like a cricket bat to the face and he reeled backwards and ducked. When he drew upright, he saw the captain's face illuminated by the leaping flames, a wide grin on his lips — wry or vaguely maniacal, it was not easy to tell.

Across the water, men were being scalded, branded, maimed, dismembered, suffocated, drowned, all as a result of this man's handiwork. Thank goodness it was the enemy doing the dying. Brand's determined visage seemed the purest expression of courage, of the will of the new Germany, for ruthlessness was the only way the Axis nations were going to overcome the odds. Kruger felt a surge of admiration for the price this U-boat captain was prepared to pay for his fatherland, a cost that was there in what his face did not, may not, reveal.

Just then, a waterspout leapt from the ocean a hundred metres off their starboard beam. '*Alarm!*' yelled the captain. 'So, the escorts are not asleep.'

Kruger caught a murky glimpse of the corvette as he leapt for the hatch, the dreaded words 'dive, dive, dive' echoing in his head and a lookout's boot crushing his fingers on a rung as he descended. Landing in the control room, he joined the stampede of crewmen racing forward to lend weight to the bows as *U-68* tipped into a crash dive.

'Shut off for *Wabos*!' yelled Lingen as watertight doors banged closed and the klaxon filled the boat with its awful knelling.

In less than forty seconds they were submerged, leaving only a swirl of foam for the enemy's guns. The hands had charged forward like a herd of spooked springbuck and Kruger followed them into the junior ranks' accommodation, hoping that his 180 pounds might make a small difference. Cursing filled the compartment as the U-boat acquired an ever-steeper bow-down angle, the sailors packed like cigarettes, the air heavy with the smell of bilge-water, oil, damp clothing, stale sweat and unwashed genitalia.

They levelled off at ninety metres and Kruger returned to the tension-filled control room, which looked like the scene from a movie in which every character had been frozen in position. The captain stood beside the chart table as though paused in mid-sentence. All was quiet: the auxiliary machinery had been switched off, as well as the fans and wireless transformer. The hydrophone operator's head leant out into the alleyway, his eyes and the captain's locked in tense telepathy.

Knock. Knock. Knock. The underwater sound of the enemy's Asdic groping for its prey. Ten seconds apart, the tap of vengeance probed and probed.

'Any time now, lads,' said Chief Hoppe from the gloom. 'Best say your prayers.'

No one responded.

Kruger pictured grey canisters splashing into the water and sinking towards them to detonate beside the U-boat, tearing open their thin metal skin, water pouring in and crazed men clawing at each other as they sank to the benighted depths.

Now came a strange rattling sound, as though pebbles were being dropped on the deck.

'Asdic has made contact with us,' said Brand for Kruger's benefit. It sent a shudder through him as he visualised the tentacles of sound reaching out to ensnare them. He found that his hands were shaking and his throat had turned to sandpaper. No one in the control room stirred, but their eyes betrayed the terror each one must be feeling. Then Kruger became aware of another sound: the propeller of an approaching corvette. *Thrum-thrum, thrum-thrum, thrum-thrum.* Closer ... closer ... overhead.

'Splashes!' hissed Zimmermann, the hydrophone operator.

Eternal seconds, then a deafening explosion that almost ruptured Kruger's eardrums. Another, and another, as though a great sledgehammer were striking the hull. His mind was in tumult. Out there: hell and damnation in balls of shattering flame, whiting out the darkness, bringing the Lord's atomized light to the deep. The submarine danced and quivered through a maelstrom of beleaguered water until, eventually, calm returned as the propeller sound receded, but reprieve was brief.

Knock. Knock. Knock. A woodpecker tapping a hole in his skull.

'Approaching from astern,' said the hydrophone operator. 'Bearing one-six-zero.'

The sound of stones dropped on the hull again, followed by the washing-machine throb of the corvette passing overhead like a low-flying bomber.

Kruger did not move a muscle, did not blink, dared not breathe. *Is this the end?* He felt desperately alone: there was no comradeship with these undersea men. Each one had retreated into his death shell, hunched in terrible anticipation, except for the captain who stood erect, shoulders back, cap askew and wearing a smirk that could have been nonchalance, indifference or defiance. How on earth did he do it?

More splashes.

Kruger heard the metallic clicks of the depth-charge pistols, followed immediately by three detonations in quick succession, then a fourth. Apocalyptic revelations, the end becoming nigh in great, water shatterings. He found that he was gripping the flag locker with both hands, his knuckles white. How much more could his nerves take? If only he could *do* something.

His mind conjured soldiers in a trench enduring a barrage: rats in a trap with nowhere to run or hide. But even in a trench you could dig deeper, your bare hands would do, clawing a hole in the earth like a mole. *Give me a rifle, give me a knife, give me a way to fight back, even if I must die trying; not like this, not here in this vast black nothingness.* Kruger was back in the cave, the sandstone walls pressing in, the light dimming. He needed to get out, get to the surface. Shutting his eyes tight, he swallowed bile, clenched his fists ... and held on.

Time had let go its moorings. He imagined *U-68*, lifeless and spent on the ocean floor, a hundred years hence: 2041. Inside her belly lay fifty-one bodies, perfectly preserved in their tomb, corpses of papery flesh and bone, the pumping of blood and heaving of lungs long abandoned; the pictures registered by those glassy eyes, the memories of those quieted brains all gone, leaked out into the great Atlantic deep, every soul committed to the great Atlantic sleep, all their loved ones, relatives and friends already dead ... except perhaps one or two babies now over a century old.

'Nothing to worry about,' said the captain dismissively. 'Our pursuer is clearly an amateur.'

Kruger looked quizzically at Brand as the throbbing receded.

'It sounds like the other U-boats are having fun, Herr Kruger. That thudding you can hear is the music of bulkheads giving way in a sinking ship.'

Kruger did not trust himself to speak. The propeller noises grew louder again: perhaps their hunter was not such an amateur.

'Four *Wabos* in the water,' hissed the hydrophone operator, dragging off the headset to protect his eardrums.

Detonations tore the ocean asunder directly above them, Thor smiting the hull four times with his hammer, followed by an almighty roaring as the Atlantic raced to fill the underwater caverns created by the explosions. How much more punishment could the boat take?

Kruger's knees had turned to jelly and he sank to the deck with his head in his hands.

'I suggest you remain standing, Herr Kruger,' said Brand. 'Not because I am a stickler for formality, but if a depth charge explodes close by while you are seated it may snap your spine.'

Kruger sprang to his feet as though he'd been stung by a scorpion.

The corvette turned to race back into the fray, a fox after a hare ... the most sluggish of hares.

'This Englishman is getting better,' said the captain. 'Switch off all unnecessary lights, we might need every drop of juice and air if this is going to be a long game.'

Another pair of ear-splitting detonations accompanied by the shattering of glass as all the remaining lights were doused. Kruger had the illusion that they were trapped at the bottom of a coal mine: black on black. *Dear Lord, if I am to drown, let it not be in Stygian darkness.* Their iron coffin was floating in the limbo of nature's purgatory — mid-ocean, mid-deep, mid-night — waiting for His final blow, or His mercy.

Torch beams. Someone shouting for fuses, then the calming voices of the captains of each station, calling from the darkness like the voices of angels: 'Engine room, all's well.' 'Motor room, all's well.' 'Fore-ends, all's well.'

Emergency lighting flickered on.

'Do not get too comfortable, they are not done with us yet,' said Brand in an offhand tone.

Kruger registered the next five minutes of silent running as the same number of hours. A turn to starboard, a turn to port and still the enemy could not be shaken. Again, the infernal knocking of the Asdic returned, a tiny hammer tapping at the anvil of his skull. Satan's tuning fork.

The sound of pebbles.

'Ha, good for him, his prolonged chase has not been in vain,' said Brand. 'Let us see if he can do any better this time.' The captain had an unearthly grimace, teeth bared like a baboon — Kruger hardly recognised the man.

Two violent detonations shook the hull, accompanied by the sound of breaking plates from the galley.

'Poor old Kombüse, he cannot take it when his precious crockery gets smashed. This might just tip him over the edge.'

Kruger did not take his eyes off Brand. If they were about to die, something in his expression would surely betray it. Kruger knew that inside the sturdy pressure hull of the captain's skull, he must be assessing their depth, course and speed, as well as that of the enemy, and the various evasive options available. All Brand had to go on was the noise of the corvette's propeller. Although this was a battle between two vessels crammed with sailors, essentially it was a duel between two blindfolded men, each trying to guess the other's next move.

'Hard a-port.'

'Hard a-port, Kapitän,' said the helmsman.

'Steer due east.'

PO Zimmermann leant out of his cubbyhole and said: 'Another ship is joining, sir, bearing one-three-zero, closing fast.'

Kruger glanced around the control room and saw the waxen looks of fear; Brand's face remained wooden. 'So, he has called a little friend to help him. That does make things more interesting.'

'How is that, Kapitän?' asked Kruger hoarsely, his voice barely above a whisper.

'When a ship approaches a U-boat, its Asdic is blind for the last few hundred metres — you see, the sonar beam cannot scan the area directly beneath it. This gives us a sporting chance to take evasive action, but if a second ship maintains contact with us from a little way off, it can guide the attacker all the way in, and stay locked onto us after the charges are dropped.'

'It evens the chances.'

'Yes, considerably, and makes the contest far more exciting, not so?' His smile appeared almost genuine.

Knock. Knock. Knock. A white stick tapping. Blind Man's Death.

As Brand predicted, the corvette raced in while the Asdic of the accompanying ship held *U-68* in its sonic embrace. Splashes. Zimmermann ripped the headphones from his ears and Kruger watched, enthralled, as the hydrophone operator's lips mouthed the seconds from entry to detonation.

Two terrible blows on a kettle drum. The boat quivered and shook. Somebody screamed.

'All right lads, we are doing just fine,' called out the captain. 'Let us take her deeper, Chief.'

Kruger's skull was an eggshell — brittle, febrile, ready to crack and spill the yolk of his beleaguered mind. An ominous silence returned, save for the slop of bilge water beneath their feet, like a calm day at Steenbokbaai, high tide lapping the beach below the house. Another world, another lifetime.

Kruger stared at the deck head above: were they so deep in the Atlantic's belly that God could no longer see or hear them? *Have we been forsaken?* No, the Lord would show His wisdom and His compassion, he must hold faith.

An interval of time passed that could have been seconds, minutes or hours. All that mattered was that the enemy was up there, waiting for the prey to betray itself. The air in the boat had become so foul and depleted of oxygen that each movement seemed to sap Kruger's willpower. Nobody knew exactly how deep their U-boat could go and how much pressure the hull could withstand. Finding out the exact depth at which a Type IX would be crushed like a paper cup could only be ascertained by experience, and no one had ever returned from the depths to divulge it.

But deeper and deeper they went, Brand having determined that it was their best chance of escape. The needle on the gauge passed 150 metres and still no order came to stop their descent. Chief Hoppe looked expectantly at Brand, but he just shook his head.

'Starboard stern gland leaking!' came a call and the chief hurried aft.

'Deeper,' said the captain, the curl of his lips perhaps as far from joy as dementia from reason.

Kruger's eyes tracked the needle as it continued its progress around the dial. Sweat beaded on his forehead, but he dared not wipe it away lest the smallest movement break the spell and scupper their luck. He'd been told the maximum recommended diving depth was 150 metres, but the needle already showed 170 and still they sank. More detonations, far above them this time: their great depth must be deceiving the hunters.

Two hundred metres now and the boat began to protest at the increased pressure, whistling like a kettle on the boil. Kruger knew that at fifty-seven metres, the grain silo in Cape Town was the tallest structure in Africa south of the Equator. He shuddered: they were more than three silos deep.

'For your information, Herr Kruger, every square metre of *U-68* is, at this very moment, withstanding a weight of 200 tons. German engineering! You have to take your hat off to those Deschimag builders in Bremen.'

Flakes of paint drifted down like snow as the hull took ever more strain, accompanied by creaking and groaning, as though the U-boat were in pain. Kruger imagined that his own body was being compressed, the air slowly squeezed from him. His breathing was short and shallow, his mouth open, a fish out of water. Every nerve in his body had migrated to his ears, registering each new sound with dread. He visualised the hull bending inwards between its frames, the Atlantic searching for the smallest weakness. Perhaps, like a balloon, all it would take was a pinprick. He pictured his ribs, the frame of his own hull, and the skin of his chest pressing between each girder, the cage that held his lungs, his heart, a cage that was about to give way.

Outside was the darkness of the deep, a night so black that no light could ever penetrate. It was like the darkness of evil and Kruger conjured in his mind's eye the light of God, a bright eye illuminating the depths, painting every corner on which His gaze fell with the brilliance of His goodness. By the Lord's grace, they would be spared.

Knock. Knock. Knock.

The Devil's gravel.

The Asdic had them once more.

The seamen's dead eyes spoke of minds that were thousands of miles away; one sailor had shrunk into a foetal position. All of them appeared braced, as if employing every sense to pinpoint the enemy, to locate the oncoming ship and its canisters of death. *May it come quickly and painlessly, may the inrush of icy water be an instant anaesthetic, a relief.*

Zimmermann reported the approach, but Brand did not alter course as the coffee-grinding sound of propellers grew louder. Kruger realised that the captain was waiting until the very last moment, when the enemy was almost upon them and committed to the attack, to change course. Brand stood with his cap pushed back, looking as though he were mulling over a mathematical problem, giving no hint that its answer determined the life or death of fifty-one men.

Splashes.

'Hard a-port, full ahead starboard motor! Pump out the bilges!'

The U-boat dragged herself into the tightest turn her length would allow.

Kruger found himself standing beside the ladder — the instinct of a doomed animal — staring blindly at the hatch above as though it might offer some fantastical salvation. He began hyperventilating, storing as much air as possible in the event that these golden breaths were his last. '*Liewe Vader*—'

A double detonation shook the hull, accompanied by the thunder of water pouring back into the excavations wrought by the blasts. Again, the shattering of gauge-glasses and light bulbs; a food locker burst open disgorging its contents. Fuses exploded like firecrackers as they blew from their junction boxes.

An inarticulate yell was wrenched from Kruger's lips. From elsewhere in the darkness came panicked shouts; one sailor broke down sobbing, followed by a heavy blow that silenced the lad. Judging by the stench, others had soiled themselves.

Torch beams darted about the control room and along the alleyway. Jets of water squirted from fissures and pipes as the crew hastened to tighten cocks and valves to stem the leaks.

'Keep your bloody voices down!' hissed the captain.

'Propellers bearing one-four-zero, growing louder,' said PO Zimmermann. 'Running in to attack.'

'Full ahead both, hard a-starboard,' said the captain.

Kruger put his hands over his ears and closed his eyes.

A murderous gyration flung him to the deck as *U-68* was yanked about like a puppet. The walls of their coffin appeared to be reverberating like the skin of a drum as blood leaked from his nose and bile rose in his throat. The sailors around him clung to their stations, trying to hold together their shredded sanity. His prayers alternated between bargaining and beseeching; in the lulls between attacks he forced his will to assert itself: *I will not be harmed for I am doing the will of my people and my God. Nothing can happen to this boat while I am aboard.*

Someone vomited, filling the control room with a sickly-sweet stench.

'Clean that up immediately,' snapped Lingen.

Kruger noticed that *U-68* was bow down and continuing its headlong descent.

'We are off the end of the depth gauge, Kapitän, but the pressure gauge reads 22 ATM, so that is 220 metres,' said Chief Hoppe.

The internal woodwork began to crack as the hull compressed, its splintering sound serving to ratchet up the terror that coursed through the boat.

'Serious leak in the motor room!'

'She will not stand any more,' said the chief.

'All right, let us level off, foreplanes hard a-rise,' said the captain.

'Foreplanes not answering, sir!' cried the planesman.

Kruger watched the gauge in horror as they continued to sink.

'Pressure reads 240 metres and still falling,' said Hoppe.

A sharp crack signalled a rivet giving way in the fore-ends. Kruger felt himself slipping into the crevice at the back of the cave, down into the darkness, red stick-figures dancing across the rock, closing in around him.

'Switch to manual,' snapped the captain. 'Both motors full astern.' But still they canted into the deep, men losing their footing on the slippery deck as they scrambled aft to offset the plunge.

'That is 270 metres now, sir, we cannot hold her,' said the chief through gritted teeth.

From somewhere came a whimpering sound, more animal than human. The rifle crack of another rivet and a thin jet of water bisected the control room like a violin string, but powerful enough to break a man's limb.

'Leutnant Bernd Hoppe, I order you to hold her.' Brand could have been demanding that the salt be passed. The chief looked at his captain with stricken eyes. Kruger's stomach had turned to water.

'She is responding!' screamed a planesman.

Kruger let out a gasp — for how long had he been holding his breath? He watched as the pressure gauge slowed and then settled. *Thank the Lord in His infinite mercy.*

'There, you see, a bunch of old hens,' grumbled the captain as one planesman broke down sobbing. Brand looked as though he was about to rebuke the lad, but let it pass as *U-68* slowly rose and levelled off at 120 metres.

Another pattern of depth charges and again Brand ordered both motors full ahead. The chief kept blasting HP air into the trimming tanks to maintain their buoyancy, but there was only so long he could keep that up before they'd be forced to surface. The air was getting fouler with each breath: oil, overheated motors, body odour, urine, faeces, vomit … and fear.

Yea, though I walk through the valley of the shadow of death, I will fear no evil, for Thou art with me. Kruger reached for some apple juice and found that his shaking hand could hardly hold the bottle steady enough to prise off the hinged cap. The taste of apples on his tongue reached him from another dimension. For a moment, he glimpsed an orchard in Elgin with the sunlight arcing through low branches, red orbs hung like Christmas decorations among dark leaves.

There were long minutes of respite: perhaps they had shaken off their attacker? Then came the dreaded tapping of the Asdic once more.

'*Gottverdammt!*' cried the captain, slamming a bulkhead with his fist, the first real demonstration of emotion.

Kruger had no idea for how many hours they'd been kept down by their torturers. With haggard grey faces, black eye sockets, red-rimmed eyes and wearing expressions of despair, the crew were slumped in attitudes of exhaustion, only stirring when the enemy passed overhead. Of course he must look the same, or worse. With little gratification, he pictured the citizens of London cowering in their Underground tunnels each night as the Luftwaffe played the role of aerial corvettes.

The next pattern of detonations was thankfully much further away.

'Bah, losing interest,' said Brand.

'Maybe they are running out of depth charges,' said Lingen.

A short while later, Zimmermann leant out of his cubbyhole and said: 'Growing fainter, we may have shaken them off.'

'Amateurs,' scoffed Brand.

As the promise of imminent death began to recede, Kruger registered the return of the world, his thoughts bending to dry land, the veld decked with spring flowers, the old house by the sunlit sea. Having felt that he was as good as dead and buried in this steel coffin, he could believe in life again. It was a sensation akin to diving under and emerging from an icy wave at Steenbokbaai. *And the Lord spake unto the fish, and it vomited out Jonah upon dry land.*

The captain announced that they would be returning to the surface. Reaching periscope depth, Kruger heard the clicking of periscope switches as Brand took a careful look around. Glancing at the clock, he realised that up there in the world it was night once more: they had been kept down for more than twenty-four hours.

'Surface!'

Donning his grey-leather bridge coat, Brand climbed the vibrating ladder into the conning tower, followed by his band of lookouts.

'Upper lid clear!' shouted the chief.

'Equalise!' called down the captain.

There was a tremendous release of pressure as the hatch swung open with a reverberating boom and each watch keeper clung onto the legs of the man above, and most firmly to the captain, lest he be ejected like a champagne cork. Foul air, thick as fog from a sewer, gushed up through the conning tower and gallons of fresh air — honeyed, tropical air — poured into the control room as if from some godly jug. All the fans were switched on, sucking in more air.

Kruger's eyes filled with tears as he gulped the nectar, intoxicated by the luxuriance of it, the decadence of it, as acolytes with upturned faces grouped around the altar of the lower hatch. It was a baptism back into life.

'Man on the bridge?'

'*Jawol, komm.*'

Kruger emerged to find a temperate night spangled into brilliance: his Maker had sown the veld of the sky with stars for daisies. A thin veil of spray passed over the bridge, anointing him. He tasted salt on his lips; everything seemed newly made. *On the third day, the Son of God shall be resurrected.*

Dolphins broke the surface and played about their bow wave like phosphorescent torpedoes. 'Too much,' whispered Kruger. 'Too much life!' Was this a sign that he'd passed some sort of test? Would he now be worthy of the task?

He looked up at the glittering heaven and mouthed the word '*Ja*'.

CHAPTER 10

HMSAS *Southern Gannet* alternated with her three sisters working forty-eight-hour anti-submarine patrols, zigzagging across the False Bay approaches and occasionally along the channel from Cape Point to Table Bay. Their most regular beat involved steaming back and forth from Rocklands Point on the west side of the bay to the mouth of the Steenbras River on its eastern flank.

Another day, another patrol. Life on board had found a comfortable rhythm. Wearing an assortment of jerseys, balaclavas and sheepskin jackets donated by the ladies of SAWAS, off-duty men gathered on the boat deck atop the boiler-room casing or beside the funnel for warmth. Everyone smoked. Below decks, stoker Jantjies sang another bawdy Afrikaans song at the top of his lungs, but only his lips betrayed the fact due to the baritone roar of the engine room.

Each evening at sea, Coxswain February opened his canteen — really just a locker — to sell cigarettes, tins of condensed milk and other treats. Pickles Brooke had been saving a parcel from his mother containing fruitcake, homemade fudge, a slab of Nestlé chocolate and boiled sweets. Happy to share with his messmates, Pickles was, for one night, the most popular sailor on *Gannet*.

After supper, the crew sat playing cards, singing and yarning. Chief McEwan often regaled them with stories about his whaling trips to the Antarctic: 'Doon south it was unimaginably cold. When someone spoke, you could read what they were saying 'cos their words froze. I remember one expedition to Kerguelen Island when there were blizzards throughout that whole summer and we had no luck catching whales. The southern-right stocks had been hammered, and the fins and blues were nowhere to be found. Och, the voyage was a dead loss, but then on our way home we bumped into an injured sperm whale whose intestines were loaded with ambergris — a sailor's gold is what that is. It paid for the whole trip and made up for all our losses.'

The coxswain also entertained the men with tales about his trawling days: 'We had brutal runs on those Irvin and Johnson boats, especially in the westerly gales,' said February, leaning against the Carley float in his oily jersey, hands in the pockets of his fearnought trousers. 'They used to pitch and roll worse than *Gannet* and if you didn't hang on tight, a big sea could easily wash you overboard. Our trawls were long, condom-shaped nets whose mouths were kept open with otter boards, just like we use for minesweeping. Working those wires in winter was horrible. Your hands froze and the trawler danced about like a drunk *droster*, the decks all slippery with fish guts, waves breaking over you, hauling in and gutting for forty hours straight. It was no joke.

'Our skipper was as tough as pig iron and never used charts for navigation. The old man could read the sea, the currents, the sky — he sailed by intuition. If we ever saw him using a chart, we got really worried 'cause then we knew he was lost. During one trip, we went so far south that we ran out of coal. On the way back, we had to burn just about everything: deck boards, panelling, bunks, you name it. Even the Bible. After that, I thought it was tickets, but the good Lord looked the other way.'

Their dull round of patrolling was sometimes enlivened by the arrival of a bigger convoy, requiring additional AS whalers and trawlers. When troop convoys comprising one or two 'monsters', such as *Queen Elizabeth* or *Île de France*, passed the Cape, Admiral Pembroke made sure that extra patrols were instituted, defences doubled and extensive aerial patrols flown during daylight hours.

The next big arrival due into Cape Town was WS.09D, one of Churchill's 'Winston's Specials', transporting 25,000 soldiers, including two Royal tank regiments, bound for Egypt. The convoy comprised, among others, the *Athlone Castle*, *Laconia*, *Oronsay*, *Durban Castle*, as well as two monsters — *Aquitania* and *Queen Mary* — requisitioned as troopships early in the war and both of them too big to fit into the harbour.

As there was a cold front brewing, which would make refuelling and victualing hazardous for ships anchored in the Cape Town roadstead, the pair were directed to the protected waters of False Bay. *Queen Mary* let out her booming siren which echoed off the bastions of Table Mountain as she raised anchor and headed down the swept channel, followed by *Aquitania*.

As for 'loose lips sink ships', every city resident — and every German spy south of the Limpopo — was aware of Cape Town's illustrious guests. Jack's flotilla conducted an anti-submarine sweep ahead and to seaward of the two giants while their own destroyer screen remained in close attendance and Ansons circled overhead.

A few hours later, the liners were safely anchored in the lee of Simonsberg, seeming to fill the hook-shaped bay. Their presence had both Commodore O'Reilly and Admiral Pembroke behaving like mother hens. Even Miss Retief, who was seldom provoked into leaving her easel by comings and goings in the bay, stood on her stoep gaping at the imperial pair.

Once the Winston's Special was safely on its way up the east coast, Jack's patrols returned to their normal beat, punctuated by regular shore leave. During one such break, Clara invited him to a braai at her parents' home. He caught the train to Newlands and walked the short distance to the old house on the west bank of the Liesbeek River.

'Dear Jack, so lovely to see you,' said Clara's mother as he opened the garden gate. 'How are you and how is your dad?'

'We are both well thank you, Mrs Marais.'

'Come and get a drink,' she said, taking his arm and leading him to a table under an oak tree sprouting the first pale leaves of spring. 'Clara will be out in a minute.'

'How are things going with the SAWAS?'

'It has been unadulterated pandemonium, Jack. We've had the *Queen Mary*, *Aquitania* and a huge convoy in —'

'I know.'

'Of course you do. Well, the whole Peninsula has been a beehive. I was supervising SAWAS operations on the quayside in Cape Town with mobile canteens and comforts depots. Then we had to lay on entertainment for the troops, sightseeing excursions around the Peninsula, trips to the country, you name it.'

'My father told me; we're tremendously grateful.'

'As bad luck would have it, another convoy landed a huge contingent of Italian POWs from North Africa at the same time. It was rather tragic to see our guards confiscating all the beautiful wooden cigarette and jam tins the prisoners had carved on their dreary passage down the Indian Ocean.'

'Why on earth did they do that?'

'Oh, there was a huge to-do when the last batch of German POWs damaged the panelling of *Queen Mary*. Anyway, the

Italians are far better off being interned here than just about anywhere else in the world, don't you think?'

Just then, Clara appeared on the stoep, wiping her hands on an apron. She had curled her hair, which bobbed enchantingly in blonde ringlets beside her cheeks. 'Oh, hello, Lieutenant Jack Pembroke DSO, I was just marinating the sosaties. I see Ma has corralled you.'

'He's all yours, *skapie*,' said Mrs Marais with a wave as she tacked from group to group across the lawn.

'Your mother has been telling me about her sterling work with the SAWAS.'

'Again. She keeps roping everyone in, except Pa of course. He'd be useless anyway. Last night, instead of studying, I was on the telephone battling with a string of *platteland* exchanges trying to arrange leave homes for 250 chaps off a cruiser and a dance for her officers at the Rotunda.'

'*Platteland?*'

'Rural districts — literally the "flat land". SAWAS arranges for sailors to get some R&R in the countryside and on farms. Pa does his bit by piping up from the armchair, his cat and the *Burger* on his lap, with unhelpful comments like, "It sounds as though you're trying to win the war with holidays and dances."'

'And…'

'Oh, he gets an earful, but it doesn't stop him. I've also been enlisted to go with Ma to Groote Schuur, the Cape Town residence of Smuts and his wife, Isie, who everyone calls Ouma — Grannie.'

'The mother of the nation,' Jack said, pouring her a glass of sherry.

'Ouma is the president of our Gifts and Comforts Fund and takes a personal interest in anyone on active service. We donate books, musical instruments, games, sweets, but also practical stuff like woolly clothes, especially for the sailors. The knitting gets done by SAWAS women and Ouma has turned Groote Schuur into a comforts depot, much to her husband's consternation. But he can't say "no" to Ouma, even if he is prime minister.'

'You'd never say so from the photos. She looks like a harmless old duck.'

'Don't be fooled: rosy complexion, curly grey hair, but the brightest, bluest eyes and a will of iron. Ma and I go once a week — it's a short walk up the road to Groote Schuur — and we sit in the billiard room drinking tea, knitting and making sheepskin jackets for the sailors. Ouma regales us with marvellous stories as she trundles away on her sewing machine making "glory bags", as the comfort parcels are called.'

'I know our sailors adore her.'

'When she's out in public they swarm around her for autographs as though she's a Hollywood star. She gets literally thousands of letters and stores them in suitcases under her bed. We've pitched in to try to help her answer them all. Just think, during the Boer War, British troops were the arch enemy and her husband led a commando against them.'

The pair strolled over to the braai where Clara's brother was turning sosaties, chops and boerewors on the grid.

'How's the flying going, Pierre?' asked Jack, handing him a bottle of Lion beer.

'Still the usual coastal patrols and tedious harbour circuits. We get so bored going round and round the anchored convoys. The other day a cheeky captain asked us to switch to flying anticlockwise as we were making him dizzy.'

'And you haven't been upgraded from those wood-and-canvas crates yet?' asked Jack.

'Ansons are actually pretty reliable with good viz, but you're right, they are slow and have limited range. If we do one day manage to intercept a raider, U-boat or, heaven forbid, a pocket battleship, we hardly pack any punch at all. Our anti-submarine bomb-load — we're not even fitted with depth charges yet — is a puny 300 pounds. I doubt something like the *Admiral Scheer* would even notice if we dropped our full load on her.'

'My father tells me a new Royal Fleet Air Arm squadron has just been formed at Wingfield,' said Jack.

'Yes, 789 Squadron. They'll be flying Swordfish, Blackburn Roc and Walrus — nothing to get too excited about. We're holding thumbs for Venturas soon, and maybe Catalinas later — now that's a decent bird for coastal patrol.'

'Have you had no luck with the Hun whatsoever?'

'None. We didn't even get a sniff of that raider before you bagged it a couple of months ago and there haven't been any U-boats that we know of in our sector.'

'There was talk of Italian submarines out of Massawa coming our way, but nothing yet, thank goodness,' said Jack.

'Plenty of false alarms, mind you. Every Tom, Dick and Harry along the coast has been spotting subs and sending us on wild goose chases all over the show. Another problem is the powers that be treating coastal patrol as a sort of rest cure for pilots after a tour of duty in the Western Desert. The chaps might be good in combat, but they know next to nothing about sea patrols, often fly too high and have no submarine-spotting skills. Just when they start getting the hang of things, they're posted back up north. It's all rather vexing.'

As it was a cool evening, the braai meat was brought into the dining room and set up on the buffet by the maid. Much of the talk around the table was about rugby, the war and politics, but

Jack got to sit next to Clara and their quiet conversation was far from such things. She told him about her long afternoons in Jagger Library studying French, German and Dutch tomes, about the novels she adored and her aspiration to become a journalist. She spoke about her love of jazz, her favourite movies, the Hollywood actors she liked best, and those she liked least.

When it came time for Jack to leave for the station, the pair lingered on a bench in the garden.

Concerning the subject of their relationship, they had come to a tacit agreement that they would be taking it slowly, but taking it forward, and for now, the arrangement suited both of them. He held her close and she settled against his big frame as though it was the most natural place in the world for her to be.

She glanced up, a questioning look in her eyes … then they kissed.

For his part, Lieutenant van Zyl had hardly stopped thinking about Sylvia Goldberg, the Austrian Jewish refugee he had recently met. He wasn't sure of her feelings towards him and, due to his first-lieutenant responsibilities, had only been able to meet her on a couple of occasions. Normally confident and playful around women, he was often tongue-tied and anxious in the presence of Sylvia. She was a serious young art student dealing with a father imprisoned in a Nazi concentration camp and a mother who was trying to fend for herself in a foreign city far from the rich and glamorous Salzburg world they'd fled with nothing more than could be carried in their suitcases, south through Italy and by ship to anywhere that would have them.

Van Zyl had signed out a car from the officer pool and arrived at the Goldberg flat in Gardens in the early evening.

There was a student dance in Jameson Hall that night and some of Sylvia's Michaelis Art School friends would be there. They parked on the University of Cape Town campus, tiered on the slopes of Devil's Peak, walked to the plaza and climbed the steps hand in hand, entering through the grand colonnade just as the band struck up and began to work its way through wartime favourites. On the stage were three singers, a row of trumpeters and clarinettists, two saxophonists, a portly gent on double bass, a drummer teasing his cymbals and a pianist tinkling his keys. As the evening warmed up, they foxtrotted and jitterbugged their way around a packed dance floor, taking regular smoke breaks on Jammie steps with its magnificent view across the Cape Flats to the Hottentots Holland.

'That's your home on the other side of the flats, isn't it?' she said.

'Yes, have you never been to Stellenbosch?' He was surprised.

'No, my *Mutter* and me, we haven't done much like that since we have come to South Africa, just the basics of living and finding where our feet are.'

'You must come with me one day. I'll show you the town, the lovely Dutch architecture and my home.' Before he'd finished uttering the words came a sting of regret: what if his brother were home and saw him with a Jewish girl. Her accent and looks would immediately betray her and there'd be no end to it.

'Has there been any word about your father?'

'Nothing. And nothing from any of the other members of my family who did not get out. It is so terrible, Jannie, we fear for the worst.'

'You must stay strong and hopeful … for your ma.'

She put her head on his shoulder and closed her eyes. He pulled her close and the music dipped and swooned with the opening and closing of the doors as a half moon rose over the flats. They sat for a long time in silence, not wanting the spell to break, each one sheltering from what the world had dealt them. Every university dance ended with the waltz 'Who's Taking You Home Tonight', which now eddied from the hall.

'Come, let's grab it while we can!' said Van Zyl, taking her hand and leading her back inside where the mood was entirely changed. They joined the throng gliding around the dimly lit hall, Van Zyl feeling her small breasts against his chest, her head nestled beneath his chin. Every couple was locked in an embrace, softly singing along to the music:

> Who's taking you home tonight
> After the dance is through?
> Who's going to hold you tight
> And whisper, 'I love you, I do.'

To his consternation, Van Zyl felt tears on his shirt and pressed her close, not wanting ever to let go.

CHAPTER 11

U-68 sailed south under the cover of the last few hours of darkness and took the opportunity to reload the two fish expended on the freighter. There was considerable enthusiasm from the sailors of the forward compartment as the reconfiguration would grant them much more elbowroom. The fore-ends had to be cleared and then, after a great deal of sweaty heaving on tackle, the new torpedoes were manoeuvred into place and slid into the tubes.

While this was going on, a message came through from the *BdU* bringing them up to date with the movements of the rest of Gruppe Savanne. Their attack had been a success with five merchantmen sunk and not a single U-boat lost or badly damaged. The arrival of a hunter-killer group of destroyers from Freetown had resulted in the attack being broken off and pursuit of the main objective resumed. The boats were to make their way independently to the rendezvous with the *Milchkuh*, before proceeding to the Cape.

As *U-68* sailed deeper into the tropics, the trade winds slackened and temperatures rose. The sun was copper coloured and lazy clouds grazed above a cobalt sea. The heat had grown oppressive and, given the strict water rationing, thirst raged constantly in the crew's throats. Standing duty in the bare minimum of clothing, the sunburnt faces and shoulders of the topless lookouts peeled continually. Pouring buckets of seawater over their heads only offered the briefest alleviation.

Temperatures inside the U-boat often reached 50°C, the air was stale and reeked of perspiration, mould and mildew stained everything. Most crew wore only white naval sports vests and

PT shorts, some of them even fashioned makeshift sarongs. There were more and more cases of prickly heat, boils and rashes, with ichthyol ointment liberally applied for most ailments. One sailor was struggling more than the rest and confided in Coxswain Fischer. Captain Brand was having his morning coffee on the settee and Kruger lay on his bunk reading from the 'Book of Revelation' when the matter was brought to their attention.

'Kapitän, we have a slightly delicate matter concerning Mechaniker Krause,' said Fischer.

'*Ja*, Steuermann, what is wrong with him?'

'It is his penis, sir.'

'What about it? Not working? It happens.'

'No, sir, it has swollen to double its normal size.'

'Tell him to stop playing with it.'

'It is not that exactly, sir. I think, from my limited medical knowledge, that he has contracted syphilis.'

'Bring the offending member here, immediately.'

The mechanic was summoned, stepped into the wardroom and stood awkwardly to attention, his cheeks flushing crimson.

'So, Krause, what have you got to say for yourself.'

'Sir, I —'

'Come, no time to beat about the bush, let us take a look at it.'

'Sir?'

'Drop your shorts, Mechaniker!' barked Fischer.

Krause did as he was ordered and both captain and coxswain leaned closer to peer at the sores that decorated the mechanic's swollen appendage. After a brief examination, Brand said, 'So, Mechaniker, you will not get to see the Cape of Good Hope after all. The *Steuermann* will issue you with penicillin and then you will be transferred to the *Milchküh*. They have a doctor on board and she will head back to France as soon as our group has been resupplied.'

U-68 reached the Equator on 14 August 1941, confirmed by Lieutenant Seebohm's sextant, and a crossing-the-line ceremony was organised on deck. As required by maritime custom, the seventeen 'polliwogs' — men who had not crossed the Equator before — were to be baptised by Neptune. Kruger was glad that his two voyages to Germany absolved him and watched proceedings from the bridge where the standard of Neptune — a square flag embossed with a three-pronged fork — flew from the staff.

Lieutenant Lingen played Admiral Triton and sported a fake white beard, flowing robes and a trident fashioned from cardboard. Captain Brand summoned the initiates and introduced them one by one to Neptune and his saucy girlfriend, Thetis, who wore a blond wig, gold crown and ankle-length toga. The polliwogs were smeared with engine grease and had to endure various trials and punishments, including a circuit of the conning tower on hands and knees carrying heavy weights. Then each initiate sat on an upturned bucket for his baptism, which involved a symbolic shaving by the coxswain using a wooden razor in the shape of a fish, drinking a dubious cocktail and having putrid concoctions smeared in his hair and on his body. The cook had saved rotten eggs for the purpose and the stench, when cracked over the unfortunates' heads, made the others reel away in disgusted mirth.

Trials concluded, the polliwogs were sprayed down with a hose on the after deck. Admiral Triton closed proceedings with a poem and presented each initiate with a mug of Schnapps, a medal cut from scrap tinplate and a baptism certificate penned by Lieutenant Seebohm and decorated with illustrations of *U-68*, palm-fringed shores, mermaids and a map of Africa.

Tropical sailing. Bright sunshine, the throaty grumble of the diesels and mesmerising rise and fall of the bows, slicing into a gentle swell. Flying fish leapt from the swells at their approach and flittered downwind like miniature fighter planes. For the most part, morale remained high, despite that lack of sightings or sinkings.

'How long have you been wearing those socks, Fritz?'

'Since we left Lorient, of course.'

'They are so ripe, even the fish are getting out of our way. How about a change, for all our sakes?'

'Are you round the bend, Otto, my lucky socks! They are the only things keeping us afloat. Anyway, you're a fine one to talk. You haven't changed your underwear in weeks and your cock smells like Gorgonzola.'

'How would you know?'

The monotony was relieved by all manner of games and entertainment. Brand knew that boredom and lethargy were insidious enemies, leading to *Blechkrankheit* or 'tin-box disease', and kept coming up with new ideas to maintain morale. He organised concerts in which each crewmember got to choose a record or take the microphone and sing a song which was transmitted throughout the boat. Although American and British jazz was considered degenerate by the Nazi authorities, Brand allowed it on board, much to the disapproval of Kruger. 'Negro filth,' he muttered as yet another Duke Ellington tune echoed over the intercom. Much more to his taste was Marlene Dietrich and the oft-repeated 'Lili Marleen' that leaked through the loudspeakers:

Vor der Kaserne
Vor dem großen Tor
Stand eine Laterne
Und steht sie noch davor
So woll'n wir uns da wieder she'n
Bei der Laterne wollen wir steh'n
Wie einst Lili Marleen
Wie einst Lili Marleen.

Outside the barracks
By the corner light
I always stand and wait for you at night
We will create a world for two
I'll wait for you, the whole night through
For you, Lili Marleen
For you, Lili Marleen.

Regular quizzes were organised with a popular first prize being the captain taking over the winner's watch. Indeed, although eccentric, Brand was a well-liked leader. With Seebohm's help, he penned a weekly newsletter — featuring on-board gossip, poems by the crew, cartoons, a crossword with specific relevance to their boat and reports from home — pinned up in the control room for all to read. There were also regular drills, the test firing of armaments and, whenever they were far enough from land, the men were allowed to sunbathe on deck and take showers on the aft casing using a hosepipe attached to the rail of the conning tower.

Despite the cook's best efforts, after nearly a month at sea, the menu suffered from a boring regularity and was devoid of fresh ingredients. Breakfast usually comprised powdered scrambled eggs with canned bread, rancid butter, black coffee and the daily dose of lemon juice to prevent scurvy. For main meals, there were the ubiquitous sausages (now grown mouldy), salted pork or hogshead brawn, often served with gherkins, canned sauerkraut and pickled onions. Desserts were tinned fruit or handfuls of prunes from a crate available to all. One afternoon, to Kombüse Schneider's delight, some of the crew managed to net a turtle, drag it aboard and butcher it on deck. The soup that night was, everyone agreed, delicious.

Kruger stood smoking in the *Wintergarten*, engrossed by the play of light upon the sea, the suck and wash of foamy water along the saddle tanks and the ever-changing white calligraphy of their wake, a squiggling line that stretched all the way back to a concrete dock on the west coast of France. Each day, each mile, brought him closer to home.

He flexed his thighs as the boat rolled: despite regular callisthenics, his muscles were flaccid from so much time sitting on his arse. Feeling like a caged animal, he knew he needed to be fit, strong and ready when he landed on South African shores. The crew were filled with amusement as they sidestepped his daily press-ups, sit ups and burpees in the alleyway and endless jogging on the spot in the wardroom. But his toned, rugby-flanker body, honed by his training in Germany, was nowhere near what it should be. He was going to need a tough exercise regime when he reached land.

Oh, how he longed to be running the farm roads once again, climbing its koppies and surveying the Atlantic from those rocky heights rather than this pitching, iron pedestal.

At midnight on 22 August, *U-68* approached the rendezvous zone at 20-degrees south on naval-grid square GG1998 where the replenishment submarine would be waiting. The milk cow made a brief, short-range homing signal — just enough to give them a fix but not enough to be detected by the enemy. It had been cushy for the sailors in the fore-ends since the torpedoes had been fired, but now they were about to take on more eels and lose their lounge suite.

'Pack away the damask tablecloth and family silver, Gustav, we are getting company.'

'It is not fair.'

'Don't complain, Otto, more fish with which to fry the enemy.'

The replenishment of Gruppe Savanne took place over two days. The *Milchküh* carried nearly 500 tons of extra fuel, food, torpedoes and spare parts. She even had a bakery and the men of *U-68* were eagerly looking forward to fresh bread. Kruger made sure he was on the bridge at dawn when the milk cow appeared out of the gloom.

'Pass up the signal lamp,' called Brand.

Moments later, the quartermaster clacked out the call sign and received an immediate reply, a pinprick winking in the murk.

'It is *U-459*, sir,' said PO Schmitt.

'Very good, exactly where we were told she would be grazing.'

The two submarines — one sleek and deadly, the other portly and cumbersome — closed to within hailing distance.

Kruger watched figures busily moving about the opposite afterdeck, the glint of a brass nozzle as a pythonic fuel pipe was manhandled into position. *U-68* would be taken in tow by the bigger submarine during the refuelling procedure.

'Fancy meeting you here, Fregattenkapitän Brand!' came the shout from a loudhailer.

'*Guten tag*, Kapitän Oelrich! We were just passing your neighbourhood and thought to ourselves, why not drop in?'

'Most kind of you. Tea? Schnapps?'

'Both, gladly. But first some of your milk and honey please. I will come over once the transfer is underway.'

The ailing Mechanic Krause was transferred to the *Milchküh* and a replacement mechanic came aboard. The replenishment operation lasted four hours during which time *U-68* took on 104 tons of diesel, 3 tons of lubricating oil and 3 tons of provisions, much of it ferried between the submarines in rubber dinghies. As a special treat, courtesy of Captain Oelrich, they received frozen lobsters from *U-459*'s refrigerators.

Transferring the torpedoes was the trickiest of the manoeuvres. Kruger watched as a party from *U-68* swam the thirty metres to the U-tanker where one eel had been hauled up onto the casing. The men then pushed their deflated lifejackets under the torpedo and re-inflated them, after which the forward main ballast tanks were flooded so the milk cow's deck dipped below the surface, allowing the eel to float free and be swum across to *U-68*, whose forward ballast tanks were also flooded and the procedure repeated.

U-156 arrived just as they were finishing the transfer. This gave Brand the chance to discuss the Cape mission with Korvettenkapitän Nagel, who would share the information with the other boats if they reached the rendezvous in time, or with the captain of the *Milchküh* to be passed on if they did not.

Nagel came aboard *U-68* and joined Brand in the navigation alcove to finalise the attack plan, a pivoted electric lamp pulled low and casting a warm glow over the chart. They agreed on a submerged approach to the *Schwerpunkt* and settled on a provisional zero hour for the Cape Town attack, but also the circumstances under which it would be aborted, such as if the AS defences of Table Bay were too strong or if they encountered an effective net barrage. Brand would do the initial scouting of the target area.

Half of *U-68*'s crew were invited for coffee aboard Nagel's boat and half his crew made the opposite journey. The cooks on both sides competed to produce tarts and cakes for the happy meeting, which was over all too soon as neither captain wanted to linger.

'Slow ahead together.'

'Good hunting and rich booty!' came a cry from the milk cow as they drew away.

'Safe journey home! Give the girls in Bordeaux our love!'

A week later, they made landfall off the diamond-mining settlement of Oranjemund and followed the shoreline southward. Brand gathered his officers around the navigation desk and, pencil in hand, leant over a chart of South Africa's west coast.

'According to the plan, we will drop our esteemed passenger on a stretch of coast owned by his father,' he said. 'Herr Kruger…'

'Yes, our farm, Steenbokbaai, is here,' he said, pointing to a tiny notch in the shoreline.

'As you know the area well, you can assist Leutnant Seebohm with the inshore navigation,' said Brand.

'Certainly, Kapitän.'

They discussed various scenarios and contingencies, and confirmed the plan of approach and landing. The officers adjourned to their posts and Kruger stayed behind to pore over the naval charts marked with their grids of numbered squares, noting the pencil line that indicated their progress. On the right-hand margin of the latest chart, finally, a strip of coast, but devoid of roads or features — a sailor's view of the land. Looking closer at the indentation they were aiming for, he noticed a tiny black square denoting a house: Steenbokbaai. From the fore-ends came the homesick lilt of a mouthorgan, echoing down the alleyway to quicken his yearning.

Late one afternoon, sailing towards Lambert's Bay, *U-68* turned east and began to close with the coast. Kruger washed and shaved, removing the unkempt beard that was fashionable on all U-boats, before joining the officers for his last supper. Kombüse Schneider had pulled out all available stops, providing a meal of tinned knuckle of pork, roast potatoes and Brussels sprouts. He deposited the aluminium dish on the wardroom table with a flourish: gobbets of pork and slices of onion like islands on a sea of boiled sauerkraut. Brand handed Kruger a precious bottle of beer.

'You are most kind, Kapitän. You have all been very good to me.'

'Nonsense, we are just terribly pleased to be getting rid of you,' said Brand. 'It is like babysitting: you never know when to change the nappies and how long before the parents come home.'

Kruger flushed. 'I am not a sea creature.'

'Ha, ha, nonsense. We have made a sailor of you.'

'This is not true, but thank you, for everything.'

'It is nothing. Now listen, Herr Kruger, we will surface shortly and wait for the signal from your people. Do you have everything ready for a speedy departure?'

'*Ja*, I am all set.'

'Good. Two *Matrosen* will paddle you ashore; there must be no lingering. Now, drink up that beer.'

Kruger took a swig and looked around the table at the men he had grown to know over the past seven weeks, sharing an intimacy unusual in the life of the land. They were gaunt, bearded, with blue stains beneath their eyes from lack of sleep, but brave men, faithfully serving the Führer so many thousands of miles from home.

As they approached the shore, the control room grew silent, the tension as thick as its fetid air. Kruger was dressed in black, a knitted, U-boat-issue *Pudelmütze* with pom-pom on his head. He could feel sweat trickling down his spine as Brand peered through the periscope.

'There! I can see the house with the white gable,' said the captain. 'Well done, Seebohm.'

'Thank you, sir,' mumbled the navigator, removing the pencil from between his teeth.

'Bootsmann, tell the dinghy party they must be in and out as fast as possible. If things get hot, I will not hang about waiting for them.'

'*Ja*, Kapitän.'

'All right, it looks clear. Surface!'

Chief Hoppe called for the fore- and after-planes to rise and sang out, 'Blow all main ballast!'

Kruger was ashen faced, his body wound to a pitch of anticipation as compressed air roared into the tanks. *Why so much bloody noise?*

'Do not worry, Herr Kruger,' said Brand, reading his mind. 'It is deafening in here, but up there we are barely audible beyond a cable's length.'

Kruger forced a smile, but his mind was already ashore. What would be waiting for him: a breakdown in the chain of secrecy, a burst of gunfire, his mission over before it had begun?

Brand was first up the ladder to the hatch, gripping the locking wheel, spinning it … *here we go again* … the lid tipped open to a dousing of salt water … and the captain was out, the others bursting from the conning tower like human jacks-in-the-box with Kruger at their heels. Within seconds, the three gun crews were closed up, training their weapons on the darkened coast.

Land once more. The sound of ocean sighing against rocks, stars waltzing in the water all about them. *U-68* eased closer, the pulse of her electric motors just discernible through the soles of Kruger's boots. There was a lump in his throat as a mixture of fear and elation coursed through him: home again after two years adrift. This smell, this shore that was as familiar to him as his own body. *Vaderland*, his father's land.

The fore hatch swung open with a metallic clang and out came a deflated dinghy as spectral figures swarmed like termites across the casing. While air was pumped into the rubber craft, Kruger's baggage, explosives and transmitter, stitched into watertight bags, were hauled onto the deck.

'IWO, I do not want our bows facing the shore after the dinghy is away — too vulnerable if we need a fast exit,' said the captain.

'But, Kapitän, stern-to will not work if we need to use the main gun,' said Lingen.

'We will lie parallel so that all weapons can be brought to bear and we can still make an easy getaway.'

'Over there, sir!' cut in a lookout. 'Port bow, a flashing light!'

'Dead on time,' said Brand. The pinprick of light was coming from a rocky outcrop. 'Acknowledge please, Borchers.' Their portable lamp flashed a short response. 'IWO, train your guns on that light, just in case.'

'Twenty-five metres depth, sir,' came the call from the control room.

'Starboard twenty, stop starboard motor.' Brand spoke into the voicepipe, his eye fixed on the gyro repeater. 'All right, midships. Slow ahead starboard motor.'

Kruger saw the main gun's long muzzle pointing at right angles, aimed at the land. *Please let it not be needed.* 'Those two Norfolk pines mark the farmhouse,' said Kruger softly. 'My grandfather planted them as a landmark for the old sailing ships.'

'Well then, Herr Kruger, I suppose this is it.'

'*Ja*, at last. You have been good to put up with me, Fregattenkapitän Brand, but I cannot say I am sad to leave.'

'Best of luck to you. Strike a blow for the Führer and for your own volk.'

'*Danke schön*, and God speed.'

Kruger shook hands with the captain and each of the lookouts, then climbed down to the casing and made his way forward.

'Stop motors and slip the dinghy when ready!'

A splash, followed by the scraping of paddles against the saddle tank. Kruger turned to the conning tower, raised his right arm and called out, '*Heil Hitler!*' Two sailors were already perched in the bows and stern of the dinghy as he slid awkwardly down the side and thumped aboard. The paddlers immediately pushed off and struck out for the shore. Kruger sat in the middle with his pile of baggage and directed them around a low headland towards a protected cove. He heard waves crunching on the rocks to port and the sighing wash of the little beach he knew as if it were a part of his body. Water sloshed aboard as the sailors paddled strongly, anxious to land their cargo and get back to the U-boat as quickly as possible.

Drawing closer to the rocks, Kruger heard the faint cocking of a rifle and saw the silhouette of a figure aiming at them from an outcrop.

'Duck!' he hissed as both paddlers crouched down, knowing full well the rubber of a dinghy was as vulnerable as skin. Kruger cursed under his breath: so close and yet, perhaps, in vain.

CHAPTER 12

As *Gannet* was due for a boiler clean and minor repairs, most of the crew were given shore leave. Liberty took many forms. Some of the off-watch headed into Simon's Town in search of entertainment, while those with overnight leave took the train up the line, grabbing a glass of Cape smoke brandy or Tickey Hock in Cape Town Station's Railway Buffet before proceeding up Adderley Street where one group of Gannets ended up carousing on the Grand Hotel balcony. As a troop convoy was in town, the streets below were seething, so much so that both the hotel's lounge and balcony had to be closed. A mob of Australian soldiers was turned away and, in retaliation, set off the fire alarm. When fire engines arrived, the pongos requisitioned the ladders in order to climb to the hotel's balcony.

Later, the same bunch of Aussies, most of them three sheets to the wind, carried a baby Austin into the general post office on Adderley Street and tried to buy stamps to post it back to Australia. Meanwhile, around the corner on Strand Street, a contingent of SDF sailors that included a handful of Gannets, encountered a group of Stellenbosch students chanting *OB* slogans, resulting in a brawl that stopped traffic. The shore patrols and police had a busy afternoon.

Seaman Manley spent another eventful leave brawling, drinking and skirting both sides of the law. An oaf and a bully, the Rhodesian was nonetheless a very good hand who knew the ways of *Gannet* as well as her NCOs. He was forever appearing at the defaulters' table and Jack was thoroughly sick of his excuses and recalcitrant attitude. The end of this period of leave was no different, with Manley arriving back on board five hours late, on his hands and knees, having tried one or two other ships 'that looked the spitting image of *Gannet*', including a County-class cruiser, and been turned away.

'I was very keen to get back on board, sir, honest,' he said, somewhat self-righteously. 'Just had a bit of bother recognising the old girl in the dark, what with the blackout and all.'

Recalling his father's treatment of his own boyhood truancy, Jack adopted the pained-but-concerned parental approach. After all, the stick hadn't worked thus far; perhaps time for a carrot. 'Now look here, Manley, you're a tremendous asset to this ship and I know how much extra work you do when we're at sea. However, you simply cannot keep landing yourself in the defaulter's book. Perhaps you don't want to remain aboard the *Gannet*.'

'Oh no, sir, I like it very much here. She's a decent ship.'

'Right then, I'd like you to go for leading seaman. I think you have exactly the right qualities ... well, enough of them anyway. There's more responsibility and more pay. What do you say?'

'Me, Captain?' He looked incredulous. 'Never, sir.'

'Think it over, Manley. Either way, I don't want to see you in here again.'

Two days later, Van Zyl came to Jack with a broad smile. 'You're not going to believe this, but I've got a request-man to take the board for Leading Hand.'

'Manley?'

'Aye, sir. You must have worked some kind of magic on our black sheep.'

Although always extremely well oiled, Manley was never again late from shore leave.

Nearing the end of their time in port, Van Zyl was notified that a trio of Gannets had landed up behind bars at the Simon's Town police station for being in possession of an object that did not, despite their protestations, belong to them. The inebriated sailors had been taken into custody while walking up St Georges Street in the early hours of the morning, past the police station, in full song, carrying a gold-framed painting of the Battle of Trafalgar. Their explanation to the cops was that they had acquired the artwork from a gent they'd met in the Lord Nelson pub urinals but could not remember his name or how much they'd paid for it.

Van Zyl spent a good deal of time convincing the inspector that the trio had meant no harm, only wanted to beautify their ship, been suffering from battle fatigue, been too long at sea fighting the Hun, that it would certainly never happen again, that *Gannet*'s captain would find a more than suitable punishment and that they were due to sail on the morrow — none of which was entirely true. By this time, the sailors had sobered up and made a bedraggled spectacle following their smartly turned-out Jimmy like obedient, if scruffy, hounds, through the East Dockyard gates and down to their ship.

Jack spent his own last day of shore leave at Milkwood with his family. He'd invited Clara to join him for lunch and an evening movie at the Simon's Town bioscope. The admiral's housekeeper served a tray of drinks as they sat chatting on the stoep and taking in the views of the bay.

'How are things with your mother and the SAWAS, Clara?' asked the admiral.

'Busier than ever, thanks to all the troopships you're dumping in her lap,' she said with a twinkle in her eye.

'You must apologise unreservedly on my behalf.'

'Oh, she complains, but she loves it.'

'And you get roped in as well, Jack tells me.'

'Yes, washing dishes and waiting table at the Mayor's Garden Canteen, bed-making at the Soldiers' Club, knitting for the City Hall work party —'

'Goodness, what about your university work?' asked Imogen.

'Oh, Ma thinks I can do that in my "spare" time.'

'A woman after my own heart.' The admiral chuckled.

'Look there, isn't that the *Queen Mary* coming up the channel?' exclaimed Imogen.

'Not quite, my dear, she's the P&O liner *Strathaird*, here for dry docking,' said the admiral. 'Three funnels like *Queen Mary*, but they're actually a bit of an anomaly. She was built back when the public equated multiple funnels with power, so she was fitted with two dummy ones.'

'How will she squeeze into Selbourne Dock — she must be over 20,000 tons?' asked Jack.

'A tight fit, certainly,' said the admiral. 'Some of the dock's lower altars have been chipped away to accommodate her bilge keel.'

'It's jolly busy in Simon's Town at the moment,' said Imogen.

'Busier by the day,' said the admiral. '*And* we've got the king, crown prince and princess of Greece as our guests next week. I'll be taking them on a tour of the dockyard and the king will address the crew of HMS *Orion*.'

'The royals must have a soft spot for her after their hasty evacuation from Crete,' said Jack.

'Very much so. In the afternoon, a crash-boat from Gordon's Bay will take the royal party on a high-speed tour of the bay. Care to join us, son?'

'Alas, *Gannet* will be at sea that day.'

'I didn't say which day.' He gave a knowing smile. 'Never mind. Imogen, how about you?'

'I'll consult my diary, but it's not entirely beyond the realm of possibility.'

'Now you know what I have to put up with,' said the admiral.

Clara beamed at the old admiral. 'My ma tells me — confidentially of course — that there are transports from Egypt anchored in Table Bay crammed with survivors from Crete.'

'Yes, your indefatigable mother has been helping with entertainment.'

'Ma says they were a miserable sight when they landed. The only clothing the authorities in Alexandria could find for them was white shorts, vests and pith helmets.'

'I know. Hardly adequate for the Cape Town winter.'

'Ma put out an appeal for clothes on the wireless and the response was amazing. Their commanding officer told her he wasn't keen on his men wandering about in hand-me-downs. Well, you can just imagine what Ma had to say. His ears will be ringing all the way to Liverpool.'

'I must thank her. Simon's Town had no uniforms available and the SAWAS stepped in admirably.'

After lunch, Jack and Clara wandered along the shore, climbing over large granite boulders and down to coves of calm, luminous water and white sand, the tideline strewn with sea-urchins, limpets, periwinkles and abalone shells.

'It's so beautiful here,' she said.

'Yes, it reminds me of the Riviera, especially Cap-Ferrat, where we used to go as a family for summer hols.'

They came to Fisherman's Beach where locals were bringing in a catch. A rowing boat had encircled a shoal and returned to the shore where a group was busy dragging in the net. Jack kicked off his sandals and lent a hand, much to Clara's bemusement. Hartlaub's and kelp gulls whirled and screamed in excitement as the steenbras were landed, their shimmering bodies gyrating in the sunlight.

Later, the admiral's driver, Wren Munroe, dropped Jack and Clara at the Criterion Bioscope for the evening screening of *In the Navy* where they were lucky to get seats as the stalls were full. Holding hands and leaning into one another, they sat through the silent advertisement slides, African Mirror news and black-and-white cowboy serial. Then the reels were changed in the projector room, the auditorium darkened and the main feature commenced. Starring comedians Abbott and Costello, the Hollywood musical had a silly plot about a popular crooner who abandons his career to join the Navy, and the attractive reporter who pursues him. There was nothing in it to distract Jack from stealing glances at Clara, and the boogie-woogie soundtrack by the Andrews Sisters was at least catchy.

After the film, Jack walked Clara back down the high street to the station, a cold breeze pouring off Red Hill and promising rain. A dazzle-camouflaged corvette lay at anchor a stone's throw from where they took shelter on the platform waiting for her train. Standing hand in hand, Jack found himself tongue tied once more, despite the mountain of things he wanted to say to her. How did she still manage to have this effect on him?

'Clara, I was wondering…' he trailed off and looked at the darkened bay.

'What were you wondering, Jack?'

'I was thinking that now that I'm spending more time ashore, and we're not exactly duelling with Jerry at the moment, and there is a degree of stability, we, you and I, might consider something more formal.'

'More formal? You are the most formal person I've ever met.'

'Not that sort of formal. Relationship formal. Something permanent.'

The train rounded the last bend screechingly and came clattering into the station.

'This is mine.'

'I know. Will you consider it?'

'Yes, Jack, I will.'

'May I kiss you?'

'Not formal at all. Yes, Jack, you may.'

CHAPTER 13

'*Wie is jy* ... Who are you?' called the silhouette from the darkness, training a rifle on the dinghy.

Kruger thought he recognised the voice. 'Hans van Zyl, is that you?'

There was an agonising pause. The paddlers hunched down; everyone held their breath.

'Gerhardus?'

'*Ja!*'

A foamy wave lifted the dinghy, thrusting it past a rocky outcrop and into the shallows beside a thatched farmhouse. Feverish with excitement, Kruger directed the paddlers around a bed of kelp to a half-moon beach. Another small wave heaved them forward and the receding surge left their prow high and dry on the sand. Kruger climbed out and took a few unsteady steps before reaching down to let a handful of broken mussel shells trickle through his fingers. 'Home,' he whispered.

A stocky figure carrying a rifle approached over the ridge and Kruger withdrew his Luger, but within moments he recognised his old friend and they embraced.

'You are here at last!'

'I am here at last.'

'We have waited a long time. You've been brought safely home, *danksy die Here se genade*.' It was a joy to hear his native tongue again. Hans helped with unloading the baggage and steel cases of equipment, after which the sailors made hasty farewells, pushed the dinghy back into the shore break and were soon swallowed by the night. Kruger looked around: the old homestead, its adjacent barn, the shaggy black cut-outs of the Norfolk pines and overhead the Milky Way forming a vast, glittering umbrella.

The pair dragged the baggage higher up the beach and threw a tarpaulin over it before making their way to the eighteenth-century house with its graceful white gable set on a stone plinth above the high-water mark. Kruger climbed the slate steps as if in a dream and knocked on the door. His mother opened and fell into his arms, his father close behind, ready to shake the hand of his prodigal son. Hans hovered in the background beaming with happiness for his friend. Although it was late, supper had been prepared — Kruger didn't have the heart to tell them he'd already eaten — and they sat in the soft lamplight of the *voorkamer*, the warmth of the Aga stove filtering through from the kitchen. His father said a prayer and his mother served his favourite meal, waterblommetjie stew with pumpkin, *slaphakskeentjie* onions and *sousboontjie* beans. Filled with emotion, he drank in the scene: the paintings of Dutch forbears on the walls, the rich glow of the yellowwood floorboards, smell of wood polish, and low ceiling whose beams his great-grandfather had fashioned from salvaged wood off a shipwrecked square-rigger.

After supper, and a round of brandies beside the fire, the elder Krugers retired to bed and the two young men took a stroll along the shore. The waves sounded like branches snapping on the beach as the incoming tide hissed over the mussel-shell banks. Kruger savoured the strong aroma of sea, red bait and decaying kelp — the smells of his youth and of home. They climbed the low headland through fynbos leaking its own heady scent and their footfall disturbed a porcupine, resulting in an arched back and bristling quills, then a dash for cover.

'It has been two very long years, old friend,' said Hans.

'I know, but I learnt a great deal in the Reich and there is so much we can achieve here in the Union. It is my intention to link up with the *Ossewabrandwag* leaders, which gives us access to its 300,000 members. Radio Zeesen, with the help of Afrikaans announcers, already has a devoted following here. The conditions are ripe for a coup, we just need to light the right fire.'

'Gerhardus, I'm sorry to disappoint you, but I think the bullet is already through the church with the *Ossewabrandwag*. Van Rensburg is a timid leader, not ready or willing to take the *OB* into proper military action against Smuts.'

Kruger stopped and looked out to sea, his brow furrowed, then said: 'I'd feared as much.'

'Far more promising is the *OB*'s new militant wing, the *Stormjaers*, to which I belong.'

'It's just what I've been thinking. Willing fighters?'

'Definitely.' The pair continued walking along the headland.

'In that case, I want you to gather a small group of the best, most loyal, patriots you can find among the *Stormjaers*. They will have to be totally committed, unwavering, ready to die for the cause. Bring them here to the farm and then we can start on this journey together.'

'We will need weapons and explosives.'

'I have brought some, but we will need more, much more,' said Kruger, his land legs growing in confidence as they followed a sandy path back down to the beach.

'I know just the man, Dolf Erasmus, an ardent *Stormjaer* champing for more action. At the start of the war, Smuts passed an act allowing police to confiscate explosives and guns above 22-bore from people living in areas that might rise against the government. So, what does Dolf do? He drives around with fake police documents confiscating weapons and issuing receipts under a string of false names. He also managed to pull off a raid on an Iscor magazine and got away with a stack of dynamite. Dolf will join us, I am sure. He's already been recruited by German agents and is passing on information to Berlin, via Lourenço Marques, using a network of sympathisers and couriers.'

'Then he is a man I must meet.'

Next morning, Kruger woke in his childhood room after an unsettled night, unused to a bed that remained stationary. He drew back the curtains and pushed open the wooden shutters to reveal a crescent beach bathed in bright sunlight. Water lapped the mussel-strewn shore just metres away and he filled his lungs, relishing the sights and sounds of his childhood cove. To be home again with the future full to the brim with promise.

After breakfast, Hans returned to Stellenbosch and Kruger set about trying to establish contact with Germany. To this end, he loaded the radio equipment on the back of his father's Ford *bakkie* and drove inland through a sea of yellow daisies and pink vygies to a sandstone koppie. The isolated location was ideal, for Kruger knew that his powerful German transmitter sent a signal that could be detected to a radius of many miles. His father's vast farm offered good protection from any mobile direction-finding units the authorities might deploy to pinpoint the source of transmissions.

With the help of two trusted labourers, certain to keep mum as their families had worked at Steenbokbaai for generations, he unloaded the green cases from their waterproof canvas, took out the transmitter, receiver and batteries, and carried them into the mouth of the cave. The strange paintings that haunted his dreams were still there, as they had been for countless centuries, but he chose to ignore them: there was important work to be done. The men set about erecting two tall aerials, comprising lengths of metal pipe fitted together to support a wire antenna strung between them, and connecting the transmitter to a set of batteries and a transformer.

Late that night, Kruger returned to the koppie alone, wired up the transmitter and receiver, and was delighted at the first crackle of static in his headphones. As arranged, he knew Berlin would receive on the prearranged frequency at 0100 on designated nights, as long as the ionosphere played along, which could be very hit and miss. He tapped out the encoded message: 'Agent safely in Union. Operation *Weerlig* underway.' After a brief acknowledgement, he switched off the set and returned to the homestead, thrilled at having been able to make contact on his first attempt.

That weekend, Hans returned to Steenbokbaai accompanied by eleven *Stormjaers*, suitably primed and burning to join the cause. They were given places to sleep in the barn, crammed with bunks and beds for the Christmas holidays when Kruger family members from all corners of the country descended on the farm. At a late-night gathering under the bare beams of the 'longhouse', Kruger sketched the outline of his vision, backed by a swastika strung across the shuttered window behind him. The young men sat around a large table lit with paraffin lanterns as a bottle of Van Rhyn's brandy passed from hand to hand.

'*Ons volk is weer op trek* ... our people are on trek again,' said Kruger, his voice low and passionate. 'We must stand shoulder to shoulder, mobilise as a *volk* and undertake another Great Trek, this time into a new dawn of Afrikaner nationalism. There will be many sacrifices along the way. Some of us may lose our lives, but I can tell you for certain that there is a promised land at the end of this road. God imbues all history with meaning. The history of our people leads us to believe that Afrikanerdom is not the work of men, but the creation of God.

'As you know, the *Ossewabrandwag* is sympathetic to Germany and is passing information to the Reich via its contacts, but it will not commit to any *real* action. The *Stormjaers* are prepared to grab the nettle, but they still take their orders from Van Rensburg and he is weak. However, the brave men gathered here tonight *are* ready to take the fight to the British.'

There were murmurs of assent.

'If we can cause enough disruption to swing the Afrikaner… If a sympathetic government replaced Smuts and his henchmen, just think what can be achieved: the opening of the Cape sea route to German ships, the withdrawal of Union troops from North Africa, German access to South Africa's mineral wealth and the liberation of South West Africa — "the diamond in the Reich's colonial crown". Indeed, South West only needs the lighting of a match, especially after Smuts arrested 3,000 of its German citizens at the beginning of the war. There are also thousands of Germans in South Africa, many of them committed National Socialists and, as you all know, there is brooding resentment towards the British among much of the Afrikaner population. At least half the police force will come over to our side.' Kruger paused to look around the room at the ardent faces glowing in the soft light of the lanterns.

'I have witnessed the transformation of Germany with my own eyes and it is a miracle. I have never seen people so free, so happy, so prosperous. Next, it will be our turn to fulfil our promise as a volk, free of Britain. Then we will unite with Germany to help fight the tyranny of the Soviet Union, which threatens to destroy everything we hold dear. I truly believe that the only answer to the dangers posed by Great Britain and Communism is the brand of Nationalist Socialism preached by Adolf Hitler.' There was a gleam in Kruger's eyes and an increasing breathlessness about his speech.

'Brothers, we will plant the seed of freedom once more in South Africa ... and sow terror among our enemies: sabotage, kidnapping, assassination, armed robbery — nothing will stop us as we stoke the flames of rebellion.' His voice was hoarse with emotion. 'It begins with us, right here, right now, in this room. It will spread across the country like a runaway veld fire as we recruit more and more fighters to the cause.'

After another round of brandies, Kruger explained how each recruit must sign an oath with his own blood, after which there could be no turning back. Now was the time for anyone with doubts or misgivings to step aside. No one voiced dissent. Then the first *Stormjaer* stood up and placed a hand on the Bible. Kruger pulled out his Luger and pointed it at the initiate's chest; Hans aimed a revolver at the back of the young man's head.

'You will read this declaration of allegiance and then sign it,' Kruger ordered.

The tall, blond recruit took the paper and read aloud with a trembling voice: 'My aim and struggle are for the freedom of the Afrikaner nation and the establishment of a National Socialist state with the ideals of Adolf Hitler adapted to the character of the Afrikaner. I admit that only nations that fight for their freedom have a right to survive.

'I stand before God and swear this holy oath that I will faithfully serve the Afrikaner nation with my whole heart, mind, body and soul in the direction given to me by my leader, Gerhardus Kruger, from now until death. The deep seriousness with which I declare myself a National Socialist finds expression in the blood with which I bind my person forever through this signature.

'I am nothing; my nation is everything. God be with us.' He cut his finger without flinching and signed with his own blood.

'Now you will read the oath in the presence of your comrades,' said Kruger, handing him a second sheet of paper.

'I solemnly promise before the Almighty that I will subject myself to the demands which my people's God-given calling requires of me. I am prepared to sacrifice my life for the freedom of my people. May the thought of treason never occur to me, in the full knowledge that I will automatically become prey to the vengeance of my *Weerlig* brothers. May God grant that I will be able to exclaim with my comrades:

If I advance, follow me!

If I retreat, shoot me!

If I die, avenge me!

So help me God.'

The room shook with the repeated oath, shouted by every man around the table.

'Long live the Boer nation! Long live the Afrikaner volk! *Heil Hitler!*' barked Kruger.

As one, they raised their arms in the outstretched salute and roared, '*Heil Hitler!*'

CHAPTER 14

After landing Kruger at Steenbokbaai, *U-68* reconnoitred south of Cape Columbine, making note of traffic entering and leaving Saldanha Bay. Brand spotted a large, two-funnelled ship in Hoedjes Bay and noted what looked like a pair of patrol boats off Dassen Island, before making a wide seaward loop to approach Cape Town from the northwest.

A specially encrypted signal came through on the WT and Telegraphist Wichmann called for an officer to do the deciphering. Lingen set up the Enigma machine on the wardroom table once more and began to decode the signal using the day's settings recorded, for security, on soluble paper. Brand stood at his shoulder and grabbed it the moment Lingen had finished.

'At last, IWO, the Konteradmiral has given us exact details. The first three U-boats are to attack Cape Town at midnight on 11 September. The other two boats have been delayed and will join for the next phase.'

He gathered Lingen, Seebohm and Hoppe around the chart table. 'We will approach Table Bay from the northwest, Kapitän Nagel from the north and Kapitän Beckmann from the southwest. Our boat will enter the anchorage first and assess the situation on the day before the attack.'

'What if the roadstead is empty, sir?' asked Hoppe.

'We wait twenty-four hours and see if more traffic arrives.'

'And if it does not, Kapitän?'

'Then we have a free hand to attack independent targets in the vicinity.'

Later that afternoon, Brand peered through the periscope, noting the purple serration of a mountain range to the east and, further south, the unmistakable aircraft-carrier shape of Table Mountain catching the last rays of the setting sun, its western ramparts painted tangerine and a wispy tuft of cloud growing from its crown. He switched the periscope to full power and picked out a red-and-white-striped lighthouse on the headland closest to them. 'Bearing now?'

Seebohm replied 'One-four-zero, sir.'

'That is Green Point Lighthouse. IWO, take us back down to forty metres.' U-68 spent the next hour creeping towards the mouth of Table Bay.

'Periscope depth,' said the captain. Nearing the surface, Brand ducked down as the column hissed from its well. His jaw clamped like a vice and his hands sweating on the handles, he made a quick scan of Table Mountain, the harbour and Robben Island. Although the port looked full of ships, the anchorage was empty.

That evening, U-68 stayed deep, edging ever closer to the Table Bay entrance. At 2330 the preliminary order for surfacing was announced over the intercom. Lookouts mustered in the control room as they levelled off at twenty metres and the hydrophone operator conducted a careful sweep. Then the U-boat rose cautiously to periscope depth and Brand pressed his face to the rubber eyepieces once more to marvel at the incongruous spectacle of a city fully illuminated.

'Surface!'

High-pressure air roared into the ballast tanks as the hull emerged from the deep in the mouth of Table Bay, the very doorstep of the enemy.

'Upper lid clear, equalise pressure!' called the chief.

The captain spun the hand wheel and the hatch sprang open as cool air poured into the control room. He did a quick, 360-degree binocular pan of the bay as his lookouts emerged to take up their positions. 'Engine-room to remain at diving stations,' he said into the voicepipe. 'We cannot take any chances, Chief.'

There was fortunately enough cloud cover to obscure the waning moon and help hide their presence. Every ten seconds, Brand flinched as the beam of Green Point Lighthouse played across the bridge: no submariner appreciates any form of illumination while surfaced in enemy waters. It seemed as though Cape Town was busy with an air-raid exercise of some sort and he spotted a target plane circling above the city, chased by the long, groping fingers of searchlights. *U-68* remained trimmed right down, her decks awash, showing very little of herself above the surface and pointing her bows at Green Point to present a minimal silhouette.

'Lookouts, keep your eyes peeled for fishing boats or other small craft,' said the captain.

The skin of Table Bay was smooth as silk, black and viscous. Brand surveyed the shoreline of Sea Point with its brightly lit blocks of flats and promenade. 'It is another universe,' he muttered, barely able to drag his eyes from the scene. In his mind's eye he was hand in hand with Greta — before the war, before the disillusionment — staring across the water at the dazzling lights of Hamburg, the flashing colours of the advertisements.

'Stop motors.' The playful slapping of chop against their ballast tanks took over and then, very faintly, the sounds of the city above the soft crumpling of surf along the shore. The U-boat was so close now that Brand could hear traffic; the dulcet music of a car horn, as mournful and beautiful as an oboe, reaching out to them across the water. And towering above the tableau, the craggy bulk of Table Mountain, brooding over this miraculous city at the southern tip of Africa. '*Mein Gott*,' he murmured.

Brand summoned the crew up to the bridge in pairs to witness the sight: something to tell the *enkelkinder*. His men stood gaping, dazzled by the lights and drinking in the heady scent of land, the rich tang of the kelp beds, tainted by a strong fish smell from the docks. The bejewelled vista held them entranced until they were cajoled and elbowed below to let the next pair up. Looking at his pale, hollow-eyed men in their tattered clothes, Brand was struck by the juxtaposition. If Kruger were here, he'd be spouting some guff about the Promised Land, but in truth Brand did feel a pang of guilt about showing these steel-coffin prisoners a glimpse of 'paradise'. It was almost enough to turn a weak man from the cause, or even capsize his mind.

After an hour, *U-68* dived and crept further into the anchorage. Brand raised the periscope for a few brief seconds at a time and spotted the dim navigation lights of an approaching coaster. Fearing mines, he followed her up the swept channel to get a closer look at the harbour. The raider *Sturmvogel* had been sunk off the Cape three months earlier and the *BdU* was not certain how many mines she had laid or how close to the anchorage. It was better to be safe than sorry. What's more, he did not know whether the South Africans had laid any protective minefields of their own in Table Bay.

'What is that noise, PO Zimmermann?' Brand snapped as a faint whining became audible in the control room.

'Just a fishing craft, Kapitän,' said the hydrophone operator from his cubbyhole. Brand grabbed another brief look through the periscope and spotted a bluff-nosed boat chugging past Green Point Lighthouse.

'And a second one at one-five-zero,' said Zimmermann. 'And a third.'

'It is like Berlin Hauptbahnhof, and that third one is an anti-submarine vessel,' he said, turning his boat about and making for deeper water. His plan was to spend the daylight hours on the ocean floor between Green Point and Robben Island.

'Try to put her down gently, Chief, we don't want a hole in our bottom.'

'I will do my best, sir. Let us hope it is sandy.'

With a light jolt and then a heavier thud, *U-68* settled on the seabed.

'All right, now we get a few hours of peace and quiet,' said Brand. But their stay on the floor of Table Bay was far from restful, given the strong current from the south and a building swell from the west, the boat constantly shifting and bumping on the bottom.

Brand could not sleep, so he switched on the lamp and reached for his leather-bound journal to bring the entries up to date. He pressed his knees under the little desk and felt the bristles of his beard against the ruff of his polo-neck jersey as he leant forward and began to write: 'The air was clear and Cape Town lit up like a Christmas tree with Table Mountain so near I could almost reach out and touch it. The streetlights along the Peninsula were like glittering pearl necklaces. I could hardly believe the existence of those happy streets — bioscopes, restaurants, playhouses — just a stone's throw away. How marvellous to think of a city at peace, here at the bottom of Africa, and how I wish we could go ashore. Perhaps, in my wildest fantasy, with Greta. The Cape is a thing of magnificence and, strangely, of hope. Last night I tried, just for a few moments, to fill myself with its beauty rather than the brutality of this wretched war.'

Now that the crew had seen Cape Town with their own eyes, the prospect of an imminent attack raised their spirits. They struggled to sleep as the current jostled their boat throughout the day, at times lifting the hull and thumping it back down on an uneven bottom. They listened with half an ear to the coming and going of traffic above, everything from the heavy throb of big merchantmen to the light beat of fishing craft.

Mid-afternoon, *U-68* blew her tanks and rose cautiously, the long-range groundswell making it difficult to keep her at a steady periscope depth. Brand's eyepiece offered a kaleidoscopic world of dazzling sunshine and blue sea, the flat-topped mountain standing out like a giant folly in the magic lantern's midst. They approached to within a few hundred metres of the main shipping channel and Brand watched in fascination as prize after prize coasted through his sights, each one a sitting duck. The temptation to loose a few tin fish was almost too much to bear. He was itching for a kill, but he had his orders: he must wait. Instead, he took the bearings of the entrance and exit channels and studied the harbour installations in more detail, including the bristling guns of Fort Wynyard.

'Down periscope,' he said, snapping closed the handles. He looked around the control room at his haggard, unwashed men with their careworn faces and felt a strange sadness once more. All the sunshine and fresh air they needed was just metres above their heads, but those few metres entailed an impossible journey. He sighed. 'Take her back down, IWO.'

They spent the rest of the afternoon bumping on the bottom, the interior clammy and dank with all unnecessary fans and lights switched off to minimise noise and conserve power. Brand was disappointed that the roadstead remained empty and wondered how long they might have to wait for a convoy to arrive. Each hour of loitering posed the risk of detection, and that irritating AS whaler passing back and forth between Robben Island and Sea Point was a worry. The B-Dienst had assured Dönitz Cape Town's roadstead would be crammed with up to fifty ships, but luck was not on their side.

U-68 spent another night spying out the anchorage and, on the morning of 11 September, followed a pair of minesweepers down the swept channel and out to sea. Having sent the briefest of reports to the BdU from far offshore, Brand received the following reply:

1358 hrs W/T signal: Gruppe Savanne
Order fixing D-Day 11.09.41 is cancelled due to empty roadstead
On account of Brand, independent attacks allowed for all U-boats commencing 12.09.41 — 0000 hrs

Although disappointed by the empty anchorage, a second signal from the *BdU* that night changed everything. Kernével had received an urgent message from agent Kruger with intelligence that, due to a full harbour in Simon's Town, the heavy cruiser HMS *Buckinghamshire* was currently anchored in Simon's Bay. While the other two U-boats were to initiate plan B — independent targets off Cape Town — *U-68* was ordered to proceed to False Bay and attempt to sink the cruiser. All attacks would commence at midnight on 12 September.

Brand's mind turned over the variables and possibilities, elated and nervous at the good fortune that had fallen into his lap. He must not squander this chance at glory for himself, his boat and his men. HMS Buckinghamshire was a powerful cruiser and a mainstay of the South Atlantic fleet: 10,000 tons,

190 metres long with four pairs of 8-inch guns and eight 4-inch guns, a complement of 715 men and a speed of 32 knots. Heavy cruisers like her were the Royal Navy's backbone, controlling the high seas far from home and vital to the long-range war effort. To sink such an important ship in Britain's most heavily defended port in the southern hemisphere would strike a mighty blow and send shock waves to all corners of the Empire.

The following morning, U-68 moved down the flank of the Peninsula and late afternoon found her idling and submerged south of Cape Point. Through the periscope, Brand surveyed the grey cliffs of this, the south-western tip of Africa. He had memorised every inch of the False Bay chart and there were many decisions to be made: where were the best defences, was there an underwater loop, how strong were the AS patrols, had the enemy laid minefields? Should he enter the bay through its deep middle section, cross to the far side and sneak in via Cape Hangklip, or follow the western shore past Smitswinkel Bay?

Tension grew among the crew at the prospect of the coming attack, audacious in its ambition, perhaps even suicidal. Every sailor had, many times in the past, made his own arrangement with fate or God or whatever he believed in and now, approaching the lion's den of Simon's Town, each man nervously renewed his vows. Surely Dönitz wouldn't risk throwing away a good U-boat on a fanciful whim? Surely success was at least possible, even if the odds were not in their favour? The waiting was the worst part — the gnawing, fear-drenched hours that stole painfully by as they crept into False Bay.

'Take her down to thirty metres. Seebohm, how are we doing for depth?'

'All right sir, it is still more than sixty metres here and we are well clear of Whittle Rock, but it will soon be thirty-five or less.' They tucked into the convenient slipstream of a minesweeper chugging back up the channel towards the naval base at dusk. She was making a sedate six knots which suited Brand perfectly, but when an anti-submarine vessel approached on a reciprocal course, he turned *U-68* towards the rocky shallows of the bay's western flank. In deviating from the swept channel, his greatest worry now was mines.

Nearing Castle Rock, and as if in response to his fears, there was a sharp clang on their port side and all heads in the control room jerked anxiously in the direction of the sound: metal on metal.

'Stop motors! Shut all watertight doors.' Brand's mind was racing: could it be a mine wire snagging the hull? Perhaps it had hooked on a bow plane and they were now busy dragging the lethal orb towards them? The faces around him were taut with fear as the scraping noise began to make its way along the saddle tank like a metallic claw.

'Starboard ten,' said Brand. Lingen stared at the deckhead; Seebohm closed his eyes. If it was a mine, they would know nothing about its detonation as their extinction would be instant. The wire reached the stern plane and emitted a loud scratching sound as if to detain the U-boat ... then suddenly they were free. The control room remained silent, but each man's face betrayed a brief journey to hell and back.

'Probably just a buoy,' muttered the captain.

U-68 continued her slow passage up False Bay's western shore. Brand raised the periscope for only a few seconds at a time, gleaning all he could from glimpses, sweat making his grip slippery on the handles. He spotted a dark shape in the gloom over to starboard, but even with the lens at full power it was hard to make out — probably an anti-submarine vessel pinging her way across towards Gordon's Bay.

'Alter course twenty degrees to port,' he said as the U-boat edged even closer to the shore, an enormous shark gliding stealthily past Miller's Point.

'Up periscope,' said Brand, bent double, flipping out the handles and meeting the eyepiece as the shaft rose from its well. A quick circuit, spinning through 360 degrees, before raising the periscope completely: a car with dimmed headlights making its way along the coast, a few white cottages and the black mass of Swartkop Peak looming above; off the port bow, a rectangular white rock which the chart told him was Noah's Ark. Brand's eye suddenly glowed bright white as a searchlight poured its glare down the tube and through the lens.

'Down periscope!' he yelled as the bronze column hissed into its well and the light beam passed over them. Taking a few seconds to recover from the momentary blinding, he pictured the lookout posts and gun batteries that must line their final approach. Eyes, eyes everywhere. How long could their ration of good fortune last?

'Vessel approaching from astern, sir,' called out PO Zimmermann from the hydrophone alcove.

'*Scheiße*,' said Brand through gritted teeth.

Soon everyone could hear the rhythmic churning of the enemy propeller, faint at first, but growing louder.

'What do you think, Zimmermann?'

'Small patrol boat, sir, maybe a launch. Closing on our starboard quarter. She is speeding up.'

'Thirty metres,' said Brand.

'We might hit the bottom!' Seebohm protested in a high-pitched voice.

'Thirty metres, I said!'

Levelling off, the captain ordered: 'Stop both. Not a sound from anyone.'

The propeller noise rose to a crescendo and Brand imagined a giant dental drill. It was right above them now. Ashen faces glanced up, waiting for the inevitable splashes. Brand clamped his jaw so tight it began to ache.

'Going away,' gasped Zimmermann. 'Fading.'

Slowly, cautiously, U-68 returned to periscope depth and resumed her tiptoeing towards the enemy's lair. Brand could scarcely believe he had made it this far without being discovered. Before him lay the Scapa Flow of the South Atlantic and tonight he had the opportunity to repeat, in modest measure, the feat of his hero, Günther Prien.

'Listen up, everyone,' he said to those present. 'I hardly need to tell you that our boat is about to make history.' The beaming faces were damp with sweat, eyes shining with anticipation and a burning trust in him. This moment was the culmination of all they had trained for, the price each one of them had paid to be here. 'I have complete confidence in every man aboard this U-boat, as does Konteradmiral Dönitz. Now, let us go to work.'

Brand climbed into the conning tower, reversed his cap and took a seat on the attack-periscope saddle, his feet resting on pedals that allowed the rapid rotation of the shaft. He called down for dead slow to reduce the size of the periscope's feather. First, he saw a glimmer of grey, then bubbles, as the metallic proboscis broke the surface. He took a hasty look around: glassy water under low cloud and Simon's Town blacked out but the crags of Simonsberg, towering above the anchorage, marking his course.

Brand noticed the tremble in his hands as he clicked the lens to full power … and, suddenly, impossibly, there she was, in his sights and ripe for the taking: HMS *Buckinghamshire*. Three funnels, two tall masts, floatplane mounted on a catapult high amidships — unmistakeable. She lay at anchor just off the harbour entrance, the muted gleam of Roman Rock Lighthouse pulsing every six seconds to faintly illuminate his target. No perimeter patrol, no anti-submarine nets: he could scarcely credit his luck, or was fate playing some deadly trick on him?

'Stand by tubes one, two, three and four. We will not get a second chance.' Enemy speed zero, bearing 285, range 2,500, torpedo depth 5 metres — a sitting duck. Lingen fed the information into the electromechanical attack computer. A few moments later the lights on the control board switched from red to green and a rating sang out their readiness.

'Open bow caps,' called the captain.

'Bow caps open, sir.'

They slid closer and Brand licked parched lips, his pulse throbbing like a bilge pump in his ears. Now or never.

'Fire one! Fire two! Fire three! Fire four!'

The rating punched the firing buttons on the control panel, followed by four muffled thuds.

'Salvo fired, sir!'

The chief immediately flooded tanks to compensate for the loss of weight and prevent their prow from breaking surface.

'All torpedoes running!' called Zimmermann from the hydrophone alcove.

'Hard a-port, full ahead,' said Brand, anxious to put as much distance between himself and the harbour before the inevitable counterattack. There was complete silence in the U-boat, the men hunched like runners awaiting a start gun. Chief Hoppe stared fixedly at the hand of his stopwatch, calling the time: 'Thirty seconds ... one minute ... ninety seconds.' The silence was unbearable; the waiting was torture.

Then it came: a rumble, followed by a second, and a third. *U-68* erupted into wild cheering, hugging and whooping. The fourth rumble came a little later: the torpedo exploding in the shallows of Long Beach beside the railway station and briefly disturbing the business of the knocking shops on Paradise Road.

CHAPTER 15

Jack was wrenched from a recurring nightmare of *Havoc*'s sinking by the sound of explosions echoing off Red Hill. He threw off the twisted sheets, leapt from his bed, flung open the French doors and ran barefoot across the dew-damp lawn, ducking under the fig tree's branches. He came to a stop at the garden's edge and stared down at the bay, trying to take in the magnitude of the disaster he was witnessing. By the look of it, HMS *Buckinghamshire* had been hit in three places — one torpedo striking below 'B' turret, one amidships and one aft.

Jack's fevered mind tried to picture the scene below decks on the damaged cruiser: sailors tumbling from hammocks and scrambling up listing decks, frantic to escape. The electricity would have failed and survivors would be groping in the dark, desperate to find their way along alleyways and up tilting ladders. The explosion below 'B' turret seemed to have penetrated the forward magazines and ignited cordite charges, sending fire tearing through the accommodation spaces and out the portholes. Jack imagined flames stripping flesh clean off the sailors trying to escape. The second torpedo had blasted open the main fuel tank, and Jack could see oil pouring from a large hole in the ship's side to engulf survivors in the water.

Mortally wounded, the cruiser turned slowly onto her side as men, most of them wearing only shorts and vests, scrambled like ants across the superstructure and down her flank, slipping on the slimy growth below the waterline and sliding across barnacle-encrusted plates, tearing clothes, gouging open buttocks and genitals. *You are the lucky ones*, thought Jack, remembering his own leap from the doomed *Havoc*. Hundreds of men remained trapped inside the hull as the cruiser turned turtle and dipped beneath the peaceful waters of Simon's Bay. Jack felt utterly, bitterly helpless. If only he could do something, help the rescue or set sail immediately to hunt down the hunter, but most of his crew were on shore leave and *Gannet* was not ready for sea.

The bay teemed with survivors trying to escape the poisonous treacle that clung to their bodies and sloshed into mouths and nostrils, suffocating them. The red safety lamps of lifejackets decorated the water like a strange marine bloom and plaintive voices — fear, pain, encouragement — echoed across the water. A few managed to reach other anchored vessels and were being dragged aboard, their oil-coated bodies resembling shiny black seals, but most waited for the rescue craft which were soon streaming out of the harbour, led by one of the tugs. Jack tore himself away from the macabre spectacle, ran inside and pulled on his uniform: he needed to get down to the harbour and to *Gannet*, send out a general recall to his men, and prepare to strike back.

Meanwhile, the retreating *U-68* stole from the bay — 'like a thief in the night', thought Brand — while PO Zimmermann's electric ears listened for the arrival of the hunters. They had kicked the beehive, but the response of the anti-submarine vessels was slow, giving the U-boat a good head start. What's more, the hunt wasn't co-ordinated and not one of the ships searched the western shallows. False Bay reverberated to the booming of vengeful craft, but the depth charges fell far from *U-68* — more scare tactic than contact-related, unless they were chasing whales. A quick look through the periscope revealed searchlight blades playing across the water, all of them in the wrong places. Brand allowed himself to start believing they had robbed the bank … and got away.

U-68 left False Bay in the early hours of 13 September and headed south, putting considerable distance between herself and the land. That night's attacks by the other two U-boats of Gruppe Savanne had also been successful. *U-156* had sunk the Dutch merchantman SS *Giesbeek* off Sea Point and later caught up with the Belgian freighter MV *Rotselaar* due west of the Cape of Good Hope and dispatched her with three torpedoes. Elsewhere around the Peninsula, *U-504* managed to sink two Allied ships, including the 13,000-ton merchantman, *City of Nairobi*, her guns and camouflage betraying the fact that she was acting as a troop transport.

The Cape's defences appeared to be in disarray. It was clear from the panicked radio traffic that there would be a few days of easy pickings as dozens of lone merchantmen rounding the Cape were thrown into confusion. Many had not even received the warning messages and sailed headlong into the jaws of danger with their navigation lights still blazing. Despite the empty Table Bay anchorage, this was exactly the *Paukenschlag* that *SKL* had hoped for.

Late in the afternoon of 13 September, about ninety miles south of Cape Point, one of *U-68*'s lookouts spotted a mast to the east. Brand quickly ascertained that she was a large vessel sailing in zigzags at about twelve knots and turned to intercept her. Nearing the target, he could see that she was a petrol tanker of some 12,000 tons — another valuable prize.

'Ha, excellent, into the spider's web she sails. Our luck holds. We will dive and attack, IWO.'

'Stand by all vents,' said Chief Hoppe as Brand landed in the control room.

'Vents ready,' came the call.

'Open all vents,' said the captain.

'Flood!' called the chief. Brand watched through his periscope as the sea surged into the free-flood spaces of the casing. The flipper-like fore-planes tilted downwards and bit into the next swell, speeding their descent. Now the foredeck was awash as sea surged across the casing towards him and pockets of air escaped in flurries. Brand always found it a disconcerting sensation to witness this moment of drowning and he realised, yet again, that he was inadvertently holding his breath.

At fifteen metres, Chief Hoppe called out 'Blow Q' accompanied by the hissing of compressed air as seawater was forced out of the quick-diving tanks and the boat levelled off. 'Up periscope.' The column hissed from its well, droplets of greasy water shining on the smooth bronze shaft. Brand crouched low, his fingers snapping the handles into place as the lens poked above the waves. He swung the eye in a full circle, then twisted the right handle towards him, increasing the magnification. With the left handle, he swivelled the top lens upward to sweep the sky for aircraft.

'Accurate depth, *Gottverdammt*, Chief!' hissed Brand. 'Woe betide you break surface so close to the enemy. She is armed.'

'That is all very well for you to say in this bloody swell,' Hoppe muttered.

'What was that, Chief?'

'Nothing, sir.' Hoppe kept his eyes glued to the Papenberg as Brand climbed the ladder to his attack station in the conning tower with the first lieutenant at his heels. The approach was slow, deliberate and executed like clockwork.

'Stand by to fire tubes two and four, single shots,' called the captain, his eye socket illuminated by the brilliance of the spring day above. He experienced a moment of self-reproach at the thought of the destruction he was about to unleash on the peaceful scene. For a few minutes more, the tanker would sail on unmolested, not a care in the world, delicately poised between insouciance and annihilation.

'Enemy speed eleven knots, range one thousand metres, bearing three-one-zero.'

'Tubes two and four ready,' said the first lieutenant.

'Damn this swell,' said the captain as a comber broke ahead of them, submerging the periscope. Regaining equilibrium, Brand fed bearings to Lingen who was bent over the deflection calculator which transmitted its readings electronically to the torpedoes.

'Open bow caps,' said Brand. 'Stand by number two tube.' Then a few seconds later, 'Number two tube: *los*! Lock on number four.' A few more seconds. 'Number four tube: *los*!'

Once more, the boat was shrouded in silence as one hundred ears listened intently, counting off the seconds in their heads, yearning for the sound of impact. Brand raised the periscope just in time to see a column of water towering over the ship, followed almost immediately by smoke, flames and a low rumbling that was met by cheering and whooping from the fore-ends. The second torpedo missed or was faulty, so Brand ordered the firing of a third which struck home after fifty seconds, eliciting another bout of celebration. He watched through his glass eye as the tanker erupted amidships, sending a red fireball high into the sky, a vision of horror and beauty.

U-68 surfaced, Brand threw open the upper lid and climbed onto the bridge, followed by his lookouts and gun crews. 'Blow to full buoyancy with diesel!' he called down the voicepipe.

Scarlet tongues licked around the ship as thick gouts of oil bled from her wounds. Brand called for the switching off of ventilators to prevent the putrid fumes from being sucked below. Flames spat and crackled like the resin of pines feeding a forest fire. The sea all around the stricken tanker was alight and in it were men, marionette figures whose arms jerked exaggeratedly as the fire engulfed them, human torches thrashing out their last moments in unimaginable agony. Brand noticed that there were still crew aboard the ship. A burning sailor ran along a burning deck and jumped into a burning sea. He thought he could just make out a scream above the roaring of the flames but dismissed it as unlikely.

'She managed to transmit an SOS on the 630-meter band, Kapitän,' said Wichmann, poking his head from the hatch.

'Then we can expect visitors, and this bloody bonfire can be seen for miles.'

Brand looked at the apocalypse he had wrought and felt disgust and awe. Like the God of Herr Kruger, he had turned water into oil lit with flames the colour of wine. From ocean he maketh fire. Of course he had every right to incinerate the enemy: it is exactly what the RAF was doing to German civilians. This war they had been dragged into by Britain and France consumed everything.

'Swimmers!' cried a watch keeper.

'Perhaps we could pull them clear of the flames, sir,' said Lingen.

'I did not take you for a sentimentalist, IWO, but yes, let us try.' Brand gave steering orders and they approached a pod of men who had managed to escape the inferno.

'Alaaarm!' yelled a lookout. 'Aircraft on the starboard beam!'

The twin-engine plane swooped out of a cloud bank and would be upon them before Brand could get his gunners below and dive. As the klaxon began its demented blaring, he made a split-second decision and shouted: 'Stop, we will fight on the surface! Full ahead, hard a-port! Fire at will!'

Both the 20mm and 37mm anti-aircraft guns opened up simultaneously, venting a hail of tracer. The Anson jinked left and right, then described a shallow dive, firing the Vickers machine gun in its nose as .303 rounds picked at the sea ahead of the U-boat and pinged off the foredeck. The guttural throb of its engines filled Brand's head and he ducked instinctively as the aircraft roared past at just fifty metres, releasing four bombs. But the pilot had been forced wide by their accurate fire and the bombs struck the water off their starboard bow, engulfing them in spray, but causing no damage. With one of its engines spluttering and trailing smoke, the Anson made off towards land, chased by a few 37mm rounds.

'Dive, dive, dive! Open all main vents!' shouted Brand as lookouts and gunners bundled down the ladder. He took one last look around as the sea rose to meet him and banged closed the hatch.

'Now that they know our position, let us hope they do not bring the whole fleet down on us,' said Lingen as his captain landed like a paratrooper in the control room.

CHAPTER 16

Jack paced the bridge, unable to remain in his cabin, his short temper and brusque commands betraying his impatience to slip the moorings and take up the chase. Much of the morning was needed to round up *Gannet*'s crew and prepare her for sea. Broadcasts on the radio, announcements at all NAAFI halls and places of entertainment, including interruptions to bioscope performances, had seen sailors flooding back to Simon's Town from all corners of the Peninsula. Every available ship and aircraft was to take part in the search, and *Gannet* was finally able to leave port in the early afternoon, heading out of False Bay and turning southeast to scour her designated search area off Quoin Point.

In the late afternoon, a signal came through reporting that an aircraft had made an attack on a U-boat which was thought to be heading east. The coordinates were not too far from *Gannet*'s current position and Jack gave the order to proceed at full speed with Robinson calculating the enemy's possible trajectory and plotting a number of interception options.

Dusk fell and they settled into a box search, working a widening tract of ocean towards Cape Agulhas. AB Potgieter sat for hours at a stretch, hunched before the dial of his Asdic set, turning the hand wheel that swung the beam back and forth, combing the three-dimensional world below. The pings came at regular intervals, like a slow heartbeat, the pulses probing the deep from the dome on *Gannet*'s keel. Always he waited for the bouncing-ball echo — 'ping ... ga' — that would announce a target and give his captain the chance to hit back. The constant sound of the Asdic never let anyone within earshot of the wheelhouse forget the hunt: those pings were their means of attack and defence, their *raison d'être*.

The following day, while cruising well to the east of her pursuers, *U-68* received a message from the *BdU*. Admiral Dönitz was pleased with Gruppe Savanne's achievements thus far: the sinking without loss of a valuable cruiser and twelve merchantmen for a total of nearly 90,000 tons in less than three days. However, given the strengthening of anti-submarine measures around the Cape, the group had permission to range independently and more widely in search of easier targets. In addition, Kruger had managed to supply his handlers in Berlin with particulars concerning Path Six, the coastal route currently being used by merchantmen sailing to Durban, and details of the imminent departure of a convoy.

Brand had been pushing his men hard since arriving in South African waters and sensed that they were both mentally and physically spent. He decided to proceed further eastward at a leisurely pace, giving himself the chance to decide his next move and the crew a period of rest.

That evening, a second signal came through from the *BdU* commending *U-68*'s captain once again on the sinking of HMS *Buckinghamshire* and awarding him the Knight's Cross of the Iron Cross, with congratulations from the Führer and a personal message from Admiral Dönitz: 'Well done, warrior Brand, continue to expend your rage on the enemy.'

Lingen broadcast the good tidings over the intercom to a roar of approval that rang throughout the length of the boat as though a cup-winning goal had been scored. Caught unawares, Brand was sitting on his bunk writing in his journal when the announcement was made. He took off his cap, laid it on the blanket beside him and stared at the photograph of his wife, momentarily at a loss.

When he entered the control room, there was loud applause. '*Danke schön*, thank you, everyone. I am humbled, but you know as well as I do that this honour is for every single man on this boat. There are no individual glories to be had in a submarine.' The cook set about baking a cake decorated with a large black cross and, with Brand's permission, hauled out twenty-five beers — half a bottle per man — for the celebratory toast.

In the early hours of Wednesday 17 September, sailing under a waning crescent moon 140 miles southeast of Cape Agulhas, one of the lookouts spotted a lone merchant vessel. *U-68* approached on the surface at top speed, trying to beat the dawn that would betray her presence.

'She is travelling slowly, without zigzagging, not a care in the world,' said Brand. 'Don't they know there is a war on?'

The freighter was making a lot of smoke and her lookouts did not spot the U-boat scything towards them on their port bow.

'Two masts, five loading hatches, about 9,000 tons,' said Lingen. 'She cannot be doing more than six knots: maybe she has engine trouble.'

'She will have a lot more trouble shortly,' said the captain. To preserve his eels, and seeing that the ocean was as calm as an Elbe backwater, Brand opted for gunnery. Given the liveliness of a U-boat's gun platform, even in the mildest swell, glassy conditions made for the most accurate shooting and he wanted to give his 10.5cm crew some practice.

'Action stations!'

Helmeted gunners and bearers of shells, extracted from the ammunition locker beneath the deck plates, scrambled to their positions in the dark.

The steamer, now 5,000 yards off, finally spotted the U-boat and turned away. She carried one ancient, 4-inch gun in a 'bathtub' on her stern — Brand hadn't noticed it in the dark — and managed to fire the first shot, which passed over their heads with the sound of tearing silk.

'Well, that makes things a little more sporting,' he said, observing his gunnery team as the loader opened the breech, received a round from a handler, then slammed closed the breechblock. Brand waited until the aimer and layer were ready.

'Open fire!' he shouted and almost immediately the 10.5cm barked, its shell whining away to fall well short, a thin plume of white in the darkness. No matter, he knew well enough the first round was unlikely to hit as it had to cope with a cold gun as well as water or anything else that had found its way into the barrel while submerged.

'Up four hundred!' Brand shouted down to the crew.

The second shot, ten seconds later, was closer and the third found its mark: an orange flash on the superstructure and billowing smoke. The ship's return fire was inaccurate, while the U-boat continued to score hits as she closed with the enemy. The freighter's radio operator tapped out an urgent, plain-language, 'SSSS', denoting a submarine attack, as shrapnel peppered the bulkheads around him, while on *U-68*, PO Wichmann was effectively jamming the distress signal. The next shell toppled the ship's mast and all transmissions halted abruptly.

Their tenth shell scored a direct hit on the bathtub, silencing the gun and killing its crew: all resistance ceased and lifeboats began to be lowered.

'Stop firing!' shouted Brand. 'Let them abandon ship, then we will finish her off.'

As the survivors rowed clear, *U-68* closed to 500 yards and resumed firing with both the 37mm and 20mm joining in, their pyrotechnics lighting up the predawn sky. When a zephyr drew back the smoke like a curtain, Brand could see the wreckage his guns had wrought, the funnel canted over like a broken top hat and the gouges in her superstructure as though a giant can-opener had been at work.

'This is excellent target practice, and not bad shooting!' Brand shouted above the noise, his unkempt beard tinged scarlet by the flames and making him appear demonic.

A lucky shot from the 10.5 took out the boiler which erupted, forming a mushroom cloud above the ship. Eight more rounds went home along the waterline and she was done for. Her stern lifted, as though shoved from below, until it stood over them like a toothy iceberg. The hull teetered, amazingly upright, as though a statement of defiance, or hate, then slid beneath the waves. Below decks on *U-68*, the crew enjoyed the sounds of her death throes: the grating of metal like the tearing of cardboard, the low booming of a shunting yard. 'Those will be the bulkheads giving way,' said Coxswain Fischer. 'Music to my ears!'

A drowned sheep was brought onto the foredeck by the gun crew, much to the satisfaction of the cook who set about butchering it on the spot. The survivors, some of them in pyjamas, filled two lifeboats and two rafts and included the captain's wife, who had been serving as a stewardess. The U-boat idled towards them and Lingen shouted questions, finding out that their prey had been the Greek freighter, SS *Skiathos*, 7,600 tons, from Haifa bound for Liverpool, carrying 2,500 tons of chrome bars, 2,000 tons of potash, assorted cargo and two German tanks captured in North Africa.

'Our humble contribution to Rommel's campaign,' said Brand. 'The *Generalleutnant* owes us one.'

'Two,' said Lingen.

U-68 edged closer to the lifeboats and a few packets of cigarettes, two cans of black bread, some hard sausage and drinking water were passed to the survivors. Lingen provided the senior officer with the course to the nearest landfall.

'Enemy ship, red one-seven-zero!' yelled a lookout.

Brand swung his binoculars onto the grey mote emerging from the murk of dawn.

'Alarm! Dive, dive, dive! Open all main vents!'

Gunners and lookouts scrambled for the ladder and water was already inundating the bridge when Brand slammed the hatch closed. Once submerged, they headed at their full underwater speed of seven knots in the opposite direction.

'Do you think we were spotted?' asked Hoppe.

'Definitely,' said Brand.

'What was she?'

'Probably an anti-submarine whaler.'

A little later, the hydrophone operator made the feared announcement: 'Propeller noise, single screw, bearing three-one-zero.'

'Faint?' asked Brand.

'Yes, sir, but growing stronger.' The captain knelt beside Zimmermann, who removed his headset and twisted one earphone so Brand could listen.

'Mmm, I hear so, thank you, PO.'

Knock-knock-knock. The tocking of a Black Forest woodpecker, a sound to drive a hole in your skull.

'Silent running,' hissed the captain.

Now came the chomping sound of the propeller on its methodical approach, like a tracker dog sniffing every bush, every burrow. It increased speed ... closer ... splashes.

Four depth charges exploded close by, then a pattern of six even closer. Asdic conditions were good and this enemy captain appeared to know what he was about. Again and again, he attacked. It seemed to Brand that with each pass the hunter was growing in confidence and getting close to the mark. He tried going very deep, then shallow, to no avail: the terrier had its bone and would not let go.

On the next pass, *U-68* was straddled, the eruptions tearing at her from all sides. Men covered their ears as they were plucked off their feet and dashed to the deck. Glass shattered and the lights went out; water jetted from leaks in the diesel room, hissing on the engine as though it were a red-hot stove. 'No, no, not again,' whimpered a stoker, his facial muscles quivering with shock.

Brand retreated once more into mathematics: depth, speed, bearings, angles. 'Hard a-port,' he said, but the enemy had anticipated his move and passed directly overhead without dropping any charges. Perhaps the U-boat had found a hiding place beneath a temperature layer.

'Going away,' whispered Zimmermann.

They waited in absolute silence for twenty minutes.

'Cold layer, I think,' said Brand. 'We might have shaken them off. Periscope depth, if you please. Easy does it.'

The chief gave the necessary plane orders and *U-68* rose cautiously towards the surface like a basking shark. The periscope-motor hummed, as Brand extended the mechanical eye.

'*Guter Gott!* Crash dive! Take her down to ninety metres, Chief, flood Q tank!'

The chief responded instantly: 'Planes hard a-dive, full ahead both! All hands forward!'

At ninety metres they levelled off. The chief gave a few plane orders and then said softly, 'Boat trimmed, sir. Main vents shut.'

'Slow ahead both, steer one-eight-zero. Silent running.'

A few minutes later, Brand pushed his cap back and said, 'Well, that was awkward. The hunter was sitting quietly 500 metres away, engines stopped, waiting for us to show ourselves. He is a crafty bugger, that captain. I would love to put a torpedo up his arse.'

'What was she, sir?' asked Lingen.

'A submarine chaser: gun mounted on the foredeck, upright funnel. She had the number T65 on her side — look her up, will you?'

The first lieutenant opened his register and, after a short search, said: 'T65 is HMSAS *Southern Gannet*, sir, a converted whaler.'

Knock-knock, knock-knock? Questions for the deep. The men looked up involuntarily, their faces taught with fear. Then came the dreaded answer: the sound of gravel as Asdic beat a tattoo on their casing. It was as though an underwater searchlight had found them and it was once again up to Brand to wriggle free.

Now the grumble of the enemy propeller, splash of depth charges and an agonising wait for the explosions. Chief Hoppe looked at his captain's face and, for the first time, saw a tremor in the left eye, the slightest crack in his armour. The three-dimensional map of the battlefield appeared etched on his face. Every report from the hydrophone operator altered the variables. The familiar, life-or-death decisions once more: would the enemy anticipate a turn to port or starboard … or call their bluff and keep on straight? A flip of the coin.

Another pattern of detonations. Those not holding on were yanked off their feet. Men wept: some in fear, others in fury, a few in hate. One of the hydroplane operators slowly beat his crown against the bulkhead.

'Stop that!' Brand snapped. 'Pull yourself together, all of you. We have come this far and we will get through it together. Do you hear me?'

'*Ja*, Kapitän,' a few murmured.

There were leaks everywhere now — jets of high-pressure water squirting across compartments as the crew scrambled to shut valves and attend to damage under the direction of Chief Hoppe and Bosun Fuchs.

More detonations.

A racing of the motors as they doglegged to another quiet patch of ocean, hoping for escape. Calculations whirred through Brand's mind: high-speed manoeuvres ate up battery current and shortened their time underwater; oxygen and batteries, survival or death. Any crew not needed were sent to their bunks to remain immobile and conserve air as the hours dragged by. Everyone had headaches and sleep was impossible, their bodies clammy and strung with tension.

'Our chaser is trying very hard but he is not as talented as I thought, one almost wants to give him a hand,' said Brand, but this time his bravado sounded hollow. 'He is wasting precious depth charges on fish. Perhaps his crew will at least be rewarded with a good supper but, unfortunately for them, not the filleted U-boat they desire.' He emitted a high-pitched, almost girlish, laugh.

U-68 went deeper, increased speed and zigzagged, but the enemy could not be shaken off and Brand again reduced speed, defeated, as the propeller sound trailed them. The next salvo rattled the deck plates but was not dangerously close and, taking advantage of the noise and turbulence, *U-68* went full ahead and pumped out the bilges, before reverting to silent running.

'He is tenacious, this South African captain, I will give him that,' said Brand as the whaler came in for another attack. 'Let us hope we are not playing Hansel and Gretel and leaking oil to show him the way.'

Just then a giant fist connected with the U-boat, keeling her over on her side. The needle on the depth gauge jumped as men were tossed to the deck. Glass shattered, smoke billowed from the engine room and there was a scramble to douse the flames. Brand stared at the deckhead above him as he clung to the periscope, the twitch in his left eye now discernible to everyone in the control room.

'Propellers faint and going away at zero-six-zero,' said Zimmermann.

Perhaps the last salvo had been a final throw of the dice; perhaps the enemy had run out of depth charges. Brand panted shallowly as sweat dripped from his face. Could the attack be over, or was this another ruse?

CHAPTER 17

For the previous eight hours, Jack had been on the tail of the U-boat that sank the *Skiathos*. He had disregarded the survivors in their boats and rafts — *Gannet* would return for them later — and gone straight for the kill, locking horns with his underwater adversary. Again and again, Jack raced in on the contact but each time the U-boat passed into the Asdic's shadow, the enemy had second-guessed him and slipped away. Later, contact would be regained — a long *p-i-i-i-ng* followed by the sharp pip of an echo. 'Target bearing port twenty, range 700 yards, moving right!' sang out AB Potgieter.

'Stand by for medium pattern!' Jack called into his voicepipe, the thump of his heart detonating in his ears. Out of the corner of his eye he registered a Wilson's storm petrel — rounded wings, long spindly legs — skimming across the wave tops and made an almost subconscious note to add it to his pelagic list.

'Medium pattern standing by,' called PO Combrink from the quarterdeck, his men crouched beside their racks and throwers in tense anticipation.

'Contact bearing port ten, range 400.'

'Very good.'

'Range close,' said Potgieter. 'Asdic temporarily not functioning.'

Gannet had entered the shadow and it was over to Jack's intuition once more.

'Prepare to fire.'

What would the enemy captain do this time?

'Starboard twenty and ... fire!' bellowed Jack from the bridge wing as Van Zyl pressed the electric buzzer to signal the release of depth charges. Jack heard them rumbling off their racks and the cough of throwers as canisters arced away from his ship and splashed into the sea fifty yards off her quarters. He counted the ponderous seconds until a patch of sea in their wake erupted in a great water tower, rising and expanding in white violence, accompanied by a muffled boom as though monsters of the deep had come to blows. Another aquatic volcano hard upon it, then another: teetering perpendiculars, hillocks of sea hanging in the air upshunned, ungravitied, before collapsing in torrential waterfalls. Again and again, his pocket monsoons abused the ocean, to no avail.

'Hard a-starboard.' Jack willed *Gannet* through her laborious U-turn, knowing all the while that if the enemy had not been maimed, she could be making off in any given direction as he struggled to regain contact. He stared aft, willing the sight of a U-boat breaking the surface like a wounded whale, aching for the sound of his guns finishing her off, but the sea had returned to its placid, implacable self, with not the slightest stain of oil for reward.

And so the day wore on with the hare always one step ahead of the fox. All they managed to kill were some fish and a pair of Cape gannets that had been diving for them. Jack was upset by the slain seabirds, their limp wings outstretched on the surface in a crucificial pose, their beautiful yellow heads submerged.

After prolonged Asdic silence, they returned to rescue the survivors of *Skiathos* before making for home. Shaken but only superficially damaged, *U-68* continued on her way and found sanctuary in the great blue waste of the Indian Ocean in unimaginably deep water off the southern end of the continental shelf.

Back in Simon's Town, Jack accompanied his father on the admiral's constitutional walk from Milkwood along the coast road to Miller's Point. It was a blustery evening with a cloudbank pouring over Simonsberg like a great, foaming wave and the road already deep in shadow.

'The sinking of *Buckinghamshire* was a bloody disaster,' lamented the admiral. 'So many dead, the town in mourning, morale in tatters.'

'It was terrible. I hear the hospital is full.'

'Full to overflowing. A desperately dark day for the South Atlantic station … and some of the blame must rest on my shoulders.'

'Nonsense, Father, without forewarning from Freetown, a U-boat attack was always going to be a complete surprise.'

'But our countermeasures were wholly inadequate. Some vessels had to help with the rescue, others with close-in anti-submarine patrol, which left only a destroyer, a corvette and two whalers to chase the wretched Hun, until you managed to put to sea.'

'I wish *Gannet* and *Belle* had been ready on the night of the sinking.'

'So do I. Since the attacks, we've tried to hurry through a whole raft of emergency measures. The use of coastal and harbour-navigation lights, radio beacons and fog signals have been discontinued. We've dimmed all the lighthouse beams and I've suggested a total blackout for Cape Town and Durban, but that has been vetoed in favour of a partial reduction of shore lighting. Fat good that's going to do.'

'Too little, too late,' said Jack, his eyes tracking two fishing boats heading back to Kalk Bay.

'The use of Saldanha will help reduce the number of ships needing to anchor in Table Bay and I've introduced double-banking in Cape Town harbour until the fuss has blown over. I want nothing parked in the roadstead acting as bait. But it's creating enormous congestion and gumming up the works, which is exactly what the Boche wants. And there's a huge knock-on effect in all the other harbours.'

'That scoundrel Dönitz knows what he's about.'

'He does. I've also postponed all sailings for another week and rerouted what vessels I can. It's bloody chaos. Wireless messages were sent to all ships warning them not to approach within a hundred miles of Cape Town during the hours of darkness.'

'If only the SAAF was equipped for night operations,' Jack lamented.

'When the radar stations are established and we get round-the-clock air cover, the combination will be very effective.'

'In the meantime, what about forming coastal convoys?' asked Jack. 'My flotilla is ready.'

'We're in the process of organising a convoy system for as many ships as possible, but some will still have to use their speed and chance their luck with as much daytime air cover as we can provide.'

The pair stopped at a bend in the road to look down on the granite boulders of Miller's Point and take in the vista of the southern arms of False Bay, bookended by Cape Hangklip and Cape Point. They stood for a long while in silence, then turned back.

'Son, you're not going to believe this, but there's been a hullabaloo about your capturing of those Vichy-French ships a few months back.'

'How preposterous: they were carrying contraband from Madagascar to France, destined for the Reich. They were legitimate targets.'

'You don't need to tell me, Jack. But Vichy noses are thoroughly out of joint.'

'As they should be.'

'I couldn't agree more, but now intelligence tells me that the French have ordered two submarines, *Le Glorieux* and *Le Héros*, to sink Allied shipping in South African waters.'

'That's absurd! Glorious and heroic Frogs my arse. After the BEF's efforts in France, after all those men sacrificed, after Dunkirk!'

'I'm afraid so. As if we didn't have enough on our plate with Hun and Itie submarines. Who knows, if Japan enters the ring, we might even have their long-range subs to deal with.'

Back at Milkwood, a fire crackled in the lounge where they were joined by Imogen and sat having a whisky before dinner. The admiral was onto one of his pet topics again: 'There are spies everywhere. Our "loose lips sink ships" campaign isn't an idle crusade: maritime information *is* being passed on by German agents and it's costing lives. I've just received a report with the names of suspected agents operating around the Cape Peninsula — a list as long as my arm! There's even a governess to a prominent Simon's Town family and a ladies' hairdresser in Fish Hoek on the list. You know, Jack, sometimes when I drive through Glencairn —'

'You mean when Wren Munroe drives you through Glencairn,' interrupted Imogen.

'Quite so, my dear: when Wren Munroe drives me through Glencairn, at one point the voices on the car radio always became weaker. She says it only happens at that particular bend in the road. I'll be damned if there isn't a radio transmitter in one of those houses. I'm going to inform the Royal Navy's Y boys.'

'Y boys?' asked Jack, taking a sip of whisky.

'Oh, very hush-hush. The Y organisation has been set up to monitor enemy wireless comms. A certain Lieutenant Bennett has established a Y station in Simon's Town and is trying to intercept U-boat chatter and illicit transmissions by agents in South Africa. Bennett has also set up stations in Cape Town, Durban, Port Elizabeth and Bulawayo. The huff-duff chaps —'

'What on earth is huff-duff, Papa?' asked Imogen. 'It sounds like a brand of snuff.'

'If I tell you I'll have to shoot you.'

'Oh, spare me,' she sighed, rolling her eyes to his obvious delight.

'Huff-duff — or HF/DF — is high-frequency direction finding. It helps us locate the U-boats when they communicate by radio with their HQ.'

'Has Bennett's team had any luck?' Jack asked, reaching over to throw another log on the fire.

'Yes, they've started getting fairly good fixes on U-boats off our coast. The Hun must have kept mum on his journey south.'

'And what about your cloak-and-dagger spies, Papa?' asked Imogen.

'As a matter of fact, them too. Bennett has picked up powerful transmissions coming from somewhere near Lambert's Bay on the West Coast. The messages are very brief, so we haven't been able to triangulate the position exactly, but the Y chaps are working on it and Bennett will be sending mobile DF units up there to see if we can't sniff out the bugger.'

'Lots of Nazi sympathisers up the West Coast,' said Jack. 'What are the messages saying?'

'We don't know. They get sent to our boffins in London to see if they can decipher them. Apart from spies leaking shipping information, we're increasingly worried about sabotage. I've helped set up the Essential Service Protection Corps — mostly military veterans — to guard key installations, especially around the ports, and we've placed sentries on the gangways of all merchant ships.'

'You're taking the threat seriously then,' said Jack.

'Extremely seriously.'

Clara invited Jack to tea with her brother at the council-run European Pavilion Tea Room, built on the sea side of the railway platform in Kalk Bay. He was somewhat taken aback to find that Pierre's pilot friend, Henry, who'd accompanied Clara to the Admiralty House dance, was included. Jack sat next to Pierre facing the bay and found himself cornered into a long conversation about the SAAF, while Clara and Henry chatted animatedly about mutual friends and a recent dance.

Pierre monopolised Jack's attention and was excited to tell him about a recent brush with the enemy. 'My navigator spotted the U-boat soon after it torpedoed that tanker south of Cape Point and I immediately found some cloud cover to approach undetected. We dropped out of the clouds about two miles shy, made a turn to starboard and dived to attack her quarter.' Pierre used his hand and two teacups to denote Anson, U-boat and tanker. 'It didn't submerge —'

'Her captain must have thought he hadn't enough time,' said Jack distractedly, glancing across at Clara, head back, laughing at one of Henry's feeble witticisms.

'Probably,' said Pierre. 'I opened fire with my Vickers and I thought I had him. We were close enough to see the brown overalls and flat blue caps of the gun crews and my navigator swears he saw the whites of the captain's eyes. I certainly caused some discomfort with my machine gun and we landed four bombs fairly close.'

'Any damage?' asked Jack.

'I think we may have wet them, but nothing mortal. They returned fire and unfortunately scored a few hits on my port engine. So I dropped flare- and smoke-floats and limped back to Wingfield, hoping the relieving Anson, which I'd whistled up, would find her. But no luck.'

The tea ended too soon with Jack hardly having had a chance to say more than a few words to Clara. He hoped they might take a stroll on the harbour wall — perhaps Clara could stay behind and take the train back to Newlands — but she had to get home to swot for a French test and they had come together in Henry's convertible. To Jack it seemed as though she was enjoying rather too much having a pair of adoring officers in orbit. Yet he ached to be alone with her, tell her as best he could how his feelings towards her were deepening … and she was playing the fool. Clara had opened a door in his heart that he could not afford to leave ajar, not with his demons forever loitering and the sea war having returned in earnest to their doorstep. He sat on the train to Simon's Town with his head bowed and his emotions in turmoil.

Jannie van Zyl returned once more to his home in Stellenbosch for a night of shore leave. He stepped off the train and walked into town past a Jewish-owned shop that had been firebombed and swastikas daubed on the charred walls. It made him sick to the stomach to think that his brother supported this kind of barbarity. He often wondered how the Van Zyl family had produced such diametrically opposing positions and blamed his arrogant, nationalistic father.

Arriving back at the house on Neethling Street, he found that Hans was unfortunately home, accompanied by ardent right-winger and old university friend, Gerhardus Kruger. The greetings were cool, Kruger doubtlessly taking exception to Jannie's SDF uniform. To his mother's disappointment, he decided not to stay for supper and joined a group of school friends at De Akker pub rather than have to endure the dinner-table conversation at home.

Hoping to find everyone asleep, he returned late, letting himself in quietly and tiptoeing across the creaky boards. The door to the lounge was ajar and he heard voices from within. A glimpse revealed three seated figures around the hearth and he paused in the darkened hallway to listen. The large Pye wireless on the mantelshelf was tuned to a talk in Afrikaans on Radio Zeesen, the broadcaster touting the Gouritz River bridge and railway line between Pietermaritzburg and Durban as appropriate targets for sabotage.

Far more disturbing was the talk he overheard in his family living room. From the gist of the conversation, he ascertained that the third man, Dolf, had just signed some sort of oath. Hardly breathing, Jannie pressed himself against the wall and listened.

'… as you know, our Glencairn informant was instrumental in the sinking of HMS *Buckinghamshire*,' said Kruger.

'The lighthouse keeper at Slangkop is also proving useful when it comes to convoy intelligence,' said Hans. 'Through him and other local agents, Gerhardus will be able to start sending very precise information on tonnage, cargo, destinations, sailing times and so on to Berlin.'

'Direct contact with the Reich will be much more effective, thanks to Gerhardus,' said Dolf. 'Up till now, our agents have had to send coded intelligence via the German consulate in LM using couriers or disguised in death notices in the *Sunday Times*. It's then passed on to Berlin using diplomatic cipher, a laborious process that gets the information to the *BdU* far too late to be acted upon. I mean, we ourselves have to wait to hear the song "*Opsaal Boere*" on Radio Zeesen before we know that the message has got through.'

'By then, the horses have long bolted,' said Hans.

The trio discussed a list of potential recruits, Dolf assuring them that he knew of many fit, intelligent, patriotic students in other provinces who were burning to take up arms. They talked about setting up secret training camps on various farms around the country to teach recruits hand-to-hand combat, how to make hand grenades and bombs, how to build road obstacles and blow up railway lines. Meanwhile in the background, Lord Haw-Haw's chilling drawl announced the Nazi version of the news.

Conversation turned to determining where, when and how to begin the sabotage campaign that would, as Hans put it, 'signal the coming of freedom to the Afrikaner volk'.

'Our first strike must be an earth-shattering blow,' said Kruger.

'How about the assassination of a politician or prominent Jewish capitalist?' said Dolf.

'Perhaps, but I was thinking more along the lines of shipping, given the critical situation in North Africa,' said Kruger. 'Having seen the havoc caused by the loss of HMS *Buckinghamshire*, right under British noses in Simon's Town, I was wondering about something similar.'

'But the defences have been greatly strengthened and Simon's Town is now surely impregnable,' said Dolf.

'I wasn't thinking of Simon's Town,' said Kruger. 'What about sinking one of the great liners in Cape Town harbour with the whole city looking on. It would make a powerful statement about the enemy's vulnerability.'

'But how, security is tight?' asked Hans.

Van Zyl grew fearful: the things he was hearing placed him in terrible danger.

'We have an agent working in the docks who is well placed to steal shipping documents and find out about security measures, sentries and so on,' said Dolf.

'We can certainly make use of him,' said Kruger.

'And I can supply explosives for…' Dolf hesitated. 'What was that noise?'

'What noise?' asked Hans.

'Creaking.'

'Probably the cat.'

'Are you sure?'

'Let me check.' Kruger stood up, grabbed a poker from beside the fire and approached the door. He darted into the hallway, metal rod raised to strike … there was no one there.

CHAPTER 18

Admiral Pembroke and his team worked rapidly to institute a convoy system, particularly for slower vessels that normally sailed independently between local ports but were now extremely vulnerable. Jack's flotilla was tasked with escorting convoy CD.03, a relatively large and diverse group of fifteen merchantmen, from Cape Town to Durban. The Royal Navy had been responsible for convoys up until now but at Admiral Pembroke's insistence, SNO Simon's Town agreed to try out an all-South African escort. However, the convoy would remain under O'Reilly's operational control, not the SDF.

Jack and his three captains attended a pre-sailing conference at Seaward House in Cape Town harbour along with the masters of the merchant ships. Hosted by the Naval Control Service and convoy commodore, it was at this briefing that each captain received his sailing orders, escort-screening diagrams, lists of call signs and enemy reports. The gathering was called to order by an effete lieutenant-commander from Naval Control who outlined the proposed route before handing over to the convoy commodore, Oscar Jones, to go into more detail and take questions.

'You all know the great danger of falling behind,' said the grey-bearded commodore at the lectern, 'and I'm sure our escort commander, Lieutenant Pembroke, will not be stopping for laggards. The passage should take us five days and, in the event of an attack, the folders you've been given contain instructions concerning signal codes to use in case of emergency, evasive tactics, et cetera.'

Jack eyed the commodore closely from his seat in the front row, knowing he would need to develop a good working relationship with the man over the coming days. Jones had recently retired from the merchant navy but returned to do his bit, with the acting rank of Commodore RNR, and would be wearing the broad pennant aboard the convoy flagship, SS *Sapphire*. Jones's duty was to see to the discipline and manoeuvring of the merchantmen while Jack, as escort commander, was responsible for their defence. But where exactly the responsibility of the commodore ended and his began, Jack was not altogether sure, and the fact that the tall and rather forbidding greybeard was four decades his senior added to the complications that turned over in his mind. If Jones were to stand on the letter of the law and seniority, Jack was not sure what he would do.

The commodore came to the end of his briefing: 'May God grant us a safe, if bumpy, passage to Durban. We'll have some pretty foul weather to contend with, but this is an urgent convoy and we can't wait for the elements.'

It was Jack's turn and he had to suppress the jitters as he took the lectern. 'Gentlemen, as you know, coastal convoys have been instituted due to the possible presence of the U-boats that were recently active off the Cape.' His voice was higher pitched than usual, betraying his nerves. 'Intelligence suggests that the enemy may be moving into the Indian Ocean. This morning, I would like to talk about procedures should we encounter U-boats. We can assume that any attack would most likely occur at night and probably on the surface. It is thus my intention to plaster the area of the enemy's presumed location with illumination to force them under. Use every form of flare, rocket or star shell you have at your disposal to make things uncomfortable on the surface.' He looked at the blank faces and could see no hint of either approval or disapproval.

Clearing his throat, he continued, 'As you know, a submerged U-boat can only travel at a maximum of six or seven knots — slower than this convoy — is easier to deal with and brings our Asdics into play. If we keep their heads down long enough, it gives us a chance to put distance between the threat and the convoy. We will maintain radio silence at all times unless we have been located by the enemy. If and when the cat is out the bag, escorts will communicate by radio.'

'What if a ship is hit?' asked one of the captains.

'That presents added problems for the escorts but the principal remains the same: rockets, flares, searchlights — turn the surfaced U-boat's night into day and force him under. The picking up of survivors will be ad hoc depending on the threat level, but we will of course do absolutely everything we can.'

The meeting came to an end, chairs scraped, the captains shook hands solemnly and gradually took their leave while chatting among themselves. Jack was impressed by their unassuming manner and all-in-a-day's-work attitude, given the danger and importance of the task at hand. Commodore O'Reilly, who had arrived late and sat at the back, came up to Jack.

'How did your first convoy conference go?'

'All right I think, sir, although I must be the youngest captain here.'

'Never mind that, not your problem if they have a problem with it,' he said dismissively. 'Listen, I wanted to remind you that your first duty is to the convoy. I don't want you haring off all over the show chasing phantom U-boats and leaving the merchants exposed.'

'Of course not, sir, but in certain cases I do believe it better to hold the Hun at bay, keep his head down, rather than simply present sitting ducks.'

'It's not about bloody sitting ducks, Pembroke, it's your duty to remain close. We can only assign four escorts, at best, to these coastal convoys. If we had a dedicated hunter-killer group, that would be a different story, but we don't. So stay close and protect your brood, understood?'

'Yes, sir.' With that, O'Reilly turned on his heel and swept out of the room, trailing two of his aides. Jack stood with his cheeks flushed, feeling yet again like a schoolboy reprimanded by the headmaster.

'You're Douglas Pembroke's boy, aren't you?' said Commodore Jones, reaching out a craggy hand.

'Yes, sir, pleased to meet you,' said Jack, trying to regain composure.

'RNVR, not so?'

'Aye, sir, HMS *King Alfred*.'

'I've got nothing against Saturday-afternoon sailors. You've proved your worth in the current show, and then some.'

Jack did not respond.

'I'm sure we're going to get along just fine, Pembroke, just so long as you obey my orders.' Commodore Jones watched the clouds gather behind Jack's eyes. 'Just kidding, old chap! We'll work marvellously together, don't you worry.'

'I'd like that, sir.'

'Splendid, splendid…' The commodore moved off to ambush another pod of captains and Jack left the room feeling he'd been wrong-footed at almost every turn.

Convoy CD.03 comprised an odd assortment of bedfellows. Among them were the commodore's flagship, SS *Sapphire*, transporting troops, passengers and general cargo; the British merchant ship SS *Karachi*, 5,971 tons, carrying assorted livestock; the Panamanian merchantman, MV *Firetree*, 4,700 tons, with a deck cargo of tanks and war materiel; the Norwegian steamship SS *Glomfjord*, 3,876 tons, sailing in ballast without cargo; the British freighter SS *Pearlvale*, 5,820 tons, carrying cotton, rubber and general cargo; the British steamship SS *City of Salisbury*, 6,597 tons, with a cargo of military stores, two locomotives and packed with explosives; the Dutch steamship SS *Gaasterdal*, 7,621 tons, from Rio de Janeiro, transporting timber, palm oil, coffee and rice; the Canadian SS *Hibiscus*, 6,581 tons, with a mixed cargo below and large barrels of petrol stacked on her main deck. The *Kilimanjaro* — a modern, medium-sized British tanker — would be placed in the centre of the convoy, along with *City of Salisbury*, as they deserved the most protection.

Jack was worried about the two dead-beat coastal tramps whose worn-out engines might struggle to keep up. One of them was the Greek SS *Pavlos*, 5,505 tons, carrying a cargo of maize — an old coal burner whose black smoke might betray their position. The other was the geriatric South African steam coaster, *Helderland*, built in Scotland in 1907, employed in moving military hardware up the east coast and currently laden with explosives.

It was the escort commander's job to make sure they all reached Durban safely, where some were to remain, some would join bigger convoys and others would follow individual routings to Egypt, the Middle East and India. Their vastly differing speeds, sizes and manoeuvrability were going to make Jack's task all the more difficult, particularly with a gale in the offing.

Somewhere in the early hours of Monday morning, Jack wrenched himself awake with a strangled cry. His dreams had again been ransacked by an explosion tearing open the ship and ravenous water surging in to inundate his world. No way out, his body sucked under, water filling his lungs and the fight going out of him as the light faded to blue, to black. *Havoc! Havoc!*

Bathed in sweat and trembling, he untangled himself from sheets that had once again managed to ensnare him. Air, he needed air. Throwing open a scuttle, he stuck his head out and drank in the smell of the sea, the peace of Simon's Town's basin, darkened battlewagons nestled against the embracing arms of stone.

By mid-morning, the escort group was ready for sea. Stores and ammunition had been loaded, fuel and water pumped into tanks and equipment checked. Jack moved to the centre of the bridge and despite feeling rough from lack of sleep and filled with apprehension at what lay ahead, he was equally charged with the exhilaration he had come to expect upon going to sea. By his side stood Van Zyl, Bunts and a lookout on each wing; below him at their designated stations, a crew of good men. *Gannet* vibrated softly, ready to head once more into the Atlantic to do her work. Jack felt the responsibility keenly, intensified by the three whalers that would be following him out through the bullnose, soon to be vastly compounded by their attachment to convoy CD.03.

Sub-Lieutenant Robinson and four seamen, neatly turned out for harbour stations, stood on the bandstand beside the twelve-pounder as *Gannet* throbbed across the basin, creasing a pencil wake.

'Starboard twenty,' Jack called into the voicepipe.

'Twenty of starboard wheel, sir,' came February's dependable baritone.

'Midships.'

'Wheel amidships, sir.'

Passing Selbourne Lighthouse at the elbow of the harbour wall, *Gannet* increased revolutions and eased into a gentle swell. Jack looked aft at Alstad taking station behind him, a mirror, a twin. He admired *Belle*'s flowing lines, from her flared prow, along a low-cut waist to her graceful, cruiser stern — naval grey, pugnacious, willing. Her quarterdeck settled deeper, her nose lifted and a frothy white bow wave made her look like a dog with a bone. The flotilla formed up line astern and steamed down the western side of False Bay before rounding Cape Point and making for Cape Town.

The four whalers arrived off Green Point just as the anchored merchantmen began shortening in and getting ready to weigh. Those berthed in Duncan Dock prepared to cast off their wires and ropes, while the commodore's flagship, SS *Sapphire*, edged away from the wharf, attended by tugs. At her captain's command, the handles of the telegraphs were pulled over, calling for slow ahead both engines. The great shafts began to turn as the liner, drab in her wartime livery but still a thing of elegance, sailed out the harbour into the bay, her rails lined with passengers and troops staring back at the Tavern of the Seas and the mighty sandstone hulk that towered over it.

Jack paid close attention as his disparate charges gradually assembled. The merchantmen were led by SS *Sapphire* bearing Commodore Jones who, Jack had deduced at the briefing, was old-school and probably set in the aspic of the last war. Once the ships had reached the end of the swept channel, the commodore's first task was to form them up in five columns spaced three cables apart. Jack decided to hold back, watch and hope for the best as signal flags fluttered above the liner's bridge. The central column was led by the flagship, followed by the tanker, *Kilimanjaro*, and then the ammunition ship, *City of Salisbury*. To Jack it seemed to take an eternity, and countless signals, to get them into their ocean-going formation. He was reminded of herding cows back on the family estate in Hampshire, each animal with a mind and pace of its own.

As they aimed the little armada south, Jack told his two officers to impress increased vigilance upon *Gannet*'s lookouts: the early glimpse of a periscope or torpedo track might save countless lives. Later, he noticed that Robinson was having the convoy's zigzag quietly explained to him once more by a patient, long-suffering Van Zyl. To his credit, Robinson was jotting down the times and alterations in his notebook: the young sub would get there in the end.

The ships shouldered into a beam sea — Cape rollers steaming out of the west in the shape of muscular, grey-green hills — as they sailed down the Peninsula towards the Cape of Good Hope. Each turn of their zigzagging course was controlled by the commodore, the hauling down of flags on *Sapphire* signalling the start of a turn. Every change of course was a major operation, one wing having to reduce speed and the other maintain it. The lead ship in each column had to put its helm over gently and each ship follow in turn, resisting the temptation to cut the corner.

Jack soon spotted trouble with one merchantman turning too early, dangerous bunching in the second column and another vessel coming altogether adrift from the tail of her column. He held off making a signal, leaving it to the commodore to sort out the mess. Although a semblance of order was regained, every course alteration resulted in a period of lesser or greater confusion.

As Jack was quickly learning, in every convoy there were slow ships and fast ships, absentminded ships and overeager ships. He watched their performance with growing concern, particularly given the approaching dusk and gathering cold front. Never mind the threat of U-boats, he dreaded what the night's station keeping might hold. Signals streamed back and forth continuously and Jack needed to be aware of all of them, reacting where necessary, trying to bite his tongue where not.

'Number 53 is out of station.'

'Number 32, why are you not answering my signals?'

'Number 13 is making too much smoke.'

In the first hours out of Cape Town, Jack kept every ship on its toes, testing wireless and lamp communication and exercising guns, and all the while *Gannet* raced up and down the columns. He realised he was making himself unpopular, but knew its absolute necessity. By evening, the strengthening blow had begun to sing in the rigging and the merchantmen were taking white water aboard as they rounded the tip of the Peninsula and wallowed their way southeast towards Cape Agulhas. Jack and the commodore agreed to desist from zigzagging at night, particularly given the brewing weather.

'Darken ship' was piped on *Gannet* and Jack felt the grim foreboding of the dusk, the coming gale, three treacherous capes to navigate in the night and U-boats somewhere out there in the blackening deep. Throughout the whaler, deadlights were being dropped and screwed home, the shutters of the wheelhouse secured and the galley stove damped down as PO Cummins did his rounds to make sure not a sliver of light showed, apart from a dim stern lamp for station keeping.

Gannet's deck rose and fell beneath Jack's feet, a dance he'd long since mastered and no longer needed a handhold in anything but the heaviest seaway. He watched the prow's metronomic rise and fall, carving a groove in the ocean, feeling the deck vibrate as she punched through each successive crest. Torrents of spray spurted up through hawse pipes and scuppers, sending water cascading across the decks. In the stomach of the ship, McEwan and his stokers toiled in a shadowy world, nursing their engine and boilers like worshippers at a shrine. The chief was bleeding from a blow to the head as he watched the dials and valves, the dancing steel limbs and piston rods, listening for any false note in his engine's music.

Gannet was out in front, patrolling back and forth, her Asdic sweeping across the convoy's wide path. *Belle* and *Langeberg* sailed up and down the flanks, trying to keep ships in line, while *Waterberg* crisscrossed their stern playing tail-end Charlie and maintaining a 180-degree sweep behind them. With only four escorts, Jack felt it imperative that the whalers 'make themselves big' by moving about their stations, pinging as wide an acreage of ocean as possible.

Many of the freighters had begun to labour, the spray flying over cargo hatches to reach their bridges. On board *Sapphire*, the grey-bearded commodore stared apprehensively at the gathering swells, his face bathed in the dim red light of the wheelhouse. His navigator leant over the mahogany plotting table in the adjacent chartroom, pencil marks indicating their laborious progress towards Danger Point. Meanwhile, the master of SS *Hibiscus* was at that moment looking anxiously at his cargo of petrol barrels lashed to the forward well deck. He did not like the thought of what a proper spring gale off the Cape of Storms might do to that lot.

The first twelve hours were a time of great anxiety for Jack, as he tried to come to grips with being in charge of such a large body of ships. He soon discovered which vessels were unable to maintain the nine knots they'd claimed achievable at the convoy conference. Allowances and cajoling, carrot and stick. Many of the masters were more than twice his age, had been in the merchant marine since before he was born, and would not always take kindly to a Wavy Navy whippersnapper telling them what to do. Convoy CD.03's problem child was the *Helderland*, christened 'Puffing Billy' by Jack due to the amount of smoke she disgorged. The tramp was long in the tooth with a straight prow, tall funnel, cruiser stern and upright features better suited to the last century. Her Welsh captain was a stocky gent with a tapering beard and bowler hat with whom Jack feared he might have to cross swords.

On that first evening out of Cape Town, dark smoke billowed from her funnel as she fought to keep up with the sedate pace of the convoy. Jack tried encouragement, commands and then veiled threats, but the old girl was not to be bullied. *Gannet* drew alongside and Jack wielded his loudhailer: 'Can't you eke another knot out of her, Captain?'

'My chief tells me she will rattle herself to pieces!' shouted the Welshman, shrugging exaggeratedly.

'Do your best!'

'Aye, that I will!' He lifted his bowler hat and *Gannet* raced back to the head of the convoy.

The responsibilities bore upon Jack with increasing weight as the night wore on. He had to communicate with the commodore, keep an eye on the weather, on ships out of station, on signals. There was never a moment to free his mind from the convoy shackles, never a moment when he was not holding the disposition, readiness, course, speed and manoeuvrability of all nineteen ships in his mind.

His escorts were also struggling to find their feet, not helped by the deteriorating conditions. For the bridge officers and lookouts, it meant hours of concentrating on blurred shapes or dark smudges glimpsed through binoculars. Given the waning visibility, each zig and zag had to be worked out according to the clock. For the flank escorts, this meant running an outward course for a set number of minutes until the convoy was well out of sight, then running back until they met it again, praying they didn't collide with a blacked-out freighter.

At midnight, a coded 'all-ships weather forecast' came through on the wireless from Simon's Town.

Sparks had his pencil and message pad ready, his headphones on, as the Morse bleated in his ears. He ran to the bridge with news his captain would not want to hear: the gale forecast had been upgraded to a storm warning with winds gusting to hurricane force.

CHAPTER 19

Tuesday's dawn broke on an awful sea south of Danger Point, the swell having grown out of all proportion in the night. After consultation with Jack, the convoy commodore dispensed with the idea of resuming daylight zigzagging. Fortunately, there was only one straggler, Puffing Billy, and *Waterberg* was dispatched to chivvy her.

'Can you squeeze a few more revs?'

'I *am* squeezing!' came the Welshman's blunt reply.

Gannet performed an exaggerated dance as she patrolled back and forth across the van of the convoy. Travelling on a more or less easterly course at almost the same speed as the Cape rollers, her rudder had ceased to have much effect. As waves attacked her quarter, *Gannet* would occasionally broach, swinging round onto her beam ends, gunwales under and the heart of every crew member in his mouth.

The freighters lifted their sterns to the swells, baring barnacled bottoms, then slid off their backs with bows pointing at the sky in an extravagant, corkscrewing jig. To Jack, from his position on the seesawing bridge, the convoy's discordant up-and-down motion looked like the pistons of an engine in slow motion. Weeping white water from their scuppers, ships would pause on a crest, then subside with a sighing grace into the ensuing trough, the smaller merchantmen disappearing altogether. None of Jack's charges was in position, each one thrown out of alignment by mountains of water, each reacting to the conditions in ways determined by their vastly different shapes, sizes, engines, cargos and crews. Ungainly and high-sided, they were like zeppelins in a gale, bucking and rearing, their propellers sometimes completely exposed, answering neither helm nor engine. Jack pitied the masters who had to control them.

While the merchantmen lumbered on, conditions aboard the four escorts were even more lively. Jack could see the masts of his flotilla gyrating as they rolled and lunged, throwing sheets of green water over themselves. He rued his bad luck to have to deal with a storm while rounding Agulhas, one of the most treacherous capes in Africa, but was comforted by the knowledge that U-boats would find it almost impossible to attack.

Moving about *Gannet* required the utmost care, judging when to make a dash across the upper deck and when to take cover. Seaman Booysen was standing aft lookout and glanced up, aghast, to find a green monster looming above him, teetering, poised to strike, to trap his ship in the yawing trough, slew her over, capsize her. At the very last instant, *Gannet*'s stern rose to meet it and the giant melted beneath his feet. But some waves came aboard the quarterdeck and a petrified Booysen would hang on to his lifeline for all he was worth as white water boiled up and around his waist.

For the most part, Jack and February were able to read the following seas and *Gannet* managed to ride all but the biggest mountains. Captain and coxswain had learnt that too much speed meant the stern would swing around and threaten a broach; too little speed made a target for the breaking waves that gnashed at their quarterdeck. Somewhere in the narrow margin between, the two sailors found *Gannet*'s place, rolling and side-slipping, but dodging the worst of the blows.

The south-westerly wind pushed against the opposing Agulhas Current piling up outsized waves, the surface of the ocean lashed into white by the fury of the storm. Jack watched as a ship entered a squall, its charcoal outline dissolving as the dubious smudge that was once a freighter became nothing, wiped away by the amoral force of the elements that bore down upon the convoy, and upon him personally, or so it seemed. A little while later, the tumult would mercifully resolve itself back into a thing of steel.

The following seas put tremendous strain on the steering gear of the older merchantmen and many captains prayed that their rudders would hold. By afternoon, the conditions were so imperilling the convoy that the commodore, in consultation with Jack, ordered them to heave to, turning their bows into the wind to ride out the worst of it off Stilbaai. But turning a group of closely packed merchantmen around in such weather was a manoeuvre fraught with peril. Swinging slowly through 180 degrees, each with a different turning circle, some almost out of control as beam seas tried to swamp them, the freighters laboured around.

That evening, they further separated for safety, yet each still tried to hold onto the blue stern-light of a neighbour in the howling wilderness of the dark. Lonely steel sentinels off the southern tip of Africa, they shouldered the Agulhas Bank's dreaded rollers that lumbered out of the darkness, threatening to inundate them.

Tuesday night was terrible. On the open bridges of the whalers, neither oilskins nor sheepskin jackets, mittens or seaboots could keep out the driving rain and spray. Red-eyed lookouts strained to spot their consorts, or the needle of a U-boat's eye, impossibly hidden in the storm. They knew the enemy could escape the torment by diving deep and that their Asdics were unreliable in such weather, but there could be no let-up in their vigilance.

Sub-Lieutenant Robinson had been seasick since the beginning of the gale, yet somehow managed to keep doing his duty, appearing on the bridge ashen faced and occasionally putting his head over the side to lose whatever food he'd tried to keep down. Through a force of will, he saw out his four hours before stumbling below to his bunk and the chance to blot out the misery with sleep. All too soon, he would be shaken for his next trick and it was with the utmost despair that he dragged his body back up the ladder into the howling wind and horizontal rain. Jack was concerned for his lieutenant, but also pleased at the young man's tenacity, his unwillingness to miss a watch and let the others down. The shame of it would be worse than the seasickness, fatigue and desolation he felt.

For Jack, there could be no fixed watch, no four hours in his bunk, for he was carrying the convoy on his shoulders. The crew of *Gannet* had grown to depend on his presence on the bridge. It was not that they didn't trust Van Zyl or Robinson, more that the tall, talismanic figure standing behind the binnacle or sitting in his straight-backed bridge chair had become the dependable, still centre of their world. With a face like a statue, a determined jaw and narrowed eyes staring ahead, their captain appeared resolute, decisive and uncomplaining, and in such times his men had begun to look up to him with a kind of awe. The new hands were also starting to learn what having a Pembroke at the con meant to the rest of the men and to the flotilla.

Throughout the convoy, there was carnage below decks. The crews had little opportunity to dry their sodden clothes and seasickness was rife, particularly among the passengers and troops on the commodore's flagship. Tempers flared and fear continued to build with each hour of rising seas and the certainty that no air cover would be available in such conditions.

Meals had become a trial with food sliding from plates, airborne soup and dishes smashing to the deck; even some seasoned salts were unable to keep their food down and mess decks were awash with vomit. On *Gannet*, Porky had given up serving hot food and resorted to corned-dog sandwiches. The men stumbled to and from meals and watches in a daze of fatigue that dulled their senses. Water cascaded upon the ratings every time the mess-deck hatch was opened and the air in the closed compartment grew foul. Sleep in their broncoing bunks was fitful, legs and arms braced even in slumber lest they be ejected by a rogue wave.

Even the simple act of putting on or taking off clothes had acquired a Herculean dimension. Men struggled to don oilskins in the sharp-edged mess deck as though engaged in a wrestling match, arriving on deck bruised and irritable for their next watch. With so little rest, they had become zombie-like, but the punishment for falling asleep on watch was severe — up to twenty-eight days in detention quarters. Nerves were stretched taut and on a couple of occasions the bosun had to stop scuffles that had broken out over some triviality.

The pitching and rolling was the worst many of the crew had experienced. They couldn't escape the ceaseless pendulum motion and, whether awake or asleep, had to be alive to where in the cycle of the roll they found themselves. If you neglected your balance for even a moment, the roll could set a myriad of booby-traps, making you sit down when you wanted to stand up or throwing you through hatchways and against bulkheads. Furniture came adrift, clothing floated back and forth across the deck. The men were beaten, cut and battered by the onslaught, and worn down by the certainty that nothing would ever, even for a moment, *stay still*.

Jack remained at his post throughout, ever watchful of his seesawing charges that came and went in the mountainous seas. Icy water found its way through all his defences — neck, wrists and boots — and he stood there, soaked to the marrow, ducking as each wave sent curtains of spray over the bridge. His lips were salt cracked, his eyeballs were peeled litchis, but he endured. The soundtrack of his vigil was the roar of the gale, like the combined string and wind instruments of an orchestra holding one interminable note, offset by the sorrowful whining of the signal halyards. Jack watched in awe as seventy-knot gusts screamed through the convoy like ethereal cavalry, tearing water from his eyes and stinging any flesh left bare. 'Don't open your mouths,' he shouted to the lookouts between gusts, 'or your teeth will be dislodged!'

The arrival of dawn brought an easing of conditions and the convoy turned to resume its passage to Durban. Jack happened to glance astern and saw a squall of outlandish proportions and venom bearing down on them. Against the black of the clouds and olive-green of the sea, the squall was white as death, forming a band across the western horizon and approaching at speed.

Jack watched as it caught *Waterberg* and enveloped her: one moment she was there, the next she'd been whited out. The squall tore through the convoy, snuffing out ships. It struck *Gannet* at the same moment as a huge wave which tossed the whaler onto her side in a sickening broach, water boiling over the leeward rail and every man holding on, white-knuckled, for his life.

Gannet stayed hard over for appalling seconds as the ocean poured into her forward mess deck. Then slowly, ponderously, she righted herself, slewing around to face the next wave, before making a full circle using the shield of the ensuing trough before the convoy was upon her.

Full daylight found Jack sweeping his binoculars across the western horizon in search of his charges. The escorts were hard at work rounding up the flock, torn from the convoy's bosom by the previous night's conditions. Everyone was still afloat and accounted for, including the Puffing Billy. The geriatric laggard had kept losing her grip on the tail of the convoy during the night, leaving *Waterberg* to nurse and cajole her back, or remain with her while she regained her breath. Jack could not be angry with her master as he was a first-class sailor and was pushing the old girl only as much as she could bear.

The weather remained foul, but there was a perceptible abating of the storm. Jack prayed for a glimpse of the sun so that Robinson could get a decent sighting before they ran aground on St Francis or Recife, two notorious capes reaching into the Indian Ocean ahead of them. Accurate navigation had proved impossible over the last two days with no stars at night and no midday sun to shoot. Robinson regularly went aft to read the quarterdeck log and relied on dead reckoning to guess their position, but he might as well have been playing 'pin the tail on the donkey'.

Jack climbed gingerly down to his cabin, the old leg injury asserting itself, to try to get a spell of rest. Peeling off his oilskins, he sat down heavily on his cot feeling icy toes squelching in his sea-boots. He dragged them off and tipped out the water, then sat massaging his feet while Fido rubbed her furry frame against his hip. He pulled on a clean pair of sea-boot stockings — oh the impossible luxury of warm, soft, oiled wool on his flesh.

Keeling over, he was asleep within seconds, his back against the bulkhead and knees crooked so that his thighs lay athwartships, preventing his ejection on the roll. Fido chose a neckline position, akin to a motorised stole, but Jack heard nothing of her purring engine, nor felt her paws affectionately kneading his cheek.

Two hours of comatose oblivion was all he allowed himself before returning to the bridge to resume his vigil. A frosty wind slapped his face and stung his eyes as he glanced around: the hooded, gnomic figure bent over the compass binnacle must be Van Zyl; the lookouts were dark statues scanning either bow; *ping, ping, ping* went the Asdic.

'Everyone on station, Number One?' asked Jack as he climbed stiffly into the wooden chair bolted beside the port rail.

'Oh, hello, Captain, didn't see you come up. Aye, looks like it. A couple of wayward chaps, but *Waterberg* and the commodore seem to be on it.'

Sparks appeared on the bridge: 'Urgent signal from SNO, sir. Huff-duff reports enemy chatter ahead of the convoy and suggests a sharp change of course.'

'Thank you, Thomas.' Jack's heart upped its revolutions.

'A wolf pack, sir?' asked Van Zyl, his tone betraying anxiety.

'Perhaps,' muttered Jack, his brow creased. 'Get Bunts up here and let's signal the commodore to turn this lot away. We might be able to give the buggers the slip.'

Once the signals had been made, the convoy lumbered through a turn to the south-southeast, away from danger, all the while maintaining radio silence.

'I wish we had some air cover,' said Van Zyl.

'Conditions are still too bad,' said Jack, pondering his options. He had to decide whether to send an escort to investigate the suspected U-boats, or follow the more prudent course of keeping them close. Offensive lunge, or perimeter defence? Caught in the fog of indecision, he chose the latter.

Over the previous two days, SS *Hibiscus* had developed an appalling roll that threatened her cargo. Now a particularly steep wave swept clean over her decks, unseating one of the barrels of petrol which broke free with a dull booming before being swept overboard. Others threatened to come adrift and there was no option but to leave her column and heave to while her crew tried to lash down the barrels. With deep foreboding, her Canadian captain informed the commodore, his signal flags stiff as bars on the halyard.

'We cannot wait,' came the terse reply from *Sapphire*. 'Good luck.'

Waterberg sidled up to *Hibiscus* and her master appeared on the bridge wing putting both hands aloft in a shrug that suggested the situation was out of his hands.

'How long?' shouted Cowley through the loudhailer.

'Don't know, doing our best!' came the faint cry.

Jack ordered *Waterberg* to remain with the straggler while oilskinned men fought to secure the deck cargo and the convoy steamed over the horizon. The crew of *Hibiscus* fought the chaos as barrels heaved themselves this way and that, trying to break free. Wet, frozen and exhausted, their fingers crushed and hands bleeding, they reeled about the deck like drunkards, the breath torn from them in wheezing rasps, corralling and lashing as though their lives depended on this one task. Some were badly injured, one took a nasty blow to the head and was carried unconscious into the saloon. But after six hours, the barrels were secured and, accompanied by *Waterberg*, the *Hibiscus* made best speed to catch up with the convoy.

By Wednesday evening, the wind had moderated and the hilly seas now passed mercifully under their sterns rather than breaking upon them. Although many ships showed signs of storm damage and looked the worse for wear, the convoy was in relatively good shape. But there was still no rest for Jack. The steady flow of signals, renewed zigzagging, instructions to his three escorts and the chasing of stragglers kept him permanently occupied, but at least it appeared they had given the enemy the slip. Jack looked astern — each ship in position, no one making too much smoke — Durban-bound and all was well. Despite his exhaustion, he took pride in this great oceanic enterprise that his *Gannet* was a part of, was in the vanguard of.

Jack left the bridge carrying a heavy torch to conduct an inspection of his ship, starting in the forward mess where the men had made an attempt to clean up after the storm. The compartment still had a certain bomb-damage air and a whiff of vomit, but Jack ignored it, smiled, chatted to the off-watch and offered words of encouragement.

Next, he went aft, looking in on Porky in the galley and the PO's mess; then he climbed gingerly down into the engine room, nursing his leg, the old wound having started to ache again during his long spells on the bridge. He was struck once more by the urgency of sound and moving parts in McEwan's dungeon. The chief gave him a broad smile and a wink, but was too hard of hearing to catch Jack's words above the din. All seemed in order though, despite the obvious exhaustion of the 'black gang'.

On Thursday morning in brighter weather off Port Alfred, lookout Pickles Brooke spotted a twin-engine aircraft coming in from the north. Bunts made the challenge with his Aldis lamp and received the requisite answer. The Maryland from Port Elizabeth swooped low over *Gannet* dipping its wings and then began to make leisurely loops and figure of eights around the convoy. Marylands had better range than Ansons and were able to loiter for longer periods. When fuel ran low, it was replaced by another to continue providing cover for the convoy.

Puffing Billy was again making too much smoke, the result of straining her engine to keep pace with their increased speed, and the commodore had the signal flags 'Make less smoke' flying once more, although it was redundant as no captain wanted to advertise his position to the Kriegsmarine.

'Can't you stop that smoke!' shouted Cowley through his loudhailer as *Waterberg* drew level.

'Listen here, young raglaw, I make speed with smoke!' called back the captain. 'What do you want of me?'

Cowley didn't respond and *Waterberg* surged ahead, pinging her Asdic warily in every direction.

It had turned into an idyllic spring day of dazzling sunshine and indigo sea. As *Gannet* cut back and forth across the van of the convoy, Jack thought what a fine sight his four grey escorts made, zigzagging around the box of ships, lamps flashing, signal flags streaming and behaving like the well-trained terriers that they were.

In the late afternoon, their winged escort had to return to its Port Elizabeth nest and, as it disappeared over the horizon and the sun slipped towards its own nest, an uneasiness settled over the convoy.

Jack found his muscles perpetually tensed, as though bracing for a strike that could come without warning and from any quarter. He spared a thought for the merchant captains who had to remain on station no matter what, even if the ship ahead or astern was torpedoed. Naked, unarmed, sailing on and praying that their vessel would not be next. At least escorts had the consolation of action, manoeuvrability and the means to defend themselves.

As dusk action stations were sounded, Jack looked at the tanker in the middle of the central column, loaded deep with benzene, and a shudder ran through him: he knew the horror of a flaming sea and the living faggots of a tanker crew.

'Do you see anything strange about all those bonfires on the shore, Number One?' asked Jack as they cruised along the East London coast.

'No, sir, not especially.'

'It might be coincidence but there are nineteen fires and we are nineteen ships.'

'Very odd, sir.'

'Yes, well, there's nothing we can do about it.'

CHAPTER 20

Later on Thursday night, as the convoy sailed past Morgan's Bay, a lookout on *Waterberg* thought he glimpsed the conning tower of a tailing U-boat. The unconfirmed sighting was immediately reported to *Gannet*, leading Jack to surmise that German headquarters might have been alerted and a wolf pack could already be homing in on his flock.

'Number One, warn the crew that action stations are likely during the night,' said Jack. 'I want AB Potgieter ready to take over if we make contact. We'll need our best ears on the Asdic.'

On the quarterdeck, PO Combrink rechecked his depth-charge equipment after the shake-up of the storm. February was on standby to take the wheel, while deep in *Gannet*'s bowels, Chief McEwan was ready to assume charge of the engine the moment alarm bells sounded. Whether or not contact was made, no one was going to get much sleep. They did not have long to wait.

'Hello *Gannet*, hello *Gannet*, this is *Belle*, distant echo, bearing three-one-five,' Alstad's voice crackled over the radio. 'Request permission to investigate.'

Belle was the port-wing ship and itching to engage, but could Jack afford to let her go and weaken the screen? Perhaps it wasn't a U-boat, or maybe it was a decoy to lure his escorts away. Four ships were barely enough to give the convoy all-round protection: remove one and you opened a hole for the enemy to exploit. But the chance of a kill... Yes or no to Alstad? And what was the U-boat, if it was a U-boat, doing? Was her captain using his greater speed to get ahead of them and let the targets come to him? If only Alstad could force him to dive, and the convoy turned ninety degrees to starboard, it might buy them enough time to slip away. This was the moment for Jack to make a quick decision, but he was in two minds.

The options gnawed at him a while longer, then he picked up the RT phone and said: 'Hello *Belle*, *Gannet* here, permission granted.' Over to port, he could just make out *Belle* peeling away from the convoy, a wave detonating on her bridge as she raced towards the contact. The radio crackled again. 'Hello *Gannet*, *Waterberg* here, permission to join *Belle*?' came the voice of Cowley from astern of the convoy.

'Permission denied. *Waterberg* to close up port screen.' Jack's intonation was flat and dispassionate, pronouncing each word clearly. His orders must be served cold, with no need for repetition or explanation, no room for interpretation. 'Sound action stations if you please, Number One.'

Alarm bells jangled throughout *Gannet* as men grabbed lifebelts and tin hats and ran to their stations.

The convoy steamed away from the receding *Belle*, each minute that passed leaving them increasingly vulnerable. After half an hour, Jack radioed Alstad: '*Gannet* to *Belle*, any luck?'

'Negative, sir.'

Jack's mind was racing: whale, school of fish, layer of cold water to offer hiding?

'I'd like to keep trying, sir.'

'All right, *Belle*, a little longer.'

If he allowed Alstad more leash to prolong the hunt into daylight, and the air and batteries of the U-boat (if it was a U-boat) became exhausted, and aircraft were added to the mix, and the enemy were forced to surface… But no, O'Reilly had stressed defence over offence: he couldn't afford to be without an escort for that long.

'*Belle* to rejoin convoy and take up previous station. *Waterberg* to resume tail escort.'

The moon was a powerful searchlight on high and the ocean aglitter with stars — a perfect night for the hunters. Jack was practically asleep on his feet, the monotonous pinging of the Asdic dipping and rising like the call of a deep-sea creature. He had barely left the bridge since Cape Town, save for a few hours of fully dressed, comatose sleep. Not for one moment had there been any lessening of the strain. He was ravenous, but the notion of food was somehow alien, as though belonging to another world. The idea of a plate of bacon, eggs and toast both stimulated and sickened him.

As if anticipating his thoughts, Hendricks appeared at his shoulder. 'Some more kye to lift yer spirits, sir,' he said, handing Jack a steaming mug of cocoa, 'and I added a drop of sauce to keep you on the ball.'

'Thank you, Hendricks, just the ticket.'

Through waves of fatigue, Jack's mind kept returning to an image of Clara, climbing the mountain in a summer dress. She wore an air of lightness, juxtaposed with the overwhelming leadenness that weighed him down. He wanted to hold onto this talismanic vision of her, but it took him away from the press of the moment, the fight at hand and its latent brutality.

Jack was conscious of an unnameable sadness that was stalking him with as much power and deadliness as a U-boat. He did not know where it came from, what it meant, exactly, and how to get rid of it, but the night's inky shadows and the threat of the deep had him in their grip, threatening to drag him under. He craved action to shake himself free. He craved Clara.

The rest of the men of *Gannet* were also out on their feet, drained by the storm, by pent-up adrenalin, sleeplessness and the perpetual, gnawing tension.

'From flag, sir, periscope spotted!' called out Bunts.

Sapphire's masthead lookout had spied the fleeting feather of a periscope three points on the starboard bow. The officer of the watch had immediately called the captain and roused Commodore Jones, who arrived on the bridge moments later with his uniform jacket over his pyjamas. The periscope had disappeared, but the alarm had been sounded and the escort leader alerted.

Jack leaned over AB Potgieter, willing the young operator to offer him an echo. Responsibility for the whole convoy now seemed to rest on the shoulders of this lanky, scruffy teenager whose ears were currently their most important weapon. His training in False Bay had brought him to the point where he could discern the variations in pitch that denoted a submarine changing speed and course, her bearing and range. But until now, he had not heard the sound of an enemy propeller. Shoulders tensed, Potgieter slowly turned his dial, probing the deep with his pings.

Langeberg was the first to pick up an echo and requested permission to investigate, thrusting Jack back onto dilemma's horns: should he lunge at the U-boat with one or even two escorts, thus weakening the screen and laying the convoy open to attack? *But the chance of a kill.* There was also the morale of the merchantmen to think about if they saw escorts steaming away on what might be a wild-goose chase. Knowing that his whalers' top speed was, at best, equivalent to that of a surfaced U-boat, he knew that the enemy could flee on the surface, drawing the pursuers far from the convoy while other wolves sneaked in through the open door. All aspects weighed and considered, despite his offensive inclination, and with O'Reilly's injunction ringing in his ears, Jack again chose compromise: dispatch one hunter.

'Hello *Langeberg*, permission granted.'

Jack positioned *Gannet* just ahead of the starboard bow of the convoy, instructing *Belle* to move to the port bow, while *Langeberg* raced off to investigate the contact. He was standing on the bridge scanning the merchantmen with his binoculars when two white rockets arced into the air above the port column, followed by a blinding flash and the sound of thunder. It took him a moment to realise that one of the freighters had been hit. His worst fear had been realised and the gap he'd created by releasing *Langeberg* had been devastatingly exploited. He noticed the winking of a signal from *Sapphire* and the rattle of the shutters on Bunts's hooded blue lamp acknowledging it.

'Message from Commodore, sir, general alarm,' said Leading Seaman Gilbert.

'Very well.' Jack's mind went blank and his body trembled: the howl of a gull-winged Stuka, bomb pregnant, clad in the vestments of death, diving towards him; climbing with leaden legs down the ladder into his shell, hard-hatted, safety-seeking, his mind momentarily slipped of its moorings to drift upon the bossing tide, *Havoc* pointing the shame of her bows at the sky, the befouling stench of oil and blackened survivors all about him clinging, drowning, dying… *Think, act!*

'Sir?' Van Zyl was looking at his captain, desperation etched on his face. 'Sir!'

Jack ran a hand across his eyes, then said as firmly as his voice would allow: 'Sound action stations, Number One, and get PO February on the helm.'

'He's already there, sir.'

'Good. Good.'

Star shells, snowflakes and rockets soared over the convoy like a grotesque fireworks display, Jack's imagination replacing the ships with clay targets in a shooting gallery.

'Sparks, inform Commander-in-Chief South Atlantic and Simon's Town that we're under U-boat attack,' he said into the pipe, trying, despite his racing mind, to keep his voice as deadpan as possible. '*Pearlvale* has been hit, Robinson to provide coordinates, escort disposition and sea state.'

The torpedo had struck the freighter on her port side forward, blasting a gash in her number-one hold big enough to drive a London bus. A hundred tons of cargo erupted from the hold and rained down on the ship and surrounding sea; derricks, beams and hatches were reduced to a twisted mess of steel. A second torpedo struck amidships and broke *Pearlvale*'s back, the two halves jack-knifing before she slipped beneath the waves, her smoking superstructure disappearing in a welter of hissing and boiling, followed by large, oily bubbles rising to the surface.

'*Belle* to *Gannet*, lookouts have spotted a faint object on my port bow moving west, suspected U-boat. Permission to attack.'

Jack was once again torn. Should he engage the U-boat on the port side of the convoy, allowing *Belle* to have one sharp crack, forcing her to dive and slow her down? Or deny *Belle*, recall *Langeberg*, and resort to pure defence?

'*Gannet* to *Belle*, negative. Maintain your position on the port screen but adjust according to the threat.' Jack's hands were tied. '*Gannet* to *Langeberg*, any luck?' His mind was being pulled in all directions, its elastic stretched to breaking point.

'We're attacking a strong contact,' said Fourie.

'Abort and rejoin the convoy.'

'Sir?'

'Repeat: abort and rejoin.'

'Aye aye, sir.' Fourie's tone was deadpan but failed to hide his disappointment.

Meanwhile the disaster of the torpedoed freighter was playing out far in the convoy's wake with *Waterberg* detached to conduct the rescue.

'*Gannet* to *Waterberg*, as soon as you've secured survivors, return to convoy at best speed.'

Just then, in another perverse incarnation of Guy Fawkes, the night was lit by star shells and rockets fired at the furthest point from *Gannet* on the convoy's vast chess board.

Jack slammed the rail with his fist, realising that a U-boat had broken through the feeble screen — weakened by his decisions — and was among the merchantmen, a fox in the hen coop. Brilliant white lights, suspended by their parachutes, drifted festively down as two columns of water rose from the flank of another merchantman, accompanied by the rumble of the double strike. Jack gritted his teeth until his jaw hurt.

In the bowels of *Gannet*, the chief and his stokers heard the explosions and instantly the telegraph beside them rang for full ahead. Everyone in the engine room knew its meaning, and that a torpedo might be knifing towards them at that very moment.

Langeberg was still a few miles adrift, so *Gannet* would have to attend to the latest casualty. 'Hard a-starboard!' said Jack as they turned into the oncoming sea and took a wave over the starboard bow, the wall of water exploding on the gun shield and swamping the foredeck. The whaler shouldered it off and straightened for the next wave. Now Jack could see the wounded freighter, *Gaasterdal*, slowing down and edging out of the starboard column, and the vessel astern of her altering course to avoid collision.

Gannet raced towards the lead ship in the starboard column, passing within a hundred yards on a reciprocal course and Jack glanced at her rusty outline dipping a straight prow into the swell. He couldn't remember her name. She was brown and worn, slow and ponderous, but it was ships like her, flying the Red Duster, that were holding the line against Hitler and he felt a momentary surge of pride. In a flash, she'd been swallowed by the night.

Following Jack's prearranged plan, escorts and merchantmen were sending fireworks of every kind into the sky, trying to illuminate all the possible attack and escape routes of surfaced U-boats. But could he risk stopping *Gannet* to pick up survivors with the enemy among them? Should he jeopardise the lives of his own crew for the sake of saving a few more? The decision was his alone and the equation played itself over in his mind, but without result, as they approached the stricken ship.

Another explosion in one of *Gaasterdal*'s holds sent a shock wave over *Gannet*, then the freighter began to sink, slowly and gracefully at first, as though tired of her work.

'There's no time to stop and lower a boat, not with Jerry about. As she's settling on an even keel, I intend to go alongside to take off survivors, Number One.'

'Which side, sir?'

'Port, to shield us from that sub if she's still lurking.'

'It won't do our paintwork any good.'

'Relatively calm sea, worth a go. We haven't got time to let them sort out lifeboats. Bunts, ask her if she's carrying any explosives or hazardous material. We don't want to become part of the conflagration while alongside.'

LS Gilbert flashed the signal, but there was no reply. *Gannet* closed with *Gaasterdal*'s quarter and stopped, her prow almost touching the Dutchman. Survivors would have to jump from the stricken vessel's stern to the forecastle of the whaler, whose bows now crashed agonisingly against the merchant's quarterdeck and figures began leaping.

Jack heard cries in Dutch and saw anxious faces lit by flames that licked around the superstructure as sailors waited for the right moment to jump. The rise and fall of the two ships seldom coincided and the distance from crest to trough was more than twenty feet. The speed with which the seesawing decks passed each other added to the peril and some of the jumpers were injured. One sailor nonchalantly traversed a two-foot gap as though stepping into an elevator, another fell soundlessly to his death between the scything hulls.

Jack looked up to see a flash from the returning *Langeberg*, followed by a bang, then a star shell illuminating the whaler and a vanishing conning tower in the middle distance. Fourie was closer than expected, the U-boat even closer: Jack had briefly lost touch with the chessboard.

'Full astern!' he shouted, gritting his teeth and trying to ignore the desperate cries from *Gaasterdal*'s quarter. The enemy must have been stalking them during the rescue and he was lucky *Langeberg* had spotted the danger. 'Anything on Asdic, Number One?'

His first lieutenant was down to Potgieter and back on the bridge in a matter of seconds. 'Yes sir, one echo, very faint on our port beam,' said Van Zyl.

'My God, two of them. They nearly caught us with our trousers down. Tell Sparks to radio *Gaasterdal*'s position to SNO and tell the Port Elizabeth crash boats to get here at first light for the last survivors.'

Van Zyl could see the cost of those words etched on his captain's face as *Gannet* slewed round to face the enemy.

'There, sir!' shouted Booysen, pointing to the small black fin.

'Enemy bearing broad on the starboard bow, range three thousand yards,' said Van Zyl.

'Open fire!' Jack shouted and the twelve-pounder belched a tongue of flame to the sound of a loud crack.

Jack was momentarily blinded by the flash and when his vision returned, he saw the spout, well short of the conning tower. He became aware of the loud tonking of *Gannet*'s pom-pom as scarlet tracer streaked across the wave tops to pepper the sea ahead of the U-boat. But the enemy remained elusive, well trimmed down and moving away at speed. Another crash from the twelve-pounder and a saltwater column rose beside the conning tower. *That's much better.* Then, as if a magic trick, the enemy vanished in a frothing welter of white water.

'Anything on Asdic?'

'Not yet, sir.'

Jack's eye marked the position of the foamy swirl as *Gannet* raced in to lay her eggs. The U-boat would be fleeing at a speed of up to seven knots in any direction and depth from that spot. Each moment that passed, the concentric circles of possible escape increased; within a minute it would be a square mile whose radius required a three-square-mile search and all the while the convoy would be steaming away over the horizon. He imagined the radiating circles, like those of a pebble dropped in a pond, each minute diminishing his chances.

Jack leaned out of the bridge wing and looked aft where he could see the sailors at battle stations beside the depth-charge throwers. To join the hunt, to hit back, the primal ache for revenge, for what had just been done to the merchant sailors

... they all felt it. First *Gannet* and then *Langeberg* ran over the U-boat's track and dropped a pattern each — white fireballs lighting the deep with preternatural fireworks.

'Anything yet, Potgieter?' he called down to the Asdic operator.

'Nothing sir, just heavy interference.'

Jack knew he had to break off the hunt and get back to the imperilled convoy with all dispatch. 'Damn and blast!' There was spittle on his lips as he tried to control his rage.

Dawn broke over a diminished convoy, sailing in tight formation south of Coffee Bay. Jack was exhausted, his feet were concrete blocks, his calves and thighs had barely the strength to raise his legs. But he had to keep thinking — coldly, rationally, methodically — making sure he did everything possible to protect the remaining ships. He had to ignore the fatigue that prowled like a circling U-boat, ready to torpedo his judgement at the critical moment. *Stay focused, stay alive to all threats, all possibilities.*

'You have to get some rest, Number One,' he said as a misshapen sun rose out of the ocean.

'What about you, sir?' Van Zyl said, looking at his captain's ashen face and red-rimmed eyes.

'I'll sleep in Durban. *Gannet* needs one of us to be fresh and thinking straight for the next round and that better be you. Get something to eat as well. Go on, Number One.'

Van Zyl was too spent to protest and made his way gingerly down the ladder.

Throughout the warm spring day, they sailed close inshore along the Wild Coast taking advantage of the counter current and reassured by the constant drone of air cover. Jack hoped they had outrun the U-boats in the night and, if not, the circling Ansons would keep them submerged, blind and too slow to retain contact. But the boats of Gruppe Savanne had headed far out to sea and easily maintained their pursuit by following the smoke trails.

At sunset, the aircraft returned to Durban and Jack felt a familiar foreboding. To add to his worries, engine trouble in two freighters meant the convoy was forced to reduce speed. At dusk, a lookout on *Langeberg* spotted a distant U-boat, trimmed down and approaching from the east. It was time for decisions once again. *Waterberg* or *Gannet* could join *Langeberg* and run down on the spot where the enemy dived, but it would draw escorts away from the convoy just as darkness fell.

Jack opted to release only *Langeberg* and watched as Fourie eked every last revolution from his engine as he raced to intercept, opening fire with his twelve-pounder as he went. The U-boat captain made a sharp about turn and was lost in the gathering gloom, using his superior speed to outrun the slowest of the four whalers. Realising the chase was fruitless, Jack recalled *Langeberg*, despite the almost audible champing of Fourie's bit over the RT.

Moments later, *Waterberg* reported a tiny shape trailing the convoy. Jack sensed he was being goaded into making a bold lunge, but nonetheless authorised a short, sharp attack by Cowley to force their shadower under. Through his binoculars Jack could just make out columns of water in the gloom far astern of the convoy, but not the sparkle and momentary glow that denoted a hit ... and now the speck was gone, back into the lair of the deep. *Waterberg* was duly recalled. *Thrust-parry, thrust-parry, when would it end?*

Boom!

Jack spun around, appalled to see a white tower climbing from the ammunition ship, the most valuable, and dangerous, vessel in the convoy.

CHAPTER 21

Gannet was at the port end of her zigzag and the closest escort to the wounded *City of Salisbury* which had begun to slide out of line just astern of the commodore's flagship. Jack swung *Gannet* through 180 degrees, narrowly crossing the path of a merchantman, treating the whaler like the greyhound she wasn't. Many ships were out of station and it was a headlong rush into uncertainty as dark shapes loomed and veered around the escort. Like dodgem cars at the Oxford fairground, thought Jack, as he conned *Gannet* through the white-lipped throng, knifing across the bows of one, shaving past the stern of another.

'Vessel on the starboard beam, sir!' The lookout's voice was shrill with fear.

Jack turned to see the bows of a merchantman rearing to strike. Booysen had obviously been distracted by the grotesque son et lumière of the ammunition ship and spotted the danger too late.

February was already spinning the wheel as Jack bellowed: 'Hard a-starboard!'

The freighter's bows rose like a monstrous cleaver, scything towards *Gannet*, poised to slice her in two.

Jack watched as excruciating seconds stretched the possibilities of time. At the last instant, his depth-charge-packed stern slewed out of the way and was elbowed aside by the bow wave. The merchantman's flank streaked by and he looked up to see the face of her master, staring down at him incredulously from a heavenly perch on the bridge wing. In a matter of seconds, she was gone, swallowed back down the throat of the night as *Gannet* stumbled across her agitated wake. Now came rockets and gunfire from the port inner column. Jack could not worry about that just yet: Alstad would have to handle that threat on his own.

The first torpedo had struck the stern of the *City of Salisbury* and blown off her screw, killing nine men instantly and trapping fifteen others who were freed by one of her officers who broke open a skylight. The engine room was slowly flooding through the shaft tunnel and it looked as though the ship would have to be abandoned. Slowing as he approached, Jack wondered whether it might be possible to tow her to Durban, or at least secure the wounded ship until dawn when a salvage tug might reach her.

Just then, a second torpedo struck the *City of Salisbury* and she erupted, sending a ball of fire hundreds of feet into the sky and illuminating the entire convoy with the brilliance of daylight. The explosion was clearly heard by the lighthouse keeper at Port St Johns, more than fifty miles away. Blazing woodwork, white-hot chunks of metal, steel plates like sheets of paper and dismembered body parts rained down on the sea around *Gannet*. Jack stood aghast: the ammunition ship had been obliterated.

Miraculously, some of her crew who had gathered near the stern had been blown into the water and survived. *Gannet* edged closer, searching for human shapes among the debris. The lights of Mae Wests flickered on the water, but precious few offered signs of life.

'Side netting, Number One, quick as you can!' said Jack, conscious of the enemy's presence but unwilling to abandon these men.

Gannet stopped her engine and an eerie silence descended as swimmers struck out for the whaler and lines were thrown to assist the wounded. The rescuers found it desperately hard to land survivors who were weak, trembling from shock and coated in oil.

All the while *Gannet* lay helpless, a sitting duck lit by a flaming sea. Fear clawed at Jack. He felt certain they were snared in a periscope's sights and a tin fish was about to pierce *Gannet*'s skin. What must the chief and his stokers be feeling, confined to the engine room with almost no chance of escape? How long should he risk his ship before giving up, knowing that there were probably still survivors out there, watching him go, watching him rob them of their last chance, left to the mercy of the ocean and the sharks?

Jack lifted the loudhailer and called, 'How much longer, Number One?'

'Just a few minutes, sir!' Van Zyl shouted from the waist. 'A couple of swimmers coming up aft. We've got a man in the water helping him. And a Labrador!'

'What the hell?'

'Ship's dog, sir, coming aboard with the men.'

'We don't bloody well have time for pets, Number One!'

'Yes, we do, sir!' Van Zyl was smiling uncertainly up at his captain.

Jack was about to berate him, then said: 'Of course, Jannie, bring the hound aboard, but for God's sake, hurry up.'

The dog's weak barking echoed from the quarterdeck, then came Van Zyl's cry of 'All aboard, sir!'

The ensuing throb of *Gannet*'s engine was the sound of pure relief as she pulled away from the burning debris into the safety of darkness, her speed increasing as she aimed northeast in pursuit of the convoy.

Gannet's Asdic operator picked up a contact and called out: 'Strong echo bearing four-five degrees, sir! Approximately 2,000 yards, moving east to west.'

'What's your interpretation, Potgieter?' asked Jack.

'Very positive, sir, it's a submarine.'

'All right then, let's go and get the bastard.'

Gannet increased revolutions and raced into the attack, her prow carving tall, white bow waves, her white ensign stiff and quivering from the mizzenmast.

Jack bent to the voicepipe and said, 'Sparks, make to flag: "Have strong echo, probable U-boat, am attacking. Convoy to alter course ninety degrees starboard for six miles, then resume present course."'

All was quiet on the bridge, save for the pulse of the Asdic and its thrilling echo. Jack aimed his ship ahead of the target, the way a hunter leads a pheasant with his gun, as the interval between each ping and its echo narrowed. Closer.

'Are you ready, Guns?' said Jack into the adjacent voicepipe.

'Affirmative, sir,' came the thick Afrikaans accent of PO Combrink from the quarterdeck.

Gannet passed into the Asdic's shadow and Jack ordered twenty degrees to port, then, at Potgieter's prompting, he called, 'Fire one!'

Seaman Rademan yanked down on the green lever to drop the first charge from the starboard stern rack. Jack could just make out a faint rattle and splash as the canister tumbled into the sea.

'Fire two!'

The red lever was pulled and the port-side rack dropped its load.

'Fire three and four!'

Rademan pushed two buttons above the levers and the throwers coughed loudly, sending depth charges high into the air on either side of *Gannet*.

'Fire five and six!'

Another two canisters rolled off the stern to complete a full pattern as the sea began to erupt, *Gannet* bucking and trembling to the blows. Again and again, the ocean was lit from below before erupting in great, phosphorescent geysers.

Jack opened the distance between himself and the target so the Asdic could find her again, then carved around, searching for the echo he craved, hoping to renew the attack. More sea fire, more forcing water into inverted pyramids, more ponderous subsidence. Jack stared unblinkingly astern, willing a sign, a chunk of German debris, anything to reward his labour. But the U-boat had, it seemed, found sanctuary beneath the convoy and was lost in the propeller din, no doubt awaiting the right moment to rise and strike again.

'Torpedo to starboard!' shrieked Booysen from *Gannet*'s bridge wing.

'Full ahead! Hard a-starboard!' called out Jack, instinctively wanting to comb the wake and present his narrow bows to the projectile. Now he saw it, a streak of bubbles powering towards them, etched in the face of a swell. *Gannet* was not coming round fast enough and the torpedo would strike somewhere aft. Jack clenched the rail, fingernails biting into the wood, bracing for the hit. His mind pictured a Stuka falling out of the sun and the banshee wailing as his old ship tried to evade her fate.

'Straighten, February.' Jack was hoarse. 'Do you see it?'

'Aye, sir, got it,' came the coxswain's baritone voice.

The torpedo rose on a crest and almost broke surface, but the moment before it struck their quarter, a swell nudged the whaler over a little more and the eel slipped past their stern with feet to spare. But the torpedo was not done and raced on: perhaps *Gannet* had never been its target.

The explosion ripped the stern off SS *Karachi* in a powerful detonation. Jack watched her crab out of line and pictured hundreds of tons of seawater gushing into the hole, smashing open watertight doors and inundating the engine room.

Karachi's bows reared up, pointing skyward, buoyed by trapped air, before the skyscraper of steel arrowed into the deep. A few survivors dotted the sea around the monstrous grave.

As *Langeberg* moved in to the rescue, Jack reported the worsening situation to SNO Simon's Town, asking for orders and wanting to know whether he should turn the convoy back to East London or press on for Durban.

'Distressed by news,' came O'Reilly's reply. 'Imperative maintain course. Support from Durban will be dispatched. Best wishes to Commodore Jones.'

Jack was close to despair: the escorts had no Asdic contacts but the U-boats remained like barnacles, probably loitering just out of sight on the surface ... or directly beneath them amid the convoy's noise. He craved daylight like a burning thirst.

Wracking his exhausted brain, he tried to think of some way to prevent the loss of more ships and resorted to ordering the escorts to race back and forth across their quadrants, dropping the occasional depth charge and keeping the sharpest lookout for tell-tale wakes. Although the sea was relatively calm and the night bejewelled, the waters off the coast of southern Natal were alive with shoals of fish, sending back echoes that had to be listened to and tested in case they were fanged and German.

To no avail. The torpedo struck *Sapphire* amidships and Jack felt the shock on *Gannet* as the explosion tore open the night and sent a sheet of flame climbing into the sky. Panicked voices echoed across the water as passengers, troops and crew scrambled to their lifeboat stations and 'Abandon ship!' was repeated over and over on the PA system. The boat deck was a scene of pandemonium conducted in a host of different languages as sailors cast loose the lanyards that secured the lifeboat covers and manned the davits.

Gannet, *Waterberg* and *Belle* closed with the liner, while *Langeberg* dropped deterrent depth charges down the convoy's vulnerable left flank. At last, some lifeboats began to descend, passing the riveted plates of the ship's side like open-air elevators. One set of falls jammed in the sheave, then snapped and the lifeboat tipped out its passengers who plummeted to the water far below.

Sapphire was listing more severely, some out-slung lifeboats almost touching the water, and Jack could see figures sliding down the deck, struggling to maintain their grip. He watched anxiously as a sailor hacked at the belly band securing his packed lifeboat to the falls and managed to push his little craft away from a davit reaching down to crush them. Thankfully oars quickly materialised and they pulled free like a disjointed insect — the last lifeboat to get away.

There came a great hissing and roaring as imprisoned air burst from the hull and the liner slowly dipped beneath the waves. The oil and scum on the water eerily reflected the moonlight as dozens of survivors crammed the rafts and lifeboats, and countless more floated in their lifejackets awaiting rescue. The sea was littered with corpses, their lifelike bobbing on the easy swell raising the hopes of the rescuers until a searchlight revealed the truth. Jack focused on the task at hand and the position of every ship, trying to ignore the distant cries for help from the darkness, pleading voices that could be mistaken for the keening of the wind. At the edge of his consciousness lay the stricken *Havoc*, a steeply tilted deck and the unearthly howling of the Valkyries.

The three whalers moved slowly through the wreckage. Weighed down by oil-soaked clothes, many survivors were too weak to pull themselves aboard, their arms too slippery to be lifted. Rescuers climbed down into the netting to help them over the gunwale and onto the waist, the badly wounded being taken to the warmth and relative comfort of the messes.

Decks were soon covered in a thin film of blood and oil coughed up from poisoned stomachs. A young girl was plucked from the waves by Pickles and Booysen, but died within minutes, her long blonde hair curling across the deck.

The whalers' decks had turned into slums: some survivors lay wounded, some hugged meagre possessions to their chests, others stared vacantly into space, but there was always a smile or joke to reveal humanity amid the pathos.

However, there were still hundreds in the water. Jack and Robinson bent over the chart table, trying to work out how far and how widely dispersed survivors would drift in the strong current, while on deck all eyes continued to strain against the dark, searching for signs of life, everyone conscious that time was running out.

Jack knew that his first responsibility was to the convoy and after half an hour, he pulled the plug on *Gannet*'s search and hastened back to shepherd his charges on the last leg to Durban. There was not a heart on his ship that was not torn by the necessity of leaving while so many were still in the water.

Thankfully help, in the shape of two RN destroyers, was already on its way from Durban to join *Waterberg* and *Belle* with the final stages of the rescue. In the early hours of Saturday morning, the pair swept past the convoy at thirty knots, their enormous bow waves and dark, slender frames looking angelic to Jack.

CHAPTER 22

Indian Ocean dawn. From the east came an easing of the darkness, the horizon assuming a harder outline, the ships slowly taking shape. Jack could begin to read the expressions of the bridge party: exhausted, grey faces. It had been the longest night of his life and although he was not a religious man, this particularly hard-won dawn filled him with profound relief and sorrow, but also indefinable gratitude.

Van Zyl stepped onto the bridge to take over the watch from Robinson and all three officers said good morning to each other in a formal and, to Jack's ear, heartfelt manner. They had somehow lasted out this night of long knives and arrived at the portal of the day. They had survived where so many had not.

Jack normally sounded action stations at first light, but in this case his crew had already been at their posts for countless hours. He would not, dared not, stand them down just yet. The sea grew brighter, adopting a pearlescent glow, and the air warmed as a friendly fireball lifted off the horizon … and here was Hendricks bearing a steaming mug of tea, as always sweetened with too many sugars.

Soon after sunrise, an Anson arrived to accompany the convoy and a Fleet Air Arm Walrus passed them to cover the rescue ships further south. Jack looked astern at the battered merchantmen that continued to follow him like obedient sheep, and felt once more the deadweight of responsibility that seemed to merge with the heaviness of his own body, weighed down with fatigue and strain. When last had he eaten a proper meal? As far as he could recall, he'd had nothing but sandwiches and hot drinks since Cape Town. And how long had February been at the wheel: could it be days? But his coxswain was made of other stuff — indestructible, indefatigable — the still centre of HMSAS *Southern Gannet*.

An air of peace hung about the convoy as they closed with Durban, but also a pall of grief for the good ships and good men they had lost. Jack thought of the hundreds of miles they had covered, of the wreckage and corpses they'd left in their straggling wake. It had been a devastating week and the crews of *Gannet* and her three sisters had been pushed to the limit, each sailor keyed up for the jangle of alarm bells that might mean sudden — or slow — death. Far below Jack's feet, Chief McEwan and his stokers, blind to the world above, had toiled at their posts, never knowing the proximity of the end. He felt a surge of affection for the old Scot in his cave, nursing his beloved engines, ensuring a steady feed of oil, watching over its pumps and glands, and being a father to his gang.

For now, the danger had almost passed. Jack watched as a pair of Durban minesweepers came huffing towards them across a glassy sea. A pod of bottlenose dolphins joined *Gannet*, riding her bow wave and adjacent swells, leaping from the crests and twisting in the air, effortlessly keeping pace with the whale catcher. Chief McEwan emerged on deck in his grease-stained overalls, a ball of cotton-waste absentmindedly in hand and a pencil behind his ear. As he leant against the rail watching the dolphins at play and the fair green hills of Natal rolling closer, Jack could faintly make out the words he sang to himself:

'Ay when you're sailing up the Clyde, sailing up the Clyde,

Back to Bonnie Scotland where the auld folk bide,

There's a lump comes in your throat and a tear ye cannie hide,

And ye're rolling back tae Scotland an yir ain fireside.'

Approaching the Bluff, the convoy narrowed its formation into pairs and Jack sailed *Gannet* up the middle to bid farewell. To his relief, Puffing Billy had managed to cling onto the tail of the convoy and somehow avoided being sent to the bottom. Jack watched as her elderly captain stepped onto the bridge wing and tipped his bowler hat. As they surged past, he noticed the signal flags on her yardarm: 'Thank you, Jack.'

Now that the convoy was safe, he felt only admiration for these freighters and their crews that formed the backbone of the Empire's war effort. Although he'd been frustrated beyond measure by those who could not hold station, could not keep up and vented more smoke than Mount Etna, he'd grown to respect these doughty ships. At this critical time in the war, U-boats were sinking more than one merchantman a day and yet there was never any lack of men to sail them. No ship in all the British Empire ever remained in port because she could not find enough crew; quite the opposite.

Jack felt a lump in his throat as he thought of the many merchant sailors who'd already died in their thousands, and how many more would perish before the race was run. These were not soldiers, but their bravery never faltered, and were it not for their tenacity and good seamanship, the war would be lost. Nominally, Jack had been their warden for the past five days, but in a deeper sense they were equals and he felt only brotherly respect for the masters and men of these rust-stained slabs of steel.

'*Efcharistó polý*, thank you, *Gannet*!' came the cry from the Greek captain on *Pavlos*, his battered cap held aloft.

Jack saluted and smiled, a weary smile full of pride and regret.

They reached the harbour entrance and *Gannet* let out three long blasts from her horn, taken up by each ship in the convoy. It was a mournful sound that echoed the loss of those who had not survived Convoy CD.03, who had died terrible deaths but whose courage lived on, as indestructible as the ocean herself. *Gannet* crossed the bar and idled across the glassy water of the channel to her berth at Maydon Wharf. As soon as mooring lines were secured, hospital orderlies hastened aboard with stretchers to take off the wounded.

When Jack gave the order 'finished with main engine', he let out a prolonged sigh that reflected the feeling that he'd aged as many years as the days they'd spent at sea. The voyage had sapped him of almost every ounce of endurance, but there had been plenty of lessons too. The officers and men of his flotilla had done everything that could be asked of them; it was his own decision making that had fallen short. The escorts had failed in their duty and he knew there would be much agonising over how many lives might have been saved with a different set of actions and reactions.

On a happier note, the Labrador — dubbed 'Bagheera' by the crew — had taken a liking to *Gannet* and her humans and was a welcome addition until a Durban home could be found for him. After Porky and Hendricks had rubbed the dog down with paraffin to remove the oil, it turned out he was not in fact black, but an attractive chocolate colour. When Jack finally made it to his cabin to get some rest, he discovered Fido and Bagheera curled up in yin-yang bliss on his cot.

'How is this even possible?' he called to his steward. 'Fido *hates* dogs.'

'Apparently, it's not a blanket hatred, sir. I'll remove the pair immediately.'

'Oh, never mind, I'll try to work around them. Do you think this means she'll tolerate Just Nuisance?'

'No, sir, different category altogether. She's just being hospitable because of Bagheera's trauma and all. It's not a new leaf being turned on the canine front, so to speak.'

'I see, thank you, Hendricks.'

At last, *Gannet*'s captain was able to wallow in a hot bath, stretch out on (part of) his cot, enjoy the hedonistic luxury of pyjamas, and then sleep — almost twenty-four hours of proper, blissful, uninterrupted sleep.

Jack woke the following afternoon to the smell of roasting meat. Porky was making up for so many days unable to provide decent meals and every now and then his oven door would swing open, allowing the aroma to waft from the galley. Sweat poured from him in the sticky Durban heat, but nothing would stop him producing proper slap-up nosh for 'his lads'. *Gannet*'s sailors, who had themselves slept long and deep, began to make the mess decks shipshape again, clearing away the debris of the voyage and of the many extra passengers they'd acquired.

That evening, Jack gathered Van Zyl and his three captains around the polished table in *Gannet*'s tiny wardroom. There was the clinking of glasses and the chance to be together, talk, console each other and laugh once more. Even as he sat enjoying the slow working of the gin, his mind kept slipping back to the endless hours on the bridge — cold and wet, straining to see the ships astern of them, braced for the hollow detonations of a merchantman exploding, willing more speed from his charges as the wolves circled, just out of reach, ready to strike when they chose. But at least for now his whalers were snug at their berths, the rest of the convoy was safe and the company around the wardroom table was exactly as he would have wished it. The worn faces of his officers bore the marks of men in command at sea in war, faces etched with weariness, the weight of responsibility and the losses they had suffered.

The escorts' home-from-home in Durban was the RNVR base on the Esplanade and Jack reported daily to the Royal Navy headquarters in Tribune House. For the men of his flotilla, the city was a revelation: warm and humid, lively and bursting with entertainment.

The crews went ashore in their white tropical rig, enjoyed meals at the service canteen or steak with all the trimmings at the Playhouse Grillroom, took rides in rickshaws drawn by Zulu men with colourful headdresses, danced with local young women at the Amphitheatre on Marine Parade and went carousing at various sailors' pubs; some of them made it to South Beach for a swim in the balmy water and a couple even tried, unsuccessfully, to ride the waves on a borrowed wooden board. All seemed determined to put the horrors of the convoy behind them, but their stay in Durban was short and after minor repairs to the storm damage, they took on fuel and provisions at Q shed and made ready for the return voyage.

Before setting sail, Jack badly wanted to make a telephone call. Clara had lingered at the back of his mind almost every moment of the passage to Durban and their brushes with disaster had made the need to contact her more pressing. He had come to a decision about Clara: there was no more time for prevarication, for 'an understanding' or 'taking it slowly'. Fortunately, a sympathetic Wren at Tribune House agreed to let him use the telephone in the commander's office during lunch when the staff were out. Noting his creased brow and nervous look as he lifted the black handset, the Wren said she would knock three times if the commander returned and closed the door.

'*Nommer asseblief,* number please?' said the operator and Jack booked a trunk call to a house on Main Street, Newlands. He did not have long to wait before Clara's voice crackled on the end of the line: 'Where on earth are you?'

'In Durban.'

'Durban! Why?'

'It's one hell of a story and of course I can't say anything over the telephone, but the long and short of it is I needed to tell you something. I needed —'

'Are you all right, Jack?'

'Yes, yes. Our convoy got shot up, which I shouldn't be divulging, and all I could think of, almost all the time, was, was—'

'You sound a bit funny.'

'Not funny at all. Deadly serious, I'm afraid. Was you, Clara. You.'

There was a long silence.

'I thought deep down you were married to your boat and the sea and the war.'

'Now I know I'm not. I know it with a great certainty.'

'I see.'

'I hope that you do and that we can be together, properly.'

There were three urgent taps at the door.

'Oh, God, I've got to go. Would you come away with me, for a night, somewhere out of town, just the two of us?'

'Oh Jack, you know my mother would never allow it.'

His mind was racing: 'We could make something up: a story.'

'You mean deception, Jack, and this from an officer and gentleman of the Royal Navy?'

'Yes.'

'How the mighty hath fallen.' She giggled and his heart melted at its faint, tinkling sound down the long-distance line.

'Look, Clara, I've got to go. I'm not really supposed to be using this telephone. Will you at least think about it?'

'Yes, Jack, I'll think about it.'

'Promise?'

'Promise.'

CHAPTER 23

Captain Brand, Lingen and the chief stood beside the chart table watching as Seebohm manoeuvred his parallel rulers and dividers. Beside them, the metal chest containing charts for every corner of the globe they might need stood open. Today's chart was marked out with quadrant KP of the Kriegsmarine grid — the northern Natal and southern Mozambique zone. *U-68*'s movement through the water produced only the gentlest of vibrations as they headed northeast at a depth of forty metres. Brand ran his eye along the pencil line, each small cross marking one of Seebohm's fixes.

'So, gentlemen, what next?' Brand rubbed his hands together. 'Radio traffic tells us Durban, like Cape Town, has become a viper's nest, so we need to shift our attack elsewhere.'

'Back to Cape Agulhas, sir,' suggested Hoppe. 'The traffic bottlenecks around there.'

'Yes, maybe. What do *you* suggest, Seebohm?' Not expecting the spotlight, the young lieutenant blushed.

'Ah, well, sir, we could try the west coast again and hit the inshore route to Walvis Bay, or the deep-ocean route to Freetown.'

'And what about you, IWO?'

'I think we should head further up the coast, into the Mozambique Channel,' said Lingen. 'They will not expect us there and the South African Air Force might have difficulty patrolling far from home over Portuguese territorial waters.'

'What about fuel, Chief?' asked Brand.

'*Ja*, I suppose we could do it, thanks to the *Milchküh*,' said Hoppe, pushing back his cap and scratching the few remaining tufts. 'As long as you do not act like a lunatic and run us at full power the whole time.'

'Who Chief? Me Chief? Never, Chief!' Brand guffawed. Hoppe sighed.

Two days later, while cruising on the surface in neutral waters east of Inhaca Island, one of *U-68*'s lookouts spotted a possible target. 'From the bridge, sir, smoke to the northwest,' Lingen called down to the control room. Brand grabbed his binoculars and made for the ladder.

'How does she bear?' he said as he emerged from the hatch.

'Over there, sir, port bow,' said lookout Meckmann. 'She is heading south.'

Brand trained his binoculars in the direction the lookout was pointing.

'Ah, yes, now I have her, well spotted, Meckmann.' He refocused his lenses on the faint spindle of smoke, then said: 'Steer two-seven-zero, half ahead both.'

After watching the vessel for a few minutes, he made up his mind. 'Lingen, I am pretty sure it is something important sailing independently. She is moving fast, zigzagging, but I think we are well placed to intercept.'

'Very good, Kapitän.' The first lieutenant could barely hide the excitement in his voice.

'Full ahead, steer two-one-zero,' said Brand. 'We will attack.' Moments later, the pulse of the engines increased and the prow cut waves shaped like big wood shavings as the submarine rose and dipped on an easy swell.

In Brand's sights was HMT *Calgary*, an elegant, straight-prowed liner of 18,250 tons requisitioned by the British Ministry of War Transport, on passage from Suez to Liverpool with 1,497 passengers, more than half of them Italian POWs guarded by 98 Polish soldiers, as well as 2,400 tons of cargo, including tens of thousands of oranges and 1,800 bags of mail.

U-68 dived and Brand made a perfect, angled approach so that he was positioned to let the liner come gliding into the crosshairs of his periscope. 'Tubes one and three ready,' said the first lieutenant. Brand fed the bearings to Lingen, bent over his deflection calculator.

'Open bow caps,' said the captain. 'Stand by number one and number three tubes.'

'One and three standing by,' said Lingen. They stole closer until Brand could make out the faces of passengers on deck with his attack periscope.

'Number one tube: *los*! Lock on number three.' A few more seconds, then: 'Number three tube: *los*!'

The colossus was hit on her port side, the first torpedo striking forward in her number two hold and the second aft in number six hold. Coming slowly to a halt, the liner settled in a shroud of smoke. *U-68* surfaced and slunk towards the scene of destruction as *Calgary*'s crew prepared to launch lifeboats.

'She is trying to send a distress signal, sir,' called out Wichmann.

'Then jam it, PO,' said Lingen.

Aboard the stricken liner, Captain Bradley ordered abandon ship with women, children and the injured first into the boats. The Italian POWs were left locked in the holds while some of those who escaped and tried to board the lifeboats were shot or bayoneted by their Polish guards. However, the liner refused to sink and Brand couldn't afford to hang about waiting for everyone to abandon. He hit her amidships with a third torpedo which resulted in an almighty explosion that sent fragments hurtling through the air and a great tower of black smoke fed by roaring fires.

'Good, that will be her engine room,' said Brand.

With no bulkheads in the ship's bowels, it was carnage below with pipes bursting and stokers scalded, their skin flayed as boilers vented super-heated steam and panic-stricken survivors scrambled to escape up the only ladder. Many passengers and crew were still trapped behind watertight doors that had buckled in the explosions. Others were doomed by the sheer weight of numbers trying to escape up listing stairs and companionways. There were extreme acts of bravery and cowardice during the liner's last moments, as men gave up lifejackets to the wounded or clawed and beat their way over their messmates to reach the exits.

Calgary turned turtle, presenting her monstrous belly to the sky, then dipped beneath the waves, creating a suction that dragged under those who had not managed to swim clear. The sea was littered with thousands of oranges which bobbed against the U-boat's saddle tanks and sluiced jauntily by, adding a surreal air to the encounter as they approached the lifeboats and survivors bobbing in their Mae Wests, many of them calling and waving agitatedly — not the usual reaction of enemy survivors.

'Stop engines.'

As they coasted towards the throng, Brand leaned over the bridge rail and shouted through a loudhailer, 'What is the name of your ship?'

'*Queen Mary*, you Nazi bastard!' shouted a British sailor.

'HMS *Lord Nelson*!'

'The *Ark* fucking *Royal*!'

'*Calgary! Calgary!*' came the cries in a foreign accent, drowning out the others. 'We are Italian prisoners of war, *Kamerad*.'

'How many are there of you?'

'Many, many are Italian. Hundreds! You must help us, *Kamerad.*' The magnitude of the disaster began to dawn on Brand.

'*Scheiße, scheiße, scheiße!*' he hammered the rail with his fist. 'This is the last thing we need.'

'What do we do now, Kapitän?' asked Lingen.

'Do you know something, IWO, I have absolutely no idea. We could leave these poor sods — our glorious allies — to drown, along with the women and children over there, or we could whistle up assistance.'

'But we are close to South African waters. Enemy aircraft could get here in no time.'

'I know, I know. Suppose we radio in plain language, giving our position and stating that we will not fire on rescuers. If the Portuguese get here first from LM, there is no problem.'

'Or we could sneak away and let them die,' said Lingen. 'The sharks are already having a go.'

'Not a happy situation.'

Wichmann was called to the bridge. 'Take this down, PO,' said Brand. 'Urgent signal to *BdU*: "Three torpedoes fired at troopship *Calgary*, approx. 20,000 grt. Sunk position KP6371. Many Italian prisoners of war among survivors. Request orders."'

With swimmers attempting to climb onto the saddle tanks and having to be shoved off with boathooks, *U-68* moved away from the throng. Brand tried to block out the sound of screaming as sharks, growing in number and boldness, glided in to attack. A few seconds of frantic terror as a swimmer was yanked under, then, buoyed by the lifejacket, a legless torso would pop to the surface like a cork, surrounded by a widening stain of blood.

'Reply from *BdU*, sir!' Wichmann stuck his head through the hatch and handed the slip of paper to Brand.

'Well, that decides it: "No rescue attempt. Continue operating. Waging war comes first."'

Lingen looked despairingly at the scene, then back at his captain, whose jaw was set.

'Slow ahead both,' said Brand in a flat tone. 'Set a course due southeast.'

As they drew away, a few survivors made a desperate effort to swim after them and cling to the hull. Torn between obeying his orders and the humanitarian crisis unfolding in his wake, Brand radioed the Portuguese authorities in Lourenço Marques, who immediately dispatched the sloop *Afonso de Almeida* and notified the South Africans.

The sloop arrived late that afternoon to a scene of carnage with hundreds of corpses bobbing about in clusters. The oceanic white-tipped sharks had done their work among the survivors and many died an agonising death, others were barely hanging on, the blood of severed limbs attracting ever more sharks. The sloop managed to rescue 120 Italian internees, 41 Polish guards, 67 crew and 44 passengers.

Meanwhile further south, Jack's flotilla had just left Durban on passage to Cape Town. *Waterberg* and *Southern Belle* were diverted to the scene of the sinking, but were unable to find any more survivors or hint of the U-boat. Miraculously, one additional survivor, an Italian POW, was to spend the next nine days drifting on a life raft that eventually washed ashore near Kosi Bay on the Natal coast.

The sunlight turned to milk in eerie foreboding as *U-68* headed back down the South African coast towards Agulhas into a gathering spring gale. The U-boat began to labour as the swell increased and the wind sang a grim threnody in the jumping wire. The sea state deteriorated through the day with streaks of foam shredded from the wave tops and the wind-fired rain peppering the lookouts' faces with tiny darts.

The prow punched through the crests, a third of the hull hanging in mid-air, before hurling herself into the dirty-green troughs to the sound of a great fist striking the keel. With each plunge, the exhaust and air-induction valves on the aft casing submerged, forcing the diesel engines to use the air inside the hull until they breasted another crest and causing the crew to suffer as their eardrums tried to adjust to the pressure fluctuations.

'It is the North Sea in January topside, sir,' said Lieutenant Seebohm, descending from his watch and pulling off soaked oilskins. Brand sighed as he dragged on damp sea-boots, thick jersey, sheepskin waistcoat, woollen muffler and tied a sou'wester under his chin. Wasn't Africa supposed to be balmy and tropical? He emerged on the bridge to find a tormented sea. It seemed as though he was in a chariot ridden by six men, charging at the oncoming waves with reckless abandon. Brand was reminded of the overture of Wagner's *Der Fliegende Holländer*, a tirade of wind and string instruments appropriate to this sublime ocean, this frenzied sky.

'The gale is shaking the soul out of my body!' yelled Lingen.

'You have a soul, IWO?' shouted Brand. 'How very touching, and perhaps naïve.'

'At least the weather will keep the South African Air Force grounded ... again.'

'Small mercies, IWO, very small.'

As the prow dipped, the lookouts automatically ducked behind the bridge casing as torrents of spray passed over them. Their eyes stung from the salt and water found its way past sou'westers, rubberised jackets and terry-towels wrapped around their necks to further chill their shivering bodies. The hands that gripped wet binoculars were red as lobster claws. There was no point in trying to dry the lenses with chamois as any effort was rendered futile moments later.

Heading further southwest and deeper into the gale, the waves grew steeper, swamping the bridge and leaving the watch keepers waist deep as the water drained away. Each man had to be secured with a safety belt around the waist. Up the side of a mountain they went, thirty degrees to the sea on a gondola ride to the summit, there to view snow-capped ranges in every direction. The nearer alps were green and veined with white, the distant ones bled into a wash of shifting grey. Then down they'd go once more, aiming at the pit of the trough like a careening freight train. Brand felt that with a bit more speed, they might keep going, ploughing through the base of the trough, burrowing deeper and deeper, straight to the ocean floor.

'This is why they call them submarines!' he yelled with a maniacal look. 'As much at home above the sea as below, or a little bit of both at the same time.'

Below decks, the U-boat was filled with the din of waves breaking on the casing, interspersed with the crash of the prow striking an oncoming wave like a giant axe, the hull noises varying from metallic clanging to sonorous, bass-drum booming.

'It sounds like a whale is trying to mate with us,' complained Schmitt.

'*Ja*, a whole randy school of them,' said Fischer.

The loose equipment, clothes and belongings that littered the ratings' mess looked like the result of vandalism. Hanging sausages swung madly back and forth, bilge water sloshed loudly beneath the gratings, bookcases ejected their contents, coats unhooked themselves and cooking utensils clattered across the deck. With so much water cascading down the conning tower, even the men in the control room wore oilskins and the bilge pumps worked continually.

The cook fitted the wardroom table with fiddles to stop plates and dishes growing wings, but still a fair amount of food landed in the officers' laps. During one meal, a dish slid from the table and the steward hurriedly mopped up the mess of potatoes, meat and tinned carrots which looked like extravagant vomit. 'Much more of this and I will apply for a transfer to the Luftwaffe,' grumbled the *Kombüse*.

Coming off watch, the lookouts arrived in the control room as if from another dimension, their faces scarlet from driven spray. They removed sou'westers and helped each other out of rubber leggings like a slow-motion, comedy turn. Pulling off sea-boots, they emptied the water into the bilges, then dragged off their socks and wrung them out. Some couldn't face the rigmarole of undressing, so collapsed fully clad in the engine room to thaw and doze in its muggy warmth. All too soon, they'd have to climb the ladder for another stint in purgatory, seldom having eaten anything more than a slice or two of bread.

Brand lengthened the daily trim dives by a few hours to grant the crew respite from the buffeting and allow some rest. As they submerged, the sea's roar would be replaced by the hiss of compressed air, then a deafening silence. Like an elevator descending to a quiet basement, all violent motion eased, but even at thirty metres they could feel the effects of the swell, so Brand took them down to sixty metres and only then could they find the peace of the ocean's womb.

'There!' he said to the control room. 'Now you can all stop whining like a bunch of old tarts. Tell the *mademoiselles* I will be in my bunk.'

The return to the surface was a return to madness. Brand signalled with his thumb for the periscope to be raised and held tight to the handles as the boat began to buck and yaw once more. First, he saw only exploding spray, then the soaring face of an oncoming breaker which made him instinctively recoil from the eyepieces. Extending the periscope, he gained a better picture of the maelstrom, noting grimly that conditions had deteriorated.

'Surface!'

He picked exactly the wrong moment to go topside and received a full dousing as his head poked through the upper hatchway. Raising himself upright with difficulty, he looked forward into the stinging rain only to find that the sea had disappeared. *U-68*'s bows were pointing at the heavens and, with the inexorability of a pendulum, began to fall as the boat careened into a deep valley. Descending the windward slope, Brand had time to marvel at the peaks around him being torn asunder in veils of spindrift.

Before him towered the biggest wave he'd ever seen. Made ponderous by its own immensity, it appeared to grow in stature with each passing second. It had a grey-green face and sweeping mane of white hair: an old, craggy giant lumbering towards them with careless malevolence. Down in the trough, there was no wind, as though they'd momentarily entered the eye of the swell. It was a terrifying sensation. The four lookouts cringed at their posts. Brand watched as long as he dared as the white-fanged beast straightened its approach, teetered, poised to detonate upon them. He yelled an unintelligible order into the voicepipe, then he too cowered behind the bridge coaming, filling his lungs with air, bracing for impact.

The U-boat penetrated a great white wall as tons of water inundated the bridge. Watch keepers were knocked off their feet, engulfed in the swirling tumult. Like probationary drownees, they remained submerged for a full twenty seconds, holding their breaths in their terrifying, icy aquarium. One lookout lost his grip and was swept over the rail. It seemed an eternity before *U-68* shook herself free, burst through the back of the wave and careered down the monster's back. The lookout was found, barely conscious, dangling from his belt off the back of the conning tower, and hastily dragged back onto the bridge by his three mates, then bundled below to be revived and thawed.

That evening, Brand wedged himself in the corner of his cabin to write in the log:

1605 — Slow ahead into a building sea. Tried increasing to 280 revs but not viable. Grid quadrant KZ2413, due east of Coffee Bay and about 80 nautical miles out to sea.

2340 — Gyro compass defective due to heavy rolling. Steering by magnetic compass.

0800 — Steep seas.

1630 — Strong current from the northeast. Navigation concerns.

2100 — Steep seas continually breaking over bridge.

0750 — No sight of land, sun, moon or stars for two days.

1130 — Current very strong and the Agulhas Bank fails to give protection against heavy western seas, but produces a substantial ground swell.

The entry in his personal journal was more candid: 'We have sailed far to the south and this wretched gale is destroying our will and driving us insane. Mountainous waves take hold of the boat, lift it up like a toy and throw it into the abysmal depths. Everything that is not securely fastened is smashed to bits. The bridge is a swimming pool; the bilge pumps work incessantly; the men are shattered. This is hell.'

Nearing Mossel Bay at the tail end of the gale, *U-68* received a signal from the *BdU* ordering a secret rendezvous on a deserted stretch of coast near the mouth of the Breede River. Two possible nights, a recognition code and coordinates were provided, but no further details, other than that stores would be available to extend their patrol. The sandy cove lay to the east of a protected headland marked on the chart as 'Skipskop' and the U-boat cautiously approached the coast on the night of 29 September.

'It is shallow, sir, but there is hardly any current and the bottom is sandy,' said Seebohm, bent over the chart table. 'Not much swell running after the gale, so we should be able to anchor quite comfortably and fairly close.'

'All right, let us take her in,' said Brand. 'IWO, I want silence, guns manned and every precaution.'

The big, black fin of the conning tower stole towards the shore on a calm, windless night, a half moon suspended between drifting clouds. At Brand's instruction, PO Schmitt aimed his shaded signal lamp at a low headland on the starboard bow and flashed the code. There was no response. The submarine slid further into the shallows, her escape routes and possibilities diminishing with each minute.

'I do not like this. Could be a trap. Schmitt, signal again.' The shutters of the portable lamp slapped out the code once more.

'Stop motors.' *U-68* coasted towards a small bay and slowed to a halt: water lapping against the saddle tanks, wavelets caressing a beach, the stifled cough of a lookout.

'This does not feel right,' muttered Brand.

'Sir!' hissed Schmitt. 'They are replying!' Morse flickered from a torch on the headland. 'The code is correct.'

A few minutes later, they made out a rowing boat with three figures coming towards them with an easy dipping of oars. The fishing *bakkie* nudged alongside and was held by boathooks as a man stepped across the gap, made his way towards the conning tower and climbed the ladder to the bridge.

'*Herrje*, it is you!' Brand was the first to speak.

'*Ja*, Kapitän, it's me,' said Kruger. 'Dr Livingstone, I presume?'

'What?'

'Never mind. Welcome to the Overberg.' They shook hands warmly.

'We must stop meeting like this.'

Kruger wasted no time in outlining his proposal for the night. A larger fishing boat would ferry stores and drums of fuel to be pumped by hand into their tanks, a process that would take many hours. Brand was invited to join Kruger at the local farmer's homestead while the operation was in progress. If there was time before dawn, the crew could be brought ashore in watches to stretch their legs and enjoy refreshments on the beach. Kruger went on to allay Brand's worries about safety while at anchor, saying that *Weerlig* lookouts were posted on surrounding hills and besides, the stretch of coastline west of the Breede River was one of the most remote and desolate in South Africa.

'In any case, most farmers in this district are *Ossewabrandwag* and support the greater National Socialist cause,' said Kruger. 'They would be only too happy to help us.'

After briefing his officers, Brand had a basin bath and changed into regulation naval attire, choosing his tropical service dress: single-breasted, open-necked tunic in tan denim with blue braid shoulder straps and tan trousers. Appraising his haggard reflection in the mirror, he applied Brylcreem and ran a comb through his long ginger-blonde hair, but there was no time to trim the wayward beard. He joined Kruger topside and they climbed down the conning tower into the rowing boat.

Lingen was left to oversee the fuel pumping and loading of stores. To Kombüse Schneider's delight, much of it was fresh produce from the farm, including crates of onions and cabbages, a barrel of wine, two sheep carcasses and a sack of biltong. The cook tried biting into the latter but found it very tough, so he boiled a batch for the next few hours, without success. One of the crew, who'd grown up in South West Africa, got to hear of Schneider's culinary troubles and put him right. The dried-meat delicacy caught on and soon the men were grabbing handfuls from the sack between duties.

It was a short row to the beach across a glassy sea glittering with shards of moonlight. The *bakkie*'s prow bit into the sand and Brand jumped ashore without wetting his shoes, but his first steps were staccato, his legs trying to adjust to the land's immobility. After sixty-eight days at sea, the aroma of vegetation was as heady as expensive Riesling. Brand looked back at his U-boat, an upright black shape married to the darkness, and could hardly believe how small his home was — his entire world for the past two months.

A Chevrolet truck was parked at the top of the beach beside a sandy track that snaked inland. The farmer's son was at the wheel and they bounced over a dune and past a lagoon. Brand drank in the delicious sounds and scents of this strange land: the silhouette of an owl on a branch, the symphony of frogs and crickets among the reeds, the startled face of a small antelope in their headlights. They passed a barn with black swastikas set in white roundels painted on the doors and approached a Cape Dutch homestead surrounded by outbuildings that looked much like the thatched cottages of his childhood holidays on the island of Sylt.

'Buffelsvlei dates back to the eighteenth century and the farmer's name is Hendrik Uys,' said Kruger as they drove across a *werf* planted with fig trees and drew up in front of the gabled manor house. 'Uys is of German heritage, a loyal patriot and staunch supporter of *Weerlig*. Fortunately, farmers are permitted to order large quantities of fuel for their equipment. The diesel gets stockpiled in an underground storage tank and is finding a new home in your boat.'

They got out and took the stairs to the front door, its open half leaking golden light. The large *voorkamer* was lit with lanterns and a handful of men had gathered, mostly local farmers by the look of it, their rifles leaning against a wall. Enthusiastic introductions were made, the Afrikaners thrilled to meet a heroic U-boat captain in the flesh.

'Thank you for welcoming me into your home, Herr Uys, and for your generous provisioning of my boat,' said Brand in clipped English.

'It's a privilege to serve the Reich, and Gerhardus Kruger also pays well.' The balding man with the Overberg drawl chuckled. 'Come and grab yourself a glass and a plate of food. My wife and the maids have been cooking all afternoon.'

Kruger and Brand loaded their plates with hearty *boerekos* from the buffet and went to sit at one end of a long yellowwood table. The farmer's wife and daughter came into the room to be introduced to the 'illustrious captain', the daughter all blushes and darting eyes. Brand breathed in as she shook his hand and the scent of her was intoxicating. His mind flew the length of Africa to settle for a moment in another time: his young wife in her white summer dress with the floral pattern. That smell, like the scent of Greta's hair, produced such a powerful ache that he had to shut it out quickly. During his last home leave, his wife's eyes had betrayed how much water had passed under the bridge, how unattainable his dreams had become. There would be no going home in any meaningful sense ever again.

'*Zum Whol*, to your health,' said Kruger, lifting his brandy and clinking Brand's glass. 'Now, to business. The main reason you have been asked to land here is so that I can hand over this package.' He reached into a leather satchel at his feet and brought out a small, canvas container, which he shook to the sound of stones in a tin.

'What is it?' asked Brand, raising an eyebrow.

'Industrial diamonds, desperately needed in Germany.'

'So now I have become a diamond smuggler.' He grinned impishly. 'How did you come by them, Herr Kruger?'

'I bought some on the black market with money provided by the *Abwehr*, but most were stolen by our friends. A man will come aboard and receive them as soon as you dock in Lorient.'

'Whenever that may be,' muttered Brand.

'Well, the re-provisioning extends your patrol. *U-156* is due here in the next few days and we will resupply Kapitän Nagel too.'

'I assume the other three boats will be returning to France, unless they send another *Milchküh*.'

'Or ask for our help again. You know, Kapitän, I just wish we could communicate directly with U-boats in South African waters and not have to pass everything via *BdU*. I have local knowledge and a perfect transmitter setup at Steenbokbaai — we will never get caught.'

'Dönitz wants to pull the strings himself. The great puppeteer would never allow a third party to dictate naval targets and naval strategy —'

'Third party, pah!'

'You understand his position, surely?' Brand's tone had acquired an edge.

'*Ja, ja*, but really. At some stage you're going to have to trust us. Things are moving so fast here and targets change by the day. As a matter of fact, we are planning an imminent *Weerlig* strike on a liner in Cape Town which will transform the situation in the Union and sow panic among the enemy.'

'I am pleased for you, Herr Kruger. You have been needing a chance like this to enter the fight.' Brand had finished his bobotie and sat back in his chair, lighting a cigarette.

'And there is another excellent opportunity for you, which I'm sure *BdU* will inform you about,' said Kruger. 'Our agent in Cape Town harbour has gained intelligence about an important convoy to Walvis Bay. It will include a number of ships that would normally have sailed unescorted to Freetown, but the C-in-C South Atlantic considers them too valuable and has placed them in a coastal convoy, provisionally designated CN.04. From our agents, we know that its escort group will be the same as the one used for the recent Durban convoy that was attacked.'

'That *is* good news. It was us doing the attacking. Most of the time, the escorts did not know their arses from their elbows. We easily outmanoeuvred those old whale catchers.'

The pair talked long into the night, making a sizeable dent in the bottle of brandy. Kruger was able to give Brand detailed information on Cape Town's searched channels, the strength of its anti-submarine patrols and particulars regarding the convoy. According to the informer, CN.04 would comprise nine ships, two bound for South West Africa, the other seven, including a trooper and two tankers, for a deep-sea dispersal point off Walvis Bay, where they would be met by a heavier escort for onward passage to Freetown. Kruger's contact had even provided a chart showing the secret merchant-shipping route to be used from Cape Town to Walvis.

While they were discussing the coming attacks, the U-boat crew completed the loading and refuelling. Each watch was then allowed ashore in turns, where crates of beer and food were provided by *Weerlig* commandos, excited to meet the brave Germans from the sea. One crewmember produced a soccer ball, eliciting an impromptu game by the light of the moon, a double row of lanterns and a truck's headlights, directed at the beach. It was *Kriegsmarine* versus *Weerlig*, but the latter were all rugby players and their soccer skills rudimentary. Despite flaccid sea legs, the sailors ran rings around the burly Afrikaners, until one frustrated *boer* picked up the ball and ran to score an imaginary try, to the cheering of his fellows and bemused looks of the U-boat men. This slightly awkward diplomatic incident was resolved with another round of beers and the laughter and camaraderie was soon restored. The first lightening of the eastern sky and the return of Brand saw the men embracing, offering sincere thanks and lifelong friendship, before being ferried back to their boat to sail for the Cape and take up the fight once more.

CHAPTER 24

After an uneventful passage from Durban, the escort flotilla was back in Simon's Town where *Belle* and *Waterberg* were due to have their boilers cleaned. For the crews, it was a chance to relax back into port routine. Days returned to their natural rhythm with hands falling in at 0630 to wash down the upper deck, colours at 0800 followed by the day's work, interrupted by stand easy and up spirits — the issue of a rum tot to every man — at 1030.

Jack caught up on his pile of paperwork, Van Zyl and the bosun attended to a list of minor repairs, Robinson brought the corrections to his charts up to date, Combrink oversaw the stripping and cleaning of weapons, Sparks Thomas landed his wet cell batteries for overhaul and updated the codebooks. Work ended at 1600, when liberty-men went ashore to sample the delights of Simon's Town or beyond, and the duty watch settled in for a night on board. Officer's rounds, the checking of mooring lines and making sure *Gannet* was properly darkened marked the close of the day.

Most evenings, Thomas would borrow Van Zyl's gramophone and play records over the PA system, alternating with radio programmes such as the BBC news or Cecil Wightman's *Snoektown Calling*, until lights out at 2130. One downside, as far as some of the crew were concerned, was Thomas's deep affection for the song 'I'm Popeye the Sailor Man'. Seaman Manley had developed such a hatred for it that one evening he burst into the wireless cabin cursing wildly, tore the record from the turntable, broke it over his knee and threw the two halves overboard.

Not long after the unfortunate incident, the crew were listening to the BBC's *Forces Favourites* after supper when the announcer said: 'The next song is for the brave sailors of HMSAS *Southern Gannet* requested by their telegraphist, Leading Seaman Douglas Thomas, who has chosen…' at which point nothing further could be heard as everyone in the mess deck yelled, 'I'm Popeye the Sailor Man' and erupted in hysterical laughter. To his credit, Seaman Manley collapsed on his bunk in a fit of mirth as the jaunty tune echoed through the ship.

'What's all the commotion below?' asked Jack as Hendricks brought him a mug of Milo.

'Just Popeye again, sir.'

'Ah, that's all right then.'

Jack was called to O'Reilly's office, fully expecting a dressing down or worse for his handling of the convoy.

'I've read your report, Pembroke…' said the commodore, running his eye over the sheaf in his hand, then taking off his spectacles. 'As you know, Commodore Jones was sadly not among the survivors of the *Sapphire*.'

'Yes sir, I was very sorry to hear it.'

'Damned tricky business with so few escorts. Still, there has been at least one piece of good fortune. One of *Sapphire*'s lifeboats with eight survivors got lost in the confusion of the rescue, but managed to make it ashore at South Sand Bluff — a wild, inhospitable stretch of coast, not a white man in sight. They traded their boat for food and clothes from the local Pondo tribe, slept a night in huts provided by the chief and were taken by ox wagon through the bush to Umtata.'

'That is good news, sir. I think we did all we could in the rescue and for the rest, I tried to keep my flotilla in close support as you requested.'

'Perhaps you did. Nevertheless, I'm not convinced by your tactics when the U-boats were in contact. Sometimes you attacked when you should have defended.'

'Staying tethered we were sitting ducks, sir, so I made thrusts to keep their heads down.'

'But you lost five bloody ships, Pembroke!'

'I know, sir, but we might have lost more if we'd sat tight. They weren't all wild-goose chases: I think we broke up some of the attacks and I'm sure we caused some damage which they'll find difficult to repair so far from home.'

There was a long silence.

'I see your point, and I acknowledge your offensive spirit ... not entirely unlike your father, I might add.' There was a wry smile. 'However, it's not the way we've been conducting these coastal escorts. The policy has been to remain tight and close, and let the air force chaps keep the Boche occupied and submerged wherever possible.'

'I understand, sir, but I can't help feeling that with a fast and hard lunge, preferably with two or even three escorts, we could get to grips with the U-boats. In future, I'd respectfully request that you give the escort leader a free hand to hunt if conditions were favourable.'

'It's too risky, Pembroke.' He saw the crestfallen look on Jack's face. 'Oh, damn it all, let me think it over.'

'Thank you, sir.'

Jack spent evenings at Milkwood dining with his father and sometimes his sister, who had acquired a busy social life, some of it involving mildly inappropriate young men who paid more attention to their wardrobe than the war effort.

'Since the attack on your convoy, we've tried to clear Durban's anchorage and bring as many ships as we can into the harbour up there,' said Admiral Pembroke, sitting on the stoep at dusk. 'We've also instituted round the clock AS patrols using four whalers, but Durban is like a shooting gallery for U-boats.'

'We saw as much,' said Jack, gazing at the ring of mauve-coloured mountains across the bay. 'Anchored ships usually lie parallel to the shore, so from seaward they present an almost unbroken line of targets nearly three miles long.'

'And boldly silhouetted by Durban's lights. I've recommended a temporary blackout for the city and no cars after dark on the Snell Parade and beachfront. I'd like to make it permanent for the duration, but the local authorities will kick up a stink.'

'How are your coastal defences coming along?' asked Jack, taking a sip of his whisky.

'Rather well, for the most part, especially around the Peninsula. I think Cape Town's four batteries are now up to scratch — Wynyard, Lion, Docks and the big 9-inch Apostle Battery above Llandudno. Hout Bay has one decent battery and Robben Island two. You know about False Bay's three — Scala, Docks and Noah's Ark— but you won't know about the pair of 6-inch guns earmarked for a new battery at Gordon's Bay. Durban and Port Elizabeth are also looking fine; East London and Walvis Bay are adequate for what they're dealing with.'

'You've been your busy self.'

'Always. And we're continuing to build observation posts all around the coast. We've now got three at Cape Point, including a fire commander's post for the Simon's Town batteries. You might have noticed one going up on the slope behind Milkwood.'

'I was wondering about that concrete carbuncle.'

'They'll provide early warning and, in the case of an enemy landing, survive long enough to sound the alarm. We're worried about Japan and the rumblings coming from the East: things could go belly-up quite suddenly in that theatre.'

'Japan's Pacific Ocean ambitions seem so remote from the Cape, but I suppose nowhere is remote anymore.'

'No, nowhere.'

Van Zyl returned to his parents' home in Stellenbosch for a night, having confirmed that Hans was out of town. He had been agonising over what he'd overheard and, despite the rupturing of the family it would cause, knew he must go to the police, but needed solid evidence. After his parents had gone to bed, Van Zyl crept into his brother's room to see if he could find clues to what might be planned by the aberrant group of *Stormjaers* or whatever they were. Quietly closing the door, he switched on the bedside lamp. The wall above the bed was adorned with an *OB* banner bearing a black eagle with outstretched wings, ox wagon and emblazoned with the words, '*My God, My Volk, My Land Suid-Afrika*'.

Van Zyl rummaged through the desk drawers, tin trunk and cupboard. Rugby ball, tennis racket, boxes of university papers, photo albums, a pile of *OB* pamphlets — nothing of any use. He looked under the bed and pulled the chest of drawers away from the wall, trying to prevent the legs squealing on the floorboards. Then he spotted it, lying in plain sight on the desk, his brother's black diary. He flicked through the weeks of late September and early October: mostly lecture times, a meeting in a pub with friends, a bioscope date. Friday 3 October had two entries in his brother's untidy scrawl: the name of a ship, 'RMS *Belgica*, 41,000 tons', and below it '10.30am, 5 Wandel Street'. A shiver ran through him: the colossal Royal Mail Ship had to be the target. Entries for Tuesday and Wednesday simply had the name 'RMS *Belgica*', presumably her period in port and the window of opportunity for an attack.

Now Van Zyl knew without a doubt he would have to inform the police and effectively accuse his brother of treason.

During their stay in port, Jack desperately wanted to escape for a night, take Clara away from the city and put all doubts to rest. It was secretly arranged that she would join him at the Hout Bay Hotel, a honeymooners' retreat on the western side of the Peninsula. Although Jack suspected that Clara had been wavering in her feelings towards him, she agreed to the tryst, which he took as a promising sign. Her mother must never get wind of the arrangement, so it was decided that he collect Clara at a friend's flat in Claremont, where she'd ostensibly be spending the night.

Jack signed out an Austin from the officers' pool and drove to town following the shoreline around False Bay and through Muizenberg to the suburbs. Clara came bouncing down the stairs of the block of flats on Bowwood Road carrying a small overnight bag. She wore a pale-blue dress to match her eyes, blonde hair clipped back, her bright red lipstick somehow making her look even younger than her eighteen years.

'Hello, stranger,' she said as she climbed in and kissed him on the cheek.

'Hello, Clara, it has been a while.'

'You look a bit different, taller even.' Her broad smile showed off her dimples.

'I'm sitting down, but yes, a rough time at sea in all respects. I think I might have been forced to grow up a bit.'

'Well, you can pack up your troubles and let your hair down for the next few hours,' she said, running her fingers through the tufts at the back of his neck.

He slipped the car into gear and pulled away, heading over Constantia Nek and down to Hout Bay valley, green and bucolic after the winter rains.

Parking beside the grand white hotel, set 200 metres from the beach and backed by the crags of Constantiaberg, Jack carried their bags past a fountain, across an oak-filled courtyard and into reception. He signed the register 'Mr and Mrs Pembroke', overseen by a concierge with a doubting, or knowing, look and they were led by a porter to a balcony room on the first floor. The Cape Dutch furniture was in dark wood with an Art Deco sofa and lamps, maroon carpet and French doors offering views up the valley to the north.

'So, alone at last,' she said after Jack had taken off his jacket.

He took both her hands in his. 'I've been dreaming about this moment during the long nights at sea.' His eyes momentarily clouded and his brow creased.

'Oh Jack, what is it taking out of you?' She put a hand to his cheek and let her fingers run gently across the scar on his temple.

'What do you mean?'

'I can see what it does to you. It's as though you're only ever partly here.'

There was a long silence.

'It makes one hard. I suppose one gets close to one's limits.'

'Is there any way you can be easier on yourself?'

'I doubt it, unless I were prepared to care less.'

'Which you can't.'

'Of course not.'

She put her arms around him and looked into his steel-blue eyes. 'You have to be the way you are, don't you?'

They both smiled.

'Perhaps one day it will be different. There's so much to keep in my head at the same time: the ship, my men, the flotilla, the convoy, the enemy, the bigger picture.'

'And don't forget your father.'

'Oh, he's always back there in the shadows somewhere, yes, and all the nautical Pembrokes behind him.' Jack wished he could tell this intelligent, intuitive young woman how much he wanted to share the burden with her, how much he longed for her to carry some of it with him. But it was too much, and he had seen his own mother recoil from the demands of the navy, withdrawing into her London world.

She was suddenly in his arms, hugging him tight.

'Clara, things were terrible in the last convoy,' he whispered, the words coming in a rush. 'The enemy were all around us; they had us on the ropes. I was caught running from pillar to post: every move I made they countered. We lost so many ships, so many brave sailors, women and children too. It was just like Dunkirk all over again and I felt completely helpless, desperate.'

'I know you, Jack,' she said, her fingers entwined behind his neck. 'You would have done everything in your power to save them.'

'It wasn't enough. And all I could think about in every spare moment, was you.' He looked into the glittering pools of her eyes and their lips met, first tentatively, then ardently, their mouths melting together. Jack peeled off her dress while she undid his shirt buttons, their lips still locked as they edged towards the bed.

'I don't think I can wait any longer,' whispered Jack.

'You don't have to.'

They fell among the pillows, knocking over a bedside lamp as they tore off the last of their garments, until Jack was inside her. He possessed Clara's exquisite, alabaster body, a possession that posed a counterpoint to the mercilessness of his war. Her body was an island — slim, supple and white as a beach; her body was all he wanted, just then, as he lost himself to her.

Later, Jack lay shipwrecked beside her, spent and content, the sun having set and twilight colours softening the room through the French doors. They smoked cigarettes from Clara's tin of Craven 'A' and asked the idlest questions, speaking innocent truths, ignoring the fears they had temporarily consigned to the dusk and wondering aloud about the dinner menu. It was time to dress and go down.

Next morning, Jack woke beside Clara as pale light filtered through the curtains onto their bed. With daylight came the weight of the war. His fingers traced the outline of her shoulder, down to her breast, coming to rest on a nipple. She opened her eyes and smiled. He kissed the tip of her nose.

'We'll have to get going, I'm afraid,' he said. 'It's back to work for me.'

'So soon.'

'Convoy prep.'

'Last night has changed things between us, hasn't it?' There was a hint of doubt in her voice.

'Yes, it has, but the fight remains, like a boulder in the road. Last night was the most perfect escape from reality.'

'I don't think I want to be placed in that category.'

'The war continues. It consumes the whole ball of wax. I wish to God I could give everything to you, but *Gannet*...'

'So where does that leave us?' Her voice was hoarse.

'You have given meaning to it all. I have to go back, changed certainly, but I don't know if I can give you everything until it's over.'

'I don't agree. I think you're afraid.' Just then, his alarm clock began its noisy trilling. 'Time to get up, Jack,' she said impassively. 'There's a war to be won.' Clara pulled on her gown and made for the bathroom, failing to hide her tears.

CHAPTER 25

Early on the morning of 6 October, Van Zyl signed out a Plymouth from the officers' pool and drove through to the city with a heavy sense of foreboding. He had previously met with the chief inspector at Wale Street police station and warned him that today might be a day of great importance and danger. Inspector Terreblanche had assured Van Zyl that he would have a team on standby to arrest the would-be saboteurs and asked him to find out as much as he could about the exact time and location of the proposed attack.

The young lieutenant parked at the corner of Dunkley Square in Gardens and got out. He wore civilian clothes, an overcoat and homburg pulled low over his eyes. Playing cloak-and-dagger spy was not something he'd ever envisaged and he loathed the idea, especially since it concerned his brother.

Loitering beneath a plane tree, he had a good view of the white wall and front door of the house on Wandel Street with Devil's Peak rising like a great fin behind it. After an hour of trying to look inconspicuous, and moving his position every few minutes, a green panel van drew up at the door and four men in blue overalls began loading wooden crates into the back. One of them was his brother and another looked like Gerhardus Kruger.

Heart in his mouth, Van Zyl wanted to get a closer look, but dared not in case he was recognised. As the men jumped into the van and pulled away, he darted across the square just in time to read the logo on the back: 'Wittenberg Shipping Engineers'.

A red telephone booth stood on the far side of the square and he yanked open the door, flipped through the chained phone book until he found the number for Wale Street police station and fed a tickey into the slot. He hastily imparted the gist of the situation to Terreblanche, then sprinted back to his car, sped down St Johns Street, doglegged to Adderley Street and headed for the harbour.

The massive bulk of RMS *Belgica* lay framed by the station building and the Coloured Soldier's Institute at the bottom of Adderley. Van Zyl turned left into Dock Road past the power station and, flashing his naval identity card, squealed through the gates onto the quayside just as two police cars stopped in front of him. Eight officers piled out, drawing .38 revolvers from their holsters as they ran for cover behind a pile of crates on the wharf.

Van Zyl threw open his door and followed, crouching down beside a crane to watch the unfolding scene, the four-funnelled liner — rust-streaked and drab in her wartime livery — towering above him. He could see one of the men in blue overalls chatting to a guard stationed at the foot of the gangway. There were smiles and laughter, a cigarette passed between the two. Meanwhile Hans, Kruger and a third man, who Van Zyl now recognised as Dolf, unloaded the crates stencilled with labels that read 'engine room' and 'tools'.

Just as the men were preparing to carry the first box up the gangway, the police burst from cover, one of them shouting '*Hande in die lug!* Hands up, you're under arrest!'

Like pigeons startled by the noonday gun, the four men took off in different directions. Kruger drew a pistol and fired as he ran, which elicited a volley of shots that echoed off the side of the ship, then more single shots. Kruger slowed, began to limp, then came to a halt and sat down, blood leaking from his thigh.

Dolf was lying face down, the third man had put up his hands, but Van Zyl's brother was still running.

'Stop, Hans, it's no bloody use!' yelled Van Zyl.

His brother glanced back and shouted a curse, but kept sprinting. More shots were fired and two policemen took up the pursuit, but Hans played first-team fullback and was a powerful runner. He soon outstripped the pair, scrambled over the perimeter fence and cut across the wasteland of the foreshore as a final shot rang out. The last Van Zyl saw of his brother was a tiny figure crossing the railway tracks and disappearing into the maze of District Six.

Back at the panel van, he found the police standing around the opened crates, packed with dynamite, batteries and pocket watches. Dolf lay in a pool of blood with a hole in the back of his head; Kruger sat on the ground in handcuffs while the third man was being loaded into a police car.

'*Fokken verraaier, ons sal jou kry* ... we'll get you, traitor,' Kruger said under his breath and spat in Van Zyl's direction.

The young lieutenant turned away, his body trembling, his footsteps ringing hollow on the concrete. Perhaps his mother might understand, but his family would never forgive him and his brother was at large and bound to seek revenge. In the Union, the punishment for treason was death by hanging, but as he made his way back to the car, it was he who felt as though he were stepping up to the gallows.

With boilers cleaned and repairs completed, all four whalers were ready for deployment and Commodore O'Reilly was putting the final touches to his plan for a convoy to Walvis Bay with Jack's flotilla as escort.

Sitting in *Gannet*'s tiny wardroom, gin and tonics in hand, Jack appraised his officers and saw two fine men, but behind their relatively neat uniforms and efficient demeanours, he saw two students: one of law, the other of architecture, young men who should be attending lectures, playing cricket or rugby, going to dances and yet here they were, good officers doing the hard work of the 'little ships', the weight of the world upon their shoulders, fighting this ruthless, interminable sea war. He was proud of Van Zyl and Robinson, these boys who had become men in a matter of months.

'For the Walvis run, I'm thinking of positioning our escorts further from the convoy to keep any lurking U-boats at bay,' said Jack. 'I want us to strike back with much more vigour and, if possible, in pairs. As I'll be explaining to Lieutenants Alstad, Fourie and Cowley in due course, I want every officer to know exactly what to do in an emergency without necessarily referring to me, or to the senior ship. We need to have a set plan, so that each of us can react immediately and instinctively without awaiting orders. At night, in the dark, in foul weather, with U-boats attacking from all sides, I want independent decision-making and aggressive action. We did not have that on the Durban run. If a U-boat is detected, I want it attacked without delay and continuously, unless or until further orders are received. Ask questions later — understood?'

'Yes, sir,' chimed the two lieutenants, stirred by their captain's zeal.

'With the Asdic of the attacking ship blind for the last few hundred yards before laying her eggs, I want a second ship standing off and maintaining the contact whenever possible. It could be even more effective if the attacker switches off her Asdic and creeps up slowly on the enemy, guided by the second ship over shortwave radio.'

'Like a boxer, sir, jab and uppercut?' said Robinson.

'Quite so, Sub.'

Next came the final preparations for sea. PO Cummins supervised the squaring off of the decks, PO Combrink oversaw the last cleaning of guns, greasing of depth-charge release gear, examination of primers and testing of electric circuits, while Leading Seaman Gilbert checked the rockets and flares. During the Durban convoy, some escorts had been forced to ration their depth charges and, not wanting to be caught short again, Jack had his whalers take on as many extra charges as they could carry. He watched Combrink supervising the loading as a crane manoeuvred the lethal canisters aboard. Meanwhile, Sub-Lieutenant Robinson was in the wardroom sprawled in an armchair reading old copies of *Reader's Digest* and dipping into *Moby Dick*, which he loved so much that he limited its consumption.

'Just listen to this, Number One,' he said to Van Zyl who was grabbing a cup of coffee, '"He piled upon the whale's white hump the sum of all the general rage and hate felt by his whole race from Adam down; and then, as if his chest had been a mortar, he burst his hot heart's shell upon it."'

'Melville again?'

'Yes, brilliant isn't it, and so apt.'

On the eve of departure, both *Gannet*'s captain and first lieutenant went ashore leaving Robinson in charge. Upset and fearful of the damage he'd caused to his family, Van Zyl needed the solace of Sylvia before going to sea again. He arranged to accompany her to the Sea Point Pavilion after her morning art classes. It was a warm, windless spring day and they met at Cape Town station where they caught a bus to the Atlantic seaboard suburb.

The pair entered the white, wedding-cake pavilion and descended the staircase to their respective changing rooms, before emerging onto the deck, heading past the children's pool to find a sandy spot among the rocks. Sylvia wore a fetching black two-piece swimsuit and Van Zyl struggled to keep his eyes off her slim figure as they settled on their towels.

'How's UCT?' he asked.

'The lectures are all right, but I love the practical side more, the making of art. It is my escape — a way for me to express the loss. The losses.'

'Graphic art?'

'Yes.'

'No colour?' He smiled.

'No. Etchings mostly. It is where I feel most comfortable, like ... how can I say ... surgery, like being a doctor. You have a needle and you scratch on a metal plate and you cannot make one single mistake in the little square where you are working. I like that. When you are busy with the needle, every part of you is engaged in the creation of this tiny thing of art. It is as though, in that moment, you are able to make a small kind of perfection, repairing the damage of the world, if only within the confines of that plate. Do you think I am mad?'

'Not at all. I think I understand, in a way.'

'Do you make art?'

'I sometimes write poems when we're at sea.'

'Ah, that is good, you must read me one of them.'

'One day, maybe... What do you like to etch?

'I love to —'

'Don't tell me: dark, brooding subjects in the style of Dürer and Goya?'

'Now you have become a mind reader.'

'Only when a mind is worth reading.' He reached over and took her hand in his.

'You are full of compliments, Jannie.'

'It's you ... I ...' He paused to look at the sun's diamond path reaching across the ocean towards them. 'Things have been terrible with my family. Not like what has happened to your family, of course, but we have also been torn apart.'

'What is wrong?' Her face was close to his, their foreheads almost touching. The sounds of the swimmers and children splashing in the shallows faded away. He told her about his brother and the betrayal, about how politics had split his family in two and how it was eating away at him. He spoke about his fears, his anger and his feeling of helplessness.

She put an arm around his shoulders and leant her thigh against his, kissing his cheek.

'It will be all right,' she said. 'You just stay close to me.'

He looked into her big, dreamy eyes and oval face framed by dark curls and allowed himself, for a few precious minutes, to be lost. When their lips met and their bodies melted against each another, the parts of their beings that were in pain found their own form of healing.

CHAPTER 26

On his last night ashore, Jack's father had to attend an event at Admiralty House, so Jack had supper with Miss Retief instead. After the meal, they sat in the two big armchairs beside the blackout curtains, the embers of a fire glowing in the grate, Miss Retief's bold Expressionist portraits staring down from the walls around them and the wireless softly leaking Tommy Handley's *It's That Man Again* comedy programme. Jack sipped his nightcap while Miss Retief knitted sea-boot stockings for her handsome lodger's men. The two cats, Smuts and Hertzog, lay curled up on a large cushion beside the fireplace.

'You'll be pleased to hear that I've joined The Good Companions Club,' said Miss Retief.

'What on earth is that?' asked Jack.

'Oh, it's a group of matriarchs who organise events for visiting sailors. We've got nearly a hundred young ladies on our books to call on for dances, either in the Soldier's and Sailors' Rest Room or in the East Dockyard Recreation Hall.'

'Do let me know when you're arranging another and I'll inform my crew.'

'I certainly will. We provide the refreshments and a band — apparently The Burchells are very popular — and to raise funds, we hold fetes on Jubilee Square, church bazaars and bingo evenings.'

'Goodness, I didn't think you'd go in for that sort of thing.'

'Too arty? Too Afrikaans?' She had a mischievous grin.

Jack blushed.

'Well, you're right, I wouldn't under normal circumstances, but I've seen what you're doing, Jack, and it has in a way inspired me to make some sort of contribution to the war effort and to Simon's Town.'

'I'm very pleased. I just hope it doesn't keep you away from your paintbrushes for too long.'

'Don't you worry: art first, war second.'

When the Tommy Handley programme ended, Jack downed his whisky and said his goodnights to Miss Retief and the cats. He hadn't let on that he was leaving on a long voyage in the morning, but his landlady could read the signs and recognise the mood. 'Sleep tight, Jack, and keep yourself safe.'

'Thank you, Miss Retief, for everything.'

He stood on the stoep before turning in, surveying the blacked-out harbour, the dark outline of False Bay, and listened to the shushing of the shore break on Long Beach. Was that the inquisitive 'hu-hooo' of a male spotted eagle owl?

Perhaps it was time, once again, on this eve of departure, to take stock of the path he had walked since the beginning of the war. The loss of his mother and his ship at Dunkirk had left him broken, but his move to the Cape had offered direction and hope. He'd found a position, a place, and he had found love, but the enemy now threatened to take all that away from him once more.

He thought of the things that brought him joy: a black-shouldered kite twitching in flight, Vivaldi's *Four Seasons* at the Queen's Hall, bouillabaisse with his family at a waterside bistro in Villefranche, a decently struck crosscourt backhand, hiking the Scottish moors with his brother and, more recently, this peninsula with its wild nature and mountains plunging into the sea. And Clara, who he knew with reinvigorated certainty that he loved and who he had unnecessarily, stupidly, hurt.

Now he was going back to sea, with the enemy lurking, and putting it all on the line once again. He would telephone Clara in the morning; he would make things right before leaving.

Next morning, before returning to his ship, Jack asked to use Miss Retief's telephone and called the Marais home in Newlands. Thankfully, Clara picked up: she was about to leave for lectures.

'Jack! Why so early? What's wrong?'

'Nothing's wrong. I'm about to go to sea — can't tell you the details, obviously — but it could be a long, hard one.'

'And I have to get cracking. Ma is giving me a lift to campus.'

'Clara, I … I just needed to apologise and say that you mean absolutely everything to me. I've been thinking a lot and come to my senses. I *do* want to make this thing between us permanent. I want to ask if you'd be prepared —'

'Jack, before you go on … I've been thinking a lot too. Things are not right between us and you're carrying too much to add me to the list.'

'That's not —'

'I can't take on the burden and I won't have my heart broken.'

'What are you saying?' His voice was tight with dread, his heart firing.

'It's not going to work between us. You have a war —'

'But Clara, my love, the war will end. I want to be with you.'

'No, I can't.'

'Is there someone else?'

'Don't ask me that.'

'Is it Henry?'

'Don't ask that. I've got to go, Ma is waiting.'

'Clara, please —'

'I'm sorry, Jack, there's nothing more to say.'

'Clara, wait —'

The line went dead. He stood holding the big black receiver for a long time, then walked slowly back to his cottage in a daze. It was time, too, for him to go.

The crew were mustered on *Gannet*'s foredeck for Jack to address them.

'I hope you have all enjoyed a well-earned rest, but it is time once again to "go down to the sea in ships" and "occupy our business in great waters". During the last convoy, we were under attack from both the elements and the enemy.' He looked around at the faces, some eager, others wary, all of them wondering what and how much their captain would ask of them this time. 'We know two things about the task before us: that U-boats are almost certainly still active in Cape waters and that the convoy we will be escorting is absolutely essential. This time, it is my intention to take the fight to the enemy whenever and wherever possible. I expect you to do your duty, proudly, selflessly and to the best of your ability, as I shall do mine. This time, we will destroy the enemy and destroy him good and proper. That is all, carry on.'

The men were still cheering when he reached his cabin.

Half an hour later they were ready for sea. 'Single up,' came the call as dock workers lifted the loops off the bollards and let the lines fall into the water before being hauled aboard through the whaler's oval fairleads.

'Let go aft.' Then a few moments later, 'Let go forward spring.'

Jack felt the familiar thrill as the last line slurped aboard: the land forsaken, the sea beckoning, another chapter. *Gannet* was a thing unto herself once more, with her own rigid order and inflexible laws: a good ship and a happy ship. The stern swung away from the dock and the whaler chugged slowly astern. He would put Clara behind him, bury her deep, at least until the convoy was delivered to Walvis Bay.

'Wheelhouse, bridge,' said Jack into the voicepipe.

'Wheelhouse, aye,' growled February.

'Starboard ten.'

'Starboard ten. Ten of starboard wheel on, sir.'

'Very good.' Then a few moments later, 'Midships.'

'Wheel's amidships, Cap'n.'

Gannet sailed through the bullnose, described a graceful turn to starboard and aimed her prow at the wide-open arms of False Bay.

With their bow waves peeling like wings, the quartet of whalers made a fine sight as they steamed line astern out of Simon's Bay on that bright October morning. Jack stood at the rail admiring the neat precision of his ships, leaning into their turns, rudders biting, masts heeling. They rounded Cape Point, sailed up the Peninsula's flank and took up position off Green Point, waiting for the convoy to assemble.

Nine ships emerged from Cape Town harbour with tugs busily in attendance and formed up in pairs for the journey down the swept channel to the hundred-fathom line. *Gannet* took station one mile ahead of the lead ships as they sailed across a pewter sea towards an approaching fog bank.

Jack ordered the column to reduce to six knots, just as the eerie grey blanket began to envelop them. Looking ahead, all he could see was the chalky white of *Gannet*'s bow wave, her prow cleaving through ethereal milk, the breeze on his face carrying the damp, fresh smell of thickened air. The fog seemed like an incarnation of his doubts, indecision and fear, the enemy's natural home, its silence the foretaste of annihilation. He stuck out an arm in front of him as if to touch the very substance of it, feeling the dampness and, to his mind, the ugliness of this creeping obfuscation that threw his plans and his ships into disarray. How would he know from which direction the threat would come? How would he find his way?

The moaning of ships' horns was echoed by the low booming of Green Point Lighthouse astern of them and Robben Island's foghorn on their starboard beam. Silence settled over the convoy as the vapour swirled and eddied, the ships appearing and disappearing as they struggled to hold station in the gloom. Lookouts were placed in the bows, fog lamps were lit. Jack could not shake off the feeling of helplessness: navigation reduced to witchcraft, station keeping a game of aural direction finding and guesswork.

Convoy CN.04 emerged into a clear patch of ocean at the end of the swept channel and formed up in a box of three columns and three rows, heading northwest in the gathering dusk. After passing Cape Columbine, its lighthouse stabbing the eastern horizon, they moved further offshore. The rest of the night was mercifully clear, but in the morning another fog bank rolled in, blanketing the ships and testing Jack's nerve once more as he endeavoured to keep his flock together. The convoy groped its way north at snail's pace, each merchantman deploying a 'fog buoy', in the shape of a barrel towed astern, the next ship in line trying not to lose sight of its splash and wake.

Jack leaned over the rail but could see nothing beyond the twelve-pounder: how he loathed this tentative pawing at ethereal walls. He kept glancing astern, fearing at any moment to see the bows of a merchantman about to slice them in two. He tried to identify and measure the distance of the various horns, hooters, bells and sirens, but fog warped, magnified or deadened sound, making his job more difficult. Listening carefully to his charges — the wheezer, the boomer, the bleater — he plotted in his mind the position of each member of his herd. Just so long as every captain held his course, trusted his neighbours and *no one did anything foolish*... Despite the cold, Jack felt sweat trickling down his spine.

On one of *Gannet*'s zigzags, the helmsman let her stray too close to the lead ship of the starboard column.

'Bridge, aft lookout!' yelled Booysen. 'Ship, sir, bearing green one-three-oh!'

Jack stepped to the side of the bridge, straining his eyes. The fog parted for a moment to reveal in the sky above them two anchors bestride the rust-streaked, Damoclean blade of a merchantman poised to strike their quarterdeck.

'Hard a-port, full ahead!' shouted Jack as he watched the aft lookout dive for cover.

'Oh my God,' whimpered Robinson.

'Shut up, Sub!' Jack snapped.

The steel blade of the freighter's bows bore down on the whaler, but her helmsman's reaction was quick and decisive and the skyscraper scythed by. There was a loud crack and the excruciating sound of scraping steel as *Gannet*'s quarterdeck connected a glancing blow. Jack looked up and saw the underside of a lifeboat passing overhead like a low-flying aircraft ... and then they were clear, wallowing through the troubled water of the merchantman's wake.

'Oi, sir, what shenanigans you up to now!' came McEwan's cry up the voicepipe.

'Sorry to disturb your sleep, Chief, but we just had our arse kissed by a freighter,' said Jack, trying to make light of what must have been a terrifying few moments in the echoing tin box of the engine room: hasty orders for full ahead, the helm hard over, and then an almighty bang.

'Kindly warn us of your next hochmagandy escapade, please Cap'n.'

'Aye, Chief, but no more romancing planned from us.'

'Me and the lads would welcome that, sir.'

Sailing northwest through the day, passing in and out of fog banks, they encountered the Benguela Current's bounteous sea life in the shape of dolphins, whales, seals and vast shoals of fish. At times, the Asdic operators had to deal with pings coming from almost every direction. Passing close to a school of sardines, Jack was distracted by a flock of Cape gannets falling from the sky in a frenzy of feeding. The birds arced down like feathered dive bombers, folding their black-and-white wings and striking the water at more than fifty miles an hour with a loud slapping sound. It was a sight to lift the spirit and transport him away from convoy duties for a few precious moments.

By late afternoon, they'd reached Hondeklip Bay and were cruising along South Africa's most barren shore.

'Huff-duff report from SNO Simon's Town, sir,' said Sparks, hauling himself onto the bridge.

'Yes, what is it?'

'Foreign transmission bearing three-two-oh, range approximately twenty-five miles, sir.'

'U-boat chatter?' asked Van Zyl.

'Probably,' muttered Jack. 'How the hell did they land up exactly in our path?'

'Spies, sir?' said Van Zyl.

'I'll bet. They must have known our precise departure time and route.'

Jack was faced with a familiar dilemma: expose the convoy and attack or protect the convoy and defend? Everyone on the bridge was studiously looking in other directions, sensing their captain's indecision. He cleared his throat as if to speak and Van Zyl stiffened, but the silence of vacillation persisted. Jack couldn't afford a repeat of the Durban debacle.

'All right, damn it, full ahead, course three-two-oh!' he snapped. Yes, he would thrust, and take *Belle* with him to hopefully catch the enemy on the surface. Jack signalled *Langeberg* and *Waterberg*, instructing them to try to plug the gaps he and Alstad would leave. 'Bunts, make to *Belle*, "Take station on me, line abreast to port, two miles apart."'

He watched the tiny grey speck approaching at full speed — disappearing almost entirely in a trough, then exploding from the crest in a welter of white water. Jack was all focus, his forehead creased with determination and a burning eagerness for the chase. Chess player, swordsman, hunter. He stood beside the binnacle, hands behind his back, leaning into the swell, taking *Gannet*'s rhythm, his duffel coat unbuttoned at the throat and his mind cleared for battle.

'Number One, sound action stations,' he said matter-of-factly. Alarm bells rang throughout the ship even before his words were fully formed, boots drumming on steel as men raced to their positions.

'Coxs'n taking over the wheel, sir,' came the gruff voice of February from the voicepipe. It was one of the most comforting sounds on *Gannet*, coming with the certainty that the man at the wheel was almost telepathically linked to him.

For the next forty-five minutes, *Gannet* and *Belle* steamed northwest at seventeen knots, all lookouts on high alert and gun crews closed up. Both hulls trembled with anticipation, their prows rising and dipping through showers of spray as they galloped towards the foe. Jack was smiling, a smile that infected the others on the bridge and seemed to leak down to the men at their weapons, even, seemingly, to the 'black gang' far below in the engine room. He looked at the gun crew on the bandstand, steel-helmeted, frozen in anticipation, hands poised on the laying and training wheels … waiting to strike.

'Periscope, sir!' shouted Behardien, then tempering his tone, 'port bow, red four-oh.'

Jack was at his shoulder in a flash, binoculars raised to scan the undulating grey swells. The slender cylinder dragging a feather of spray seemed to him a thing of the purest menace — a needle of hate. Within moments, it had vanished. Jack knew that at the very least, the U-boat had to be kept submerged until the merchantmen had passed.

'Distance?'

'About three miles, sir.'

He picked up the RT phone: '*Gannet* to *Belle*, *Gannet* to *Belle*, do you read me?'

'*Belle* to *Gannet*, reading you strength four,' came Alstad's Nordic drawl.

'*Gannet* to *Belle*, I have a contact on my port bow, range less than three miles,' said Jack. 'I am reducing speed to eleven knots.'

'Contact bearing two-eight-oh, sir,' called out Potgieter.

'*Gannet* to *Belle*, I have Asdic contact. Enemy moving right to left, range 2,500 yards.'

There followed a period of tense silence on the bridge as the two whalers closed with a patch of ocean that held the object of their utmost desire.

'*Belle* to *Gannet*, I have contact.' Alstad's voice was clear as a bell. 'On my starboard bow, range fifteen hundred yards, converging.' The pincers were closing. 'Request permission to attack, sir.'

'Permission granted,' said Jack, trying to empty his voice of emotion.

The game's pieces, having appeared almost stationary during the build-up, now hurtled towards each other like cymbals about to clash.

'*Belle* to *Gannet*, contact lost.'

'I still have her,' said Jack. 'She is dead ahead of me. Take your cross bearing off *Gannet*. I am setting a deep pattern, suggest you set yours medium.'

Jack pictured fifty Germans in a steel tube somewhere beneath his feet and his two ships playing ferret, poised for the kill. *Belle* tore across *Gannet*'s bows and Jack watched as depth charges rolled off her stern and leapt from her flanks, then the sea ahead of them erupted in six almighty explosions.

Next came *Gannet*'s turn. At Jack's command, charges rumbled off their stern and throwers coughed, sending canisters high into the air. 'Load, load, load!' yelled PO Combrink, as the Atlantic was ripped asunder. After each pass, Combrink's team toiled to reload the chutes and throwers, the quarterdeck's violent roll threatening bodily harm as depth charges swung back and forth on their tackles like demented pendulums.

'Hard a-starboard,' ordered Jack as *Belle* healed over to port and slewed around to resume her attack, racing across their wake and planting another set of seeds to the tune of preternatural booming. Down in the engine room, the chief and his stokers experienced each detonation as the deafening reverberation of an enormous bell, their steel compartment trembling to the shock.

'Contact regained, sir, dead ahead!' shouted Potgieter. Then a few minutes later: 'Contact lost.'

That would put her within three hundred yards. In his head, Jack counted off the seconds of probable convergence, then called: 'Fire!'

More sea volcanoes, more frustration as their attacks remained unrewarded. Jack's mind held a three-dimensional picture of the two hunters, the quarry, their speeds and courses, moving this way and that across the board. He was trying to guess the enemy's reaction to the last pattern. The U-boat captain had probably taken her as deep as her frame allowed and would be slinking away, but in which direction? There was still too much turbulence in the water from the previous charges to get a fix and Jack waited anxiously for the sea to settle and the Asdic to find the target again. Its regular pinging had taken the place of his eyes, his ears … his pulse.

'Stand by for another deep pattern, Guns,' Jack said into the voicepipe.

'Standing by, sir,' said Combrink.

Gannet dropped her charges, then slewed round to bisect once more with *Belle* as they braided their attack. To no avail as the contact was lost yet again, seemingly for good. Aimless now: Jack and Alstad were blind men beating white sticks at the emptiness of the deep. Thankfully, the convoy had long passed, so at least they had kept the enemy down — slow, deep, toothless and unsighted — giving the merchantmen a chance to alter course and be swallowed by the fog.

Belle and *Gannet* left the scene of their disappointment and sped back towards the convoy in the twilight. Just then, to Jack's horror, the fogbank ahead was lit by internal combustion, like lightning in the belly of a thunderstorm. Out there in the flickering gloom, a ship was dying and Jack had chosen to hunt far from his flock. While he'd been chasing elusive tails, another U-boat had exploited the weakened defences.

'Signal to convoy commodore, Sparks: "Do not disperse. Am coming to your assistance."'

Jack ordered *Waterberg* to pick up survivors from the sinking ship, now coming into view, as *Gannet* and *Belle* raced to catch up with the convoy. He watched through his binoculars as the stern of SS *Paternoster*, a large merchantman carrying passengers, rose into the air. Her funnel crumpled as though made of cardboard, disgorging soot, as the Atlantic roared into her mortal wounds. The great brass propeller continued to turn grotesquely as she sank like an imploding tower, displacing a turmoil of water that swamped the two lifeboats that had been launched and engulfed the swimmers.

Waterberg would remain in attendance until deep into the night, picking up 147 souls which made for a tight squeeze on the whaler. She was ordered back to Cape Town, her crew tossing everything over the side that could be jettisoned to make room for the bedraggled survivors, packed like sardines asleep on deck or sitting comatose on benches. Waterberg's sailors provided blankets, clothes and care where they could, while the cook knuckled down to the most taxing thirty-six hours of his naval life.

The remaining three escorts kept a vigilant screen through the night and arrived at the gates of dawn off the mouth of the Orange River without having lost any more of their number. But mid-morning that all changed in the blink of an eye.

'U-boat on the surface red nine-oh!' yelled Booysen as the fog lifted briefly to reveal a dark shape six miles to the west.

'Good eyes that man!' exclaimed Jack, then down the voicepipe: 'Everything you've got, Chief.'

'Aye, Cap'n, I'll do mae best,' said the old Scot as *Gannet* turned to face the enemy and went straight to action stations.

'Battle ensign, sir?' enquired Van Zyl.

'Why not?'

Without being asked, Behardien was already scurrying down the ladder to raise the huge flag to the mizzen gaff. *Gannet* made a proud sight, her white ensign streaming, her stern tucked well down giving full purchase, her prow raised. Once again, *Belle* joined in the chase as the U-boat turned and fled, hoping to outpace her pursuers. McEwan somehow managed to squeeze the better part of an extra knot out of his engine, but *Belle* — the marginally slower sister — slipped astern. Up on the fo'c'sle, PO Combrink kept calling the range as they closed with an elusive dot shrouded in diesel fumes.

'Eleven-thousand yards, sir!'

Jack gripped the rail with both hands, his gaze locked on the enemy.

'Ten thousand five hundred!'

'Very well, that should do,' said Jack. 'Open fire!'

Crack! The bridge was swathed in cordite smoke that cleared to reveal the speck sliding beneath the waves even before the shot had landed in her wake. Jack was awash with doubt once more, but pressed on. The two escorts were again being drawn away from the convoy, and it would take nearly twenty minutes to reach the spot the U-boat had dived. In that time, she could travel at least two miles in any direction and Jack had to decide *right now* which way the enemy captain would flee. Intuition said he'd continue west, away from the coast, then turn north to stay in touch with the convoy on a parallel course. He radioed *Belle* his intentions and, when he drew closer to the hunting zone, slowed to allow the Asdic to come into play.

Jack stood behind the gyro compass wearing a look of deep concentration, his head cocked as though listening for the propeller noises of his quarry. Every few minutes he passed steering orders to February.

'Echo bearing three-one-oh!' sang out Potgieter.

'*Gannet* to *Belle*, am commencing the attack,' said Jack into the RT phone.

The whaler surged towards the contact, quivering to the beat of her engine as she loped over an easy grey sea. The Asdic beam echoed off the U-boat's hull with a most satisfying metallic sound, coming faster and clearer as they approached the target.

'Stand by for a full pattern, PO,' Jack called into the voicepipe.

'Fire!'

Six depth charges tumbled off the stern or shot into the air from the quarterdeck, followed by a few seconds of pregnant silence. Then the pressure waves struck *Gannet*'s hull and monstrous detonations roared in Jack's ears as the sea was torn open and hurled aloft. *Belle* joined the fray to sow destruction in an adjacent patch of ocean, but there was no debris to show for their labours, so round they came again … and again.

Jack knew he was dealing with a canny opponent who wasn't being panicked into any rash moves and continued to run silently, varying his depth after each attack and skilfully using the hunters' blind moments to evade them. But with many hours of daylight ahead, Jack was content to settle into the fight for as long as it took: this fish was not going to get away. All through the afternoon they toiled, sometimes lying in silence, waiting to regain contact, sometimes weaving madly and laying profligate eggs.

Although Asdic could not provide Jack with the U-boat's depth, he surmised that the German captain had taken her very deep. He radioed Alstad and suggested a barrage by both ships sailing line abreast, dropping a large pattern set to 550 feet at six-second intervals. *Belle* swept alongside and they sailed together, laying the charges as they went. The sea boiled and writhed as explosion after explosion ripped the Atlantic apart in a terrible display of firepower that shook both escorts from keelson to truck. What it was doing to the U-boat, Jack could hardly imagine.

To no avail.

The U-boat captain doubled back, lay doggo or used cold layers to hide, before being found once more to resume the dance, the depth charges sometimes falling close, more often wide of the mark, but the pursuers never growing tired, circling back across each other's paths, calling bearings and courses, sticking doggedly to the hunt. Time and again, they lunged, ravaged the ocean, wheeled around and lunged once more.

Jack began to suspect that the U-boat was even deeper than the settings on his depth charges would allow. So he tried other methods to force the enemy's hand, like running in at speed on dummy attacks, encouraging the U-boat to take sharp evasive action and use up battery power. The hours dragged by and although the convoy was by now far to the north, Jack hoped that below his feet men would shortly be running out of air. Another consideration was that *Belle* was low on depth charges and might soon have to resort to pairs or even single charges to stay in the fight.

The afternoon drew to a close and the sun found a resting place somewhere in the grey eiderdown of the west. They would have to give up and re-join the convoy before dark, but Jack wanted one last crack and opted for the creeping attack he'd discussed with his captains but not had time to train for. The idea was for *Belle* to hold the contact at about a thousand yards and direct *Gannet* — Asdic silenced and travelling at less than five knots — as she stole up behind the enemy, her quiet approach from dead astern theoretically masked by the sound of the U-boat's own propellers.

When contact was regained, Jack put his plan into action. Alstad conned him into position over the RT, nudging him this way and that as the three-vessel ballet developed. Jack gripped the compass binnacle, his mind emptied of everything but the quarry, as *Gannet* inched quietly up the U-boat's wake, waiting for *Belle*'s command. At any moment, the enemy might get wise to the trap and take evasive action.

'Stand by,' said Jack, his voice hoarse.

'You are directly above the U-boat now,' Alstad's voice crackled through the telephone. *Gannet* would need to get ahead of the enemy before releasing her charges and Jack waited with agonising impatience as they edged painstakingly ahead of their quarry, ten yards, twenty, thirty… At fifty yards he bellowed, 'Fire!' as a full pattern set at maximum depth splashed down in their wake. The quarterdeck party reloaded feverishly to be ready again in fifteen seconds. 'Fire!' Another pattern was released. Now came the torment of the seas, as charge after charge detonated.

'I'm prepared to stake a wager on that lot, Number One!' he shouted above the din. 'If not, we're sure to have shaken the teeth out of some Nazi gums.'

The submarine surfaced without preamble, bursting from the deep like a champagne cork to the surprise and shock of the onlookers. Her bows hung in the air for a moment before her body splashed down. Jack stared in disbelief at the loathsome object — a dark-finned, salivating death-maker — the incarnation of his fears, dragged from subconscious depths and exposed to the light of day. *He must destroy it.*

The gate-crashing U-boat caught the gun crews on both escorts momentarily off guard as tiny figures poured from the conning tower to man their weapons. Jack watched as the enemy turned away, bent on outrunning her pursuers in the gathering mist and gloom of the east. *Gannet*'s twelve-pounder spat: a tongue of flame, a stinging waft of cordite and afar the salty pillar of white beside the enemy. The flash and bang filled Jack's mind with images that he immediately staunched. *Concentrate, focus, watertight!*

The two whalers steamed forward, grey ghosts gliding through the threadbare drifts like hunting dogs with prey in their nostrils. Black attack flags flying and battle ensigns streaming sacramental and white, they tore towards the dark-hulled adversary. Jack's bloodlust was up: the many ships sunk and good men lost on his watch weighing heavily as he raced on. He looked down at his gun crew — tin-hatted like medieval lancers marching towards the enemy pikes — as they fed their pills into the breech. Yes, a two-horse cavalry charge across soft fields of grey, riding down upon the Gothic foe.

'Sound trumpets, let our bloody colours wave, and either victory, or else a grave,' Jack murmured through clenched teeth.

Bang! Another round.

The enemy appeared unable to dive and the whalers began scoring near misses that slowed her escape as the U-boat twisted and writhed to evade their fire. Bright red tracers lifted from the enemy's 37mm and 20mm guns, arcing lazily through the air, then coming home in a rush as the sea around *Gannet* was peppered with the deadly dance of water sprites. Now the maniacal squeal of ricochets and clang of body blows. Tracer streamed aboard, plucking Seaman Manley from the twelve-pounder, a shell opening a steaming hole in his stomach as he was flung to the deck. Another sailor quickly ducked behind the gun shield to take his place. Jack spotted Porky with a field dressing bent over the burly, oafish, headstrong, Rhodesian — poor, beautiful Manley — as blood pooled on the deck around them. After a few moments of frantic activity, Porky shook his head and looked at the sky.

Belle veered slightly to port and *Gannet* to starboard so that both ships could bring their secondary armaments to bear. Pickles, sat behind his pom-pom, cursed oaths of great filth as his short-necked beast spat its venom, sending red tracer on a low trajectory towards the submarine. The two-pounder shells were lightweight but repeated blows tore at the enemy's skin and ate at her vitals as metal flew from bright-flashed hits. Pickles's handiwork gutted a German gunner, his intestines snaking across the slimy afterdeck. More men poured from the conning tower but were plucked aside and asunder until blood streamed from the U-boat's decks.

Gannet's twelve-pounder cracked again, followed by another dull bang from *Belle*. Through his binoculars, Jack saw a bright red flash leap from the conning tower as the ready-use ammunition was set ablaze. Like a cornered animal, the U-boat turned to face the attackers and Jack could clearly make out her number, *U-156*, as tracer continued to pepper the casing with sparkles of light.

Now the enemy lay dead in the water, too crippled to dive, her guns cleared of men by accurate fire and bodies strewn about her deck. As *Gannet* ran in at speed, Jack spotted one or two figures cowering on the bridge, possibly wounded. He altered course to pass down her flank, raking the hull with his Lewis guns and dropping a shallow pattern alongside. The detonations enveloped the U-boat in spray and, when the water subsided, she was already beginning to sink.

Gannet went about and slowed to approach the listing hull. So this, then, was the enemy Jack had cravenly hunted and whose prey he had been. Here was the enemy that had filled his waking hours and ransacked his dreams; here was the author of his torment; here was nothing. The U-boat pointed the shark-like fin of her prow at the sky and slid stern first into the Atlantic as a few figures jerked from the conning tower and threw themselves overboard. Only then did Jack become aware of the cheering from his own ship and its echo coming across the water from *Belle*, lying stationary less than a hundred yards away.

The two whalers drifted down on the survivors who were hauled aboard at the ships' low waists. These were hardly Nazi monsters: simply lads just like their own, shivering, oil-stained and shocked. The wounded were carried to the wardrooms while the remainder were herded under guard to the boat decks and given hot drinks and blankets. The U-boat's captain — Jack learnt that his name was Nagel — was not among the survivors.

CHAPTER 27

Darkness fell like the curtain at the Alhambra Theatre as *Gannet* and *Belle* closed with the convoy and took up station to continue their northbound passage. Midnight found them off Lüderitzbucht, stalked by a lone U-boat cruising out of sight on their left flank. *Belle* had just detached herself to pursue an echo that might be a pod of seals, dolphins … or a submarine. As Jack watched her dip a shoulder into the swell, a tall column of water rose forward of the bridge. For a moment, he simply stared, not quite believing what he was seeing. Then the sound of the explosion reached him and he knew immediately *Belle* was done for. The wounded whaler staggered, then swerved to port, still travelling at considerable speed as water tore into and through her.

Escorts were normally too small, agile and shallow-drafted for submarines to waste torpedoes on, but *Belle* had been passing a bigger target at exactly the wrong moment. Jack wheeled *Gannet* around and hastened to the rescue, sending *Langeberg* to cover the left flank and fend off the attacker.

Gannet circled the scene, pinging to discourage the U-boat, as Jack stared aghast at the carnage: across the narrow gap were men like his own, shipmates, friends, brothers. Drawing closer, Jack spotted Alstad, blood streaming from his head, but still erect and holding onto the binnacle as the bridge heeled more exaggeratedly, threatening to topple him.

'Abandon ship!' came the faint cry from Alstad's loudhailer. Men began to jump off the stern into the freezing water and Jack noticed *Belle*'s navigator emerging from the wheelhouse with a wooden box in each hand — the ship's sextant and chronometer.

'Come on in, Captain, the water's lovely!' shouted one of the swimmers.

Alstad stepped off the bridge and dropped into the sea. '*Herregud det er kaldt!*' he gasped as he broke the surface. Hands reached out and dragged him aboard the float by his lifejacket.

Belle was going down. On her stern, now rising high out of the water, the leading torpedo-man fought back the pain of his mortal injuries and went about the business of removing the primers from his depth charges, lest they explode among the survivors when the whaler sank. He worked his way methodically through the canisters and managed to neutralise the last one just as *Belle* slid beneath the waves, taking him with her in a vortex of filthy water.

Gannet made a last sweep, pinging for the enemy, then approached the dozen survivors, some on the Carley, others floating among the bodies and debris.

'Dead slow,' said Jack. 'Robinson, get down there and prepare some lines and a net. Hail me as soon as everyone's aboard.'

'Aye aye, sir,' he said, scuttling down the ladder.

'Stop engine.'

Gannet wallowed closer, the eerie silence of the mist pressing in. The pinging of the Asdic provided their only protection, sounding louder than ever, as survivors were lifted carefully aboard. To the crew of *Gannet*, they were rescuing a duplicate of themselves — a similar set of jokers, dreamers and rogues — and were all the more attentive because of it. *Belle*'s young navigator was saved, but without his precious sextant and chronometer. Alstad was in the process of being helped aboard when the rescuers lost their grip on the captain's oil-soaked arms and he fell back into the sea. Pickles threw a heaving line but, try as he might, the big Norwegian couldn't hang onto the rope due to his injuries and began to lapse into unconsciousness.

'Come on, Alstad, we won't bite!' Jack called desperately from the bridge, but the wounded captain no longer heard him and was drifting away on the current. Just then, Booysen grabbed a line and dived overboard, swimming as swiftly as he'd ever done in the shallows of Kalk Bay harbour. The young sailor secured the end of the line around the man's waist and the two were dragged aboard.

'That's all of 'em, sir!' Robinson's voice echoed in the mist.

'You sure, Sub?'

'Aye, Captain!'

As *Gannet* pulled away, the survivors were helped to peel off their oil-caked clothing and given blankets. Hendricks served mugs of sweet tea and an odd assortment of garments appeared from *Gannet*'s mess decks.

Four sailors carried Alstad to the captain's cabin and lowered him into Jack's cot. He was barely conscious and still in too much shock to feel the agony of his wounds. Porky arrived to administer morphine from his stock of syrettes and applied dressings to the Norwegian's head wound and shrapnel gash on his arm.

Jack stepped into the cabin to check on the patient.

'*Takk, takk* … Thank you, Kaptein,' murmured Alstad. There was pain and sorrow in the craggy Nordic face but the defiance remained, worn like a badge.

'I'm just glad we got you safely aboard,' said Jack.

'Take care of my boys.'

'Of course, now get some rest, you old Viking rogue.'

No sooner had Jack returned to the bridge than Potgieter yelled from the Asdic hut, 'Torpedoes fired, port beam!' followed soon after by a lookout's cry of alarm: 'One torpedo, bearing red eight-oh! Second one will pass astern!'

Jack spun round to see the bubble trails that marked the shallow-running projectiles. He could hardly credit the brazenness of his adversary. *Gannet* was still travelling too slowly and wouldn't have enough time to build up speed or even turn. Jack had a brief picture of the torpedo's impact and fiery annihilation ... the toothy prow of HMS *Havoc* pointing at the sky, dead sailors in the water all around him.

'Full ahead, hard a-port!' Then into the quarterdeck voicepipe: 'PO Combrink, depth charges, now! Shallow setting, fire at will!'

Gannet's stern was coming around painfully slowly: the arrow could not miss its mark. Only Jack's audacious gamble could save them now. There was shouting as the crew realised the inevitable meeting of ship and torpedo. Their spinning propeller tried vainly to claw them from the double danger of enemy missile and, given *Gannet*'s slow acceleration, their own shallow-set depth charges destroying the quarterdeck. Jack stared aft in horror, realising his ship would suffer both calamities — murder and suicide — at the same time. He braced himself, screwing his eyes almost shut as the men around him crouched down, hoping the bridge and funnel would shield them from the blast.

The eruptions lifted their stern bodily from the water and hurled *Gannet* forward. Jack and every other upright sailor were flung to the deck. A white skyscraper stood over the ship as tons of water cascaded down upon them. Jack's ears were ringing and his legs had turned to jelly, but he was back on his feet and looking aft, quickly assessing the situation and finding

Gannet, miraculously, intact. As he had hoped — at the limit of his wildest dreams — a depth charge had countermined the torpedo just yards from the stern. His outrageous experiment, plucked from desperation's top shelf, had saved their lives.

'Ridiculous,' Jack muttered to himself.

'Fantastic, sir,' said Van Zyl in a trembling voice as he pulled himself erect and made a mental inventory of his body parts. Damage reports streamed in: there were leaks everywhere but none of them mortal. *Gannet* would live to strike back and striking back was foremost in Jack's mind. He looked around at the faces of the men on the bridge: there was shock, certainly, but also defiance, and he could feel the ferocity growing within him. *Keep a lid on it, use it, don't let it use you.*

'One starts to take it personally, Number One,' said Jack. With his cap blown off, his hair a mess and blood running down his cheek, *Gannet*'s master looked more pirate than RNVR lieutenant. 'Let's go and get the bastard.'

'Aye aye, sir!' The mad gleam in Van Zyl's eye matched that of his dishevelled captain.

'AB Hendricks regrets to announce that almost every plate, mug, glass and bottle has been smashed,' said Robinson, appearing on the bridge. 'We'll be eating off tin plates until we get home.'

'We can borrow crockery from some of our flock when we get to Walvis,' said Jack. 'They're going to owe us one after we sink this Nazi bastard.'

'I see, sir,' said Robinson, catching the infectious spirit of retribution that hung about the bridge of HMSAS *Southern Gannet* on a foggy October night somewhere off Hottentots Point, South West Africa.

Jack set about a box search, fully aware that with each passing minute the enemy would slip further from his grasp as the convoy, his singular responsibility, sailed over the horizon. And what if there were another U-boat or, God forbid, a wolf pack lying in wait further north? His instinct told him not, and that this was the target that counted, and that now was the time.

'Asdic report: contact bearing oh-four-oh, 900 yards!' called out Potgieter.

'Deepest setting, if you will, Guns,' said Jack into the voicepipe as relief and adrenalin poured through him with the force of opened seacocks.

'Aye aye, sir, deep setting,' answered PO Combrink.

'Asdic reports contact dead ahead.'

Closer.

'Asdic reports contact lost.'

It was over to Jack. Would the enemy turn to port, to starboard or hold steady? Jack decided on the bluff and held his course.

'Open fire,' said Jack.

'Fire one!' barked PO Combrink. 'Fire two! Fire three!'

Jack leant far out from the bridge wing as the canisters sank to their predetermined depths. The explosions were lower in pitch and more muffled, like the belching of an abyssal creature, their preternatural light flickering way down in the deep. Jack opened the range to 1,000 yards to regain contact, then carved *Gannet* around and back into the melee for another thrust.

But the first salvo had been lucky and Jack was again caught wrong-footed as a U-boat's prow burst from the sea shedding torrents like a breaching whale before splashing down on an even keel. Jack read her name, *U-68*, as the conning-tower hatch sprang open and sailors poured out to man the guns.

'Fire as you bear!' bellowed Jack. *Cry* Havoc *and let slip the dogs of war.* He watched the enemy's 10.5 traversing to take aim at his ship. The Germans fired hastily over open sights, the shell whining past their bridge as *Gannet*'s own gunners raced to bring the twelve-pounder to bear. The second German shell carried away their foremast, a piece of it crashing against the bridge wing, narrowly missing Jack and the lookout as it went over the side in a tangle of wire and splintered wood.

But *Gannet* was hitting back. Seaman Malan on the Lewis gun and Pickles on the pom-pom vented streams of tracer across the narrowing gap and plucked the foredeck gunners from their unprotected mount until the casing was a bloody charnel house. More men tried to reach the 10.5, but were killed or turned back by the lethal hail of lead. *Gannet* increased speed to ram and Jack warned the engine room to stand by for impact. Unable to dive and with nowhere to run, the U-boat veered sharply, inside the whaler's turning circle and too close now for either pom-pom or twelve-pounder to depress far enough. McEwan kept the engines at full power as February carved the tightest circle his ship could manage.

Jack could see the white cap of the opposing captain, staring back at him across the shrinking gyre of their mutual hate. The U-boat was a hooked shark, thrashing about on the end of a line, but still lethal. *Gannet*'s Lewis gun continued to pour bursts of lead onto the conning tower to prevent the secondary guns from being manned, but doing no serious damage to the hull. For a moment, it looked as though the U-boat might turn sharply enough to ram her pursuer, the German captain perhaps rolling his last dice. Jack watched, mesmerised, as his opponent dragged a decapitated gunner from the 20mm, took aim at *Gannet* and opened fire. Sparks flew as rounds clanged and ricocheted off the bridge; Behardien fell to the deck screaming with a shell through his shoulder.

'Full astern!' Jack shouted, knowing full well the consternation it would cause McEwan.

The sudden change momentarily threw off the enemy's fire as *Gannet* shuddered down her full length, clawing inside the U-boat's turning circle, her bows edged round to aim at the submarine's low silhouette. The distance closed rapidly and the 20mm fell silent as both Lewis guns hosed the conning tower with tracer and the German captain ducked for cover.

The old scar on Jack's temple burnt hot. He wiped a sleeve across his eyes to clear the sweat and the images that whirled behind the light of their fire. *Gannet* was so close now that her high prow obscured the target and all guns fell silent as the whaler bore down on her prey. Jack was momentarily awed by the impending collision of his ardent desire with the ugliness of the kill.

Their bows rose on a swell and the forefoot came down like a guillotine, striking the U-boat just forward of her conning tower and slicing through the toughened steel of the pressure hull with the ease of a flensing knife. The impact sent *Gannet*'s crew sprawling as *U-68* rolled beneath them and scraped along the keel like a mortally wounded whale. Emerging from *Gannet*'s stern the U-boat briefly righted herself before subsiding beneath the waves.

'Fire one and two!' Jack shouted into the quarterdeck voicepipe, sending a pair of depth charges after his stricken foe.

Inside the U-boat, all was chaos, terror and death. The fore-ends had been carved open and the sea poured in, drowning everyone within. As the boat rolled over under the weight of *Gannet*'s blow, those in the control room and remaining watertight compartments were hurled against bulkheads and machinery as items tore themselves loose and tumbled with the men to the scream of tortured metal. Lingen was dashed against the ladder, his face opened to the bone; Hoppe's body was broken upon his beloved diesel engines; Kombüse Schneider was crushed to death by an oven freed of its mountings.

A dazed, but miraculously unharmed Captain Brand looked around at the carnage of the righted control room, the blood splattered instruments, his wounded men, and listened to the roaring of water inundating the fore-ends. Then he heard the splash of depth charges beside his boat. He drew the Luger from its holster and, taking one more glance around him, put the barrel to his temple, muttered '*Heil Hitler*', and squeezed the trigger a second before *U-68* was eviscerated.

On *Gannet*'s bridge, Jack saw an orange flash in the depths that looked like undersea lightning, and the rumble of aquatic thunder. Giant air bubbles and gouts of oil resembling clotted blood rose to the surface. Potgieter reported breaking-up noises as the U-boat, sinking into the midnight deep, was squeezed until the last of its watertight compartments imploded. A straggling cheer erupted from the foredeck and was taken up throughout the ship. The men of *Gannet* celebrated with unrestrained passion, a passion borne of their terrible losses, of their fear, and of relief — blessed, overwhelming relief.

Incredibly, one German sailor managed to escape the U-boat and *Gannet* idled closer to rescue him. The naked rating was crying, '*Hilfe! Hilfe!*', as Seaman Rademan reached down with a boat hook to try to pull the lad closer. Only then did he notice one arm missing and the stub gushing blood. Stoker Hughes grabbed the good arm and, ignoring the screams, dragged the survivor aboard. Porky tried to staunch the bleeding with dressings from his first aid box, but it was no use. The German teenager's sobbing diminished to a hoarse keening of '*Mama, Mama, Mama,*' his face turning grey as he slipped life's mooring lines and drifted away.

'Oh God in bloody heaven, I hate this shit,' said Porky, staring at his blood-soaked hands as if they didn't belong to him. He rubbed a sleeve across his eyes, stood up slowly and walked back to the galley with hunched shoulders.

Jack ordered the ship's boat lowered to pick up debris — a soccer ball, two tins of coffee, the photograph of a young woman, a human lung — evidence to prove to O'Reilly that Davy Jones had indeed received the new intake of fifty recruits. Presented with the macabre collection, Jack felt numb. His anger had drained like water from *Gannet*'s decks. All the accumulated tension of the recent months — the training, the weight of command and dreadful sacrifices — had culminated in this triumphant moment, but all he felt was emptiness and exhaustion. This battle was won, but he stood alone, still burdened with the great responsibility of the convoy, still without Clara, without a true harbour. The befogged darkness pressed in around the bridge, soulless and absolute.

Jack's body trembled from the cold and delayed reaction to the duel. His heart ached for *Belle*, the doughty whaler that now rested on the seabed. Dozens of sailors had died a terrible death at his hand this night, and somehow he needed to believe it was a victory. Because it *was* a victory. He willed himself to quell the doubts and hold on to his dutiful role of fighting commander of a fighting ship … *just like clipping on his gilded officer's sword.*

'Damage report, Number One, and then let's catch up with that damn convoy as quick as we can.'

By sunrise, the fog had lifted and Jack's flock was in sight. Soon after, a tiny speck appeared in the northern sky: an Anson from Rooikop to offer daytime protection for the last leg to Walvis. *Gannet* caught up with the convoy and sailed down its left flank with the desert sands, salmon-coloured in the early light, forming a handsome backdrop. Each ship in turn sounded her horn giving thanks as she passed — a protracted moaning that reminded Jack once again of the cows on their Hampshire estate.

'Very well done, sir,' said Van Zyl, hoarse with emotion or lack of sleep, Jack couldn't tell.

'Well done to all of us, and especially to you, Number One.'

Van Zyl's face lit up and just then he looked more Stellenbosch schoolboy than first lieutenant with the weight of the war, and who knew what else, on his shoulders.

'I'm going below for a bit. Take station two miles ahead of the leading ship of the second column. And a damage report, please.'

Jack climbed stiffly down to the wardroom where Behardien was laid out on a settee covered in blankets, his shoulder bandaged, his face pale. 'How's he doing, Porky?'

'Not great, sir, but he'll pull through.'

'That's good news,' Jack said, laying a hand on the young man's forehead.

'I'll be back on the bridge with you in no time, sir,' said Behardien haltingly through chattering teeth.

'Of course you will, Mohammed. Now get some rest.'

Twenty minutes later, Van Zyl presented Jack with a list of *Gannet*'s wounds. Her forefoot was crumpled, the bosun's and ammunition stores were leaking badly and the Asdic dome had been scraped clean off her bottom. Jack grimaced: he would have a lot of explaining to do to Commander Dalgleish, but at least he had a scalp to show for his vandalism.

'Thank you, Number One.' Jack leaned over the rail and noticed Pickles with a pot and a brush painting the silhouette of one and a half submarines on the side of the wheelhouse.

'Now that was a proper, old-fashioned bump,' said Jack.

'What's a bump?' asked Van Zyl at his shoulder.

'Oh, in Oxford we have rowing regattas where boats line up one behind the other on the Isis and the objective is to try to bump the eight in front of you. If you succeed, in the following race, you move one position up the line on the river.'

'Sounds weird, sir, and dangerous.'

'Not really, it's actually damn good fun. My boat got three bumps in the last Summer Eights before the war. That all seems like another epoch now, a dream.'

'Signal from Simon's Town, sir,' said Sparks, appearing on the bridge.

'Yes, what's the commodore say?'

'It reads: "Congratulations from SNO and C-in-C South Atlantic to Lieutenant Pembroke and his Gannets."'

'I think that calls for a splicing of the main brace, don't you, Number One?' Up came the jars of rum and February wasn't too fastidious about the size of tots sloshed into the crew's mugs as he went about the ship from station to station.

Jack stood on the bridge staring ahead, the golden sands of the Namib Desert spooling by on their beam, the low sun already warm on his face. Here was all his world: *Gannet* with her brave men, her dead, her wounded, her survivors. Over to starboard, *Langeberg* was a thing of stub-nosed, pugnacious beauty, catching the morning light as she turned at the end of her zigzag. Behind him, a procession of merchantmen, his particular charges, his reason for being here.

Havoc and his mother, and perhaps also Clara, were lost, but there was finally a degree of clarity — he could see that now — in this thing he was doing, was perhaps always meant to be doing. He would see it through to the end, come what may: this fight, this great sea fight, taking *Gannet* and her courageous sailors into harm's way until the job was done. Until light had been shone into every deep corner of the darkness; until the fog had lifted.

Pelican Point Lighthouse rose out of the ocean to the northeast, a black-and-white banded tower on a lonely sand spit at the entrance to Walvis Bay. The two grey vessels bustling towards them would be *Aristea* and *Goulding*, the lead minesweeper flashing a signal as she approached. Filling in for the wounded Behardien, Leading Seaman Thomas stood beside the Aldis lamp, ready to make the reply.

'What's she say?' asked Jack.

'Ships entering Walvis to form single column astern of us, sir,' answered Thomas.

'Acknowledge,' said Jack.

GLOSSARY

AB — Able Seaman
Abwehr — German Military Intelligence
Afrikaanse Nasionale Studentebond — Afrikaans National Student Union
the Andrew — nickname for the Royal Navy
AS — anti-submarine
Asdic — an early form of sonar used to detect submarines by the reflection of sound waves
B-Dienst — the *Beobachtungsdienst* (observation service) was a department of the German Naval Intelligence Service that intercepted and decoded enemy radio communications
BdU — the *Befehlshaber der U-Boote* was the Command HQ of the German Navy's U-boat arm
black gang — stokers who worked in the engine room, so called because of the soot, grease and coal dust that blackened their skin
BEF — British Expeditionary Force
Bosun or **Boatswain** — usually a petty officer, responsible for the efficient seamanship functions of the ship
braaivleis or **braai** — barbecue
Bunts — signalman specialising in visual signals such as flags, lights and semaphore (literally 'bunting tosser')
C-in-C — Commander in Chief
CD.03 — the letters CD denote a convoy from Cape Town to Durban
CN.04 — the letters CN denote a convoy northbound from Cape Town, often to Freetown, sometimes via Walvis Bay
corned dog — tinned bully beef

CPO — Chief Petty Officer

Davy Jones's locker — the bottom of the ocean; the grave of those drowned at sea

DSO — Distinguished Service Order

ERA — Engine Room Artificer

HE — hydrophone effect

head — naval term for a ship's toilet

hensopper — literally a 'hands upper', a Boer soldier who surrendered to the British during the Anglo-Boer War

HF/DF or **huff-duff** — high-frequency direction finding was used to locate enemy wireless units that transmitted on a high frequency over great distances. DF stations around southern Africa were manned day and night by operators proficient in Morse code. Each station took the bearing of an enemy transmission and the intersection of these lines marked the target's location, be it a U-boat or land-based spy sending intelligence to Germany

HMS *King Alfred* — training depot in Hove, Sussex, for officers of the Royal Navy Volunteer Reserve

Iscor — South Africa's state-owned Iron and Steel Corporation

IWO — first watch officer, or Number One, on a U-boat

the Jimmy — also known as the First Lieutenant, Number One or Jimmy-the-One; the second-in-command of a warship

Kombüse — German naval slang for 'cook'

kye — sweet hot chocolate, often served on board at night

Lordships — U-boat slang for seamen

LS — Leading Seaman

Mae West — nickname for an inflatable life jacket

OB or *Ossewabrandwag* — the 'Ox-wagon Sentinel' was formed by Hans van Rensburg to formally represent the increasing Afrikaner nationalism inspired by the Great Trek centenary celebrations of 1938. The *OB* rapidly evolved from a cultural organisation into a political voice and by 1941 its membership had swelled to approximately 350,000. During the early years of World War II, the *Ossewabrandwag* became more militaristic with an extreme right-wing paramilitary sub-group, the *Stormjaers*

OKM — *Oberkommando der Marine* (Nazi Germany's Naval High Command)

oppo — chum, special friend, buddy (literally your 'opposite number', the person on watch when you are off)

PO — Petty Officer

Pompey — sailors' nickname for Portsmouth

Pongo — soldier; slang for any member of the British Army (troops rarely washed in the field, hence 'where the wind blows, the pong goes')

Radio Zeesen — a Nazi propaganda shortwave radio station (broadcasting from a village near Berlin) listened to worldwide and popular in many Afrikaans households

RAF — Royal Air Force

RN — Royal Navy

RNR — Royal Naval Reserve

RNVR — Royal Navy Volunteer Reserve

RNVR SA — South African Royal Navy Volunteer Reserve

RT — radio-telephony

SAAF — South African Air Force

SAWAS — South African Women's Auxiliary Services

Schwerpunkt — 'centre of gravity'; a popular term used by German strategists denoting concentration on and maintenance of the objective

SDF — Seaward Defence Force; forerunner of the South African Navy

Sicherheitsdienst — German Secret Service

SKL — *Seekriegsleitung* (operational staff of *OKM*)
SNO — Senior Naval Officer
Snoektown or **Snoekie** — sailors' nickname for Simon's Town
Sparks — radio operator; telegraphist specialising in wireless communication
splice the main brace — the order given to issue a ship's crew with alcohol
Steuermann — coxswain in a German warship
Stormjaers — a paramilitary sub-group of the *OB* modelled on the Nazi's *Sturmabteilung* or Brown Shirts. During World War II, the *Stormjaers* carried out sabotage within South Africa as a protest against Jan Smuts's United Party government, which supported the British
Sturmabteilung — this 'Storm Detachment' or Brown Shirts was the Nazi Party's original paramilitary wing
U-68 — all the U-boats named in this novel are alternative versions of similar submarines that operated in the South Atlantic and off the South African coast during World War II
UZO or ***U-Bootzieloptik*** — a large pair of binoculars mounted on a pedestal on the bridge of a U-boat to form an aiming device whose data was transmitted to the attack computer below
Wabos or ***Wasserbomben*** — depth charges
WRENS — Women's Royal Naval Service
WT — wireless-telephony

HISTORICAL NOTES

On 16 October 1985, while serving as an officer in the film unit of the South African Navy, I was asked to record the destruction of a target ship. Our team boarded a Puma helicopter in Simon's Town and rendezvoused with the submarine SAS *Johanna van der Merwe* southwest of Cape Point. I prepared my video equipment as the pilot hovered closer to the *Harvest Warrior*, an old Irvin & Johnson trawler destined for the seabed.

The submarine dived and turned to fire a stern torpedo, which detonated beneath the ship's keel. The *Harvest Warrior* was lifted from the water by the explosion, which broke her back, and the two halves sank in less than four minutes. I was stunned by the destructive power of that single torpedo and reminded of the many ships that had met a similar fate off the Cape Peninsula during World War II. Watching the demise of the *Harvest Warrior* laid the seed for this novel.

When South Africa declared war on Germany on 6 September 1939, it is said that Hitler burst out laughing. At the time, South Africa's permanent naval force consisted of only two officers and three ratings. The Cape of Good Hope was a critical strategic point on the sea route around the continent and would be vital during the coming North African and Asian campaigns. Once Italy entered the war in 1940, the Mediterranean became extremely dangerous for Allied convoys and most were rerouted around the Cape. Much preparation was needed before Nazi warships made their way to Africa's southern tip. The Royal Navy base in Simon's Town had to be expanded and reinforced, and a fledgling South African navy created almost from scratch.

First came the German surface raiders, then the submarines. During one particularly successful four-day period in 1942, the Eisbär U-boat group sank fourteen ships in the vicinity of Cape Town. In another highly profitable attack, *U-160* managed to torpedo six ships in a convoy south of Durban during a single night. Over the course of the war, the Kriegsmarine employed twenty-eight U-boats off our coast, sinking over a hundred merchantmen (all enemy action in South African waters accounted for more than 150 vessels and nearly a million tons of shipping). It's an episode in the country's history that went largely undocumented. During the war, this was justified given the need to maintain morale and keep ship movements secret. After coming to power in 1948, the Nazi-sympathising Nationalist Party did not wish to celebrate, or even acknowledge, South Africa's war achievements. For them, the future of the country looked not dissimilar to Hitler's Germany, with racial segregation being central to their post-war plans.

Defending against the U-boat threat and protecting convoys around our coast fell to the Royal Navy — mostly ships based in Simon's Town — and to the fledgling South African Navy, initially named the Seaward Defence Force. This is the story of one such anti-submarine flotilla, commanded by Lieutenant Jack Pembroke DSO RNVR, operating in the stormy seas off the southern tip of Africa in 1941.

A NOTE TO THE READER

Dear Reader,

Thank you for taking the time to read the second Jack Pembroke naval adventure. I do hope you enjoyed it. In this series, I will be tracking Jack's story through World War II and although each novel may be read as a stand-alone, it will follow on directly in time from the previous novel, just as *The Wolf Hunt* picked up Jack's story in the months after the events of *The Cape Raider*. Book three in the series will tell the tale of escorts operating between Alexandria and Tobruk in North Africa during the winter of 1942. Jack and the good ship *Gannet* will be trying to protect coastal convoys from the threat of Axis aircraft, E-boats, U-boats and destroyers operating in the Eastern Mediterranean.

In this series, I have chosen a British hero and placed him on a South African ship initially stationed in a Royal Navy base at the southern tip of the continent. It has provided me with the opportunity to marry parts of my own background: my time in the South African Navy as a citizen-force officer, my university education in England and my love of the Cape and its stormy ocean.

Since I was a boy, I have adored nautical yarns and grew up reading the likes of Alexander Fullerton, Nicholas Monsarrat, Patrick O'Brian and Douglas Reeman. But I always lamented the fact that none of these naval adventures were set in my home, the Cape, despite the presence of an important Royal Navy base in Simon's Town. The Jack Pembroke series is an attempt to bring the South African maritime story of World War II to life. Future books could see Jack serving on the dangerous Malta convoys, clandestine operations in the Mediterranean, or even in the oft-forgotten Madagascar campaign.

Nowadays, reviews by knowledgeable readers are essential to an author's success, so if you enjoyed the novel I shall be in your debt if you would spare a moment to post a short review on **Amazon** or **Goodreads**. I love hearing from readers, and you can connect with me through my **Facebook page**, **Instagram**, **Twitter** or my **website**.

I hope we'll meet again in the pages of the next Jack Pembroke adventure on the high seas.

Justin Fox

Sapere Books is an exciting new publisher of brilliant fiction and popular history.

To find out more about our latest releases and our monthly bargain books visit our website: **saperebooks.com**

Printed in Great Britain
by Amazon

26747341R00188